Three Generations

by Yom Sang-seop

—

Translated from the Korean by Yu Young-nan

Afterword by Kim Chi-sou

archipelago books

YOM

Library of Congress Cataloging-in-Publication Data
Yæom, Sang-sæop, 1897-1963.
[Samdae. English]
Three generations / by Yom Sang-seop ;
translated by Yu Young-nan. — 1st ed.
p. cm.
ISBN 0-9749680-0-5
I. Yu, Young-nan. II. Title.
PL991.92.S3S24I3 2005
895.7'33 — dc22
2004021832

Published by Archipelago Books
25 Jay St. #203
Brooklyn, NY 11201
www.archipelagobooks.org

Distributed by Consortium Book Sales and Distribution
1045 Westgate Drive
St. Paul, MN 55114
www.cbsd.com

Jacket art: *Riding the Streetcar to School*, Unknown. Circa 1936–1939.
Copyright © Jang Gil-jun

Book Design by David Bullen Design

*This publication is made possible with public funds from Lannan Foundation,
the New York State Council on the Arts, a State agency, and with the support
of the Korea Literature Translation Institute.*

NYSCA

Three Generations

—

Translator's note

For the Romanization of the Korean alphabet, the new system issued by the South Korean government in 2000 was used. For the transliteration of the author's name, however, we accepted the wishes of his family.   *Yu Young-nan*

Two Friends

—

Standing on the stone step in front of the inner quarters, Deok-gi watched a manservant packing a quilt and pillow for him on the veranda. His grandfather came in from the outer quarters, his hands clasped behind his back. Seeing Deok-gi, he frowned and started grumbling.

"Deok-gi, someone's here looking for you. Who is this guy? His hair is a mess. You know it's important to have good friends. Why do all your friends who come around look like that?" His eyes widened as he caught sight of the quilt the manservant was wrapping. He stepped closer and touched it. "What's this? What's the good quilt—" Then he exploded. "How dare you! What's this three-colored silk doing here? Silk is for your elders. You can't take this all the way to a foreign country—you'll just get it dirty! You're just a student—are you crazy?" He shifted his gaze over to his granddaughter-in-law, who was standing in the kitchen without budging, and glared at her, too.

While his grandfather's tongue-lashing focused on this new target, Deok-gi snuck away to the outer quarters, where he suspected—from the mention of disheveled hair and shabby looks—he would find that his visitor was Kim Byeong-hwa.

"Hey, I was going to stop by your place after dinner," Deok-gi said, welcoming the friend he had seen just two days earlier.

"Oh, sure, a bourgeois like you coming to pay a visit to the likes of me! If

—
3

you're going to say good-bye to anyone, you might as well start with the head of the Bank of Korea." Byeong-hwa burst into laughter as he stood there, tall with hands buried deep in the pockets of his dusty overcoat.

"You just can't help being a wiseass every time we get together, can you? Cut it out, all right?" Deok-gi disliked being called a bourgeois. Not that he didn't feel fortunate to have enough to live on, but times being what they were, he didn't enjoy such sarcasm. "Come on in."

"What's the use of staying in?" Byeong-hwa said. "Let's go out. I'm hungry, I'm dying for a drink, and I don't want to go back to my boarding house for a miserable dinner with the family there. Anyway, they feed me only once a day — if I'm lucky — so why don't you pay, and I'll take you to a decent place? How does that sound?"

"How about I take you out and *you* pay?" Deok-gi went into the room that he was using for the time being.

"Give me a cigarette, will you? My mouth keeps telling me to put something in it." Byeong-hwa stretched out his hand and peered into the room.

"You go without cigarettes when I'm away, don't you?" Deok-gi tossed him the pack of Pigeons lying on the desk. "Seems you're only happy when you're bumming something off me, aren't you? Even if it's just a cigarette. How about we trade places in the exploiter-exploited class relationship?" Deok-gi hastily took off his Korean clothes as he spoke.

"You're getting upset about a cigarette? Like grandfather, like grandson!" Byeong-hwa inhaled slowly, savoring the flavor of the tobacco. "I'll wait outside. If the old man comes in and gives me the evil eye, it'll ruin our plans." He sauntered outside, beyond the gate of the outer quarters.

Actually, Deok-gi was also hoping to get away before his grandfather returned. Thinking about what Byeong-hwa had just said, Deok-gi snorted as he took the student uniform down from where it hung on the wall and put it on as fast as he could. He rushed out, overcoat in hand. His grandfather would almost certainly assume from Byeong-hwa's state of disarray that he was the kind of person who'd try to get something from his grandson or worse, tempt him to drink and squander money.

"What time do you leave tomorrow?"

"Probably in the evening." Deok-gi, born into a leisure-class family, hadn't yet decided which train to take, and had left his plans vague. He figured he could just as soon leave the following day if he didn't get it together tomorrow, or even the day after that if something else delayed him.

"Well, I don't care when you leave. He must have given you quite a bit, huh?"

"Do you really think the old man would give me anything without counting down to the last coin on his abacus?"

"Stop whining. Are you afraid someone's going to ask you for a handout?"

"What have I got to hand out?"

"Come on! I won't let you leave until you give me enough to keep me fed for at least a month. If the landlord actually had something, he'd let me eat even if I couldn't pay, but his daughter works in a factory, and they can only afford to buy rice by the handful, even though rice prices have come down so much lately. I can't stand idly by."

Deok-gi looked sympathetic, but then he laughed and said, "They really made a mistake when they took you in!"

"That's how people like me get by, you know."

"You said it!"

"You just can't bring yourself to admit that it's a mistake being friends with someone like me. Am I right?" Byeong-hwa continued.

"You took the words right out of my mouth," Deok-gi said.

"You know that if it weren't for me, you wouldn't have anyone following you around and hitting you up for drinks."

"Yeah, right! And the great revolutionary of our generation must be so ashamed to admit to being friends with someone so green, so fresh out of secondary school. I'm truly honored by your presence, really."

Nowadays, the two friends saw each other only once or twice a year. They traded sarcastic remarks every time they met, but they'd never actually been really angry at one another. Their friendship had begun thanks to their similar family backgrounds, when they were bright young students vying for first place in their class, and now nothing could break the deep understanding and sympathy that had developed despite their differences.

Neither was more intelligent nor more articulate than the other, but the fair-skinned Deok-gi was from a rich family and had an air of calm about him. Byeong-hwa was dark and brazen, with a stubborn streak. Deok-gi was not overly cheerful, in spite of having grown up sheltered in an affluent household. He regarded Byeong-hwa, who seemed to have become more cynical in the past couple of years, with aloofness.

"So where are we going?" Deok-gi asked. "You don't look like you're in the mood for Chinese or for Japanese fish-cake soup. How about we go to _____House and hire a *gisaeng*, too?" Deok-gi had never been to a restaurant where *gisaeng* served.

"Do you think I'm some sort of lackey who wants to follow his rich friends around, squeezing as much out of them as possible? That kind of place is too good for me."

"Didn't you just tell me that I should be grateful for the privilege of buying you drinks? And now all you want to do is go to a cheap bar?"

"Exactly. You give me money for drinks, and you can go to the *gisaeng* house by yourself."

The two young men made their way toward Jingogae.

"Now don't be stubborn. Let's just go in and eat. You should have a good meal at least once a day." Not one for drinking, Deok-gi stopped suddenly in front of a Western-style restaurant that he knew and tried to pull his friend inside.

"No, no. I know a better place farther down. I'm not sure who she is, but there's this knockout who works there, two of them actually, and . . ." The truth was, Byeong-hwa was more interested in alcohol than food.

"Now I get it. You're really a secret playboy, and I can guess what kind of a place you're dragging me to." Deok-gi laughed and followed his friend.

"Someone took me to this place yesterday. It's called Bacchus. Isn't that an excellent name? It's a nice place. For some reason, they even seemed glad to see an unemployed guy like me. They probably liked my looks. I haven't gotten such a welcome anywhere else in town." Byeong-hwa suddenly sounded proud of himself.

Deok-gi was doubtful but followed his friend into Bacchus.

He could see what Byeong-hwa meant about not wanting to tag along with rich friends just to be fed and not belonging in fancy places, but his feelings were hurt all the same. He felt as if his friend were criticizing him. Byeong-hwa complained out of one side of his mouth and then ate whatever Deok-gi paid for with the other. Like most people who are well-off, he would have been happier if Byeong-hwa had just gone along with everything he said.

Naïve though he was, Deok-gi at least tried to understand how humiliating it might be for someone who didn't have money to hobnob with those who did, tagging along like a footman, and how he would tire of acquiescing to his wealthier friend, allowing his pride to be stepped on.

The proprietor brought out a tray with a bowl of steaming fish-cake soup and two glasses filled with yellowish liquor. Deok-gi didn't care much for alcohol, and the mere sight of the large, clumsy glasses chafed against his natural dignity; he couldn't help but frown.

She had a dark complexion and small, sharp features, but her clear eyes were those of an educated woman, and the way she pursed her lips into a friendly, ever-so-delicate smile gave her an air of intelligence.

Byeong-hwa gulped down his drink before the proprietor had even left. After a minute, Deok-gi asked, "Is she your knockout?"

Byeong-hwa couldn't answer right away. "No," he mumbled between bites of his fish cake. "But I should've asked where she's gone to." Still munching away, he clapped his hands to summon the proprietor. Even though Byeong-hwa had mentioned the beauty to his friend, he was not particularly interested in having her presence at the bar.

As she approached, Byeong-hwa finally swallowed. "What happened to that other girl?" he asked.

"She just left for the bathhouse. She should be back soon." The proprietor stopped in the middle of the hall, her eyes on Deok-gi.

To her, he seemed fair, handsome, and intelligent. She didn't particularly mind Koreans, but assuming he was from a wealthy family—a young man in an expensive well-cut suit, though only a student uniform—she looked down on him somewhat. Byeong-hwa, on the other hand, didn't seem such a trifling person. She had seen him a few times at the bar, and thought that if those two were drinking buddies, then Deok-gi surely couldn't be just a "modern boy," the darling of some rich family. The woman had opened up her business the previous fall, and perhaps because her sensitivity hadn't yet been dulled by the flood of business, she measured the value of each man who came in with the curiosity of an ordinary woman.

She thought of O Jeong-ja, the eldest daughter of a judge from a district court in Korea. Although O was his surname, he was Japanese, and in that language his name was pronounced Kure. The proprietor had once been the head nurse of a charity hospital in the same district, and when Jeong-ja was hospitalized for some ailment, the two had grown close.

Now why did I think of Jeong-ja? she asked herself. This young man and

Jeong-ja looked like siblings, but that was ridiculous. They weren't even the same nationality.

When discussing society and politics with the confident Jeong-ja, the proprietor would agree with her or at least listen with an understanding smile. She liked to believe she wasn't completely out of touch when it came to fashionable ways of thinking. So when the disheveled young man had come in with his friends, and they had begun talking among themselves in Japanese, she had felt a certain affinity toward them. Even so, she condescendingly considered the young men "Marxist boys" and assumed now that Deok-gi might be one of them, too—and her mind jumped to Jeong-ja, whom she sometimes called the "Marxist girl."

Hong Gyeong-ae

——

Noticing that her customers were beginning to look bored, the proprietor pulled up a stool between them.

"Are you going to make trouble again today?" She smiled. "I'll have to kick you out if you do."

"When have I ever made trouble?" The other day Byeong-hwa had skipped lunch and dinner and had had too much to drink. He vaguely remembered being drunk. Perhaps he had flirted a little, though he didn't usually pay much attention to the opposite sex.

"Don't pretend you were so drunk you don't remember!" She continued to talk about his drunken behavior to keep the conversation going.

"I'm not pretending anything. But with someone like you next to me, I might have easily misbehaved." He laughed.

"Oh? Well, if you really had, I wouldn't have stood idly by."

"*Tadaima*," a woman called out in Japanese as she came in, dressed in a Japanese outfit and holding a bath bowl. She stopped short when she saw the customers.

Looking up, Deok-gi winced as if ice had been dropped down his neck, his eyes darting back to his drink. The woman seemed to cringe as well; she abruptly turned on her heels and slipped out.

Gyeong-ae! Deok-gi's heart sank. Moisture filled his eyes, though tears did not surface. His glass, three-quarters full, seemed to dance up and down. Although he was sensitive to alcohol, he knew he wasn't drunk, but he nevertheless felt dizzy, and the room seemed to whirl around him.

"What do you think? Is she a knockout or what?" Byeong-hwa laughed. "My eyes are as sharp as yours, no?" He laughed again, oblivious to his friend's thoughts.

"When you see a beautiful girl, you say she's beautiful," the proprietor rebuffed. "But what's all this about a knockout?" She sounded somewhat jealous.

"Oba-san, more liquor. And ask Aiko-san to come out quickly," Byeong-hwa said.

Aiko-san was a Japanese name derived from the "ae" in Gyeong-ae's name. The proprietor jumped to her feet and went inside.

"Tell me, do you know who she is?" asked Byeong-hwa, smiling.

"Who?" Deok-gi asked, his voice barely escaping his tightly clenched teeth, afraid that his friend might know about her background.

"I bet you think she's Japanese." Byeong-hwa was still smiling.

"So . . . she's Korean?" Deok-gi's heart grew heavy; his eyes had not deceived him.

Byeong-hwa laughed. "When I first saw her, I didn't know either, but then I found out that she's *a traveler from Suwon* as the song goes — actually, a woman from Suwon. Her name's Hong Gyeong-ae."

Deok-gi's heart began to race, hearing the girl's real name from another's mouth. He was speechless.

Byeong-hwa had expected Deok-gi to be surprised by her background, but instead he saw his friend's face, flushed a moment ago from the alcohol, turn pale. Byeong-hwa stared at him, baffled by his reaction.

"Do you know her?" Byeong-hwa asked.

"No," Deok-gi answered, his voice unsteady. Realizing that Byeong-hwa might catch on from the expression on his face, he quickly picked up his glass and tossed back more than half his drink.

Byeong-hwa had never seen him drink like that. *Something was up.*

He clapped his hands again for service. It was not Aiko who brought out the drinks but the proprietor who appeared, apologizing.

"Where's Ai-san?" Byeong-hwa asked.

"She's combing her hair. She'll be out shortly."

The proprietor poured another drink for Deok-gi. He had finished his glass, and under different circumstances he would have refused another, but now he just sat in silence, uncertain what to do. He wanted to persuade Byeong-hwa to leave with him immediately, but he had an irresistible urge to see the beauty once more.

"What do you say we go get something to eat now?" No matter how he thought about it, leaving was the right thing to do. He felt he had regained his composure to some extent.

"What's the matter with you? You've come all this way and now you want to leave without even meeting her?" Byeong-hwa knocked back his second glass in high spirits; leaving was the last thing on his mind. "Come on, drink up. We're going to get drunk tonight. After tomorrow, we won't see each other for a long time."

"Is the young man going somewhere?" The proprietor glanced at Deok-gi with a friendly smile.

"Well, you see," said Byeong-hwa, laughing, "I missed my young son here, so I called him home from school during winter break, but now I have to send him off again tomorrow. This is his farewell party."

"Father and son get along famously, I see!" The proprietor joined in the laughter.

"You're crazy!" Deok-gi snorted.

"And what school do you go to?" she asked.

"Kyoto Prep School Number 3," answered Byeong-hwa as Deok-gi sat silently, his thoughts elsewhere.

"Ah, Kyoto. Have you been there long?" She seemed interested, and she took a closer look at Deok-gi.

Deok-gi gave her a blank look before answering. "Yes, about two years," he said, then turned to Byeong-hwa again. "Come on, let's go."

"Why do you keep saying that? You just got here."

"I have to pack, and I think we'd better eat something," Deok-gi said. He thought it would be better not to meet Gyeong-ae. He didn't have any particular feelings for her, but the thought of meeting her under these circumstances pained him. It was so shocking to see her like this, as a hostess in a bar. She certainly wouldn't want to see him. It was best that they leave as soon as possible.

"You eat every day. Sit down, will you?"

"You just don't know when to stop drinking. Do you want to pickle that formidable young brain of yours?" Deok-gi sounded angry.

"You know, I don't get meals every day like some people we know, and I don't always have someone buying me drinks, so what am I supposed to do? What's a guy supposed to do if he can't get a few drinks every now and then? Live on cold water alone? Are you telling me I shouldn't drink?"

"Of course you should! Especially when you're in such a good mood!" exclaimed Aiko-san as she hurried in. She stood next to the proprietor without so much as a glance at Deok-gi. "Kin-san!" She addressed Byeong-hwa, "Why are you preaching to a young gentleman like him? Come on, drink up!" She picked up the bottle.

"Ai-san's right. You drink first," Byeong-hwa said, offering her his empty glass.

"All right," Gyeong-ae said, readily exchanging the bottle for the glass, into which Byeong-hwa poured her a drink.

Deok-gi averted his eyes as she accepted the drink. Her flirtatious behavior filled him with shock, aversion, contempt, and sympathy. He wished his father could see her now and felt a stronger sense of rebellion against him than ever before.

Deok-gi wasn't the only one surprised by Gyeong-ae's abandon. The proprietor had been watching with a smile, thinking that Gyeong-ae was flirting harmlessly, but when half the drink disappeared, she was astonished.

"What are you doing? What's wrong with you?" she exclaimed, as she snatched away the glass. "You can't drink this much! Will you be all right?" she asked, her eyes gauging how much Gyeong-ae had drunk. This wasn't simply an owner chastising an employee. She sounded genuinely concerned. Hearing her, the two men appreciated her thoughtfulness as though they themselves were the ones being scolded.

"I can handle much more than that," Gyeong-ae said in a Japanese so perfect it was almost uncanny. She smiled slyly, like a child who was proud of a prank she had pulled. Then she pulled out a Pigeon.

Deok-gi stole a glance at her as she lit her cigarette. Perhaps he imagined it, but her eyes, glowing from the light of the match, seemed to be brimming over.

So she does shed tears, he thought.

They had gone to the same elementary school and the same church, and look how far she had fallen! It might be out of bitterness that she drank and helped herself to her customer's cigarettes like a low-class barmaid, but her tears seemed to say that she hadn't fallen all the way. The more he thought about it, the more he pitied her.

"Give me the glass! You're all keeping me from drinking! Ai-san, drink up and give me my glass." Byeong-hwa urged her on, ill at ease, sensing the tension.

"I'm not drinking any more. Take the glass. You can't refuse to share it even if you think it's filthy, because you've accepted drinks from a rich master, right?" Gyeong-ae blurted out, pushing her glass toward Byeong-hwa. She had come around the table and was sitting between Byeong-hwa and Deok-gi.

Deok-gi was taken aback by her flippant remarks, tossed off as if she had no idea who he was. His spirits sinking, he stole a quick glance at her. He was beginning to feel afraid of this woman. Who was she, really?

"Drink up!" said Gyeong-ae, refilling the glass.

As though he had been waiting for just such encouragement, Byeong-hwa picked up the drink and gulped it down.

"Let's get out of here," Deok-gi said, before Byeong-hwa even had a chance to reach for a snack to go with his drink. Deok-gi felt as if he had been duped by a conniving spirit, and he couldn't stand being there any longer.

"Now, you stop right there. As Aiko-san said, it's not easy to get a rich gentleman to pay for drinks. I'll go when I'm ready," retorted Byeong-hwa, who was getting increasingly drunk. He bit greedily into another fish cake.

The proprietor burst out laughing, and Deok-gi was embarrassed. In fact, it was the ravenous way Byeong-hwa was eating that made her laugh, but Deok-gi felt she was mocking him, like the other two were. He had no choice but to stay put and listen to their banter, but whichever way he looked, the others seemed to belong to an entirely different world as they chatted among themselves. It was unnerving.

"Have some more yourself, young man," said the proprietor to Deok-gi in a friendly tone. "Don't act like a girl!"

"How can we force such a young gentleman to drink? I'll drink it myself!" Gyeong-ae picked up the glass in front of Deok-gi and whispered low in Korean, so that only Deok-gi could hear, "I'll suck up every single drop of the *buja*'s blood if I can." She sat up straight. It was not clear whether by *buja* she meant "father and son" or "rich man."

Gyeong-ae didn't raise the glass to her lips, having snatched it from Deok-gi only to say what was on her mind. She had uttered the words aggressively; she definitely recognized him. *This glass belongs to Jo Deok-gi, the son of Jo Sang-hun*—she hadn't forgotten that.

Who was Sang-hun and who was Deok-gi? As it happens, she had once been the father's mistress, and although the son had once been a school friend of hers, he was supposed to have been like a son to her. This thought lodged itself in her mind.

Deok-gi was so bewildered that he just sat, scared stiff that Gyeong-ae might really get drunk and spill the story of her past.

"Aiko-san, what's the matter with you? You're not thinking of your lost love again, are you?" The proprietor smiled at Gyeong-ae.

Thinking of her love! Deok-gi felt his heart sink again.

"Don't be silly! I'm in a better mood today than I've been in ages." Gyeong-ae took Deok-gi's glass and poured out the contents into the ashtray before pushing it toward Byeong-hwa. She asked him to fill it up.

This time Byeong-hwa poured until the glass was only half full.

"What are you doing? Emptying a customer's glass!" the proprietor scolded Gyeong-ae.

Gyeong-ae didn't respond but turned to Deok-gi and, every bit as sociable as she might be with any customer, said, "My dear Mr. Scholar! Since you're not drinking, it's all right, isn't it?"

Deok-gi blushed and mumbled something or other, maybe "yeah," or maybe a more formal "yes."

"People will say I'm a fallen woman if I keep drinking like this. But does a woman drink because she's fallen, or is she fallen because she drinks? I say neither! If a woman's fallen because she drinks, then all drinking men are fallen, too, and all nondrinkers, like ministers, will go to Heaven, right? Kin-san, isn't that right?" She slapped Byeong-hwa on the thigh.

The more she drank, the more talkative she became, and her coquettish manners grew even more appealing.

At the mention of ministers, however, Byeong-hwa bit back something that was on the tip of his tongue. He just nodded, looking at Deok-gi.

Byeong-hwa's father was a church elder, and Deok-gi's father, although he held no official post, was also involved in church work. Her remark didn't sound like deliberate criticism to Byeong-hwa, who didn't see how she could possibly know their fathers, but her words stung him because he had severed all ties with his father following an ideological clash. For Deok-gi,

Gyeong-ae's words were far from idle chitchat. He knew they were aimed directly at him, and he began to panic, realizing that he really must leave before she blurted out anything else.

"No, I'm no fallen woman, and even if I were, I wouldn't blame anyone. And supposing that I was, what about all those bastards and bitches out there? I wouldn't choose to go to Heaven if you paid me—not even if they had a spot ready and waiting for me. No way!" Gyeong-ae's speech was beginning to slur.

Byeong-hwa thought she must have gone to a mission school from all her talk of ministers and Heaven. "I agree with you, one hundred percent," he said. "But you can't go saying such things out loud. We all do what we have to do. Now promise me you'll always live courageously and never give up your convictions!" His face flushed redder as he grew more excited.

"And what do you do for a living?" Gyeong-ae abruptly asked him, suddenly eager to change the subject.

"Me? Well, what does it look like I do?" Byeong-hwa was beaming.

The conversation was cut short, however. The door flew open, and a handful of new customers came in.

Next Day

———

"Wake up! Your mother is here."

Deok-gi managed to drag himself out of bed only after his wife had run to his window to alert him.

"You must have had a late night. Are you leaving today?" his mother asked as she came in. She wanted to see her son before he left.

"I'll probably leave tomorrow," Deok-gi answered, stifling a yawn.

His wife followed his mother inside to fold up his bedding and quickly stow it away.

The occupant of the main room, Deok-gi's step-grandmother, didn't bother to look out. Deok-gi's mother had no intention of paying respects to her new mother-in-law, and the younger mother-in-law, for her part, assumed that her daughter-in-law would come in to greet her.

It had been five years since Deok-gi's step-grandmother moved into the main room and his parents moved out. Deok-gi's mother was loath to eat from the same rice pot as her new mother-in-law, who was five years younger than herself. The dislike was mutual.

The same was true for father and son. The old man was partial to his grandson, Deok-gi, but frowned on his own child, whom he drove out of the house in order to set up house with his precious young wife. But even before she had arrived, the two generations had felt uncomfortable living together.

After the old man turned seventy, his wife gave birth to his only daughter, Gwi-sun, who was now four years old.

———

Deok-gi, a secondary-school student at the time, had left with his parents as a matter of course, but when he himself got married during his fourth year of secondary school, he had moved back in with his grandfather after living only six months with his parents. Deok-gi's mother had been reluctant to let her son and daughter-in-law leave, and the bride's family didn't like the idea of their daughter living under the thumb of a young new grandmother-in-law. Still, they could hardly defy the grandfather's stern order. It was quite convenient for his new wife to have the young couple there to order around, and as a bonus she could make her daughter-in-law, whom she disliked the most, feel lonely.

As for the old man, it's possible that he took in his grandson and granddaughter-in-law out of affection. Deok-gi, for his part, liked his grandfather more than he did his own father. He knew, furthermore, that the family assets were still in his grandfather's hands and that he dispensed all the money, down to the last coin. Deok-gi felt it would be wise to follow his grandfather's wishes.

A year after the wedding, a baby's cry was also heard in Deok-gi's room. It was a son. The whole household was abuzz over such good fortune. But the excitement rested merely on the surface. Deok-gi's step-grandmother, narrow-minded and lacking a good upbringing, was jealous of the baby in Deok-gi's room, her great-grandson, for no reason. As her four-year-old daughter and Deok-gi's three-year-old son grew up, they played and fought with each other, sparking unpleasant exchanges among the adults.

Whenever the old man held his great-grandson, his wife would shoot him a reproachful glance. He did not intend to be unfair, but it was simply too tiresome. When all was said and done, he preferred his own daughter, and his affections tended toward his young wife.

"Is Father home?" Deok-gi asked his mother with another yawn, venturing out to the veranda. He considered visiting his father to pay his respects before his departure.

"I'm not sure. If he's not in the outer quarters, he may have gone out somewhere." His mother's answer was indifferent.

The middle-aged couple were husband and wife in name only. Deok-gi's father ate, slept, and even washed his face in the outer quarters. Days would pass without his wife catching even a glimpse of him. Yet, to the outside world, they seemed to get along well enough, since they rarely revealed their feelings. Perhaps it was because the husband, who was serving as a son of God, didn't care about worldly matters. Or perhaps he kept his distance from his wife in order to uphold his sense of morality. His wife, who was just over forty years old, both disliked and resented her husband, whose face she had almost forgotten.

"Where's the baby?" Deok-gi's mother asked.

"The maid went out, carrying him on her back. He's probably playing in the outer quarters."

Deok-gi's wife called out to the maid, asking her to find the baby. As the maid left with the little girl strapped to her back, Deok-gi's wife whispered to her, "When you get to the outer quarters, tell the master of the house that the madam from Hwagae-dong is here." It was intended as a thoughtful gesture to give her mother-in-law an opportunity to pay her respects to her grandfather-in-law.

No sooner had the maid left than the old man appeared. He was not especially eager to see his daughter-in-law, but he had nothing much to do during the day, so he spent his time wandering between the inner and outer quarters. Impatient by nature, he came over as soon as he heard his daughter-in-law had arrived.

When he cleared his throat at the gate leading to the inner quarters, his daughter-in-law came out of Deok-gi's room.

"Hmmm," he grunted as he glanced at her. When he caught sight of Deok-gi, who was still in his pajamas, washing his face on the edge of the veranda, he began to scold him. "Do you plan to wear those all day long?"

Then he got really angry. "Where did you go yesterday, and when did you get home?" He already knew what time Deok-gi had come in because his wife had told him. Deok-gi had no choice but to stand quietly, eyes averted, face dripping wet.

The old man entered the main room. His daughter-in-law followed and offered a deep bow. Only then did she come face-to-face with her stepmother-in-law.

"You're all right, then?" The old man rarely ventured out of his house, and his daughter-in-law was reluctant to visit him unless she had to. She paid her respects on an average of once a month.

"Will you stay until the memorial, the day after tomorrow?" the father-in-law asked her, all of a sudden.

She stood for a moment without answering. Then she remembered that the memorial rite for the old man's father was to be held in two days.

"If you don't have anything important to do, why don't you just stay here instead of traveling back and forth? We can't leave all the work to the young ones."

The daughter-in-law couldn't bring herself to say yes, and her father-in-law was offended.

"Of course, you should be the one to help prepare it," his wife broke in from the corner, where she was sitting with her face turned away. "What can I do when the days are so short and I have a baby?" She was disturbed by the old man's comment, which sounded almost as if he were insulting her in front of his daughter-in-law.

Deok-gi's mother remained as silent as if she'd been caught swallowing a mouthful of stolen honey. She didn't appreciate her stepmother-in-law using the form of speech reserved for addressing younger people. She was tempted to respond in kind, but she knew it would accomplish nothing in the end, which made her furious.

Granted, she's just a second wife, but if she had some manners and proper upbring-

ing, there would be no reason she couldn't take charge of the rite. After all, it isn't as special as the first or second anniversary of the dead. And why this excuse about the baby? Does she really think that a woman raising children can't make time for anything else?

"I know you people don't care about ancestral rites since you've become involved in Christianity and whatnot," the old man said. "But there's nothing you can do about it while I'm still alive!"

He looked with disapproval at his daughter-in-law standing there mute. Though he tried to repress a surge of anger, his wrinkled face colored as he remembered the annual conflict with his son over the ancestral rites. The daughter-in-law was frightened, but she didn't feel free to speak.

"So now you've gone and become a Catholic yourself? Will you offer me even a drop of ceremonial water after I die?" His voice grew louder.

The Suwon woman—the stepmother-in-law was from Suwon—was quite pleased with the old man's scolding tone. She thought it would be amusing if his daughter-in-law answered back.

And she did at last. "I came here fully intending to help with the preparations, sir. I was going to see my son off and then return home after the ancestral rite."

Faced with this unexpectedly docile reply, the old man felt somewhat deflated and was no longer angry. But his wife felt cheated, as if she had chased a fire truck hoping to see a full blaze only to return home after settling for just a few wisps of smoke.

The old man began his usual sermon. "Even if you believe in Christianity, or something more important than that, there's nothing wrong with holding memorial rites for your parents. They say Jesus didn't know who his father was, but he was born thanks to his parents, wasn't he? Deok-gi, you listen carefully!" he shouted toward the veranda. He went on grumbling about Christianity, then moved to the topic of his son.

"Deok-gi!" he called to his grandson, who was drying his face with a towel in his room.

"Yes, sir," Deok-gi answered, entering the main room.

"Take that Japanese robe off, will you? You should be more careful about what you wear." He broke off his scolding with a strict order: "Leave after the rite!"

"Yes, sir." Deok-gi was exhausted. He was also upset that he could do nothing for Gyeong-ae, so this command was, in fact, a relief. He knew he shouldn't feel disturbed by Gyeong-ae's circumstances, and it was certainly no reason to put off his departure, but he welcomed the delay nonetheless.

On the other hand, staying meant hearing his grandfather disparage his father, which Deok-gi hated. He never took sides, but his grandfather's all-too-frequent sermons on Christianity gave him a headache. He had heard it so often since childhood that if his grandfather's words were nails, his ears would be stuffed with them. Several times a year, when it was time to observe the ancestral rites, it got even worse.

During the memorial for Deok-gi's grandmother, the whole house was turned upside down. Deok-gi's father never attended his mother's rite, which was hosted by the old man and attended by Deok-gi, his mother, and numerous cousins.

"The bastard doesn't even respect his own mother!" the old man would spit out a hundred times a day, as he trotted back and forth between the inner and outer quarters, calming down only on the night after all the guests left.

"The master and his wife got along so well," the young women would say within earshot of the Suwon woman. Deok-gi's mother would join in by mocking her husband: "It's no wonder they did—just look at the frightfully gentle and wise son they gave birth to."

The Suwon woman would retreat to her room to sulk and then lash out at the children. The women didn't approve of her behavior, so they giggled and made a racket while preparing the feast. All night long, they would make disrespectful remarks just loud enough for her to hear — that the old gentleman paid far more attention to his first wife's rite than to that of his own father, that a woman could wish for nothing more if she knew her husband would prepare such a ceremony for her after her death, that the first wife's spirit would visit the main room to spend a restful night there.

This time, listening to his grandfather rattle on about how everyone lacked the proper devotion for the rite, Deok-gi could only think, *Should I go to Bacchus again tonight?* His head throbbed. He gazed blankly at his grandfather's eyes, flaring behind his glasses, as if he were staring at the horizon.

The tirade concluded with the warning that Deok-gi shouldn't party all night with the likes of that good-for-nothing who had come the day before. Deok-gi and his mother were dismissed, and they returned to his room.

Deok-gi sat before the meal that his wife had brought in on a tray. As he watched his mother, who positioned herself silently next to the portable brazier with a cigarette between her lips, he thought about Gyeong-ae.

Does Mother know about her? What really happened? Why did Father and Gyeong-ae split up? I heard there was a child, my half-sister. I've never seen her, nor do I want to.

Deok-gi felt as if his tongue had dissolved into little pieces and an earthquake had erupted in his head. He busied himself with his rice, which he had dumped into a bowl of water. He could think of only one thing: *Should I ask Mother about it?*

In the end, he decided not to; it was too cruel.

But who can I ask about it? This wasn't an urgent matter, but his curiosity was piqued. He suddenly felt frustrated. He could hardly question his father directly, and apart from him, there was no one.

It occurred to him that he could get the information he wanted from one of his father's friends. He considered which one would be best but soon stopped himself, realizing that it would only cause trouble were it to be known that he'd been probing into the past. The affair must be the greatest secret of his father's life. It had taken place between two churchgoers, and although he still enjoyed the trust of the church, his actions had been scandalous at the time. It was certainly not something to bring up recklessly, if Deok-gi cared anything at all about his father's honor.

Oddly enough, the more he tried to care for his father, the more his old hatred for him surged up, in place of the natural feelings one might expect between a son and his father. He felt sorry for his mother and also for Gyeong-ae. He felt bad for the daughter Gyeong-ae had given birth to, be she alive or dead, the little sister that he had never met. He even pitied his own sister and himself.

His father was not a remarkable man, but he might have been happy if he had his son's respect.

Deok-gi struggled with himself. *It is true that Grandfather isn't the most understanding person in the world, but if Father hadn't had the affair, Mother might actually have been happy, and we might have been a happy family. Gyeong-ae might have been better off, too.*

With the coming of the Western New Year, Deok-gi had turned twenty-three — old enough to have a good grasp of the evils of the world but young enough not to be influenced by them.

"Mother, has Father been drinking recently?" Deok-gi stopped sipping his rice tea and looked at his mother, who was turned away from him.

"Who cares what he's been doing? He could be out drinking or visiting *gisaeng* houses." She may have realized that her snub was too harsh and added with a smile, "He probably hasn't been drinking. He never asks us to bring out the liquor tray for him."

Deok-gi thought he heard a hint of mockery in his mother's remark.

Sitting on the colder side of the room with the brazier between her and her mother-in-law, Deok-gi's wife chimed in, "Don't worry about Father's drinking. You just worry about yourself."

"Stop nagging!" Deok-gi rebuffed as he tried to light a cigarette from the ashes of the flame.

His mother, somewhat surprised, looked at him. "Have you been drinking, too?"

"Last night he came home dead drunk in the middle of the night," his wife said. Afraid of her husband's reproach, she left the room quickly with the meal tray in her hands.

"There's not much you can do when it runs in the family, but it's not a good idea for you to start drinking at your age," his mother scolded gently.

"It wasn't my fault. A friend took me . . . Anyway, a few drinks don't make you a drunk and . . ." Deok-gi trailed off, and his mother waited a moment for what might come next but then jumped in, "Are you worried about your father? Well, that's just the way he is."

"I wouldn't really care about it if he didn't write those articles in the newspaper promoting abstinence. If he didn't talk about these things and stopped attending church, I wouldn't care. But he gives moralizing speeches all day long, morning till night, and then he goes prowling from dive to dive. You think people don't know about it? It'll come out sooner or later. It might be different if our financial situation forced him to cling to his religion just to beg for handouts from Westerners."

Deok-gi spoke in a firm but low voice, his anger kept barely under wraps. He remembered how excitedly Byeong-hwa had reported seeing Deok-gi's father in a sleazy bar near Naeng-dong, outside Saemun.

"Why are you telling me all this?" his mother retorted. "Why don't you find your father and tell him what's on your mind to his face?"

Well, what about you, Mother? Deok-gi was tempted to reply. *Instead of behaving like a stranger, pretending you don't care what your husband does, what if you actually made an effort to look after Father properly and discouraged him from such behavior? Don't you think that might help Father's situation, not to mention the situation with the rest of the family?*

Deok-gi bit his tongue, and the conversation came to a halt. Mother and son sat quietly and smoked.

The baby started crying loudly from somewhere near the middle gate. Deok-gi's mother looked out the front window and scolded the maid, "Why are you running around in this cold weather?" She then soothed the child from where she was sitting. "Don't worry, honey. It's all right, stop crying. It's all right, it's all right now, that's enough."

Deok-gi's wife ran outside and returned with the crying child in her arms, followed by the maid. The grandmother held out her hand, but the baby nuzzled his face in his mother's chest and kept crying.

"What are you doing? Why won't you say hello to Grandma?" The mother was hesitant as she talked to her baby, probably shy about exposing her breasts.

"Go ahead and nurse him," Deok-gi's mother said, looking at her precious grandson.

The baby closed his eyes with the nipple in his mouth.

"He was just tired," commented his grandmother.

"It's no wonder. He wakes up at dawn, ready and eager to play," her daughter-in-law replied.

As if nothing more were left to say, the two women stopped talking. The maid, bored by the silence, left the room and headed to the veranda. The mother-in-law struck up a new conversation.

"It must be hard for you in this cold weather. The backs of your hands look frostbitten." Frowning, Deok-gi's mother stared at her daughter-in-law sitting with the baby held in her reddened hands.

27

"They're not too bad," replied the daughter-in-law with a smile, as if it were nothing out of the ordinary.

"So the Main Room sweeps everything in your direction and pretends she doesn't know how to manage, right?"

"That's exactly what she does!" Tears welled up in the young woman's eyes at her mother-in-law's kind words. "She never even leaves her room. All she does is play with that child day and night."

"The maid, too?"

"Of course. From the very beginning, she never properly instructed the maid as to what she should and shouldn't do."

"What about the new maidservant?"

"Well, she cooks, but she's a piece of work. After only a few days here, she started to kiss up to the Main Room. She's in and out of there constantly."

"Who brought her in?"

"I don't know for sure. Grandfather brought her from the outer quarters and told us that she would be with us from then on, so probably a guest in the outer quarters did."

"It's a shame."

"What do you mean?"

"With the maidservant getting so close to the Main Room, as if she were her personal attendant, it must be difficult for you, to be caught in the middle."

Deok-gi's wife didn't reply, but sniffled with her head bowed, apparently moved to tears by her mother-in-law's sympathetic reaction.

"The servant thumbs her nose at you because you're young. And your elder behaves so atrociously. I know how hard it must be on you. I wouldn't have a single worry or complaint if only you could live with me! But this is my fate, I suppose," her mother-in-law added—instead of saying, "It's all God's will," since she was not Christian.

Deok-gi stood up, refusing to listen any further. He wanted to tell his wife to stop her useless prattle but kept quiet while his mother was still present. Walking out to the outer quarters, he heaved a deep sigh. What would happen to the family if things went on like this?

On the shoe ledge at the outer quarters lay four or five pairs of inexpensive rubber shoes. With his grandfather's tightfisted way of running the household, sixty-year-old Secretary Ji was the only one designated to take care of the outer quarters. But several old acquaintances gathered there anyway, those who had nowhere else to go for a free meal. Deok-gi entered his room, lay down, and thought about what he had just heard in the inner quarters.

His grandfather had made a great fuss about finding a suitable girl for him from the right family and had forced him to marry. Deok-gi had liked his bride at first, but by the time he went to Japan he had begun to lose interest, and now he felt sorry for her, thinking how hard it must have been for her to put up with her step-grandmother-in-law while he was away.

His wife tolerated the situation because she had been raised by an old-fashioned family and had only gone to elementary school. A modern woman would have caused plenty of trouble. Deok-gi had hated the idea of marrying an uneducated woman, but given the circumstances he thought it was better that she hadn't received a modern education.

Before he knew it, he had fallen into a deep sleep.

"I told Deok-gi to leave after the ancestral rite."

Startled, Deok-gi opened his eyes. Was he dreaming? He thought he had heard his grandfather's voice. Sunlight streamed in from the window high above his head. It was after three o'clock. Still hung over after breakfast, he had lain down on the warm floor and fallen asleep. As he raised his head, it cleared and his body seemed lighter.

"I told your wife to stay. So, are you going to stop by the day after tomorrow? Although what use would you be anyway?" His grandfather's disapproving tone smacked of sarcasm, as though he were intent on making a scene.

Guessing his father had arrived, Deok-gi looked out through the tiny glass panel. The back of a slender man in a black coat with an otter-fur collar was visible in front of the main veranda on the other side the yard. Facing him was his grandfather, sitting in the room with the window open. Deok-gi felt the urge to venture out and greet his father but restrained himself, deciding to go out after his grandfather closed the window.

"I'll be here, but why does Deok-gi have to stay? He's a student. We should send him off as soon as possible, no matter how urgent the matter."

It was his father's voice. His slow, careful way of speaking gave an impression completely different from the thin, nervous figure he presented. Deok-gi always thought that his father's gentle voice and measured speech must be something he had acquired since becoming a Christian, though it was possible that he had spoken this way all his life. In contrast, the grandfather's voice was high-strung and tense—exactly what you would expect from the way he looked.

"What do you mean, no matter how urgent?" Grandfather's voice rose a notch, as if he were happy at the chance to start an argument. Deok-gi's father stood in silence.

"If a woman made him stay, would that be urgent enough? Or if his father or mother dies?"

"Why get so worked up over something so trivial?" The voice was still calm. It sounded as if he had made a point of speaking only a certain number of syllables a minute. But the old man couldn't appreciate his son's meticulousness; on the contrary, he thought his son was trying to provoke him.

"What are you trying to say? Would you even blink if I died this very moment? You ignore your own mother's memorial. Why did we even bother to give you an education?"

Deok-gi's grandfather pounded the ashtray with the long pipe he had been holding in his mouth. The old guests, who had been sitting with the old man, sat quietly with their heads bowed down as if in slumber, occasionally rubbing their hands together. They couldn't judge whether the elderly master of the household was right or wrong, but they believed his remarks made some sense.

Deok-gi's father responded, "Even if a person doesn't perform ancestral rites because he believes in a different religion, that doesn't mean that he wouldn't sit at his father's deathbed."

The old guests thought that the son made sense, too, though they believed the master of the household was right to scold his son for not attending the ceremony.

"How dare you say that to me! Shut up and get out of here! Do you think you're going to turn your son into the spitting image of you? You were responsible for his birth, but that's all. I raised him and I'm paying for his tuition. Did you feed him even once with your own hands when he was a child? Did you contribute anything toward his schooling? I couldn't possibly do a worse job raising him than I did raising you! Now stop talking shit and get out! Do you actually think the world will be a better place if you keep up this empty moralizing about philanthropy and salvation while you fail to teach your own son a single thing?"

The guests had heard the old man say this many times. They thought that he was in the right again.

"Please calm down, sir," said the oldest of the guests. "Everything you say is justified, but your son doesn't attend the ancestral rites because of his work in society. No one has said that he's against the rites." The guest was biding his time, his stomach rumbling, hoping that a liquor tray might suddenly materialize after some of the other guests left for their evening meals.

Deok-gi came out of his room, unable to stand listening to this any longer.

"I was going to pay you a visit today, Father. I think I'll leave in about three days or so." Deok-gi invited his father to come in.

The father regarded his son silently, doffed his hat, and bowed toward the room. Then he proceeded out the front gate without stopping at the inner quarters.

The old man slammed his window shut. Deok-gi was dismayed as he watched his father walk away, the father who was scolded whenever he visited and who always left quickly without venturing into the inner quarters.

Father was, of course, to blame, but he wasn't an evil man or a world-class hypocrite. If one weighed him against all the people in the world, there might be a difference of a tiny stone, not enough to make any noticeable difference. Like so many young men of his generation struggling to cast off the burdens of a feudal society, Deok-gi's father had stepped forward as a young patriot. Many of those men had flocked to the altar, kneeling before it as political possibilities dwindled. That was how Deok-gi's father had taken his first step toward religious life. If, instead, he had chosen to "come to terms with his past," to use today's parlance, and had learned to distance himself from it, he might have succeeded in making the ideological transition into a new era. And he might have developed a lifestyle more suitable to his character, instead of leading a double life.

"It's not that I don't understand how you feel. I'm not blind to the reality of society. But I want to find some common ground between the ideals of my era and those of yours. In simple terms, I'm hoping for the so-called Third Empire where your ideology and mine can meet. It's true that you've advanced a step and I've fallen a step behind. But when you take another step forward, who's to say that you won't need the ideology of my era, even if only a small part of it? I believe this could happen, and I am actually looking forward to it."

This was what his father had said to him recently, when Deok-gi returned from Japan and had asked him to give up his religion. He had been talking with his father and Byeong-hwa, and the conversation had drifted to current events and social activism.

Deok-gi was inclined to contradict his father, but custom would not permit him to do so, and he had no talent for long, circumlocutory arguments. He decided to shrug it off instead. He was glad at least to find, against all expectation, that his father was not completely clueless about, or uninterested in, modern ideological trends and social phenomena. This made him feel closer to him. Deok-gi pictured his father standing on a narrow log, linking the feudal era to modern times. It occurred to him that his father was himself in a similarly awkward position in the family, stuck between his own father and Deok-gi. Deok-gi could side with neither. He knew his father agonized over social issues, his own family, and his beliefs, and therefore often found himself pitying or sympathizing with him, while from time to time experiencing a surge of antipathy toward him as well.

Deok-gi entered the inner quarters and changed into the Western suit he had worn the night before. He didn't feel like sitting alone in the outer quarters or staying inside to listen to his mother and wife discuss the Main Room or his father.

"Where are you going? You didn't even eat your dinner!" Mother's tone was almost reproachful.

"I'll be back soon. I just want to get some fresh air."

"Aren't you going to see your father?"

"He was just here."

"What?" His mother pursed her lips. She figured her husband had wanted to avoid her.

"Then why didn't he stop by?" asked Deok-gi's wife, disappointed on behalf of her mother-in-law.

"He must be busy," Deok-gi snapped, not wanting to offer a long explanation. But he could see that he had hurt his mother's feelings. No doubt she was thinking, *So you're on your father's side!*

"Mother, will you stay overnight?"

"What else can I do? I may be over forty, but I'm still under the iron thumb of my in-laws." She stopped complaining to ask her son to stop by the Hwagae-dong house on his way out to inform the household of her plans and to ask that Deok-gi's sister be sent over.

"I don't know whether I'll have time. I'll try, but why don't you send a messenger over anyway?"

Deok-gi had no particular plans, but he didn't want to go all the way to Hwagae-dong. As he left, he mentally calculated how much money he had left in his wallet. He hadn't yet received travel expenses and the money for his tuition, so it would be difficult to give Byeong-hwa enough for a month's worth of meals.

Boarding House

———

Maybe I'll go up to Jingogae and buy something. Deok-gi had nothing particular in mind, but was merely entertaining a thought typical of the idle rich. Then it occurred to him: *Will Byeong-hwa be waiting for me if he thinks I'm leaving today?* He vaguely remembered promising over drinks the previous night that he would bring money to Byeong-hwa's boarding house.

Deok-gi hopped on a passing streetcar, got off at Seodaemun, and had to ask several times for directions before reaching Hongpa-dong. He took out his address book as he meandered from one alley to another, negotiating a maze of streets as twisted as animal's innards. He had grown up in Seoul and lived there for more than twenty years, but never had he been to this kind of neighborhood. He wandered for more than half an hour until he found himself at a tiny gate perched on a rocky hillside. The winter sun was slowly descending below the horizon. He had seen many such houses in the neighborhood but had assumed that a boarding house would look better.

The place was a wreck. It wasn't a hovel, strictly speaking, because there was a gate, albeit one on the verge of collapse. The entire house was wrapped in blackish, rotting straw mats, like a *kimchi* jar insulated against the cold.

So this is where he's holed up, where he gets free meals! The thought made Deok-gi more inclined to despise Byeong-hwa, rather than sympathize with him.

He called out for his friend several times, but no one answered. He knew his voice had carried, for the yard was no bigger than a cat's forehead. Finally he heard a voice ask, "Who is it?" He had not detected any movement on the other side of the gate, but when he peered in through its gap, he saw a disheveled woman, who, were it not for her pale face, might have passed for a weasel plucked straight from a chimney. She looked as short and skinny as a dark leg warmer. This, and the sound of her voice, suggested she was over thirty.

"Mr. Kim? He's still in bed. He's not feeling well."

Deok-gi's face brightened at the news that his friend was home. Since Byeong-hwa hadn't come out to meet him, Deok-gi had been afraid that Byeong-hwa had already left and that the two had missed each other.

"Well, if he can't come out, may I come in?" Deok-gi asked, pushing lightly on the gate.

The woman winced with embarrassment at the thought of inviting a guest into her shabby home. She kept peering out, trying to get a good look at her visitor. "Please wait here," she said and went back inside.

In a few minutes, one of the windows slid open, and Deok-gi heard Byeong-hwa's husky voice: "Is that you, Jo? Come on in!"

Deok-gi cleared his throat and entered the house. The housewife looked back at the guest as she opened the door to the main room. Deok-gi automatically returned her gaze. She looked like a gentle woman, after all, and he felt sorry for her.

Is her daughter not at home? Judging from the mother, I bet the daughter has a pretty face and is sweet, too.

Deok-gi stood smiling at Byeong-hwa for a while before he said, "What's the matter? Does wine-loving Chinese poet Li Bai sometimes get hungover after having a few drinks?" He remained at the doorway, put off by the shabbiness of the veranda and the cavernous room.

"Come on in. It's freezing out there!" Byeong-hwa shook his shoulders and buried his hands deep into the pockets of the pants he had slept in — the only pants he owned. Deok-gi gazed at the dusty trousers with a look of pity.

"Why are you standing there with your mouth hanging open? Does everything look that pathetic to you?" Byeong-hwa asked in the gravelly voice of someone who had drunk too much rice wine.

"Let's go out."

"We can go out, but why don't you come in first? I can't move a muscle yet. I'm sick and starving," Byeong-hwa whined.

Deok-gi was at a loss. He noticed someone watching through a tiny glass pane in the main room and wondered whether it was the daughter of the family, who, according to Byeong-hwa, worked at a factory. He began to feel self-conscious.

"If you're sick, take some medicine." With this advice, Deok-gi jumped onto the narrow veranda.

"I'm starving to death. What medicine can cure that?" Byeong-hwa muttered angrily, as if his friend were to blame for how he felt.

"That's why I'm saying we should go out. Get some cheap drinks or some beef soup." He finally entered the room from the veranda. The floor under his feet was icy cold.

His friend had been covering himself with a quilt, but it was so soiled that it was impossible to say which side was the cover and which the lining. A chill rose up through Deok-gi's body, and a quintessentially male odor, a mixture of grease and old sweat, assaulted his nose and made his stomach turn.

Deok-gi stuck a cigarette between his lips and picked up a box of matches from the desktop. Several magazines were strewn about, but other than that the desk held only a bottle of ink. Newspapers were in open disarray at the head of the bed.

I guess some people live like this.

Deok-gi was shocked, but in the end he felt sorry for his friend, and his sympathy deepened when he realized how unswerving Byeong-hwa's spirit must be for him to suffer such extreme conditions while he clung to his ideals.

I wouldn't last a day here. I would have crawled back home and would be living off my parents.

"So you don't want to go out?" Deok-gi asked again.

"I'm sure an aristocrat like you finds this place unbearable for even a minute, but just sit down, will you?" Byeong-hwa pushed aside the quilt, but Deok-gi was reluctant to sit amid such squalor.

"Are you afraid you might catch something? I don't have lice, you know." Byeong-hwa sarcastic as ever.

"You're crazy. Cut it out and put your clothes on."

"I can't go out. My head is spinning. Are you leaving today?"

"I've got to stay three more days."

"Why?" Byeong-hwa asked in undisguised disappointment. If Deok-gi wasn't leaving today, the money he had promised him might not materialize quickly.

"My grandfather wants me to stay until after my great-grandfather's ancestral rite."

"Did you ever actually meet your great-grandfather? Did you get some radio report from Heaven or paradise that your great-grandfather, whom you never knew, will be satisfied with his ancestral rite only if he has the pleasure of your attendance?" Byeong-hwa smirked.

Deok-gi returned his grin. "You are really, really crazy!" He pretended to frown.

"Anyway, this great-grandfather of yours is going to cause me trouble."
"Why?"

"The sooner you leave, the quicker my financial situation improves."

"Are you that desperate?"

"You better believe it. The owners haven't said anything today. They're nice people, so they don't pester me. But I see what they want. That's why I stayed in bed, hoping you would come by."

Deok-gi felt bad for the family more than anything else.

"Hasn't the daughter gone off to work?"

"She seems to, but what's the use? She doesn't bring back a penny."

"What does the landlord do?"

"Absolutely nothing! His contribution to the household is reducing the number of mouths to feed by eating jail food." Byeong-hwa took a cigarette from the pack Deok-gi offered him and lit up.

"Why?" Deok-gi asked in surprise. "Is he a bum or some sort of ideologist?"

"Well, that about describes him." Byeong-hwa changed the subject to the one he found more urgent. "So you don't have any money on you?"

"I haven't gotten my travel expenses yet, but I guess I could give you five won anyway."

"Fine. I'll take it." Byeong-hwa held out his hand as if in a great hurry. He took the five won and headed for the veranda, calling out "Auntie" as he went. The woman came out to meet him, and they began whispering loud enough so that Deok-gi could hear. In a low voice the woman kept repeating, "We're so obliged to your friend."

Deok-gi was pleased to have done a good deed and happy to look good while he was at it; but it all made him rather queasy. The miserable condition of the house was too much for him.

"Okay, let's go," Byeong-hwa said, as content as if he had solved a mathematical puzzle. He threw on an overcoat and led Deok-gi outside. Deok-gi felt as if he were leaving behind something essential. Realizing he would never have any reason to come to this house again, he wanted to catch a glimpse of the landlord and, better yet, his daughter. He was curious about this young woman who earned a living for her family and was widely praised

39

among the ideologists for her intelligence. It occurred to him that half the reason for his coming here today was most likely his hope of catching a glimpse of her.

Deok-gi broke the silence after a while, but what he said was not what he had been thinking. "Your mother must know that you're here. How can she let you live like this?"

"What else can she do? After all, my mother is a daughter of God, isn't she?"

Do You Think You're the Only One Suffering?

———

Deok-gi disapproved of Byeong-hwa's mean-spirited comment, which was clearly meant to ridicule his own mother. It would have been another matter if the woman had been Byeong-hwa's stepmother, but she wasn't. During their secondary school days, Byeong-hwa's father had worked as a pastor in Hwanghae Province, so Deok-gi didn't see his friend's parents much. Although they had visited the boys' school around the time of their graduation some three years earlier, Deok-gi couldn't remember them well. He did recall, however, that Byeong-hwa's mother seemed like a nice woman. Since moving to Seoul, Byeong-hwa's father had become acquainted with Deok-gi's father. After graduation, though, Deok-gi had gone off to Kyoto for three years, and Byeong-hwa had left for Tokyo a year later and returned to Seoul only this fall — no, he should say last fall, now that they were in the new year. As a result, the two young men had not recently had many opportunities to see each other, nor spend time with each other's parents. Deok-gi didn't know the Kims well, but he doubted that Byeong-hwa's mother would turn a blind eye to her son's plight, now that they all lived in Seoul.

After graduating, the two young men had met on only three occasions — twice when Byeong-hwa had stopped off in Kyoto on his way to or from Tokyo, and this time in Seoul. While students, however, they had been particularly close, first getting acquainted through their parents, who were involved in the church, and because they themselves were churchgoers. The friendship deepened in their third year of school, when Byeong-hwa began attending Deok-gi's church.

Teenagers' friendships are supposed to be spontaneous, but theirs was cemented by their parents' religious practice. Despite their close relationship, they kept a certain distance from each other, afraid to reveal too much of their lives. In their postgraduation years, both boys drifted away from the church, and having this in common created a new bond between them.

It was around this time that Byeong-hwa failed to gain admission to the Law Department at Keijo Imperial University and so decided to join his parents, who were living in Haeju. A year later, on his way to Tokyo, where he was planning to attend university, he stopped in Kyoto and confided in Deok-gi.

"My father told me I should try to get into the Theology Department at Doshisha University, and that if I can't get in there, I should go to Tokyo to study. I said okay and left home, but I'd rather die than become a minister. A minister? I don't even have a Bible in my bag."

Deok-gi had been surprised to hear these words, and pleased. Unlike Byeong-hwa, he was hesitant about breaking away from religion, so when his old friend, whose experience was so similar to his own, voiced such opinions, he felt himself agreeing wholeheartedly.

Still, this was a matter of some concern for Deok-gi, knowing as he did that Byeong-hwa's family was not wealthy. "If you don't agree to study to be a minister, your father won't pay for your tuition. And he was probably going to try to find you a church scholarship once you had gotten into college."

"Believe me. I've thought about it more than you have. But I can't sell my soul for a few years' tuition. How can anyone just betray their convictions? What use is studying a religion you've lost faith in? Isn't that selling out Jesus? Wouldn't that make me like Judas? It'd be like preparing a funeral without the corpse. Come on. You don't make a New Year's outfit for a child that's dead and buried, though they may make a shroud for a child who's just died. Isn't that the order of things?" Byeong-hwa spoke confidently, almost arrogantly. "The world is changing, my friend. Let's say you put out a charity pot on Jongno Avenue and start to pray. Then some beggar, thinking you've dozed off for a minute, is caught taking a penny from your pot. Will you beat him up and send him to prison for stealing? Or will you pray all the more for his repentance and regeneration? You tell me. The world isn't what it used to be—beggars steal before your eyes. And as for you and me— well, for your father and my father—is it right to keep a watchful eye on that charity pot while parading around in fur coats?"

Byeong-hwa spoke with passion, spit gathering at the corners of his mouth and his hands gesturing wildly. As soon as he had graduated from secondary school, his beliefs had changed as though he had been waiting for just the right moment. His ideas, then, were like buds about to open, and he was sincere and enthusiastic, if naïve.

Today, with the same Byeong-hwa walking in front of him, Deok-gi made his way down Seokdari, outside Seodaemun, and thought about his friend's life since their last encounter.

After his brief meeting in Kyoto with Deok-gi, Byeong-hwa had indeed gone to Tokyo and attended school for about one semester, registering as a student in the Department of Political Science and Economics at Waseda University. His father, just as Deok-gi predicted, refused to pay the tuition. Byeong-hwa's father had approved of his son's original plan to apply to the Law Department at Keijo Imperial University, and had he supported Byeong-hwa on this new path, things might have sorted themselves out more smoothly. But the clash between the equally stubborn father and son meant no financial support for Byeong-hwa.

This state of affairs partly grew out of a rebellious letter Byeong-hwa had sent home. Everything might have been fine if he had just kept quiet and pretended to get along with his father, even though his view of the world was changing, but his young heart, unwilling to compromise, drove him to assert his new outlook.

As he scraped by for a year in Tokyo, barely avoiding starvation, his disposition grew ever more radical and his resolve was toughened by the kind of life he now led. Never mind that he had broken ranks with his father—what was more surprising to Deok-gi was his discovery that Byeong-hwa's ideology had undergone a radical shift from his own. Byeong-hwa, however, finally gave up and, after scrounging just enough to get from Tokyo to Kyoto, came to borrow the rest of the money to return home.

Back in Seoul, less than two months after his homecoming, Byeong-hwa had it out with his father. It all began when Byeong-hwa refused to pray before a meal. His father upbraided him, saying that if he intended to ignore paternal instruction and discard his faith, he should either move out or die.

"Well, since I'm not planning to die any time soon, I suppose I'll just have to go," replied Byeong-hwa, and he left in a fit of anger.

As the two of them walked along, Deok-gi said out of the blue, "So, my friend, I've been thinking it would have been better if you had gone to theology school."

"What? What did you say?" Byeong-hwa asked sharply, his eyes, teary from the cold wind, glistening behind his glasses. He knew Deok-gi mentioned this because his situation looked so pathetic. The thought enraged Byeong-hwa so much that if he had still had that five won in his hand, he would have thrown it back in his face. Instead, he swallowed his anger.

"Well, I was looking at your long hair from behind, and I suddenly remembered that time we met in Kyoto." Deok-gi forced a laugh. He was amused by Byeong-hwa's reaction and wanted to hear what his friend had to say. That was why he was quite deliberately, indeed mischievously, baiting him.

"So, what about it?" Byeong-hwa sounded angrier.

"Don't lose your temper. I just meant that if you'd gone to theology school, you'd be able to keep your eyes comfortably on the charity pot." Deok-gi laughed again. By repeating Byeong-hwa's own words, Deok-gi was insinuating that Byeong-hwa would have been better off had he become a minister. This didn't go over very well.

"I didn't steal your five won from the charity pot, you know. I'll give it back someday!" Byeong-hwa shouted. He wheeled around and stalked off without saying good-bye. Deok-gi looked on with a smile, then walked after him.

"Why are you acting like a child?"

"I've got a headache; I'd better go home and lie down," Byeong-hwa said. He kept walking.

"I'm sorry I said something so pointless, but why make a fuss over such a small amount of money? Do you think I brought it up because I miss it? I was only trying to convince you to change your mind and go back home a bit humbled." Deok-gi grabbed his friend's hand to try to calm him down.

Byeong-hwa stopped short. It suddenly occurred to him that he should put their friendship behind him; it would be too difficult to maintain a real relationship, or even keep up appearances, with a friend who had money. "I don't think we can go on being friends — unless you come a step closer to me or I take a step back for you. That'll be hard for both of us. If we continue to see each other, it'll be meaningless, and I'll just keep owing you money."

"Well, it's not as if I haven't ever felt the same way, but let's go out now anyway. We can at least relax and talk a bit before we say good-bye." Deok-gi held his friend's arm and headed downtown. Byeong-hwa followed quietly.

As they reached the street near the prison, they looked for a place to eat but continued on toward Namdaemun until they found themselves in front of a Japanese noodle shop. A cold evening wind swept through the darkening streets. Deok-gi led the way to the door, brightly lit with an electrical bulb. Byeong-hwa, a few steps behind, was about to enter, when he suddenly turned on his heels and walked away. Thinking his friend was being difficult again, Deok-gi followed him out. Byeong-hwa stood with his eyes on Namdaemun, where about a block away, a young woman in a white blouse, black skirt, and a scarf drawn high up to her cheeks, was approaching with quick steps. Byeong-hwa seemed to be waiting for her.

Her hair was pinned up, but she was young, only about sixteen or seventeen. Deok-gi surmised she must be Pil-sun, the daughter of the man who owned Byeong-hwa's boarding house.

"What brings you here?" Pil-sun asked Byeong-hwa, casting a sidelong glance toward Deok-gi. Recognizing him, she quickly turned away in embarrassment and looked as if she might dash off.

"Chilly night, isn't it?" Byeong-hwa was about to say more when Deok-gi caught up with him and whispered, "How about asking her to warm up inside? It's freezing out here."

That was exactly what Byeong-hwa wanted to do, though he was reluctant to take her to a restaurant with a stranger and figured she almost certainly would refuse. He also didn't think it was a good idea after having just quarreled with his friend. But Deok-gi sounded sincere, and Byeong-hwa wanted her to have something to eat before going home; she must have gone to work with little breakfast and then walked all the way from Yongsan in the cold. Besides, he had once shown her pictures of his friends, and when she commented on Deok-gi's good looks, he had joked that he'd introduce her to him the next time he came over. Come to think of it, she'd probably be quite happy to join them.

Yet Byeong-hwa still hesitated, staring at her as she walked away. At last, he took several steps after her and called, "Pil-sun, wait a minute."

"Why?" She turned swiftly.

"Just come over here for a minute, will you?"

Pil-sun slowly approached him.

"Aren't you cold? Your legs must be tired, too, from walking such a long way. Why don't you come inside with us for a while?"

"No, thanks." She looked over at Deok-gi, who was standing a few yards away.

"Don't worry. He's one of the friends I told you about. We'll just chat for a while. Come on. Warm yourself up a bit before you go home." Byeong-hwa pulled at her.

Pil-sun couldn't make up her mind. When Byeong-hwa's friends came to visit, she usually spent time with them, for they were, for the most part, her father's friends as well. She knew them all and wasn't reluctant to be with them. But now, knowing that this friend was Jo Deok-gi, the son of a rich family, she felt embarrassed by her appearance and ashamed of being taken to the shop. She was even more hesitant to go in because she was so hungry.

"Don't worry. It's not a fancy restaurant; it's only a noodle shop. Just come in and warm yourself up." Byeong-hwa had no intention of persuading her any further. He pushed her toward the shop and Pil-sun could no longer resist. She let him escort her in.

Deok-gi was already standing in front of the stove inside. When he saw them, his face lit up and he moved aside to make room. The three of them crowded around the stove.

"This friend of mine is a modern boy. His name is Jo Deok-gi. And this young woman is Yi Pil-sun. She works at a rubber factory. I wouldn't introduce you to Jo if he were a delinquent. That, at least, he is not, so I'm granting him this honor." Byeong-hwa chuckled, as if he'd forgotten all about the fit of anger he'd just had.

Deok-gi and Pil-sun smiled and bowed to each other, after which she blushed and hid her face behind the stovepipe.

Deok-gi thought Pil-sun a great beauty. He didn't dare examine her features too closely yet, but under the electric lights she looked adorable, if a little mature for her age.

She must have been cold, wearing only a thin cotton blouse, but it was clean and so were the white Korean padded socks peeking out below her black wool serge skirt. Compared to typical factory girls decked out in gaudy synthetic silk and Western-style shoes, she struck Deok-gi as simple and modest.

After they sat down, Pil-sun furtively put the small bundle she had been carrying on her lap under the table. She was being careful not to make a racket with her metal lunch box. When Byeong-hwa caught sight of it, he wondered if she had brought rice boiled the evening before, because no one in the house had eaten breakfast that morning. Pity welled up in his heart.

Byeong-hwa told Deok-gi to order rice topped with chicken for Pil-sun. But she blushed and firmly declined, afraid that he was trying to feed her rice instead of noodles because he thought she was skipping meals.

The noodles were served, followed by drinks. The savory smell whetted Pil-sun's appetite, but she found it difficult to pick up her chopsticks, wondering whether her family was sitting at home without food. Besides, she didn't want to look greedy.

"Don't worry about your family!" Byeong-hwa said quite openly. "I managed to pay them, so don't worry about it. Eat." Pil-sun was embarrassed by his remark but relieved.

Influenced as she was by her father and Byeong-hwa's friends, Pil-sun didn't think poverty was anything to be ashamed of. Yet she didn't like Byeong-hwa talking about her household affairs so candidly and explicitly in the presence of a virtual stranger. Why couldn't he have mentioned the money before they came in?

He's so thick-skinned. He is the kind of person who'd enjoy himself at any feast, no matter what other people thought of him! The more Pil-sun thought about it, the more uncomfortable she felt. She regretted joining them and wished she'd gone home.

Byeong-hwa may have given them money, but who was going to buy the rice and the firewood to cook it with? Her father had been housebound since the day before, when his only Korean coat had been taken apart to be washed. Had her mother sewn it back together? Such details worried her. She could picture her mother running back and forth in the cold, running errands. She was ill at ease and wanted to check on her parents.

All of a sudden, she asked herself where Byeong-hwa's boarding money had come from. Instantly she understood and her face reddened. If anyone noticed, she could always blame her blushing on the cold.

"Please go ahead and eat," Deok-gi said. "You'll have to come and visit me at my house sometime. You should meet my sister; she's seventeen this year. Actually, she just turned eighteen with the Western New Year."

Pil-sun nodded, though she was so lost in thought that she wasn't really paying attention to what he was saying. The money must have come from Deok-gi, and he must have invited Byeong-hwa, who was starving and staying in bed.

"Yes, eat while it's warm," said Byeong-hwa, pausing from his greedy slurping. He turned to Deok-gi. "Is your sister that old already? She and Pil-sun are the same age then. She's in the upper level at R School, right?"

"Yeah, she's about to start her fourth year."

"Tell me, though—how can this girl make friends with your sister? I'm pretty sure I can handle you, but hanging out with the precious daughter of a bourgeois family could be dangerous. Women are too easily swayed, and vanity always gets the better of them." Byeong-hwa was concerned that Pil-sun's ideology might change if she befriended the daughter of a rich family.

Deok-gi didn't appreciate this observation, but he suppressed his anger and offered a rebuttal: "What do you mean calling us bourgeois? We're not even middle class by Japanese standards, not to mention those of other countries. Anyway, my sister's not typical of the girls you see around these days."

Pil-sun was offended by Byeong-hwa's thoughtless remarks. And vanity would never get the better of her!

"Please eat. Your family will worry about you if it gets too late, and I'll feel bad about having asked you in." At Deok-gi's urging, she reluctantly picked up her chopsticks. Already anxious about being late, Pil-sun felt grateful to this young man.

Byeong-hwa didn't like seeing Pil-sun behave so timidly. She was articulate, she could talk with other men, even when meeting them for the first time, and her outspokenness had earned her the nickname "Miss Know-It-All." It didn't become her, this acting clueless like an old-fashioned woman confined to her home.

It is because he has money? Or because he's handsome? Byeong-hwa regretted introducing them. Was it jealousy? No, he was simply worried that his friend might confuse the girl or shake the ideological foundation that Byeong-hwa had been nurturing in her with such special care.

When Pil-sun had finished most of her *tempura udon*, she put down her chopsticks, quietly wiped her mouth, and whispered to Byeong-hwa that she really must go.

Deok-gi wanted to order something more for her, but Byeong-hwa said that they'd better send her home before it got too late. The two young men saw Pil-sun off at the door.

"Too bad she couldn't go back to school. She seems really bright!" Deok-gi's praise was genuine. He was touched by her situation.

"Well, if you really think so, why don't you give her the chance?"

"If that's what she wants, it shouldn't be too hard. It would be great if she came and stayed at the Hwagae-dong house. My sister feels lonely as the only child living there. Do you think we couldn't pay her tuition?"

Byeong-hwa had mentioned it offhandedly, but Deok-gi was quite serious.

"If that's the case, why don't you give me the chance instead?" Byeong-hwa said sarcastically. "It wouldn't work because I'm a man?" He went on in the same unpleasant tone. "Isn't it obvious why a man would want to pay for a girl's education? It seems you're not quite satisfied with having only your wife around. You fell for that girl the minute you saw her, didn't you? Ha!"

"Just how long are you going to go on insulting me?" Deok-gi responded sharply, but then he managed a laugh. "If you're willing to compromise with my father, why don't you tell him to clear out a room so you can stay there, too?"

"Stop it. If I could compromise with your father, I would have done it already with my own!" Byeong-hwa said. Complaining that his head hurt, he picked up his glass and tossed back his drink.

"If you drink this much, you'll have to keep drinking tomorrow because your head will still hurt. You'll never clear your mind!" said Deok-gi, looking at his friend's glass disapprovingly. He decided to offer some sincere advice. "Stop doing this to yourself. Just make peace with them and go home. How long can you go on leading a vagrant's life? What can you accomplish in such a state?"

"Make peace? More than compromising with my father, you think I should compromise with the bourgeois guard that keeps watch over the food, don't you?"

"It makes no sense to keep up this barrier between you and your father. Can't you see it as an ethical matter between father and son, instead of an undermining of your beliefs?"

"Well, whatever you want to call it, when parents drive a child away because he doesn't parrot their words and follow their faith, how else can he live his own life without being their possession or slave?" Byeong-hwa was becoming increasingly longwinded as the alcohol kicked in.

"This is an ethical matter concerning the father-son relationship. How can you talk about compromise and personal life when everything boils down to family?" Deok-gi said, fearing that Byeong-hwa might think he had originally brought up the word "compromise" in reference to the relationship between father and son.

"Stop talking bullshit! You go your way and I'll go mine."

"A little while ago, you were ranting and raving as if you were ready to sever our friendship, but I'm sure you need someone like me." Deok-gi's voice was equally cold.

"For what? Oh, I see. You mean I need to beg you for spare change every now and then, right?"

"What are you talking about? Do you actually think you're making any sense?" Deok-gi glared at Byeong-hwa.

"At any rate, being friends means that we don't take advantage of each other. That should go without saying between like-minded comrades," offered Byeong-hwa, after a moment of thought.

"Comrades? Well, I may not be a like-minded comrade, but you're not the only one suffering." Deok-gi's expression was dark.

"Oh, yes, the luxurious suffering of a bourgeois. Nothing but extravagant sentimentalism," Byeong-hwa said.

"Someone like you might see it that way, but you don't know everything that goes on among my family's three generations."

"I do know that you're able to compromise with your grandfather and father, and that's why you won't let up with me. And I also know," Byeong-hwa added spitefully, "that, in your case, you can expect an inheritance!"

Deok-gi stood up without another word and paid the bill.

A New Baby Sister

———

Two mornings later, Deok-gi snuck out of the house and spent half the day holed up in the library of the Government-General of Korea. He had nothing urgent to research, but there was nowhere else to go to pass the time. If he had stayed home on the day of the ancestral ceremony, he would have had to listen to his grandfather yell at everyone as he bustled around the house. Deok-gi also had little tolerance for the women making such a fuss in the inner quarters. Nor did he like the idea of kneeling before his grandfather to write a ritual text with one of those calligraphic brushes he so rarely used. And he wanted nothing to do with the job of arranging ceremonial food into neat piles on the ritual table. So he had left the house early, before his grandfather could begin ordering him around, and he intended to return home after dark.

Deok-gi left the library before the electric lights came on and headed for Jingogae, thinking he'd get a cup of tea somewhere. He considered trying to find Byeong-hwa, but he knew that if they met up, they'd only end up drinking. And another dose of Byeong-hwa's sarcastic remarks might give him a headache. It was much better to enjoy some peace and quiet by himself. He stopped at a bookstore, flipped through some books, and left with a couple of magazines. Amid the sounds of gramophones drifting out of several shops, he walked up the street swarming with people.

He thought of Bacchus, which he had visited a few days before with Byeong-hwa, and wondered how Gyeong-ae was doing. It felt like ages ago that they'd met, and the memory of what had happened that night had dimmed, like a faded dream. He considered dropping by once more before he left for Japan to see Gyeong-ae and get to the bottom of what had happened between her and his father. Two nights earlier, he had been tempted to go to Bacchus after eating at the noodle shop off Saemun, but with Byeong-hwa in tow, he wouldn't have been able to talk discreetly with Gyeong-ae, and it wouldn't have been a good idea to expose his father's well-guarded secret to his friend. He had resolved to go back by himself on some other occasion, but it was hard to muster the courage. From the moment his path veered toward Jingogae, however, he realized that stopping at Bacchus had been at the back of his mind.

But they only serve drinks there, no food . . . thought Deok-gi as he got closer to the bar. He decided not to go in, though he knew he was just making excuses.

If I don't go in now, I'll leave without seeing her. And she might find another job before I come home for spring vacation, which means I may never see her again . . .

Not going in did seem heartless, he thought, and it probably wasn't polite.

But why isn't it polite? The problem is between her and my father, and they'll have to solve it. If it's already been settled, then that's that . . .

He was about to give up. But if a daughter—his younger sister—indeed existed, the situation wouldn't be that simple.

What should I do? The more complicated this gets, the more difficult it'll be for me to solve. They must have tried to deal with it somehow . . . But we have the same blood . . . If both her parents died, who'd take care of the child?

Deok-gi's head throbbed. It was a delicate matter since it involved his parents. Besides, Gyeong-ae hadn't been merely his father's concubine, but Deok-gi's childhood friend as well. It wouldn't matter if he were the type of person who put things behind him once and for all, but he wasn't. He was emotional and sensitive, and he tended to worry obsessively about one thing or the other.

Well, I guess I'll have some tea and think about whether or not to go.

He walked slowly, looking for a teahouse.

"Where are you headed?"

He thought he heard a woman's voice among the crowds on Jingogae, but he kept going.

"Hey!"

The voice came from right behind him. Startled, Deok-gi spun around. It was Gyeong-ae.

She looked at him wide-eyed without even a trace of a smile on her face, as if she were about to scold him.

Deok-gi couldn't believe that they had run into each other this way.

"Where're you going?" Gyeong-ae finally permitted herself a shadow of a smile.

"I'm looking for a nice teahouse." Deok-gi smiled back.

"But why are you still in town?"

"I leave tomorrow . . ." Deok-gi hesitated, not knowing how to end his sentence. He wasn't inclined to use a formal ending, but it was difficult to justify a familiar one.

"If I weren't busy, we could go somewhere to talk, but . . ." Gyeong-ae hesitated, her eyes wide and blank.

"Well, it's not too late. How about we have dinner together somewhere nearby? I was thinking of coming to see you anyway."

"There's really not much to talk about. The child has a bad cold so I was on my way to —"

"Let's just go somewhere and sit down for a while," Deok-gi said. Hearing her mention the child, Deok-gi felt even more compelled to latch on to her and ask how they were doing.

"Well, then, maybe for just a minute," Gyeong-ae said.

As they walked side by side, Deok-gi compared the Gyeong-ae he'd once known with the woman beside him now. It had been five years since he had seen her last, but her face hadn't aged at all and her height seemed the same. What was different was her expression, the way she carried herself, the way she addressed him.

Who would believe this woman is an employee at a hole-in-the-wall bar called Bacchus? Deok-gi thought, taking in Gyeong-ae decked out in her Western outfit. In the twilight, he couldn't make out what she was wearing under her coat, but the dark orange overcoat, her fuzzy hat, and her pointed enameled shoes wouldn't be out of place on a dance floor or a stage.

"Where is the child? Is it a very bad cold?" Deok-gi said after a while.

"At my mother's in Changgol. It must be the flu. She's been sick for three days, and it's getting worse. If she's going to die, I hope it happens sooner rather than later," Gyeong-ae spat out.

Deok-gi took her to a Japanese noodle shop, thinking it would be less crowded there.

He had thought they would have a lot to discuss, but once they were finally sitting across from each other, there wasn't much to say.

"Is everyone all right?" Gyeong-ae broke the ice.

"Yes."

"Does your father still say 'Amen'?" A sneer flickered over Gyeong-ae's face.

"He does." Deok-gi answered with an embarrassed smile. It caused him pain to talk about his father.

Gyeong-ae didn't want anything from the menu, saying that she had already eaten. Deok-gi didn't feel like eating a full meal in front of her, so he just ordered a bowl of noodles.

"How did you start working where you are now?" Deok-gi was dying to know.

"Why do you want to know?" Gyeong-ae smiled fleetingly, then added: "The proprietor is a friend of mine. She asked me to work with her because she'd never run a place like that before. I was bored so I went along. It's fun." She flashed another smile.

Deok-gi found it difficult to delve further into her affairs.

"How old is the child now? A daughter, right?"

"She's five. If she were a boy, it would be more troublesome," she answered without a hint of embarrassment. "That child, she's a Jesus, a female Jesus." She sneered.

"Why is that?"

"Because she doesn't have a father."

"Why?"

"She isn't in your family registry, is she? Your father the Christian, the 'pastor,' won't put her name there because it would sully the Jo family name." As she spat out these words, a menacing look flitted across her face.

Deok-gi gulped down his noodles quickly; they left together.

"It's a little out of the way, but do you want to stop by?" Gyeong-ae said as they went down Jingogae together. "I don't want to say that I feel bad for her, but . . ."

Gyeong-ae wanted to say, "but she does have the same blood as you." She just couldn't bring herself to say it.

Although Deok-gi understood what she meant, he didn't respond right away. At first he thought that perhaps he could ignore the situation, or that at least there wouldn't be any need for him to go and see the sick child, even if the day did come when he'd meet her as a grown-up. It was his father who should go and see her out of sincerity, affection, and loyalty. It wasn't his place to make an impulsive appearance.

What does my father think about all this, and how responsible does he feel? If he doesn't include her in our family registry, what's going to happen to her when she's an adult?

He felt sorry for Gyeong-ae and the half sister to whom he had yet to be introduced. The more he pitied the mother and daughter, the more he disapproved of his father.

"Maybe you know what happened and how I ended up like this. Whether you do or not, I could just leave it at that, and it probably isn't something you should ask me about. I don't want to argue about who's right and who's wrong. But why don't you at least meet her once? It's useless, if you give it serious thought, and I'm sure it's a bother for you, but no one visits the poor thing, not even once a year. Though she's still young, I feel sorry for her." Gyeong-ae's words were unexpectedly sentimental.

She's an ordinary woman, a mother loyal to her family, Deok-gi thought, and he agreed with what she said.

"Unfortunately, I'm in a ridiculous and rather embarrassing position, but it might be a good idea for me to go and see her, as you say. Especially if my father doesn't do anything for her . . . I mean, she was born a Jo, and if she has no one to look after her in ten or twenty years, I can't ignore her then. But as long as you're raising her, you'd better do a good job of it. If we ignored her and then tried to take care of her when it's too late or who knows what, it'd only look bad." Deok-gi stammered, feeling awkward about broaching the matter. What he said was intended in part as advice that she be careful not to taint the Jo family name.

Gyeong-ae walked along slowly as she listened, but she didn't respond. Deok-gi struck her as mature for his age, and he was, to his credit, giving the matter of her child serious thought. She was grateful to him for that. Truth be told, she was taking him to see the child with every intention of entrusting her to him in lieu of his father. She was glad to learn, even before she brought up the subject, that the same idea had crossed Deok-gi's mind.

If I get him to meet her and he visits her often, he won't be able to turn his back on her!

Gyeong-ae's house was in Bungmi Changjeong, down a long alley marked by many twists and turns. Deok-gi would have a hard time finding his way out.

"Did you bring medicine?" Gyeong-ae's mother called impatiently as she came out to greet her, but on seeing Deok-gi, who was standing behind her daughter, she stopped short and stared.

The house was a tile-roofed building in fairly decent shape. Peering into the veranda, which was lit with electric lamps, Deok-gi surmised that this was not a household in need.

Who do they live with? Did my father set them up here?

Deok-gi followed Gyeong-ae onto the veranda. As soon as the child saw her mother, she began to fret, whining from the bed. She saw her mother once a day, but her mother rarely held her, so she didn't ask to be picked up.

"Don't cry, honey. Look who's here! We've got a guest!" Gyeong-ae pointed to Deok-gi.

The child stared at the stranger and burst into tears.

"Now, now, our little Miss Jesus — our Christ!" The young mother took off her coat, hung it on the wall and sat down by the child, lifting her into her lap.

Deok-gi sat at the foot of the bedding on the warm part of the floor.

"This is your brother! Your brother! You said you wanted to see your father, didn't you?" Gyeong-ae shifted the child in her arms so that Deok-gi could see her. Flushed with fever, the child stared at him, her teary eyes wide open in surprise. Then she buried her face in the crook of her mother's arm.

"What's the matter?" Gyeong-ae asked Deok-gi with a smile. "Were you expecting someone else?" She thought it was both funny and embarrassing that the word "brother" had rolled unhindered off her tongue. It sounded odd to Deok-gi's ear, too.

Deok-gi thought the little girl looked clever and pretty. He knew he couldn't keep sitting there without saying anything.

"She still seems a bit feverish. Why not use some Chinese medicine?" He looked at Gyeong-ae's mother.

The mother looked stubborn but not coarse.

She had been sitting quietly sizing up Deok-gi, but seizing the opportunity opened up by his comment, she asked her daughter, "This gentleman is the eldest son?" She threw a quick glance in Deok-gi's direction.

Gyeong-ae nodded and introduced her mother to Deok-gi. Then she mumbled in a teasing tone, "And yes, Mother, this gentleman is the eldest son."

Her mother understood who he was when Gyeong-ae first used the word "brother." Now her face clouded; she uttered an exclamatory remark and began to spout a stream of grievances. "How could that man just stop coming by all of a sudden? He could have at least shown some interest in how his child has been doing these past few years. After all, she does live in the same city. Has my daughter somehow become his enemy? I think that it's just despicable the way he. . ."

Gyeong-ae kept flashing her eyes at her mother without success, so she finally cut her off. "Why are you telling these things to this gentleman?"

Her mother stopped out of sheer surprise, but she had a hard time suppressing her anger. Her face reddening, she said to Deok-gi, "Well, just go and tell him how hard it's been for an old woman like me to raise the girl."

Deok-gi was startled at this unexpected scolding, but he sat with his head bowed, as silent as someone with a mouthful of stolen honey. He was curious to know why his father and Gyeong-ae had parted ways, but he couldn't ask either of them.

"Just because he lets us stay in this grand house of his, he thinks he doesn't have to look after the child. Why did he have the child in the first place, then?" As the mother resumed her litany, Gyeong-ae scowled and sharply told her to go to the other room. The old woman's chiding words, which were unfairly directed at Deok-gi, made him feel uncomfortable, but there was nothing he could do about it. *So this is the house my father bought for them.* He hoped the old woman would continue her rant, if only to satisfy his curiosity.

"Why can't I say what's on my mind? What have we done wrong? A son ought to hear about the misdeeds of his father. Both you and this child have the misfortune of having a bad father," she said, addressing Deok-gi but pointing to the girl on Gyeong-ae's lap. "You should take this child away with you. Looks like you've returned home from your studies. If your father won't take her in and raise her, you'll have to do it yourself. You wouldn't feel it's unfair to raise your own sister, would you?"

"Please calm down," Deok-gi finally managed to say. "I'll figure something out. But first, don't you think we should give her some medicine to make her feel better?"

"Mother, how can you say such things to someone who doesn't know the whole story? Now please go to the other room," Gyeong-ae insisted, this time deeply annoyed.

Memories

———

"Don't even think about telling your father that you saw me," said Gyeong-ae after her mother had gone. Her voice had been calm enough when she had stopped her mother from lashing out, but now it was tinged with anger. Her mother had stirred up a dormant wrath.

"If it weren't for this child, I wouldn't have stopped you in the street, let alone brought you here. Your father never thought about the baby at all. He was too afraid of rumors going around the church that he had deflowered a young girl and fathered her child. He thought everything would be fine as long as he maintained his social status, so he dumped me. I didn't beg him to take me back then, and I don't even want to speak to him now." Gyeong-ae spoke calmly, but her voice contained deep resentment.

"I know I've made mistakes," she said, after a long pause. "My mother, for all she said —" She broke off to mull something over; she picked up the small paper bag at the head of the bedding. Counting out the pills, she shouted to the maid in the other room, asking whether the water was warm yet.

By mistakes, Gyeong-ae meant that it was her own vanity that sparked the affair. Her mother hadn't acted admirably either, despite her posturing. At the time Gyeong-ae was involved with Deok-gi's father, he was a gentleman who preached eloquently, a good-looking man in his prime, less than forty years old. He had lived in America for almost two years. Thanks to the prestige of family money, he enjoyed great popularity within the church, and he caught the eye of all the young women in the community.

The maid entered with a child-sized brass bowl.

The little girl had calmed down, though she was still very congested. But when she spotted the medicine and the water bowl, she burst into tears, as if she had been burned. Somehow, Gyeong-ae managed to push three tablets down her throat as the child slid down from her mother's lap, her arms and legs flailing. Deok-gi helped get her to swallow the medicine and then smiled, proud of himself.

Deok-gi's memories of the past were vivid.

Eight or nine years had passed since Deok-gi and Gyeong-ae graduated from the elementary school near Namdaemun. Gyeong-ae joined the school in the middle of the third grade. Of course, boys and girls attended different classes, and Gyeong-ae was two years older than Deok-gi, but they were placed in the same grade.

The school was church-affiliated, and Deok-gi's father was one of the founders. Since Deok-gi was a member of the church, his father sent him to this school, far from their Hwagae-dong home, rather than to the nearby public school.

When the two met, both were acting in the annual Christmas play. Ten-year-old Deok-gi and twelve-year-old Gyeong-ae were star pupils. Both were good-looking and talented, and both excelled at singing, acting, and elocution. Deok-gi hadn't always been very aware of his fellow students, but to this day he still remembered how Gyeong-ae, a girl two years his senior, had been friendly to him.

After school, when the students would stream out in groups, the two would walk side by side up to Namdaemun. Gyeong-ae would shout, "Good-bye!" and head for Bongnaegyo. Deok-gi never knew that she was actually from Suwon, that her father was in prison, and that she lived with her maternal uncle's family near Migeun-dong.

What stood out in his memory now was a day in the fourth or fifth grade. The students had come to school to rehearse the Christmas play, and

Gyeong-ae and Deok-gi left the school grounds to buy some Japanese rice cakes, which they shared. A classmate snitched on them, and although Deok-gi escaped a scolding, Gyeong-ae was severely reprimanded by a schoolmistress, who said a big girl as old as thirteen shouldn't be buying snacks for herself or her friends against school rules. Gyeong-ae was not allowed to sing that day and stood weeping outside the classroom all afternoon. How vividly Deok-gi recalled that day!

Now Gyeong-ae was holding Deok-gi's sister in front of him and bitterness rose in him. Deok-gi wasn't sure whether to laugh or cry—had the old days been a dream or was he dreaming now?

"It all happened because we were so poor. If my father had been alive, it wouldn't have come to this. Did you ever meet him?"

Deok-gi and Gyeong-ae hadn't spoken since they graduated from elementary school. She knew he couldn't have met her father, who was in prison the whole time they were students.

"My father was generous to a fault and never paid attention to household affairs. He donated all his assets—yielding three or four hundred bags of rice a year—to a school and canceled all his tenants' debts. Before he went to prison, he was talking about making back his money by launching a new business. But after the March 1 Independence Movement in 1919, he was thrown in jail, and we had to scrounge for money to send him toiletries and food, to hire a lawyer, and so on. In the end, we sold the house and came to Seoul. Looking back, it wasn't a great idea for me to come here."

Gyeong-ae rambled on about her life and her family history as if she were telling an amusing old tale, in sharp contrast to her fierce tone a few minutes earlier. She was in large part rationalizing her current situation and Deok-gi felt little need to listen to her. It was quite unpleasant to hear Gyeong-ae grumble about his father. Nevertheless, he sat attentively, his curiosity piqued by the circumstances of her life.

"After she sold the house and settled accounts, my mother came to Seoul with about a thousand won—a lot of money. She couldn't find a house that suited us, so she stayed with her brother and entrusted him with all the money. And he up and ran off with it."

"Really!" Deok-gi was stunned. "Did he spend it all on women?"

"No. He ran away to Shanghai, and we'll never forgive him for what he did to our family."

The two now felt that the initial barrier that separated them had disappeared. They switched to a more respectful manner of speech, appropriate for old friends.

"When my father was released from prison on probation because of his illness, we were still living with my mother's family and providing three meals a day wasn't easy, never mind what it took to pay for Father's medicine. He was ill for almost a year. You can't imagine how sad it was."

Gyeong-ae suddenly seemed hesitant to talk so openly about such memories.

Deok-gi waited for her to continue. Gyeong-ae's eyes were on the child. It looked as if the little girl had fallen into a light sleep, breathing regularly, but suddenly she began screaming and rocking her body back and forth as if a heavy weight were pressing down on her.

"I should go." Deok-gi stood up.

"Are you leaving tomorrow then?" Still seated, Gyeong-ae looked up. As much as she wanted to talk, she didn't want to press him to stay.

"Well, if I come home during spring vacation, let's get together."

"I'll let you find your own way out." Gyeong-ae stood up as she comforted the crying child.

"Yes, it wouldn't be good for her to be out in the cold."

As Deok-gi was putting on his shoes, Gyeong-ae's mother came out to the veranda and said, "Be careful on your way home in the dark."

He wondered what insults she might hurl at him as he left, but her farewell was unexpectedly brief. From the inner room, he heard Gyeong-ae's voice echo, "Yes, be careful on the way home."

Released from the humid, stifling room, the cold night air felt refreshing. The chill lifted Deok-gi's spirits, and he felt as though he had just escaped captivity.

That's it! So that's when it all began. No wonder she stopped talking to me all of a sudden.

As he found his way out of the dark winding alley, Deok-gi thought back to a day some five or six years ago. Gyeong-ae had arrived at the Hwagae-dong house on a winter day to see his father when Deok-gi was still living there.

They had last seen each other three or four years earlier at elementary school. After graduation Deok-gi attended a different church in Anguk-dong, close to Hwagae-dong. To his surprise, she seemed taller and quite a bit more mature. He felt she was looking down on him somehow, as if he were a child. Although he was glad to see her, he felt ill at ease with her and was much more timid than she.

Later he asked his father why she had come by. His father said simply that Gyeong-ae's mother went to Namdaemun Church and that her father, who had been sick for nearly a year since his release from prison, was now dying. At the time, Deok-gi felt sorry for his old school friend and suspected nothing else, but now he figured she must have been sent by her mother to borrow some money.

Gyeong-ae's father was a patriot. Everyone recognized his name as a religious activist, _____ from Suwon, and he was enough of a celebrity to merit several lines in the newspapers whenever prison news was featured as well as later on when he was released on probation. Churchgoers respected Gyeong-ae's mother as his wife. The pastor even mentioned him in prayers: *Almighty Father, we ask that you let this son of yours remain longer in this world so that he can help our cause.* He went on to pray for his recovery from the grave illness that threatened his life. Gyeong-ae's mother felt privileged to be the center of so much attention, but her husband's illness continued to worry her, and she didn't really know how to take care of him. From that moment on, her stature rose within the church, and Gyeong-ae's beauty seemed to shine even more radiantly. After services, Gyeong-ae's mother, her face aglow, busily fielded a flurry of exaggerated greetings and sympathies expressed for her husband's illness from a multitude of new best friends whose names she didn't even know.

One well-wisher from the church was Deok-gi's father, Jo Sang-hun. It was especially gratifying to receive such thoughtful inquiries from a man not only generous and rich, but trusted, revered, and powerful. Jo Sang-hun was particularly kind and gentle with her. It would be an insult to his honor and character to say that he treated her with such respect only because Gyeong-ae, her daughter, was a student at his school and a young woman much admired in the church for her beauty and intelligence. No one considered Jo's kindness in this light, and certainly Jo Sang-hun himself had no ulterior motive.

Jo Sang-hun would always ask Gyeong-ae about her father's condition with genuine concern. When he saw her mother, he inquired: "Has there been any improvement? I often think of visiting him, but I'm so busy that I keep making excuses. I've never met him, but I really should call on him as one of our distinguished elders, illness aside." Could she tell him what would be a good time to visit?

After repeating these pleasantries several times, Jo Sang-hun set a time to call at Gyeong-ae's uncle's house in Migeun-dong one Sunday that early winter, along with the pastor, to comfort the sick man and to pay his respects. After the service, Gyeong-ae and her mother showed them the way.

Gyeong-ae's father was glad to see his guests and sat up in bed to welcome them. He was very ill with bronchitis and a kidney inflammation, and had been hanging on to life by dint of sheer will. Sang-hun was surprised to see that his hair was graying; he looked well over sixty, though his wife was only about forty. Gyeong-ae's mother was actually his third wife, almost like a young concubine, and Gyeong-ae was his only child. This wife had given birth to a son and a daughter but only Gyeong-ae survived.

The room wasn't warm enough to combat the cold spell before the winter solstice. Sang-hun noticed Western medicine bottles, coated with dust, at the head of the bed and frozen dregs of herbal remedies thrown into the straw basket inside the middle gate. He pitied the old patriot, who, it appeared, couldn't afford quality medical care.

Before taking his leave, he chatted with Gyeong-ae's father about life in prison, the current education system, and society in general. After he had said good-bye, Sang-hun quietly called for the patriot's wife and asked her to send her daughter or a messenger to his house after three o'clock. He repeated his address several times.

"Why? What for?" she asked, although she had her own ideas about what he had in mind.

"I think I have some medicine at home that might help your husband," Sang-hun said.

That was why Gyeong-ae had first come to Hwagae-dong.

At the time Sang-hun had given her several ginseng roots, a ticket redeemable for a large bag of rice at the Daeseong Rice Mill near Namdaemun, which his father still managed, and an envelope into which he placed ten won. He included a polite letter in his own neat handwriting so that the family wouldn't be ashamed to accept what he sent.

Sang-hun's kindness stemmed from a deep sympathy for the old patriot and regret over such a miserable end. Never had he set out to produce the baby daughter, who today was sitting in Gyeong-ae's lap, groaning with fever.

Several days later, Sang-hun paid another visit to the sick man. It wasn't his intention to hear how grateful they were for his kindness. Still, the family surrounded him and thanked him profusely, almost to the point of groveling. Sang-hun's pity for all of them was heartfelt.

In any event, the more they expressed their gratitude, the bigger his favors grew. On his second visit, he brought his own family doctor and had him examine the patient.

Gyeong-ae's father had been paroled because his condition was severe; indeed, it was terminal. Because of his advanced age, he suffered from multiple ailments, and though he saw some improvement shortly after his release, his condition soon took a turn for the worse under the pressures of poverty and the onset of winter. There wasn't much Sang-hun's doctor could do.

After New Year's, his health declined even more. Administering medicine seemed only to hasten his death. Like a lamp drained of oil, he flickered and suddenly went out. In the end, he was considered fortunate just to be able to close his eyes in peace—even if it was in his brother-in-law's house and not in his own home—rather than die alone in prison. Had he lived, he would have had to serve out his prison sentence, for there were forces jealous of his short life who would have insisted on it.

Both the pastor and Sang-hun were present at his deathbed. The dying man had no formal words to leave behind, but he was worried about his wife and daughter. He had good reason to trust Jo Sang-hun. Although they hadn't been acquainted for long, he found Sang-hun's kindness overwhelming, and he was grateful for it. It was not easy to find such men in the world, even among the religious community.

"I've prayed that God would take me peacefully, without causing trouble to you and my family, and now that time has come. I am at peace with myself as I depart this world, but those who remain behind are still so troubled. I'm leaving behind my brothers, my comrades—our society. I'm leaving this child of mine. I've thought about what my legacy will be after sixty years of living, and all I really have is this child. I know that, in effect, I'm throwing her naked into the street by leaving her behind this way, and while I have no doubt that you will each do your best for the sake of society, please take good care of this child. I know I could never thank you from the grave, Mr. Jo, and I know it is shameless to ask this of you, but I would be eternally grateful if you could, when I die, take care of my wife and child . . ."

The patient's mind was clear until he drew his last breath. Amid prayers and blessings from all those gathered around him, he uttered this long-winded last testament in the moments before he died.

Sang-hun vowed that he would abide by his wishes as much as possible. The dead man would never know whether Sang-hun kept his vow, but those who had heard him became his witnesses. And God Almighty was, needless to say, a witness equal to a million mortals.

The funeral held in Seoul was a propitious mourning, well attended and well subsidized by devoted members of the church, those connected to the school in Suwon, and other influential personalities. Sang-hun assumed the role of the funeral committee director and offered fifty won for expenses. The public ceremony was held at _____Church, but for the traditional funeral service the casket was transported all the way to Suwon, where he was buried in his family plot.

After the funeral expenses were paid, between five and six hundred won in donations were left over. During his lifetime, Gyeong-ae's father and his family had had a hard time coming up with even a handful of rice or a bundle of firewood. The deceased had invested all of his assets in institutions for social progress and education.

It was decided that the five hundred won should be used as capital, rather than for the family's everyday expenses. After consulting with Sang-hun, Gyeong-ae's mother decided to rent a small house using this capital as the deposit, because it made no sense to squander it on trivial purchases. Besides, if Gyeong-ae and her mother continued living with her brother's family, they would be expected to contribute their fair share toward the running of the household. It was Gyeong-ae's mother who made the decision to leave; it was a heartless thing to do to her brother's family, some of whom had no way of supporting themselves. She told her brother's eldest son, who was doing nothing for a living, to take care of his own brood. The hope was that when Gyeong-ae graduated from school the coming spring, she would be able to provide for her mother and herself.

Sang-hun did his best to listen to their concerns and advise them how best to proceed. If they found a house to move into, he would supply them with food until Gyeong-ae graduated two months later and landed a job. The future of mother and daughter now looked considerably brighter.

They found a small rental property in Dangju-dong and moved in. In a sense, it was the dead man's legacy, for it was thanks to him that they were able to live there. Yet it was also thanks to Sang-hun, for they wouldn't have dared to make the move without his support.

"How can we ever repay Mr. Jo?" the mother said whenever the subject came up with her daughter.

As for Sang-hun, then as now, he lived on a monthly allowance from his own father—he wasn't especially well-off. Still, he felt that he couldn't simply abandon them as long as he had gotten involved, so he sent the family rice from his father's mill on a regular basis. Actually, he sent far more than he needed to. He was not so extravagant that the mother and daughter could splurge on fancy sweets, but they were able to pay off accounts on fermented seafood and cooking oil with the leftover rice from his supply. Sang-hun continued to help the family, all quite sincerely, until Gyeong-ae graduated and started working at his school.

Sang-hun was not a merchant, nor had he mapped out a course of action. He wasn't the type of person to be guided by an ulterior motive—by the expectation, as the saying goes, that people who have eaten salty food are bound to ask for water. On the contrary, since he had lived nearly forty years without knowing any worldly difficulties, he was easygoing and good-natured in his dealings with other people. He felt a certain measure of excitement about helping those in trouble, and when the recipients of his goodwill expressed their thanks profusely, he played along with equal enthusiasm. It was cruel to suggest, but one might be inclined to wonder whether he would have behaved the same way if the family didn't have a daughter as lovely as Gyeong-ae.

In the church, people spoke highly of Sang-hun and praised his steadfast charity toward the family of the late patriot. Such words of praise, however, soon changed into jealousy and suspicion.

"Why does he have to visit them morning and night?"

"If he were as attentive to his parents, he'd be a model son."

Women began to gossip about him. The truth was that although he went to pay respects to his father once a week, sometimes twice, he called on Gyeong-ae's house, which was between the school and his own home, almost every day after work.

"Well, if it was just the old widow at home, it wouldn't be much fun, but there's the daughter, you know."

When you have friends, you have enemies as well. Even the young teachers at school whispered such jokes among themselves.

After she graduated, Gyeong-ae had joined the school's staff. Sang-hun, who still had strong ties to the school, recommended her. The faculty did not openly disapprove of this pretty new addition, but behind her back they exchanged knowing glances, rolling their eyes. New to the working world, Gyeong-ae detected nothing out of the ordinary.

Whenever she met Jo Sang-hun, Gyeong-ae treated him not only with respect and adoration, but also as her benefactor. Not only had he helped her father before and after his death, but she had grown to depend on Jo's guidance. Her trust and love for him ran deep; she wouldn't begrudge him if he were to ask her to die for him. Her mother also trusted him. For Gyeong-ae, the faith she invested in Sang-hun was like that of a girl toward her father, her brother, and her dearest friends—fused into one.

But when her colleagues sneered and insinuating remarks were brought more frequently to her attention, she was shocked and angry. She found herself gradually avoiding Sang-hun. She even felt a little afraid of him, though she had no concrete reason to be so. Still, she couldn't hate him even if she wanted to. He was the same Mr. Jo he had always been.

Her colleagues' suggestive ridicule grew more intense. She couldn't respond directly to their innuendos, so she didn't know how to defend herself. Bottled-up rage and anguish tormented her. The more she suffered, the more she avoided Mr. Jo, but in her heart her fear of him faded and her affection for him grew. Though she couldn't complain about her situation to her mother, who was the only person in the world she could really depend on, she felt she could pour out her innermost thoughts to Sang-hun. With the start of her third semester as a teacher, Gyeong-ae decided to meet with him to ask for advice. What she most wanted was to request a transfer to another school, though it was impossible for her to explain the reason. Gyeong-ae's nerves were so frayed that she didn't want to teach another day under such malicious scrutiny.

By this time, however, Mr. Jo himself seemed less friendly toward Gyeong-ae, as if he were trying to keep his distance from her, and he had stopped coming to her house altogether. If she wanted to meet him, she would have to go to his house. She didn't like the idea of running into Deok-gi, as had happened the previous winter, but in her opinion it would be far better to meet Mr. Jo at his house, away from watchful eyes, than to meet at school or at church after service. She would have preferred that he come to her house, but it would be difficult to talk in her mother's presence.

She debated with herself for some time until she heard that Mr. Jo had been home for two days with a cold. As soon as she got home and put down her books, she told her mother that she was going to pay him a visit since he was sick. Her mother was surprised at first and thought it would probably be better if she went along, too, but she quickly changed her mind and urged Gyeong-ae to go over straight away. She had to cook supper; her daughter could relay her sympathy.

Gyeong-ae ventured out with resolve. There was no reason for her to be anxious about what others might say; she was only visiting a sick colleague. Besides, she had told her mother that she was going to see him. Yet as she approached Hwagae-dong, she was ambushed by the worry that someone from church or school might be there. Having come this far, though, she couldn't turn back.

She stood at the gate but couldn't bring herself to enter. She peeked in, hoping somebody might come out of the house and see her. Luckily, the maidservant appeared carrying a large bowl of rice. It seemed that dinner was ready.

Gyeong-ae thought the maidservant would go to the inner quarters to report her arrival, but instead she went to the outer quarters, returned, and asked Gyeong-ae to come in. If the master were eating dinner, he would be in the inner quarters. If he was in the outer quarters, he must be meeting a guest. Who could it be? Had someone come from school? Although she knew she shouldn't feel uncomfortable, she was on edge as she entered. There wasn't a guest in sight, however, and the master of the house, coming out to the veranda, welcomed her warmly. From the sound of his voice, his cold didn't seem to be severe.

"I'm so sorry to keep you out in the cold, but please wait just a minute. I was on my way out to meet someone," Sang-hun said. He went back into the house and came out, hat in hand, having put on a Western-style overcoat over his Korean one.

Through the windowpane, Gyeong-ae caught sight of a dinner tray that seemed to have been brought in only minutes before.

"Oh, please finish your meal. I can't stay anyway. When Mother heard you were sick, she asked me to pay you a quick visit."

Although Gyeong-ae was simply being polite, she was relieved that she might be able to leave with him and thus avoid the eyes of Deok-gi and of any guests who might drop by. Sang-hun had something similar in mind as he hurried out of the house. He wanted to avoid his wife's nagging.

Just as he was out the door, with Gyeong-ae in front of him, the maidservant came out to serve him some rice-water. With her eyes glued to Sang-hun and Gyeong-ae, she slipped on a patch of ice at the foot of the steps.

Water splashed from the bowl and the brass tray nearly slipped from her hands.

Sang-hun and Gyeong-ae, now in front of the gate, started when they heard the maidservant shriek.

"Watch where you're going!" Sang-hun barked.

The maidservant stood there blankly, speechless, forgetting to ask whether he had finished his supper and she could clear his tray.

Afraid that they might run into Deok-gi, who hadn't come home yet, Sang-hun took the road leading to Samcheong-dong and then turned onto the main street at Yeongchumun.

The two walked in silence.

It's spilled water, thought Sang-hun as he recalled the scene he had just witnessed leaving the house, but he was surprised at how appropriately his words described his own feelings at the moment. He made excuses to himself. *But what have I spilled?* His words rang in his ears: "Watch where you're going!"

"Are you going straight home?" Sang-hun finally asked when they reached Yeongchumun.

"Yes, but I have something to tell you," Gyeong-ae said, making up her mind after a brief hesitation.

"Oh?" Sang-hun stopped in his tracks and looked into her eyes. They couldn't stand in the middle of the road, so they moved toward the Yeong-chumun wall and stood side by side. His heart raced wildly.

Sang-hun recently had been as troubled as Gyeong-ae. When he first caught wind of the rumors, he tried to turn a deaf ear to them and resolved to get on with his own work. Then, in order to clear up the misunderstandings and bolster his own standing with even more good deeds, he considered marrying Gyeong-ae off to a good family and hastily arranging a wedding ceremony, in much the way he had supervised her father's funeral. Yet when he tried to push Gyeong-ae out of his mind, his heart seemed to draw closer to her. If he had been serious about searching for prospective families for Gyeong-ae to marry into, he would have found one soon enough. The truth is he simply couldn't bring himself to do it. He rebuked himself, but the more he did so, the greater his torment grew. Even after hibernating for two days, with the pretext of a cold, he saw no way out of his predicament. He was unable to calm himself, and was so agitated when Gyeong-ae appeared, it almost seemed as though fate had directed her to do so. He might have in fact been secretly hoping that Gyeong-ae or her mother would pay him a visit when they heard he was bedridden.

"What is it?" he managed to ask. "Is something wrong?"

"I can't make up my mind about school . . . Could you find somewhere else for me to work?"

The evening wind, descending the slopes of Samgak Mountain and bouncing off the eaves of the Yeongchumun pavilion, swept away Gyeong-ae's words.

The two began to walk again.

"Why are you asking me now, out of the blue?" he asked, feigning ignorance.

Gyeong-ae didn't answer. As they reached the Government-General, a brightly lit streetcar approached from Hyoja-dong, made a stop, and then took off again. Sang-hun wasn't sure how to proceed. To have a conversation, they would have to go inside somewhere, but there was nothing in sight. He worried that if they took a streetcar toward Jingogae, they'd run into someone they knew on board.

They didn't speak again until they had walked all the way down to Hwangtohyeon. Both could hardly breathe. As Gyeong-ae followed Sang-hun, she couldn't dispel her anxiety. They could have met briefly and parted ways after exchanging a few pleasantries, but now that things had gotten to this point, she almost felt as though they were doing something wrong by evading other people. Yet, she didn't want to shake off these feelings completely. Perhaps this was the sweet scent of temptation.

Even when they passed the alley leading to her house in Dangju-dong, Gyeong-ae said nothing.

They ducked into a café next to the police station at the Hwangtohyeon intersection. Most people, at that hour, were home eating supper. The restaurant was brightly lit but had no customers, and when they walked in, several Japanese waitresses clustered around the stove jumped up to welcome them. They greeted Sang-hun cordially; he was, after all, a distinguished gentleman with a beautiful woman at his side. Gyeong-ae chose a corner table, far from the stove, and sat with her back to the rest of the restaurant.

"You must be terribly worn out from work." Sang-hun picked up where they had left off.

"Well, I am tired, and everyone there is getting on my nerves. I've been thinking of finding a job at the _____ school in Suwon." Her father had founded it and Gyeong-ae herself had gone there through the third grade.

"Well, did they offer you a job?"

"No, but . . ."

"But?" Smiling, Sang-hun studied her expression. "Even if they have a position for you, it's not a good idea to go off to Suwon now that you've set up house in Seoul. Are people talking about you at school? Are the young teachers giving you a hard time?"

"No!" Gyeong-ae blushed.

"Well, then, I don't understand." Sang-hun pretended to be completely in the dark. He didn't know why he felt like a woman with morning sickness, but he was certainly not in a position to acknowledge it and saw no other option but to feign ignorance.

"Everyone is spreading rumors about me and gossiping," she finally confessed. She seemed to have made up her mind to release her frustrations. Her lips trembled as she said, "I'm furious." She dropped her head.

"Rumors about what? Look, everything will be fine if you just ignore it, whatever they're saying about you." Sang-hun wanted to comfort her.

"I could put up with it if it were just me, but for no reason at all, you're —" Gyeong-ae finally blurted out the words she had found so impossible to utter. As tears streamed uncontrollably down her cheeks, she tried to turn her face away. She didn't know why she was crying so freely; she had only intended to have a simple conversation with him. Once she sat across from him at the table, however, all the frustrations and anger she harbored inside overwhelmed her and erupted.

"You have nothing to cry about. No matter what other people are saying, it doesn't matter as long as you haven't done anything wrong." Sang-hun spoke confidently, almost rebuking her, but he was indescribably torn, her tears seared into him—his words and his heart were poles apart. They sat facing each other, not knowing what to say next. Their food arrived.

Sang-hun hesitated slightly before ordering beer. Gyeong-ae looked up in surprise.

She didn't want to ask if he drank, nor did she disapprove of alcohol. She was merely concerned about his drinking cold beer on such a frigid day, when he was suffering from a cold.

"I don't drink normally, but a glass of beer is good when you're frustrated or when you've got heartburn." Sang-hun tried to come up with a plausible excuse.

Gyeong-ae was not prepared to watch Mr. Jo drink. Until now, she had full confidence in him, but a vague suspicion about his character was growing within her. While she didn't feel it was her place to condemn him or find fault with his behavior, she did give him a sidelong glance as he raised the full glass to his mouth and guzzled almost half of it down.

"Heartburn because of fever —?" She grimaced.

Sang-hun ignored the remark, but he picked at the snacks that accompanied the beer, as if he were angry. Gyeong-ae felt confused and uncomfortable sitting with him. Although she rarely had a chance to sample such treats, she hardly touched the Western food and sent back one plate after another almost untouched.

"You know, I really don't like getting involved with the ins and outs at school. I'd rather leave it all to the others." He had already finished the first bottle of beer, and even though he claimed he'd drink only one glass, he didn't refuse a second when it was brought to the table.

"I don't plan to be stuck at that school forever, and I know I want to do something more meaningful in the future, but these days life itself seems too much to cope with." He was steadily drowning his troubles. Seeing that he was hardly affected after tossing back two bottles, she was appalled to discover that he was such a drinker.

Gyeong-ae was feeling disillusioned by what people labeled "holy." She was under the impression that a good Christian never drank or smoked, and when it came to being intimate with women, he knew only his wife. She had even wondered on occasion how a man who read the Bible, prayed, and sang hymns could allow himself to sleep with any woman, including his wife. She couldn't imagine anything so dirty. Sitting across from this supposedly holy man, now flushed with drink, she felt ashamed for him.

Was she wrong to regard Mr. Jo and his colleagues as holy beings? Was she shocked because she was still young and didn't know much of the world? Or were those people disguising their true nature with airs of sanctity and gentility? Was she stupid for thinking otherwise, unaware that the world was such a place? Had her father been no different?

The fact that the revered Mr. Jo drank beer threw the young woman into even further confusion.

Leaving the restaurant, they headed back on the same path they had taken on the way there. Gyeong-ae wanted to take the shortcut to her house, but he suggested that they walk a bit more together, and she followed him.

"Are you so quiet because you don't approve of my drinking?" Sang-hun asked as they entered the avenue in front of the Joseon Dynasty's Six Boards government buildings.

"No," she answered automatically. It pleased her that he understood how she felt. His kindness and gentle, apologetic voice also softened her heart.

"Tighten your scarf. It's cold," said Sang-hun, as he lifted the back of it around her neck. A chill raced through her body, intensifying into an electric shock that jabbed her in the pit of her stomach.

"Be careful in this night air. You could catch a cold." His voice was affectionate, filled with concern for the young woman. Gyeong-ae felt her cheeks burning. She didn't dislike him, nor was she afraid of him. Suddenly, she had forgotten how much she had disapproved of his drinking only a few moments ago.

Why do I feel this way? All he did was lift my scarf, fearing that I might catch cold. She chided herself and tried to calm her pounding heart. When they reached the front gate of the infantry unit, Gyeong-ae wanted to say good-bye.

"Well, then, hurry on home before it's too late. And when you're at school, don't worry about anything. Things will gradually . . ." His words trailed off as he began to turn away, but then, drawn back toward Gyeong-ae, he offered to walk her home, since it was dark and probably eerie with so few people around. Gyeong-ae shook her head, but he followed her anyway. She didn't object.

"Actually, I'm upset by it all, too." Sang-hun spoke with gravity. He went on, "If anybody heard me say this, they'd probably mock me for not acting my age, but at forty I still have the feelings I had in my twenties. No one knows how much I've struggled against this passion, which shames me before my children, and if you sense it . . ." He had come out with it at last. His ears rang and his breath was labored. He couldn't believe what had come out.

Gyeong-ae felt the drunken man's warm breath on her half-exposed cheek but couldn't believe what she was hearing. Her head throbbed. Her heart pounded. She had no energy left to speak.

When they reached the edge of Dangju-dong, Gyeong-ae wanted to tell Sang-hun to go home, but the words stuck in her throat. She had no choice but to walk the dark alley with him again and try to stay a step behind.

"Let's not talk about such trivial things . . ." He stopped short and stood shoulder-to-shoulder with Gyeong-ae. "You should get married soon! Once you're married —" Abruptly he stopped talking. Gyeong-ae was a little relieved, waiting for what would come next, when all of a sudden something warm touched her hand. A shiver coursed through her body; she lost her balance and almost fell.

Gyeong-ae couldn't shake his hand away, so she took several more steps. She held her breath, although even a stunned pigeon in her place would have let out a coo. He squeezed her hand as if to crush it, and then just as abruptly released it. "Go home! Go on," he shouted, as if angry. He spun around and was gone.

Gyeong-ae looked back at the black shadow disappearing into the darkness, then letting her head drop, she stood quietly for a moment. Passers-by threw curious glances at her.

Her mind went blank. She felt like crying, but her eyes were dry.

The experience of the past few hours had changed her world in a flash. But the world didn't belong to Jo Sang-hun, so how could it suddenly seem so different? The world now eluded her; it was at once terrifying, shameful, utterly ridiculous, delightful, and full of hope.

The next day, Gyeong-ae didn't have the courage to go to work. Exhausted after a sleepless night and trying to hide her insomnia from her mother, she was afraid to face Mr. Jo, who might have gone to school that day. She felt ashamed and out of sorts. And scared. Something of the utmost importance had to be settled, but she didn't know precisely what it was.

Her mother was worried that she might have caught a cold after her outing in the chilly air the night before. She talked about running to the pharmacy to fetch some medicine, but Gyeong-ae refused everything her mother offered and stayed in bed all day. She wanted to be alone, away from her mother.

Is he insane? Or was he just drunk? What else could have made him act that way?

She came to the conclusion that Mr. Jo was not crazy. Nor had he been all that drunk.

She tried to remember his exact words about being ashamed in front of his children, but she couldn't recall them. She was sure she understood at least part of what he was trying to say to her. She certainly hadn't expected to hear that. Still, what did he mean by telling her to get married?

"Let's not talk about such trivial things . . . Once you are married . . ." She remembered how Mr. Jo had abruptly cut off his words. *What was trivial about any of this? I should get married? And then what?* Gyeong-ae was at a complete loss.

In truth, Sang-hun had been talking to himself. He had thought that if he only stopped prattling and let Gyeong-ae get married, his heart might calm down and nothing would happen between them. He decided that the only way to avoid the dangerous route his heart was leading him toward was to get Gyeong-ae married as soon as possible.

Gyeong-ae returned to school the following day. As she was about to head to second-period class, Mr. Jo entered the teachers' lounge. Since few people asked after his health, she figured he must have come to school the day before. Mr. Jo was not the Mr. Jo from the other night. He was the same Mr. Jo she had known all along. She could detect nothing different in the way he greeted her.

Gyeong-ae was once again thrown into confusion. What had happened two days earlier now seemed like a dream. To her mind, human beings protected themselves not only with layers of clothes, but also with invisible shields, hundreds and thousands of them. And Mr. Jo wasn't the only one. She took a second look at everyone she came across. She felt as naked as a newborn, and she wasn't proud of lacking her own protective shields; she thought it was odd. This was how she first learned to wear the armor of lies.

At the end of the day, Gyeong-ae quickly gathered her books and rushed out of the teachers' lounge. She ran into Mr. Jo at the door as he was coming in. His eyes darted left and right to see if anyone was around as he slipped an envelope out of his coat pocket and handed it to her. Gyeong-ae felt her face flush as she took it from him. She was delighted to receive the letter yet terrified that someone might see them together. She hid it beneath her book bundle without a word.

In the letter, Sang-hun asked why she hadn't come to school the day before and repeated several times, with great sincerity, that both of them should forget what had happened. He also asked for her forgiveness. Her heart had been racing when she opened the envelope, but now Gyeong-ae was disappointed. She had expected to read something meaningful in the letter and she felt deflated by what was missing. Not that she was desperately longing for Sang-hun and for something more profound, but this letter was so bland!

———

But who would have known all the details of what had happened five years earlier? All that Deok-gi knew, and all that Gyeong-ae's mother knew, was how it all ended, not how it started. The child who'd fallen asleep in her mother's arms revealed the outcome but not the details. To Gyeong-ae and Sang-hun, as well, it was now only a fleeting memory.

Less than five months after receiving Sang-hun's first letter, Gyeong-ae resigned from the school. Soon after that, she left Seoul, saying she was going to study in Tokyo—which sounded very nice. She did, in fact, go to Tokyo, but not for the luxury of studying abroad—she went to take reluctant refuge.

When the other teachers at school heard of her plan to study in Tokyo, they traded glances and asked, "Who's paying her tuition?" In other circles, it might not have attracted much attention, but within the church, the whispers snowballed into a full-blown scandal.

Gyeong-ae went to Tokyo and hid herself away in the outskirts of Omori for three months, feeling like a prisoner the whole time. It was not that she had to perform manual labor or that she was poverty-stricken. Rather, she felt as lonely as someone sent into exile. The pain of not being able to meet her beloved was mutual, but there was no way Sang-hun could leave Seoul. If he had quietly gotten away even for a week, the rumor that he had followed Gyeong-ae to Tokyo would have fanned the flames of gossip just when talk of the affair was dying down. Less than three months later, Gyeong-ae returned to Seoul like a fugitive. She arrived at Yongsan Station, where her mother met her and took her home in a car late at night, to avoid being seen by anyone. This was when Gyeong-ae saw for the first time the house at Bungmi Changjeong where they now lived.

This was the house Sang-hun had prepared for her. There was no good reason to find a place in this area, which was near the church and the school. After settling in Dangju-dong, Gyeong-ae's mother had attended a church nearby. She didn't want to live in her former neighborhood. The area near Samcheong-dong was simply out of the question. What Sang-hun did was force the chief clerk at Daeseong Rice Mill—who had rented this house from Sang-hun's father, the proprietor of the mill—to move out in order to let Gyeong-ae's mother move in. Once the matter had been settled, Sang-hun thought that the arrangement was rather clever, since no one would suspect they lived so close by; it's said that the ground directly beneath the lantern is always the darkest.

When Gyeong-ae moved into the new house, seven months pregnant and with a belly big enough to draw the world's attention, she felt so relieved that she was finally able to breathe easily again.

From the outset, Gyeong-ae's mother said nothing to her daughter about the affair. Nor did she say anything when she was reunited with her after the three-month interval. Was she resigned to it all, since nothing was to be gained by making a fuss? Was she willing to repay Sang-hun's kindness to her husband with her own daughter's body? Or was she making a secret calculation? Since Sang-hun had such a reputation—not that anybody really cared about that—and such wealth, when she died, even if she wasn't carried in a six-bar hearse by twelve men, she would be spared the shame of riding to her grave in a coffin with only two pallbearers. This calculation might indeed have been foremost in her mind.

This was a woman who had been an evangelist, carrying her Bible around with her in a black tote bag. But she was not a naïve woman who had forgotten what to do to ensure her own survival. Besides, she was a third wife, just a step above a concubine. If she hadn't believed in Jesus and hadn't married a man who had devoted his life to social causes, she herself might have ended up pouring wine for men in the marketplace or making a *gisaeng* out of her daughter. This is not to demean her, but rather to suggest that she was open-minded and resourceful, and that individual circumstances affect the choices people make. If her husband had left behind paddies yielding forty or fifty bags of rice a year, she would never have been indebted to Jo Sang-hun, and she would never have come to Seoul in the first place.

As it turned out, this woman became a grandmother three months after she moved into her new house. A new life had been received, shielded from the eyes of the world. But it was this infant who forced her grandmother to turn her back on the church.

The First Clash

"Whatever the reason—whether my father has become demented or he's thinking of the old days—shouldn't you discourage him from doing it?" Sang-hun said to Chang-hun, his cousin once removed.

"How can I possibly convince him, when even you can't? We're in the same boat. You can't stop him, and I can't get him to listen to me."

"Tell me, then—who's putting these ideas into his head in the first place?" Sang-hun retorted.

"You don't know what you're talking about. Does Uncle ever listen to anyone? You seem to think I have something up my sleeve. Well, I don't."

"Then explain to me his sudden extravagance at a difficult time like this. Why renovate the grave site of an ancestor who goes back ten generations, if not more?" Sang-hun had no idea whose grave it was.

"Don't you think you should ask your father, not me?" growled Chang-hun, turning purple in the face.

Because the ancestral ceremony was taking place that day, all the relatives had gathered at the house. One of the rooms in the outer quarters was almost bursting at the seams, and the air was thick with cigarette smoke. Sang-hun didn't participate in the rites, but he always sat in the outer quarters and left immediately after the final ritual, when the officiator imbibed and nibbled from the offerings on the table.

Sang-hun's father was busy in the inner quarters supervising, while the elderly and middle-aged relatives occupied the large room in the outer quarters, waiting for the food and chatting loudly among themselves. When Deok-gi returned home a little after eight, he received a good deal of scolding from his grandfather for gallivanting on the sacred day, and to make it up to him he was now helping to arrange the food on the ceremonial table in the inner quarters. The old man made sure that his grandson learned the proper procedures, such as placing fish to the east and meat to the west, and the strict rules of fruit placement: first jujubes, then chestnuts, pears, and finally persimmons arranged in order from left to right. The old man knew his son wouldn't perform the rites after he died, so he was relying on Deok-gi, his only grandson and the eldest of his generation, to carry on the family name.

The old man had already made sure that his last words would outlive him. If any bastard dared to offer up a Christian prayer for him after his death, he'd retrace his steps from the underworld and rip out the rogue's tongue with his own hands. He was terribly worried that his son would give him a Christian funeral, and in order to avoid such a horror, he had made it clear that all ceremonial procedures were to be supervised by Secretary Ji with the counsel of Chang-hun, who at the moment was arguing with Sang-hun in the smaller room of the outer quarters. The old man had told his son that when the time came he was free to do as he pleased—follow the procession in a tuxedo, ride in a carriage or an automobile, or else he could just lounge around in a *gisaeng* house, humming a tune.

The old man wanted to live another fifteen years, by which time he would be eighty-two and have a son with the Suwon woman. He fantasized that if she became pregnant now, by the time he died he would have a fifteen-year-old chief mourner to follow the procession on a pitched-roof palanquin. The old man's worries were mostly centered around this wish. If he were to find a woman who could guarantee that she'd give birth to a son, he'd happily take her in, though he didn't dare breathe a word about such dreams. Each day, Secretary Ji concocted medicines that would help prolong the old man's life for another decade or more and help him sire a son. On winter days, Ji thought his feet might fall off from spending so much time preparing these cures before the medicine chest in the freezing hallway.

But if the old man actually lived as long as he hoped to, the designated funeral master might well die before him, as he was getting up there in age, too. The same was true for Chang-hun for that matter; he was over fifty.

"Wasn't it you, Cousin, who moved the clan's temporary genealogy office here?" Sang-hun again accused his cousin.

"What are you talking about? The head of the clan decides these things. I just run errands on the old man's behalf. You nag me whenever you see me, but what have I done?" Chang-hun had recovered his composure and answered with patience.

"Your cousin is right," cut in another young cousin sitting nearby. "Where else could we have opened the office anyway?"

"How much money did you spend on the genealogy office?" Sang-hun figured his father must have squandered at least three or four thousand won in printing genealogy books alone.

"I don't know. Look, it's all been recorded in the account book. Someone else handles the expenses," Chang-hun answered icily, snorting before he added, "Do you think I went out and bought a pack of cigarettes or a bowl of rice with the money? I didn't do anything of the sort! I was born into the Jo family, and I'm obliged to do this, whether I like it or not."

Sang-hun refrained from pressing his cousin any further, but his thoughts were sharp: *I see you've replaced the Korean rubber slippers you wore when you first came to Seoul with Western shoes. Your shabby outer coat has transformed itself into a stylish wool serge, and, to top it off, you're now wearing a Western overcoat. Just where did all this come from?*

"When will you take down the genealogy office signboard?" asked Sang-hun sarcastically, after a long pause.

"Now that the printing is done, it'll be taken down even if people object," Chang-hun answered.

"So, now that you're out of work, you can't pay for your meals at the inn. That's why you came up with a new project, right?"

No one in the room answered.

It had been some time since the long, wide signboard bearing the words "_____ Jo's Genealogy Office" had been posted on the gate with the magnificent rising roof at Adviser Jo's house in Suha-dong. Two years had passed and not a single member of this particular branch of the Jo clan had failed to stop by. Those who up till now had been complete strangers flooded into the office. Sang-hun disapproved of these irritating clansmen. But the grandfather allowed these young country bumpkins, who imposed themselves on him in droves and called him "Grandfather" or "Uncle," to stay at his house for days on end. When they left, he would even send them packing with travel money.

The old man would be the first to admit that he'd taken several dubious paths. First, at the age of forty, he grabbed hold of a government position by paying twenty thousand nyang, four hundred won in today's money, amid the confusion of the 1905 Protectorate Treaty with Japan. So, although the position was bought, his current title, Adviser, was not totally unjustified. Second, he took in the Suwon woman six years ago, soon after his wife's death. The cost, twenty thousand nyang, was nothing to sneeze at, but the woman had given him a daughter—Gwi-sun—and if he hadn't taken such measures, there could be no dream of a son mourning him when he dies. All things considered, the cost of the Suwon woman had been worth it. Taking over the genealogy office was the old man's most recent indulgence. This time, he was drawn into a major venture, and spent as much as two hundred thousand nyang, ten times the amount he'd spent on the Suwon woman, to create the genealogy center. It is difficult to belittle the venture, even if it went against the spirit of the times. Though Sang-hun didn't particularly object to the genealogy office, neither did he feel any urgency to promote the new project. However, when his father put up a precious four thousand won in an effort to worm himself into this particular faction's genealogy book, Sang-hun thought he was definitely off his rocker.

Buying yangban *status!* It was humiliating to Sang-hun.

But the old man didn't mind spending the money, and he believed he could reconcile his dignity with the spirit of his father because he had earned the money himself rather than using the thousand nyang his father had left him. When a man was successful, he could arrange to confer posthumous government titles on his father and grandfather. Instead of laughing at him for spending money to become a *yangban*, wouldn't it be better for people to think he was a dutiful son? In any event, he had used the money to install the signboard on his grand gate with the same sincerity with which he might transfer his ancestors' spirit tablets to a new location. The genealogy book was printed, with his name listed as a descendant of the eldest son's branch of the ＿＿＿ Jo clan. People now began to talk about clearing the grave site of Grandfather ＿＿＿, the progenitor of this branch of Jos, after hundreds of years of its having lain in waste. They planned to erect a house on the site, bigger than the grave keeper's hut, something like an old-fashioned academic hall.

Replacing the worn-out stone statues in front of the graves, the pavilion at the grave, the paddy for ceremonial rice . . . these projects would require a budget of ten thousand won. The Jo clansmen said they'd all chip in to cover at least half the cost, and the old man was to put up the other half.

When adopted, an individual gains the right to inherit assets, but if his adoptive parents are poor, he assumes the obligation to support them. There wasn't anyone else in this particular Jo branch who could donate money. They had begun the project and fully expected the old man to go through with it. Although they promised to come up with their half, the pledge was clearly just a way of setting the bait and wringing the rest of the money from him. Unfortunately, this had been their intention all along. The Jos visited the old man frequently and bowed to him with deference and ulterior motives. The old man couldn't bring himself to refuse them. He had been putting it off, first telling them to wait until after the harvest and then until spring. That spring was just around the corner. After Lunar New Year's, less than three months away, came Hansik, the Cold Food Day.

Very recently, the Jos had sent Chang-hun, whom the old man trusted most, to advocate for their campaign, for they hoped they could move forward with the project as soon as the Hansik rite was over.

The old man said it would be rather difficult, with the price of rice having hit rock bottom, and suggested that the construction be put off until Chuseok, the Harvest Moon Festival, or until the next Hansik.

The old man was by no means naïve. On the contrary, he lived the better part of his life counting money with his arithmetic sticks and his abacus.

Secretly, he was grumbling about one large sum or another he had recently spent. Meanwhile, the Jo kinsmen were idling away their time in huge gambling parlors, even as their stomachs growled from hunger, or were spending their days playing go, holed up in someone's outer quarters. They tried to squeeze anything they could out of the old man, using the pretext of the genealogy book since they couldn't find any other way to make him loosen the strings of his money pouch. Now, Grandfather _____ was the latest fodder for the discussion of the five thousand won. Those who maintained that five thousand would be necessary for sprucing up the grave figured that by asking for five thousand, they'd end up wringing three thousand out of him, and the old man, for his part, was prepared to offer half of the five thousand. He regarded the grave renovation as a sort of commemorative project that he'd leave behind, now that his death was drawing near. He was the savior of the Jo clan after all, wasn't he?

This was why, under his relatives' incessant urging, he had recently pledged an initial thousand won, five hundred for landscaping and the rest for building a grave keeper's hut. He added that the rest of the Jos should chip in with the remainder, either with money or with labor, such as transporting dirt and grass.

He then told them that he'd buy some paddies at a later date to harvest rice for ceremonial purposes. With this maneuver, Adviser Jo calculated that he might get credit for spending two thousand won while donating only a thousand.

"But Uncle says he'll contribute only a thousand," muttered Chang-hun to himself after sitting quietly for quite some time. "We'll end up running all over the place collecting money to complete the project. Really, how can we just abandon it midstream? We'll end up dead tired, and if something goes wrong, we're the ones who'll get the blame . . ."

"Looks like you're doing great work," Sang-hun retorted. "So, did Grandfather _____ actually ask you to build a grave keeper's hut? Did he tell you he was lonely without a stone statue at his grave?"

With great difficulty, Sang-hun managed to refrain from using a verbal ending that would have indicated his lack of respect for his cousin. Bringing up Grandfather _____'s name was rather awkward. It wasn't because, as a Christian, he was unable to show respect for his ancestors, but rather because this was a totally unknown "grandfather" from some ten generations back, a man whom his father had posthumously adopted.

"How can you think of saying things like that? You may disagree with some of the traditions since you've become a Catholic, but bear in mind, we wouldn't be alive today without our ancestors. Who in the world doesn't care about his ancestors? We've got to make sure the Jos don't lag behind other clans and ensure its prosperity from generation to generation." Chang-hun had no compunction about grating on Sang-hun's nerves. He disapproved of him anyway.

Sang-hun bristled. "The prosperity of the Jo clan? Surely this ancestor that we've conveniently borrowed will reserve his blessings for his natural descendants before us . . ." He was about to continue when the room suddenly grew quiet at the sound of the old man clearing his throat coming from the edge of the veranda.

"What's all this commotion?" The old man flung open the door. The young men in the room scrambled to stand up, and Sang-hun, who was sitting on the warmest part of the floor, shifted to a cooler spot.

Cigarette smoke escaped through the doorway, along with warm air.

"It's like the inside of a chimney in here. Why do the young ones smoke so much? And what's this childish babble about?" The old man started scolding them as soon as he entered the room. He then sat down on the warmest part of the floor and continued in a hushed voice.

"Everyone sit down." He seemed to be preparing for a major scene. He had just finished setting up the ceremonial table display and had gone to the outer quarters to kill time. Having overheard the quarrel between the cousins, he rushed in to intervene because he couldn't stand it any longer.

"Why are you here? Isn't today a church day?" His face flushed with anger, the old man glared at his son, who was standing on the other side of the room.

"Get out of here! You can't just come in anytime you feel like it. You idiot! You're almost fifty years old, and what did you just blurt out in front of your young cousins? We borrowed our ancestors? Borrowed ancestors only help their natural descendants? What a fool!" The blue veins on the old man's flushed neck were throbbing, and it looked as if he were about to collapse.

Sang-hun stood in the corner, his head bowed.

"You're my own son, so you must be a human being! You should know about your ancestors. You inherited your parents' own flesh and blood! When your young cousins start babbling nonsense, it's your job to teach them a thing or two. Just think what will become of our family if you keep spouting things that even children wouldn't dare say." The old man took a deep breath before raising his voice again. "After I die, what's going to happen to this family? What'll ever become of it? Get out! Get out of here, I said! You say we borrowed our ancestors. Well, then you must have borrowed your father, too! And a borrowed father won't be of any help to you. So don't even think of coming to see me again!"

In blind fury, the old man picked up his long smoking pipe, slammed it down, picked it up again, then brandished it like a long sword.

Inwardly he was resenting the fact that four thousand won had been sucked out of him little by little, and he was worried about the future. When he heard his son making light of the project that meant so much to him, he was all the more incensed. The son had, of course, fallen out of his father's graces long ago. Everyone expected that a row would erupt even if the young man kept his opinions to himself, if only for the reason that he—the living opposition to ancestral rites—had dared to show his face on this particular day. It was too good an opportunity. The son naturally became the target of the old man's temper.

Chang-hun intervened for the sake of appearances, although he was happy with the turn of events. "He didn't mean anything like that. Uncle must have misheard what Sang-hun said."

"Misheard? Are you calling me deaf now?"

"Hold on a minute. Sang-hun must have a good reason for saying what he did. He must be worried about all the money you've had to spend in these confusing times." Chang-hun tried to make excuses. But Sang-hun hated Chang-hun more for trying to calm his father down than he hated his father for lashing out.

"Who gave you the right to worry about my money? It's not yours to spend. And what business do you have telling me how I should spend it?"

"What you're doing, Father . . ." began Sang-hun while his father, having calmed down somewhat, opened his tobacco pouch to restuff his pipe. "I don't mean to find fault with the fact that you're spending money. I'm just saying that it's wrong for people to even come up with such big unnecessary projects."

"Unnecessary?" The father's voice simmered now.

"Well, take the genealogy book, for example. I heard it cost fifty won to bind each volume. If you actually collected fifty for each copy, why did you need an extra three or four thousand?"

"Who says I spent that much?"

The old man knew his son was right, but the additional money hadn't been used for printing the genealogy books. It was used to silence those who had objected to the old man's worming his way into the registry of a sonless family, those who had worried that the increase in number would dilute the true *yangban* stock. The old man claimed that he had spent only a thousand, much like a prodigal son quoting a figure lower than what he has actually squandered. It was by exploiting this weakness that tricksters normally chiseled some money for themselves, but it was the first time the old man had played the fool over money.

An old saying tells us that the young are not supposed to offer advice to their elders. The time for such niceties was long past, but the son, though fuming, tried to treat his father with respect.

"It's not a matter of how much you spent. It's just that if you had only been using your money for a good cause . . ."

"What the hell do you mean if I used my money for a good cause? Was it for a good cause that you spent five or six thousand on a school where you went and seduced somebody's daughter, your own student?"

Everyone in the room knew that Sang-hun had been prodding his father with a hot poker.

Sang-hun was caught completely off guard and turned crimson.

By coincidence, the Suwon woman came from the same town as Gyeong-ae and her mother. Sang-hun had kept his family in the dark about the affair, but the Suwon woman had heard rumors of it from acquaintances, even though she had never laid eyes on the two of them. After Gyeong-ae had the baby, Sang-hun's entire family learned of it, including Deok-gi, who was able to piece together the gist of the story from the Suwon woman. The old man turned a blind eye while Sang-hun had several rows with his wife and never forced his son to evict Gyeong-ae and her mother from his house in Bungmi Changjeong. But now, his father, infuriated, had just announced to a crowded room that Sang-hun had wasted money on school and seduced one of his students. Mortified, the son felt his father had now gone too far.

"You're being too harsh, Father. What I mean is that there're so many things to do in the world, don't you think? Education projects, library work, and now they're even putting together a Korean language dictionary . . ." Sang-hun methodically continued his argument, carefully and calmly.

"I don't want to hear about it! Who wants to listen to a sermon from you? Now get out of here!"

"Whatever happened in the past, what sense does it make to landscape the grave site at this point? If it were just a little bit of tidying up, it would be another matter, but I really don't understand how you can seriously plan to build a Confucian academy and expect Confucianists to flock there in droves. Money aside, does it make any sense nowadays?"

"Enough! I told you to get out, but here you are still—going on and on. Why do you care what I do? Are you my supervisor? Don't you worry. I'll make sure not to leave you a penny when I die. Go ahead and starve to death. I won't give you a thing. To my mind, you don't exist any more . . . All of you, pay attention, too." He looked around at the others. "I don't have many assets, but I plan to leave half of what I do have to Deok-gi and use the rest for whatever I want to spend it on while I'm alive. If there's anything left over, I'll distribute it fairly before I die. I'll settle everything before I go, even if it means hiring a public notary or a lawyer.

"And as for you, consider yourself a stranger to me. Don't tell me that when I die you're actually going to wear hemp or let down your hair in mourning!"

The old man had been gradually transferring his land deeds to Deok-gi, and he intended to use up the rest while he was alive and leave the remainder to the Suwon woman and their daughter.

Sang-hun often heard his father talk of such things when he was drunk, but it was the first time that the old man, stone sober in consideration of the rites, spoke of them in front of the entire crowd of young relatives. All of a sudden, Sang-hun felt betrayed, as if everyone were against him. No one in his own family would be on his side, let alone the extended family present in the room.

"You don't care about your father and mother or even your wife and children. So I say you deserve a little hardship. I know the only reason you come to see me every month. What if I had nothing? You'd never visit me. You'd let me die in the woods somewhere. Now get out of here, you bastard! You're no member of the Jo family. How dare you say that we've borrowed ancestors?" The old man suddenly jumped up and charged toward his son as if he were going to bulldoze him out of the room. The young people rushed over and blocked him.

"Sang-hun, I think you should go now. He's a bit too worked up . . ." Chang-hun pulled his cousin out to the veranda.

Sang-hun thought his father might be going senile, but he was embarrassed in front of all the younger relatives, including his own son. He couldn't go into the main room in the inner quarters, nor could he move to the smaller room in the outer quarters, where the ones close to Deok-gi's age sat together. He had no choice but to put on his hat and go down to the stone step. Deok-gi came out of the smaller room and stepped into the yard.

"Please join us in here," Deok-gi stammered, but his father spun around and left without replying.

Second Clash

———

The old man woke up at the crack of dawn the following day, though he had gotten to bed at two in the morning after the rite and had slept in the main room in the inner quarters because so many visitors stayed on in the outer quarters. Before returning to the outer quarters, he had his usual three cups of morning wine. He was on his way to awaken the youngsters, who had stayed up most of the night. He knew it might not be easy. At that moment, the Suwon woman, who was sitting in the main room, heard doors slamming and raised voices. Deok-gi's wife, startled by the noise while doing the dishes that had been piled high the night before, tried to listen carefully to what was happening. She told the maidservant, who was washing rice for the morning meal, to go see what had happened.

In the main room, too, the Suwon woman ordered her maid to go and take a look. She rushed out and returned right away, crying, "*Aigo*, Madam, please go and see for yourself. How terrible! The master slipped on the ice on the shoe ledge and fell down!"

"What?" The Suwon woman, trembling with shock, ran out of the main room, slid her feet into her rubber slippers without looking down, and dashed to the outer quarters. The granddaughter-in-law and her maidservant trailed behind. The maid in the main room also rushed out. Amid all the commotion, the child woke up in the main room and began to cry.

It was only then that Deok-gi, still enjoying his sweet morning sleep, opened his eyes. Sliding open the door of his room, he asked, "What's the matter?"

From the other room, his mother shouted, "Go to the outer quarters. They say your grandfather has slipped." She wasn't able to go herself because her daughter had slept with her the night before and she was braiding the girl's hair in preparation for school. The other women who had slept in the same room couldn't come out immediately either; having lounged around gossiping so late, no one was properly dressed.

Only after Deok-gi had thrown on his shirt and pants and had rushed out did his mother and his sister, Deok-hui, manage to run to the outer quarters.

At the gate to the outer quarters Deok-gi's mother met up with those who were coming back. The Suwon woman, wearing a scowl on her face, passed right by, ignoring her. Thinking that the younger woman was disturbed because she had taken too much time to come out, Deok-gi's mother grew angry.

"How is he? Has he hurt himself?" she asked her daughter-in-law, who was walking behind her young grandmother-in-law. Deok-gi's mother was indeed concerned about her father-in-law.

"He isn't seriously injured. He's resting in his room now."

The old man, who was lying down, was troubled that his daughter-in-law had taken her time to check on him. Still, he preferred her to his own son, so he didn't show his displeasure. When his daughter-in-law inquired about his well-being with her usual morning greeting, he said, "Yes, well, my back hurts a bit, but it should be all right."

Turning to his granddaughter, he asked her kindly, "Are you going to school now? You look tired. Did you just get up?" He wondered what had kept them.

"No. We were just combing my hair. We heard you had fallen while Mother was in the middle of braiding my hair." She smiled winsomely at the old man before turning to look up at her brother standing next to them. "Only a lazybones like my brother sleeps until this hour," she teased.

"You spoiled girl!" the old man said. "At your age you don't know how to braid your own hair?"

"I can, but I have so much hair. And when I braid it myself, I just can't manage to capture that high-collar look," Deok-hui answered, giggling.

"If you're already worried at your age about looking high-collar . . . I don't think I should send you to school any more." Pleased with his grand-daughter's endearing ways, the grandfather continued the same line of conversation. Laughter and good feelings filled the room. At such times, the old man's boyish features showed through in spite of his gray hair.

The grandfather tried to straighten up a bit, but he groaned from the pain in his back, and a scowl appeared on his face.

"Give your grandfather a back massage," said the mother to Deok-hui, who obeyed and approached her grandfather.

"It's all right. You'll be late for school. They already went to fetch a doctor. He'll be here soon." The grandfather sent them back to the inner quarters and called for the Suwon woman. She came out with a change of clothes since the old man's pants and jacket had been soiled.

"How could they just sit in their room without the slightest care when the whole house was in commotion?" Referring to Deok-gi's mother and her daughter, the Suwon woman muttered loud enough for her husband to hear.

"She was braiding her daughter's hair. What does it matter anyway?"

The Suwon woman didn't like her husband talking this way. She wanted him to agree with her, and she didn't appreciate the way he was siding with his daughter-in-law.

"How can you believe her? Braiding a girl's hair when she's already old enough to get married! When your wine was served, she ignored it and stayed in her room." The Suwon woman had felt offended since early in the morning.

"Well, she probably went to bed late last night. It'd be different if her own daughter-in-law wasn't around, but Doek-gi's wife was already up and working in the kitchen."

The old man was right, but the Suwon woman sulked even more.

He said he would change into his new clothes later because his back hurt, so she sat massaging him without a word.

Although in her opinion her stepdaughter-in-law should not have taken her time, she thought it equally bothersome to massage her husband's back. She felt even less inclined to do it because he had refused to lend her a sympathetic ear. How worried she had been, rushing out after her husband's fall! But how did she feel now? Why did she think it would have been better if he had been hurt more seriously? She couldn't quite sort out her feelings.

When the doctor arrived, the Suwon woman went to the inner quarters. The old man thought it might have been better if she had remained while the doctor examined him, because there was no need for her to abide by the old custom of avoiding the opposite sex, doctor or no doctor.

The doctor said that the fall wasn't serious, but because the old man might have pulled a muscle, it would be better if he lay flat on his back for a while. The doctor applied some ointment on his back and put a hot pack under him before leaving.

In the main room, the women were talking in loud voices about the old man's fall as they ate breakfast.

One woman said, "He's lucky he wasn't hurt worse than he was. What would have happened if he had really fallen flat on the ice at his age? He could've easily damaged something internally."

The seamstress answered, "You know that old man Choe Sa-cheon? Well, he sprained his back stepping down onto a shoe ledge. He didn't slip on the ice, but he still had to stay in bed for three months."

"Choe Sa-cheon? He didn't slip on a shoe ledge. He just got a little too excited in bed with his new young wife one night. That's why he couldn't get up the next day," said a friend of the old man's late wife, laughing.

"Madam, that can't be true," said the seamstress, laughing along with her. Everyone, in fact, broke into laughter except the Suwon woman, her stepdaughter-in-law, and her stepgranddaughter-in-law. The Suwon woman flushed.

"He's still going strong. He'll easily live another ten years," said an uncle's wife.

"But madam should be careful for him," the seamstress teased.

The Suwon woman didn't feel like listening to these women any more.

"He's carrying on because he's lucky to have naturally good health, but he's not what he used to be. His age is one thing, but . . ." Deok-gi's mother spoke without any special meaning, but it didn't sound innocuous to the Suwon woman.

"I'm sure he'll live many more years," someone added. "He's rich, and he has such a precious wife and daughter . . ."

The phrase "such a precious wife" was jarring to the Suwon woman's ears. Thinking that everyone was making fun of her, she grew increasingly angry.

Deok-gi's mother again offered her opinion. "However long he lives, what more can he get out of life? When their time is up, it's best for old people to die in comfort . . . in their sleep." No particular motive was behind the remark—she must have come out with it because her own lot was so miserable—but the Suwon woman glared at her.

"How can you say that?" the Suwon woman finally exploded, after watching her stepdaughter-in-law stuff her mouth with rice.

"Whatever do you mean, dear?" asked an old woman, an aunt to Deok-gi's mother and a cousin to the Suwon woman, in a consoling tone, as though she hadn't the foggiest idea why the woman was so upset.

"Well, it sounds as if she can't wait for him to die."

"What are you talking about?" Deok-gi's mother looked up, her eyes wide open. "When did I ever say I hoped he'd pass away soon?" She gasped and said, "Why would you go and accuse an innocent person like that?" She resumed eating.

Now that these two fierce opponents were facing each other, neither would ease up. The other women were spoiling for a scene and watched, offering no discouragement. Deok-gi's wife grew anxious, not knowing what to do.

"So I'm the one who's wrong?" The Suwon woman put down her spoon and was ready to enter the fray. "You're the one who's accusing an innocent person. You might get away with that in private, but we have witnesses here. Don't bother with anyone else, just ask her." Fuming, the woman pointed to Deok-gi's wife. "You know exactly what she said. 'When your time is up, you might as well die quickly.'"

"Do you really think I said Father should die? I just meant that I feel sorry for him because he won't get much more out of life, no matter how much longer he lives." Deok-gi's mother's blood was boiling not only because her opponent had found fault in her words, but also because she realized how difficult it would be to dispel the suspicion.

"Why shouldn't he get more out of life? And who do you think would be responsible if he doesn't?"

"What do you mean, who?" Deok-gi's mother was losing her temper, too. "Do you actually believe that I'm responsible?"

"Well, you said it yourself—what a fine son he has."

"Oh, and have you given birth to that fine son? That's none of your business. All I can say is, I can't believe how some people think that their own shit doesn't smell."

"Ha! And what have you been smelling? Go ahead, just go ahead and say it," her face was blue with anger.

Deok-gi's mother was tongue-tied.

"Just admit it. You're trying to make me look bad because you want to take over the main room of this house. If that's what you're really after, why don't you just say so? Why do you have to drive me away?"

"Who said anything about wanting to take over the main room?" Deok-gi's mother demanded.

"Then what is it? What do you want from me?" The Suwon woman's voice rose, but Deok-gi's mother simply sat there, offering no response.

The elderly aunt came forward and made excuses for Deok-gi's mother. "Now, now, she spoke without thinking, and once you start arguing, one thing leads to another. Come now, dear, it's too easy to find fault with other people's words."

"But I know why she said it. Admit it. You look down on me because I was a child widow who changed my fate for the better." The Suwon woman started trembling and burst into tears, letting her grief pour out. "My lot was bad enough and that's why I ended up here. That's why I'm abused like this."

They could hear someone coming. Deok-gi's wife looked outside and saw that it was her father-in-law. Most of the women went out to greet him, but the two opponents held their ground.

Sang-hun hurried over to see how his father was, since his daughter had stopped by the house and told him about his fall. The old man, however, opened his eyes only briefly and pretended to be asleep. Sang-hun had no choice but to leave. On his way home, he stopped by the inner quarters.

"It's so cold outside. Come on in," urged the aunt, but he didn't respond.

He addressed his daughter-in-law, who had descended to the stone step. "What's going on?"

"Oh, nothing, sir."

Waves of a woman's weeping wafted out from the inner room. Sang-hun understood the situation.

"Why are you so indiscreet? Showing up everywhere and making scenes?" he shouted to his wife in the main room. Addressing his daughter-in-law, he said, "Tell your mother to go home." Then he was gone.

Deok-gi's mother went to the other room after she sensed that her husband had left.

The Suwon woman kept her mouth shut, offering not a single farewell, as the guests took their leave. She waited until everyone was gone before she returned to the outer quarters.

The old man was surprised to see her swollen red eyes. He gazed at her sitting quietly next to him and asked, "What's wrong?"

"I can't stay here any longer. I'm going to leave and stay at an inn or something." Her eyes were brimming with tears.

The old man was surprised but angry. "What nonsense is this? Why are you acting this way? Speak up!" he thundered.

"You'll find out soon enough. Anyway, I've made up my mind and I'm leaving." The Suwon woman spoke firmly; she rose to her feet.

Had the old man not been bedridden, he'd have bolted up and shaken the woman by the hair in a fiery rage. As it was, he couldn't move a muscle.

"Sit down! Why are you acting this way?" His voice soared dangerously high, all the more frustrated by his inability to move his body. The Suwon woman sat far away from him, without speaking.

"Who did you fight with? And look! Even if you did quarrel with someone, even if you did get upset, how can you talk about leaving when I'm lying here like this?" He knew that his wife and daughter-in-law didn't get along, but he didn't want to ask whether she had had a fight with her.

"Here I am living like this in your house, and how am I supposed to stay even a minute longer when I keep being insulted by an underling?"

"Who said what to you?"

"Deok-gi's mother is running off her mouth again. She says it'd be better if you died soon and that I don't know how bad my own shit smells. Is she the only one who counts in this household?"

"What are you talking about? How is all this possible? She's not the kind of person who would —" The old man curbed his anger.

"There you go again. You trust her more than me, right?"

"Enough! We have manners in this household, and we're her elders. Just because you heard something insulting, does it make any sense for you to leave? Do you think Deok-gi's mother is the only one who matters in this house and that you've got to look up to her? Think about it. Grant me that much!" The old man scolded her in a measured tone of voice.

The Suwon woman hung her head low. But did she think any differently, suddenly moved by her husband's words? The old man suspected that she simply had wanted to find a reason to stir up trouble.

"And why would she ever say that she hoped I would die soon? Even if she entertained such an evil thought, she'd never say it out loud. Who in her right mind would say such a thing in front of you, knowing that I'd hear about it right away?"

To the Suwon woman, the man sounded as if he were still siding with his daughter-in-law. "She must have said it without thinking, because she's been thinking about it constantly. She's a nasty one. When she's angry, I'm telling you, she'll say anything."

It did sound plausible. The old man lay quietly, blinking his eyes.

"So why does she want me to die?"

"Isn't it obvious? After you die, she'll kick me out of the house. Then she'll take over the main room and live happily ever after with her son's family."

This seemed to make sense, too. He tried to suppress his rage.

"And what did she say about you smelling?"

She sensed the old man was slowly coming around. The Suwon woman felt better and lifted her face.

"Who knows? She claims she noticed something evil I was doing." She pursed her lips. "She wants to drive me away. That's why she's saying things like that!"

This sounded plausible enough, as well.

"It would have been different if she'd said those things to me in private, but the room was full of guests and even your young granddaughter-in-law was there. I—" Breaking into sobs, she failed to finish her sentence. The old man felt sorry that his wife had been so harassed.

Third Clash

———

Deok-gi had to postpone his departure again for another day or two. In good conscience, he couldn't just go until he was sure that his grandfather was well and could move around a little. It would have been a different story, of course, if Deok-gi's father were tending him with a bowl of Chinese medicinal brew, but such was not the case, and Deok-gi didn't have the heart to take off when his grandfather was still confined to bed.

His grandfather told Deok-gi to go if he wanted to, but he seemed to hope that his grandson would stay.

Deok-gi didn't feel like hanging around the house, though. In the aftermath of the clash between his mother and the Suwon woman, he had no desire to watch them behave like chickens after a fight.

The next day Deok-gi went to visit his father. He wanted to talk about a number of things with him, not the least of which was the matter of Gyeong-ae, and he wanted to express his opinion about his father's clash with his grandfather two nights before.

Since his father wasn't up yet, Deok-gi went to the inner quarters. His mother inquired after his grandfather and then asked him what his step-grandmother had said about their fight. Deok-gi said he didn't know. Although he wasn't sure about exactly what the Suwon woman had said when she broke down in tears in the outer quarters the day before, he had heard about the way she'd made a nuisance of herself to his wife, pretending to be so hurt that she was going to leave the house so that they could all live happily ever after without her. She had gone so far as to accuse Deok-gi's family of putting up a united front in an attempt to drive her away. After hearing bits and pieces from his wife of what the Suwon woman had said, Deok-gi was angry but also skeptical, and in the end he decided to ignore all the rumors.

"It sounds like she's giving your wife a hard time again. Really, who cares what nonsense she whispers into your grandfather's ear, but why does she have to bully the youngest one in the family?" His mother had now found a new reason to be indignant about the woman.

"If you understand her so well, why do you have to go and provoke her the way you do? Whatever she said yesterday, couldn't you have just ignored her?"

"How can I simply sit by and let her attack me for no reason? Yesterday morning, she tried to make me look bad because I didn't scurry out to the outer quarters when your grandfather fell. Then I hear she bad-mouthed me to your wife, claiming that I wouldn't even bat an eye if my father-in-law were dying. She even said that if he were going to die anytime soon and we inherited everything, we'd all be dancing on his grave! Can you imagine? These must be her own nasty fantasies. I have no doubt she's counting down the days until your grandfather passes away, so that she can pocket her share and be rid of the Jo family once and for all before she gets too old." His mother was fuming and made no effort to conceal her bitterness.

"Don't you realize she makes these sorts of accusations against us because you accuse her of the same thing? Granted, she's only my grandfather's second wife, and she's younger than you, but how do you expect her to behave when you tell her she doesn't know how bad her own shit smells?" It wasn't that Deok-gi didn't want to take his mother's side—as the saying goes, your arm bends in, not out—but he was still unhappy about her lack of dignity, her inability to keep the Suwon woman in check.

"Do you really think I'd say something like that without good reason? On the day of the rites, for example, she kept conspiring with the maidservant while everyone else was busy working. Then, when your grandfather went out, she said some relative of hers had come to Seoul and fallen sick in an inn. She just rushed out of the house, with the excuse that she had to see how he was doing. Now tell me, how can she just take off while everyone else is so busy? Does that make any sense to you? I don't care if it was her mother on her deathbed, she just can't do that. Anyway, the woman ran off and whispered something to Clerk Choe at the gate. Then he goes into the outer quarters, and she runs down the street. I'm telling you, it's all terribly fishy. They're all up to no good, I'm sure of it. Granted, she doesn't have the slightest interest in the rites, and she doesn't know how to put in a good day's work, but can you believe she was stuck to that dressing mirror of hers until noon? Then she fumbled with the vegetables as if she didn't know what to do with them and left the trimming and the rest of the work for us. What kind of behavior is that? The maid, you know, was brought in by Clerk Choe, and it took less than a week for your stepgrandmother to become best buddies with her. And then what do you make of her whispering to Choe just before she ran out? I'm sure they're conspiring to cheat your grandfather somehow, but does he have even the slightest clue about what's going on?"

Deok-gi had heard from his wife that the Suwon woman was gone for almost an hour on the day of the rites while his grandfather was out, though he hadn't found it odd. But the way his mother told it, it did sound rather suspicious.

If Gannani, the nanny who minded Deok-gi's baby, had indeed seen something out of the ordinary and had reported it, it might very well be true that Choe and the Suwon woman had met at the gate. Although it was true that it was Choe who had introduced the Suwon woman to his grandfather, it might have been only a coincidence that they'd run into each other at the gate. The fact that they hired the maidservant on Choe's recommendation could also be a coincidence. It didn't necessarily mean that the three were conspiring in some way against Deok-gi's grandfather. As for the Suwon woman's mysterious outing on the day of the rites, some relative of hers might have caught the flu or something and sent a messenger asking her to visit. The maid could have relayed the message in whispers to the Suwon woman, who immediately ran out.

"Who did she say this relative of hers was?" Deok-gi asked.

"Her brother. But if that were true, why didn't he come directly to our outer quarters and take to bed there? Why would he just collapse at an inn? Even if it were her brother, why did she leave so frantically?" His mother remained unconvinced.

"What do we really know about other people's business? Can you be sure that your view of things is right? I bet she told Grandfather beforehand that she'd have to go out." Deok-gi wanted to discourage his mother from thinking the way she did. He didn't intend to defend the Suwon woman; he just wanted everyone to get along. His mother was displeased, though, thinking that Deok-gi was again siding with the Suwon woman.

When the conversation between mother and son came to a pause, Deok-gi stood up to go. "Grandfather said he wants you to come over today or tomorrow."

"I was planning to see how he's doing anyway, but now it sounds like he has something to tell me." She felt a twinge of guilt.

"I don't know. Maybe the Suwon woman said something to him."

"I'm sure she did, no doubt . . ." She recalled how she had spat out the remarks that ended up putting her on the defensive. Now she was worried.

In the outer quarters, Deok-gi found his father sitting in front of a meal tray.

"I'm afraid you won't be able to leave today," his father said.

"That's right."

Deok-gi would have preferred to leave right away unless his father and grandfather were actually at war with each other, but he couldn't bring himself to say it.

"You're graduating this spring, right? What next?"

It was the first time the father had asked about his son's studies. One could assume he was an advocate of absolute permissiveness. When Deok-gi had settled on a course of study and informed his grandfather of his decision, the old man agreed to pay his tuition, most likely because he didn't know much about these new studies. When Deok-gi asked his father for permission, he merely nodded in agreement. Despite having such a family, Deok-gi had come this far, partly because he wasn't stupid and partly because he had learned about the ways of the world early on.

"Actually, I was planning to enter Kyoto Imperial University."

"Is that really necessary? If you applied to Keijo Imperial University here in Seoul, the admission process wouldn't be as competitive, and in light of what's been going on in the family recently, it would be more convenient."

"Well, Keijo is a good school, too." Deok-gi wanted to stay as far away from Seoul as possible, but if he could get into Keijo, he wouldn't mind having to stay.

"Then why don't you apply? It really would be best for the family . . ." Sang-hun stopped himself from adding *and it would be best for me, too.*

The way Sang-hun figured it, if things kept going the way they were, his father would try to cut him off by using whatever legal means it might take and pass most of his assets on to Deok-gi. And given how conniving the Suwon woman was, he couldn't be sure what else might happen at a later point. With his own reputation at stake, Sang-hun couldn't afford to get involved in an ugly court fight with his father, as some did these days. Furthermore, being a religious leader, he was in no position to openly claim his father's assets. He knew that the only way things would work out in his favor was if he maintained a firm grip on Deok-gi and, manipulating him as he wished, made him fend off the interference and trickery of the Suwon woman, the other relatives, and the extended family. In order to accomplish this, he sweetened his attitude toward his son so the boy wouldn't feel alienated from him and might be inclined to listen to his father in the future.

"So, what are you thinking of majoring in?"

"I think I'll apply to the Law Department." Deok-gi hoped to concentrate on criminal law. Even if he didn't end up practicing as a specialist in this area, in light of Korea's current political situation, the field would help him find a good career.

When Deok-gi had mentioned his plans to Byeong-hwa, Byeong-hwa had mocked him. "You'll be so far from the ideological front line that we'll find you hiding behind the Red Cross flag!" He added, "It'll be like you're supervising the surgeons who are operating on the soldiers."

"Say what you will," Deok-gi replied in the same vein, "but if you become a prisoner of war on your so-called battlefront, you just may need a medic like me."

"Well, they do need guards for prisoners of war," Byeong-hwa continued in jeering tones; "It sounds like you want to become a prison guard. The job actually might suit you well."

All joking aside, Deok-gi did feel the need to be somehow connected to the movement for the disadvantaged. He wasn't exactly the type to fight for their rights on the front lines, but he thought he might do his part by looking after them as a lawyer—come to think of it, not unlike medics do on battlefields. He had no grand illusion about becoming a success, but at the same time he didn't want to end up an isolated academic. He wanted to pull his own weight by doing something helpful that suited him as well.

"How about the Economics Department or the Business Administration Department instead of the Law Department?" Deok-gi's father seemed eager to push his son into the business world. He could make the best use of him there.

"I wouldn't mind the Economics Department, but I don't really like the idea of going to the Business Department." Here, too, Deok-gi had some vague thoughts of his own.

"Do as you please," the father responded casually so as not to irritate his son. Changing the subject, he lowered his voice and asked, "Have you been to any cafés recently?"

Deok-gi was surprised. Why was his father asking him, out of the blue, about going to a café?

Did someone tell him I was there? "Yes, I have," he answered. "Kim Byeong-hwa dragged me to one." Turning bright red, he glanced at his father to see how he took it.

"Who did you meet there?" asked the father.

Deok-gi didn't know how to respond, his father had caught him off guard.

"I suspect I know who, and I don't really care, but . . ." The father tried his best to make his son talk.

"I met . . . Hong Gyeong-ae." Deok-gi felt awkward saying the name aloud.

"Which café was it?"

"It wasn't a café. It was a bar called Bacchus . . . a fish-cake soup place." Deok-gi's gaze was fixed on his father, who posed the questions without a trace of embarrassment, as if it had nothing to do with him.

"What was she doing there?" he asked after a while.

"Selling liquor."

"Does she manage the place?"

"No, I think she just works there." Deok-gi didn't want to tell his father that Gyeong-ae was doing it to pass the time as a friend of the proprietor. He wanted to paint a wretched picture, an image of a fallen woman.

It's not that he wanted to elicit his father's sympathy for Gyeong-ae. Rather, he simply wanted to make it clear that his father was responsible for her current situation.

"How did she look?"

"Not great but not terrible, either. She was wearing this Japanese gown that—" Deok-gi suddenly brought the conversation to a halt.

"Who told you I saw her?" Deok-gi asked, after a moment's pause.

"I just heard about it from someone," his father said, smiling.

Deok-gi couldn't press the issue any further, but he grew more and more curious. "Kim Byeong-hwa?"

"Where in the world would I meet Kim Byeong-hwa?" Then his father added, "I don't think you should be going out to places like that any more. What'll happen to you if you start drinking like a fish at your age?" His father admonished him gently.

Although the father was right to disapprove of his son's behavior, his words had the effect of sparking Deok-gi's rebellious urges. He wondered whether perhaps he had said something indiscreet when he was drunk that reached his father's ears. But who would have spoken to his father? He didn't have a clue.

Had he told his wife, when he came home drunk that day, that he had met Gyeong-ae? If his wife then told his mother, word might indeed have reached his father. Deok-gi was puzzled.

This was, in fact, precisely what happened.

When his mother heard her daughter-in-law mention that Deok-gi had run into someone called Hong Gyeong-ae at a Japanese bar the previous night, she felt a memory she thought had been long forgotten grip and start to shake her. Wasn't she unhappy enough as it was? Instantly, she assumed that her husband was hiding Gyeong-ae away and had given her enough seed money to manage a high-collar bar.

The mother had wanted to ask her son whether it was true that he was sympathetic to Gyeong-ae. But she hadn't found the opportunity to bring up the matter at her father-in-law's house, and she had forgotten to mention it to him later on in her room because she was wrapped up in criticizing the Suwon woman. It wasn't until the other night, when her husband had—for the first time in quite a while—entered the inner quarters to scold her for fighting with the Suwon woman, that she'd been able to bring up the topic of Hong Gyeong-ae.

The wife went on and on about how he and Gyeong-ae would never sever ties because they had a four- or five-year-old child between them. The husband didn't quite grasp why she cared so much whether he parted with Gyeong-ae or not, but assured her that he'd be glad to grant her a divorce.

Deok-gi found it difficult to approach the subject now, as he faced his father, but he forced himself to say what was on his mind. "I don't know exactly what happened between the two of you, but how can you just abandon her in light of what's happened?"

"What else can I do except leave her alone? I have to think about my own position, you know. And, besides, she's the one who made such a fuss and broke things off with me."

"That's not what she implied. Even though you're my father, I've got to say that what you've done—sacrificing others for the sole purpose of saving your own skin—is just plain wrong."

"That's none of your business!" the father shouted.

"You're right! It is none of my business. It's your responsibility, from beginning to end. And I want to know what you're going to do about it."

"Responsibility? What are you talking about? I told you—you shouldn't go poking your nose into things you know nothing about." The father's resolve to speak to his son with tact had completely disappeared.

"I'm sure that she neither initiated the affair nor ended it. It's only because word got out that—" Deok-gi said.

"Stop this nonsense! To talk to your father this way! How can someone your age be so impudent?" The father had no intention of hearing his son out and wanted him to know who was in charge.

Deok-gi felt compelled, however, to finish what he had started to say.

"Don't you feel sorry for the child? Why should she be your sacrificial lamb? I won't pass judgment on you, Father, but don't you think you should finish what you've started?"

"What do you mean, what I started? That child isn't mine."

"What do you mean? I saw her two nights ago. How can you say such a thing? I'm afraid to even ask you this question, but do you really intend to avoid your responsibility? Are you going to try to shift the blame onto Gyeong-ae?" Deok-gi was incensed.

"Don't you dare talk to me like that!" The father then tried to temper his rage, managing to lower his voice to add, "Now, get out of here! Get out!" He turned his back on Deok-gi, repeating what his own father had said to him on the day of the ancestral rites, as if he were passing down the command from one generation to the next.

Deok-gi's father was furious to learn that his son had gone to see the child, but he was nevertheless curious about the visit. He was in no position to ask for details, though.

Was he simply repeating what he used to say to the members of the church and to the outside world in order to deny the truth? He had never denied it to himself. Actually, it was Gyeong-ae, more than the child, whom he couldn't entirely forget even now, several years later. He had convinced himself that there was no need to pick at an old sore, since he didn't have the nerve to get in touch with her.

If Sang-hun could do it all over again, he would surely find a way to keep her instead of tossing her away so heartlessly. At the time, though, he hadn't had the courage. He had trembled with fear that rumors might spread all over town—throughout the church at the very least—and since he didn't know how to take responsibility for his actions, he just walked away. If only he'd had a thousand won at the time to send her away to the countryside! But it had been impossible to make his father cough up such a hefty sum without saying why he needed it, and he couldn't have raised that kind of money quickly because his father held on to the deeds of the Hwagae-dong house. While she was in Tokyo, Gyeong-ae wanted desperately to come home, and he really couldn't leave her there with her swelling stomach, so he brought her back and in a frenzy hid her at the Bungmi Changjeong house, fearing the scrutiny of women in the church who often visited Gyeong-ae's house in Dangju-dong.

Gyeong-ae's mother also feared there'd be rumors at church. She told everyone that she was moving back to Suwon, using the excuse that her daughter was still studying in Tokyo and that it was difficult for her to live in Seoul all alone. She did actually go to Suwon for a while, but she soon returned to Seoul and set up house in anticipation of Gyeong-ae's return. No one guessed that the sudden disappearance of the mother and daughter meant they had been admitted early to Heaven. A secret like Gyeong-ae's couldn't be kept for long. And Seoul was a small world. When the mother ran into friends from church on the street, her excuse that she'd come to Seoul for a short visit grew stale. The rumors began as far-flung stories but soon gravitated toward the truth. Gyeong-ae's mother felt harassed and caught in the middle, while Sang-hun went around looking gaunt and unwell. Had he openly renounced the church and its doctrines, having a concubine would no longer have seemed a sin, and he might have felt it was nothing to be ashamed of. But he couldn't find the courage to sacrifice his place in society however much he didn't want to banish Gyeong-ae or abandon her. In the midst of all this, she had the baby.

"We'll have to move somewhere far away now, and we'll need some capital to help us get settled. You can't expect us to go on living like this in Seoul, hiding out like criminals. And we can't move to Suwon. Of course, we'll raise your child for you, and by that I don't mean that we should cut off our relationship completely . . ."

Being a Christian, Sang-hun couldn't become a free man until his wife died, and because divorce wasn't allowed, he couldn't live openly with

Gyeong-ae. It might have been seen differently had Gyeong-ae been unknown to the congregation, but she was the daughter of a well-known church figure who had recently passed away. If she were to become Jo Sang-hun's concubine, it would dishonor the deceased, not to mention Sang-hun. Gyeong-ae's mother, at any rate, wanted to get out of Seoul, but at this point Sang-hun found it even more difficult to scrape together some money than when he had brought Gyeong-ae back from Tokyo. This was because the Suwon woman, having heard all the rumors from her hometown circles, had shared what she knew with the old man.

The old man never said anything directly to his son, but he tightened his purse strings even further, so the son didn't have a penny of his own. While Sang-hun was having little success raising the money he needed, rumors continued to spread, and to make matters worse, the Suwon woman maliciously mentioned the affair to Deok-gi's mother, who didn't take the news sitting down.

Deok-gi's mother went straight to the house at Bungmi Changjeong before having it out with her husband. She poured out all kinds of abuse at the women, stopping short of physically assaulting them. If they had anything more to do with her husband, she'd threatened to spread word of their affair throughout the congregation, and with the help of her stepmother-in-law's network of friends she'd make sure they'd never be allowed to set foot in Suwon again.

Since then, Sang-hun and his wife had continued to live together in the same house, but they hardly spoke.

Though Sang-hun tried to ignore the opinions of the judgmental gossips around him, it upset him that they had misconstrued his earlier kindness to Gyeong-ae's father and family as simply a means of getting his hands on the young woman. From the outset, he had helped Gyeong-ae's father because the man was a patriot and an elder, and because Sang-hun sympathized with his family's miserable condition. It was regrettable that Sang-hun had a relationship with Gyeong-ae, and he thought it was this misconception that led people to misread him.

Sang-hun was in no position to divorce a wife who was alive and well, taking into account his status as a Christian and the feelings of his grown children. Since his relationship with Gyeong-ae couldn't last long, he even considered taking away the baby as soon as possible and having someone else raise it, which would at least give Gyeong-ae the chance to marry properly. The best way to accomplish this would have been to give her some money and send her away to a small town in the country, where she could find a job as a teacher. Such a scenario, however, was not to be, and he found himself wasting a lot of time.

In the eyes of Gyeong-ae's mother, nothing could have been more unjust. Her daughter had been dishonored, and she herself was forced to live a life of confinement and to be the object of constant abuse. The only thing she had gotten out of it all was a grandchild, but the baby required constant care and attention. To top it off, they now lived in a house that didn't even belong to them. Had they not been indebted to Sang-hun for his help in the past, she might have exposed his guilt to the world, because at that point it wouldn't have mattered to her one way or the other. It was only a certain lingering loyalty to the man who had been of such assistance to her family that kept her from doing so.

She asked for a thousand won so that her family could leave Seoul, but days, then weeks went by without any word. It was unclear whether Sang-hun was finding it difficult to raise funds or whether he simply had no intention of providing the money.

One day, he came over and made something of an announcement, as if he'd come to a major decision. "Why don't you entrust the baby to someone else and go wherever you want with this money, at least for now? Anyway, there's no proof that the child is mine. Even if she were, I could pretend she was never born." He then handed over three hundred won.

He added that when Gyeong-ae's mother moved from the Dangju-dong house, she'd had five hundred in deposit money, so they must have almost a thousand, all told. But the deposit had already been spent. Although Sang-hun had helped out from time to time, his contributions were not enough, and she had had to dip into their deposit to pay for various expenses: moving, buying furniture and kitchen utensils, and for when Gyeong-ae gave birth. During the several months they had lived in the new house, apart from a little grain, Sang-hun hadn't given them even a penny. In any event, Gyeong-ae's mother was offended. She was positively speechless when he said that there was no proof that the baby was his. *Is he human?* she wondered, though the thought had crossed her mind that perhaps he just wanted to pick a fight. An argument ensued but nothing came of it. All she got was a mere three hundred won, and from that day forward, Sang-hun stopped his visits altogether.

Sang-hun thought this move of his would not only drive Gyeong-ae and him apart but also justify him in the eyes of the world. Floating the rumor that Gyeong-ae and her mother had disappeared on account of a love affair with the child's father, whoever he was, worked decidedly in his favor. He figured they would entrust someone with the baby and move to the countryside in search of a job or of an eligible man Gyeong-ae could marry. He truly believed that it was in everyone's best interest, since he couldn't take responsibility for Gyeong-ae and her child. But Gyeong-ae and her mother didn't budge from the house for the next several years.

As for Gyeong-ae's mother, her almost masculine nonchalance drove her to a rather radical way of thinking: Why even keep in touch with such a sub-human bastard? At the same time, though, she couldn't bring herself to completely sever ties with the man, remembering how they had been indebted to him in the past. She came to terms with her bitterness and let the matter stand.

One month passed, two months passed, then a year. After two years had gone by, tempers had subsided. Sang-hun assumed that Gyeong-ae and the baby were all right and made no attempt to find out more about them. He tried to forget everything that had happened, and his father didn't make an issue of the house, writing off the lost rent by pretending it remained vacant. The old man was probably unaware that his son and Gyeong-ae had parted ways, but turning a blind eye was his way of respecting his son and his honor.

Reunion

———

Deok-gi left for Kyoto three days later. His grandfather's back pain had worsened to the point that he was now confined to bed. Someone had to attend to his ablutions, but nothing else was wrong with the old man. He ate voraciously, and the doctor said that he'd be able to get up in a week or so. Deok-gi's grandfather told him to leave, which was just as well, as Deok-gi couldn't afford to miss any more school right before his graduation.

Deok-gi's mother didn't come on the day he left. It had been three days since she had paid a visit to her sick father-in-law, after Deok-gi had conveyed his grandfather's order that she do so, and when she did, he scolded her so harshly it infuriated her. She felt that he was unfair, but she was also afraid of him. If he hadn't yelled at her, she would have checked on him every day, but she sent Deok-hui instead. She had wanted to see Deok-gi off but decided against it, fearful that her father-in-law would get angry again and accuse her of coming to see her son and not him. He had lashed out at her more abusively than the Suwon woman ever had.

The old man was now saying that although he felt like banishing his daughter-in-law from the family for her public tirade, he would forgive her for the sake of her children. He told her never to come to his house again, words usually aimed at his son. That was rough enough in itself, but when he interrogated her about the Suwon woman's possibly suspicious conduct, Deok-gi's mother broke out into a sweat.

Before she was able to explain how her words had been misconstrued, the old man, still in bed, began ranting and raving, arms and legs flailing like an outraged child; so she ended up returning home without being able to make her case.

"You and that husband of yours are praying that I'll die soon! I'm sure he's praying to that of God of his, but you? Are you praying to mountain and river spirits? Who knows what a witch like you might do to me next. Poison my medicine?" It had been quite a tantrum. Deok-gi's mother was appalled by these remarks and loathed him all the more. Even though the old man blindly accepted what his young wife whispered to him and heaped scorn on his daughter-in-law, she was willing to pay the sick man a visit as soon as the following day because he was the family elder. But now she was afraid that she might be blamed for something she didn't do or be tricked in some way. What if something were to happen to the old man right after her visit? The Suwon woman wasn't to be trusted.

Annoyed by the family turbulence and knowing that his presence was of no use, Deok-gi decided to leave. When he visited the Hwagae-dong house, his mother burst into tears, lamenting how she had failed to defend herself against her father-in-law's rage. Sitting in the outer quarters with his friends, his father said coldly, "You're leaving? Well I guess I'll see you during spring vacation then." As the son was about to kneel on the floor to offer a formal bow, the father stopped him. "Don't worry about that, son. Just go on now."

Was his father being too modern? No matter where he went, Deok-gi felt downright uncomfortable, out of place. When he was about to leave, though, his father approached the edge of the veranda and asked him, in a barely audible voice, "Deok-gi, where's that bar you talked about the other day?"

"It's at Samjeongmok on Bonjeongtong."

As Deok-gi was about to return to the inner quarters, his mother, who was waiting at the outer gate to say good-bye, asked, "What were you saying about Samjeongmok?"

Without thinking, Deok-gi made a face but quickly came up with an answer. "We were talking about a bookstore."

As she followed him out to the middle gate, his mother recalled something she had heard. "Isn't that Gyeong-ae girl somewhere in a bar over there?" Caught off guard, Deok-gi said, "I don't know."

His mother's face blanched at her son's betrayal. She suspected that he was siding with his father and had decided to keep her in the dark.

After Deok-gi left, snowflakes began to fall. In the outer quarters of the Hwagae-dong house, the guests started playing mahjong. It was Friday, and as there were no activities at church, they all felt like staying on and playing a game or two on this snowy evening. Everyone hoped that Chinese food would be ordered or that they'd eventually head for that bar they sometimes went to in secret.

Outside, large snowflakes were blanketing everything in white. They lit up the gloomy room.

Since they were upstanding Christians, they took the precaution of locking the gate in the outer quarters and speaking in low voices as they played. Only the clinking of mahjong tiles drifted from the room.

"I'm sure we'll have a good harvest next year, too. Look at all the snow we've gotten this year."

"You're right. We should at least have good harvests. Though someone like Mr. Jo will certainly disagree."

"What's the use of having a good harvest in times like these?"

When the electric lights came on, the master's dinner tray was brought in, but no one showed interest in the food.

The maidservant was not pleased. Whenever they played table games, the guests usually ordered out for Chinese food, and the dinner tray would be left untouched until deep into the night, which meant that she couldn't retire to her room even on a cold night like this. If they actually ordered enough food so that she could taste a few leftovers herself, it might be a different story, but she knew these guests always licked the dishes clean, as though they were ghosts who had starved for three lifetimes.

She asked the master, "Should I take your meal back and bring it out again when you're ready to eat?"

The master told her to leave it, and after consulting with the guests in a low voice, he wrote down the names of the dishes he wanted her to order at the Chinese restaurant, just as expected.

"Lock the gate to the outer quarters. And if anyone stops by, tell them I'm not home."

Even though everyone was a brother or a sister before God, the master of this household, being a *yangban*, used a less refined form of speech when addressing his underlings at home. What's more, the maidservant thought it was rather odd that he ordered her to send away any visitors rather than simply lock the gate. She'd never received such instructions before.

Was he expecting a debt collector? Were they planning to stay up all night playing mahjong? The maidservant had her suspicions, but the truth of the matter was that on the list of Chinese dishes was six hundred grams of Chinese liquor, and they intended to enjoy it as they took in the snowy evening. If any church members outside their clique were to stop by, it would ruin the festive mood and immediately put them on the defensive.

As the second round of mahjong neared its end, the Chinese food was delivered. The keeper of the outer quarters went out to open the gate. It was dark outside and snowing less heavily.

When the keeper shouted to the inner quarters, the maidservant emerged with a tray that she set on the edge of the veranda, onto which she transferred all the food. Inside, the mahjong players hurried to finish up the game before the tray was brought in.

The outer gate squeaked open and footsteps, crunching the snow, approached. The maidservant, caught by surprise, found a man standing behind her clad in a black Western-style suit.

"Who are you?"

"Isn't the young master from the main house here?"

"Well, he was here, but he's gone now."

Inside, everyone went silent as though they were in a gambling den being raided by the police. The door opened a crack, and the visitor could see the master, still seated, frowning.

"It's just me." The visitor doffed his hat and bowed.

"Ah, I wondered who it might be. Come on in." The master stood up, seeing that it was Byeong-hwa, and a smile spread across his face, as though he were relieved, perhaps even glad, to see him.

"That's all right, sir. I heard your son was leaving today, and I just came by looking for him."

"He's already gone. He wasn't at home?"

"When I dropped by a while ago, I was told he came over here."

"It's cold out there. Please come in."

"No, thank you, sir. I'll just be on my way." Byeong-hwa's curiosity was piqued, however, by these Christians gambling behind closed doors.

"Don't be silly," the master urged him. "Come in and warm up a bit before you go. It's freezing out there."

Sang-hun was displeased with the maidservant for not locking the gate, but he was being as kind as he could, thinking he couldn't shoo this chatterbox away with all this food spread out and a liquor bottle in full view. He also had something else in mind.

The truth was that Byeong-hwa was able to get in only because the Chinese deliveryman was standing at the gate. Otherwise, he would have been sent away, covered with snow. Byeong-hwa stepped up to the veranda to join them inside.

The men in the room were once again deeply absorbed in their game and didn't bother to look up at the intruder. Byeong-hwa recognized one or two of them from his own churchgoing days.

It took a while to wrap up the games after the food was brought in. When the players finally approached the tray, they were excitedly discussing the hundreds or thousands of points, and Byeong-hwa signaled that he would go. The master wouldn't hear of it.

If Byeong-hwa wanted to go to the train station to see his friend off, the master said there was plenty of time. He offered some refreshments to Byeong-hwa, assuming that he hadn't eaten yet. Byeong-hwa figured it would be better to eat than to leave hungry, so he began to devour the food put in front of him. He also drank whenever someone offered him a cup. The men then ordered another bottle of liquor, saying that they didn't have enough to drink, though there was plenty of food. Tossing back the throat-stinging stuff as though it were water, they seemed more interested in getting drunk quickly than enjoying its flavor or savoring the moment and its snowy backdrop. Byeong-hwa shared their eagerness to get drunk, though with different motives.

"I hear you live somewhere outside Saemun," the master of the house finally addressed Byeong-hwa. Until then, not a soul had spoken, busy as they were slurping and chomping on their food.

Though Byeong-hwa was his son's friend, and Sang-hun felt comfortable with him, on this occasion Sang-hun was more solicitous than usual for he was afraid that Byeong-hwa might talk about what he'd seen.

"You seem to be doing all right, considering you're not earning any money. I met your father a while ago, you know. Why don't you just give up what you're doing now and go home?" After several drinks, Sang-hun had grown talkative.

Byeong-hwa looked around at the others in the room and said, "You know, I wouldn't mind going home if my father were more like all of you and didn't actually pray before he drinks and eats. He's well into the third stage of his opium addiction." He smiled. People often referred to religion as opium.

Many in the room were embarrassed by Byeong-hwa's remarks, but something defiant hardened their faces. Sang-hun was at a loss for words. When they sat down to eat at home, they all prayed, but they'd simply forgotten to do so here—almost as though God himself had exempted them from prayer before consuming Chinese food and booze. *You bastard!* shot out of the corners of the men's eyes.

"I hate to point this out, but it seems to me that if all of you can enjoy yourselves like this on a regular basis, you must admit to enjoying the taste of freedom, joy, and peace—the taste of real life. Now think for a moment how frustrated you would feel if you had to sit like a bride on her wedding day, with your face bearing traditional ceremonial marks, your eyes cast downward, and your body squeezed into a cumbersome ceremonial gown." This was how the tipsy Byeong-hwa assaulted them.

Offering neither opposition nor an excuse, Sang-hun responded: "It's good to break out of the mold from time to time, but you can't just abandon your self-control, drink all day, and wander around in a drunken stupor! It doesn't hurt anyone though to take a break every once in a while from the discipline of everyday life."

"I'm not talking about your drinking and having fun. I'm talking about your feelings, your conscience. To say that life can be free, fun, and peaceful only when you drink, play mahjong, and go out on the town is to take quite a decadent view of life. Ask yourselves this: What exactly is the purpose of the disciplined life you just mentioned? Suppose a more disciplined, a more arduous life than practicing religion actually exists."

As Byeong-hwa poured out this passionate speech, as befits a literature-loving youth, many sat with frowns on their faces, wondering where the second bottle was.

"Liquor here, liquor come," the Chinese deliveryman shouted in broken Korean, shaking the gate. The doors slid open and shut again, followed by a bustle of activity. Byeong-hwa wanted to talk more about his theories and annoy the others, but he wasn't given the chance.

As soon as they finished eating, Sang-hun ushered Byeong-hwa out of the room with a sense of urgency. Byeong-hwa was not drunk, but Sang-hun assumed he was and wanted to send him off quickly, before he offended anyone again with his sharp tongue.

"Why don't you spend your money on useful things instead of inviting all these people over to play mahjong? It's just a high-class way of killing time." Byeong-hwa offered Sang-hun this distasteful advice as they walked to the gate.

Spending money on useful things . . . Sang-hun remembered how he had given the same advice to his father not long ago. But he tried to come up with an excuse for himself. "Well, I wasn't dreaming of a gambling life when I set up the mahjong table. I bought the set when I went to Antung, China, this spring because people told me I could get one there cheap." Then he added, "You hold your alcohol pretty well. How about going somewhere else for another drink?"

"But your guests are still in the house. Please go back in. Besides, I have to go to the train station."

"I'm sure Deok-gi's gone by now."

"I bet I can catch him if I go right away."

"All the way to the station? Do you know what time it is?" said Sang-hun, looking at his watch. "It's past eight. Come on, let's go somewhere. Can you think of a good place?" Now that he had some alcohol in him, Sang-hun deserted his guests and followed Byeong-hwa, secretly hoping to visit Bacchus.

"I know of a place we could go." Now that it was too late to go to the station, Byeong-hwa also felt he could use a few more drinks. "I'll show you the way," Byeong-hwa let Sang-hun board the streetcar ahead of him. He wanted to take Sang-hun to Bacchus. That modern girl they called Aiko had been haunting him. He wanted to see her again. They had been in the middle of a conversation when Deok-gi had dragged him out of the bar. She didn't seem like an ordinary woman.

Sang-hun assumed Byeong-hwa would take him to Bacchus. What a perfect opportunity, he thought, but he was afraid that Gyeong-ae might act rudely in front of Byeong-hwa. And since Byeong-hwa was taking him to Bacchus only days after he had brought Deok-gi, he worried that he might lose face in front of Gyeong-ae. Then again, this might not be the case; it might not even matter. He knew it would be difficult for him to go to Bacchus sober. If he went with Byeong-hwa, it wouldn't appear to Gyeong-ae that Sang-hun was following up on rumors but had simply stumbled in by coincidence. Actually, he wasn't entirely sure of his own intentions. Cooped up in his room, Sang-hun had been thinking of Gyeong-ae all day long and had made up his mind to visit her that night. Drinking only made it easier to keep his resolve.

"So where are we going?" asked Sang-hun, feigning innocence, as they stepped off the streetcar. He wanted to hear what Byeong-hwa would say.

Byeong-hwa smiled to himself, thinking of how this man's son had asked the same question in the same anxious manner when he had tagged along several nights before. He chuckled and said, "Just follow me. It is a great place. I'll even introduce you to a girl so beautiful she could bring down an empire. Just don't go thanking God for his grace when you see her. Instead, make sure you take me out again for another night on the town."

"Hah! What use does an old man like me have for a beautiful girl?"

"You're not an old man yet, though I must say it's somewhat disheartening that older men lose their appeal to beautiful women. Our bodies may age, but our hearts stay young—isn't that how it goes? There's something quite deadly about a middle-aged love affair, don't you think?" Byeong-hwa laughed out loud, as if he were mocking his companion. Sang-hun was astonished. Suddenly he was struck by the fear that Byeong-hwa actually knew everything, that he was taking him to Bacchus to humiliate him. But he couldn't back out now.

Even if Deok-gi hadn't breathed a word to his friend for the sake of his father's honor, there was no guarantee that Byeong-hwa hadn't heard it from someone else. It was equally likely that Byeong-hwa had schemed with Gyeong-ae to arrange a meeting with Deok-gi and was now taking Sang-hun to Bacchus in order to humiliate him or force him to make up for what he had done. Sang-hun sobered up quickly, feeling like an ox approaching the slaughterhouse. But his stubbornness reasserted itself; what, after all, could they do to him? He followed Byeong-hwa inside.

The four tables in Bacchus were occupied, and the air in the room was stale with smoke. Sang-hun couldn't see anything when he stepped in because his eyeglasses immediately fogged up. He pulled them off as he moved closer to the stove.

"Don't be so rude!" cried a woman in Japanese. A familiar voice. As Sang-hun looked over, he saw Gyeong-ae standing at the far end of the corner table. Intoxicated guests sat blocking her way on the left and right, and Gyeong-ae was arguing with them, trying to make her way through.

Gyeong-ae turned her head and saw Byeong-hwa. She called out with a twinkle in her eyes, "Nice to see you again." When Sang-hun's ruddy face appeared behind him, the light went out of her eyes, and she froze. She couldn't believe it—how could he come here? Their eyes met, and both looked down.

Gyeong-ae had been about to make her way out, but she abruptly took her seat. The guests who had been pestering her had momentarily been distracted by the newcomers, but when Gyeong-ae sat down, they applauded. Byeong-hwa was irritated. Since there were no free seats, Gyeong-ae should have produced some extra chairs or at least suggested that they return later because there was no place to seat them.

"Isn't the proprietor here?" Byeong-hwa clapped his hands angrily.

The woman who ran the bar immediately materialized, saying, "How can I help you?" She was holding a paper dish with some change in it. The guests sitting next to the newcomers picked up their money and stood up.

Byeong-hwa and Sang-hun grabbed their seats. As luck would have it, Byeong-hwa found himself with his back to Gyeong-ae, while Sang-hun sat facing her. Byeong-hwa asked Sang-hun to change seats, but the older man ignored him. Gyeong-ae didn't so much as throw a glance in their direction but openly flirted with her Japanese guests. She giggled and laughed with such delight that it was clear she wanted to show off to the newcomers. Wearing a simple Japanese robe called a *kinsha* and gold-rimmed glasses, she was dressed more modestly than Sang-hun had expected. But by the tone of voice she used to welcome Byeong-hwa and by the way she now interacted with her customers, she seemed to be quite a natural—a "whore" in Korean bar slang, or what was called a low-class bar hostess in Japanese establishments. Sang-hun frowned without knowing it, and his teeth hurt as if something heavy were caught between them.

"I'll give you a reward if you down it," the customer sitting next to Gyeong-ae was saying, eager to push the glass on Gyeong-ae.

"Oh, will you now? How much?"

He pulled out a wallet, fished out a ten-won note, and put it on the table.

"Okay, I'll drink it," announced Gyeong-ae.

A peal of laughter from the customers rose and fell.

Sang-hun glanced over and saw Gyeong-ae drinking from the glass, with her chin gradually tilting upward. As half of the yellow liquid flowed at a sharp angle into her mouth, Byeong-hwa turned his head to watch. He grimaced and then threw a quick glance at Sang-hun, who hung his head in despair.

Although the glass had not been full, when she finished it off all the Japanese customers around her applauded, shouting, "Good job! Good job!"

Gyeong-ae's face was flushed, but a smile rippled over it. She sat slumped in her chair. She then helped herself to a cigarette as though it were a snack lying on the table.

"Ai-san, you shouldn't drink like that just because you're angry!" Byeong-hwa shouted in Japanese from his seat, but Gyeong-ae pretended she hadn't heard. Snubbed, Byeong-hwa returned to his drink.

"Please have a drink," he said to Sang-hun, who was gazing pensively at the flickering cigarette in his hand.

Byeong-hwa's outburst to Gyeong-ae was nagging Sang-hun, who was convinced that Byeong-hwa knew everything. But why was Gyeong-ae drinking so much? *She must be angry with me*, Sang-hun thought. *Or did she really just do it for ten won?* Everything before Sang-hun's eyes began to flicker into darkness.

Perhaps she didn't regard Sang-hun as a stranger, a mere face in a crowd who might pass her in the street. What was suspicious, though, was that she seemed to be quite friendly with Byeong-hwa. Sang-hun figured that Gyeong-ae was not responding to Byeong-hwa's overtures merely because he was there.

"How dare you hold me so cheap! Do you think I actually drank something I didn't want to just for the sake of ten won?" Gyeong-ae's shriek rang through the room. A ten-won note, crisp enough to cut a finger, fluttered down from Gyeong-ae's hand.

"Well, how about a hundred won then?" A young man sitting next to her laughed.

"Hah! What's a hundred won but ten times ten won?" Gyeong-ae laughed and glared at the man with contempt. "Do you think I'm some Chinaman playing tricks on the side of the road? A hundred won might be a hell of a lot of money, but put it back in your wallet. Buy your wife some underwear! Just because you have ten won left over from your meager bonus doesn't mean you should squander it like this. Your wife will give you hell!" With a hearty laugh, she sprang to her feet.

"Isn't she something?" Everyone around her clapped their hands and made an uproar. The snubbed young man who had put out the money sat with an awkward smile on his face. Then it suddenly dawned on him, in his drunken state, that he had been insulted, and his face turned bright red.

He blurted out, "You've got some nerve treating me with such contempt. I gave you the money because I promised it. I'm a gentleman! Do I deserve to hear such insults from the likes of you?" Nevertheless, it seemed to be so much hot air, since he had lost face in front of the other customers, who knew he had offered Gyeong-ae the money in order to win her favor.

"What a temper, eh?" Gyeong-ae said, stopping short as she wove her way out of the crowd. "Are you so flustered because I'm refusing money? You must be the kind of person who bows to a thief. In today's world, it's not easy to come across a person like you!" She laughed boisterously.

Others in the group clapped their hands and roared. "Hear, hear!" they shouted.

"Now, I don't know how much money you have, behaving the way you do, but why don't you take out all your money and treat us to something delicious?" Gyeong-ae teased.

"That's it. That's more like it. Our Ai-san is unique! Let's hear it for Ai-san!" they shouted. The young foreign men were quite taken by the witty quips of the beauty they worshipped. The young man who had just seemed offended let out a laugh, too.

"Now that it's come to this, we have no choice but to take our queen along with us! Hey, cough up that hundred won of yours. Ai-san, let's go," one young-man pressed her. Gyeong-ae didn't move, still grinning.

"Of course we should take her along—if for no other reason than to pay respects to Ai-san's great spirit. You guys spend the money, and I'll take the credit," another young man said, linking his arm with Gyeong-ae's.

"Well then let's go," Gyeong-ae shook free of the young man and rushed into the back room. As she slid by Byeong-hwa's table, she tossed him a greeting. "Sorry about this. Enjoy your drinks."

Sang-hun was utterly demoralized. He didn't feel like drinking any more.

Gyeong-ae quickly reappeared after having changed into a Western suit. The men couldn't wrest their eyes from her; she had on a warm overcoat and a black hat perched on her head at an alluring angle, her face flushed from drink.

"Okay, let's go." Gyeong-ae hurried the men.

"Come back soon," the proprietor said. "And don't drink too much. What's gotten into you recently, going out all the time like this?" Since the proprietor didn't try to deter Gyeong-ae from going out, Sang-hun assumed that she was not a regular employee.

Sang-hun and Byeong-hwa had to watch Gyeong-ae walk out on the heels of the drinkers. The two men were like dogs that had just lost a chicken after a hot pursuit.

After the group left, the bar felt deserted, as though a corner of the room had been suddenly scooped out and emptied.

"Who were they?" Byeong-hwa asked the proprietor.

"They work at the bank around the corner. Certainly are an entertaining group of boys, aren't they?"

"She must be very friendly with them."

"No, not really. She's been acting up for some reason today. I bet she'll be back soon."

"Well, it doesn't really matter," Byeong-hwa said, but he was both hurt and disappointed that he had been ignored.

"Is it your policy to turn a blind eye when customers decide to take out an employee when they please? They can't do that in a café, can they?" Sang-hun sounded as if he were a policeman investigating an infraction.

The woman peered at the stranger and replied stonily, "What's the difference? She's not an employee of mine. She's a friend."

Sang-hun and Byeong-hwa didn't want to stay any longer. Both felt snubbed, having taken pains to come all this way only to be ignored. They stood up to leave.

"Why are you leaving so soon? It's not because our heartthrob has left, I hope?" The proprietor laughed mockingly, which they found far from amusing.

The two men went to the café next door for more drinks. To Byeong-hwa's shock and dismay, Sang-hun began fondling the hostess right in front of him and then made a fool of himself by peppering his dialogue with halting Japanese. Stronger than his feeling of disgust, though, was Byeong-hwa's desire to tease the man, for he knew that Sang-hun would no doubt go to church the following day and say his prayers. But Sang-hun was his friend's father, so Byeong-hwa bit his tongue. He kept a smile on his face.

It wasn't until after eleven that they managed to tear themselves away from the café. Once in the street, Sang-hun, who seemed to have completely forgotten everything about Gyeong-ae, suggested that they return to Bacchus.

"Let's go back in again. Don't you feel offended that the bitch treated you so rudely?" Sang-hun's voice was somewhat slurred, but his steps were steady.

"Sure, let's go. But don't take it so seriously. You won't be able to fall asleep if you go home without getting the chance to hold her hand, will you?" Byeong-hwa teased Sang-hun as he led him into Bacchus.

"That bitch! There are other women in the world, you know. By the way, she's Korean, right?"

"She sure is. She knows your son pretty well, but you don't seem to have a chance with her." Byeong-hwa joked with Sang-hun to test the waters.

"Huh? What?" Sang-hun snorted.

"Aren't you disappointed?" Byeong-hwa jeered.

"Why would I be disappointed? I'd be happy to marry her off to you." The smart remarks rolled out of Sang-hun until he noticed that Gyeong-ae was not there.

The proprietor brought out some alcohol and then locked the door, since midnight was approaching.

"Why would a woman like her even look at a penniless man like me?" asked Byeong-hwa.

"Weren't you paying attention? She seems to be one of those who don't care about money, so I wouldn't worry about that. You heard her going on."

"Do you think she really meant it? Well, in that case, I hope you'll pull a few strings for me." Byeong-hwa brayed with laughter.

When the sun sets over the desert sands and night falls . . . oh, my love . . . A popular song was being sung at late-night volumes outside, when a tuneless shriek broke through the other voices. The proprietor, who was serving drinks beside Byeong-hwa and Sang-hun, recognized the bellowers. She frowned and went to the door to open it. "Are those boozers back again? What do they think they're doing out there in the middle of the street?"

The drunkards outside abruptly stopped singing and began knocking on her door, making quite a fuss. She opened the door but blocked it, saying, "We're closed now. Come back tomorrow."

Gyeong-ae slipped into the bar, humming something called "Arabian Song," but when she saw Byoeng-hwa and Sang-hun, both drunk, sitting plaintively in a flood of light, tears welled in her eyes. Hoping to hide her tears, as far gone as she was, her song grew louder and she began to dance between the tables. After making a circle around the room, she darted over to Byeong-hwa, grabbed the unsuspecting young man by the arm, and pulled him out of his seat. Before he knew it, his disheveled mess of hair was pressed up against Gyeong-ae's chest. Dragging his oversized body across the floor, she whirled around the tables.

"Snap out of it, will you? Are you made of tofu?" Stifling her tears, Gyeong-ae knocked his head with her small gloved fist, laughed, and then kept swirling around the room singing the same tune with different lyrics.

"Gazing at the waning moon above you. Will you stay up until dawn, afraid it will never come again, once the sun pushes it away? Go on and gaze until your eyes sting because it will be gone when the sun rises." Like a shaman chanting, Gyeong-ae made up the words as she went along. Glancing over at Sang-hun, she told him, "What a pathetic sight you make, sitting there with your chin in your hands." Then she pushed Byeong-hwa away and stopped, but when the drunken man seemed about to stumble, she scrambled over to hold him up.

"My poor little baby. Tell me, who did this to my big boy?" She patted him on the shoulder, as a mother would her child, then she smothered him with noisy kisses.

Sang-hun watched her every move but then averted his eyes.

Just then, the drunkards, who had been making a nuisance of themselves outside, barged into the bar past the proprietor, who had been pressing against the closed door. One of them was the young man who had offered Gyeong-ae the ten-won note.

The two Japanese men came into the center of the room, but when they spotted Gyeong-ae and Byeong-hwa embracing, they erupted. "You guys are putting on quite a show," one of them said. "No wonder you wanted to send us on our way."

"You've got yourselves a side business here!" said the other. "This is clearly a violation of business regulations. Let's just see who wins this one."

Gyeong-ae ignored them. She grabbed Byeong-hwa, who was dangling off her, and pretended to dance with him, first pushing him into a narrow corner and then yanking him out again as she stepped backward. Then she whipped around and asked, "Why the hell are you guys making so much noise? Following me around like leeches, trying to suck something out of me. Go on home to bed!"

"What? And you're going to hang on to him?"

"What's it to you? Do you think I'm your wife? Go on home . . . Who knows whose arms your wife is in while you're here. Are you practicing with me what to say to her? Shall we demonstrate some more tricks?"

Gyeong-ae bungled her performance and actually kissed Byeong-hwa. His reaction was conflicted, but he uttered no complaint.

"Are you making fun of us? You filthy pieces of shit! We're going to report you to the police!" The inebriated young men were outraged to witness such a scene at their local haunt. Their eyes burned with rage. After spending several hours together and plenty of money, they hadn't been permitted even to touch this self-styled "queen" on the hand, and yet here she was kissing a Korean stranger before their eyes—this was incomprehensible.

Humiliation

———

Though the proprietor was furious over the young men's remarks, she was willing to chalk up their offensive behavior to liquor, break up the fight, and shoo them out. But Byeong-hwa wasn't able to shrug it off. Eyes bulging with anger, he shouted, "Filthy pieces of shit? Report us to the police? What filth have you seen here? Bastards! Are you police rats?"

Byeong-hwa had pulled himself away from Gyeong-ae and was ready to lunge at them, and his opponents, undoubtedly, were spurred. Gyeong-ae threw herself between them, and held Byeong-hwa back, while the proprietor did her best to block the two young men. Sang-hun just looked on, suddenly feeling sober.

The women, however, weren't strong enough to stave off the three drunkards. When, like a signal on the battlefield, an ashtray flew past Byeong-hwa's cheek and shattered against the opposite wall, the three men sprang forward, and soon one of them was thrown to the floor. Sang-hun stood up, and when the man on the floor got to his feet and charged toward him, both were thrown to the floor. Seeing this, Byeong-hwa came to Sang-hun's side and kicked his opponent several times. He grabbed the second man by the collar and tossed him across a wobbly table and chair — his legs dangling in the air when they collapsed. The man dropped with them, unconscious.

"Well done! Well done!" shouted Gyeong-ae as if she were in a wrestling arena or at a bullfight. The proprietor, meanwhile, was safeguarding the stove, still aflame, afraid that the fighters might crash on top of it.

———

Sang-hun's coat was covered with dirt and blood ran down his right thumb, though it was not clear whether it had been bitten or crushed. He sat down, out of breath, cradling his bleeding finger, but Gyeong-ae ignored him.

Outside, passersby gathered around in the front of the bar murmuring among themselves, though no one dared to open the door.

The two young men stood up and, unable to attack their opponents again, shouted more abuse. When they seemed ready for a second round, the trembling proprietor came over to brush the dirt from their clothes, begging them to leave. Gyeong-ae, the source of all this trouble, stood by with a weak smile.

"What is the problem with you people? After young men go out drinking, they're supposed to be on their best behavior. I must say, though, you do put up a good fight. Sit down and catch your breath." Gyeong-ae pulled some Haetae cigarettes from the pocket of her overcoat and walked around the room, offering each man a smoke. The two Japanese men waved them away. She didn't offer one to Sang-hun. Byeong-hwa, however, took one and used her lighter. Gyeong-ae lit one, too.

"Now, what is this? Fighting indoors on a beautiful night like this with so much snow on the ground? The thing to do would be to go over to the fields at the Drill Camp or, even better, to Keijo Gymnasium or to the pine groves at Jangchungdan, where you could fight a real duel." Gyeong-ae continued to provoke them.

"I'm all for it. Someone's got to teach you a lesson." One of the men leapt toward Byeong-hwa and held him.

"Let's go! But where to?"

"We won't rush to the police like a bunch of cowards. Let's go and settle scores at the Grand Gate."

"Sounds good," Byeong-hwa said, pulling off his torn coat.

Just then, there was a knock at the door. It was a policeman, shouting for them to open up. The proprietor ran to the door, as if he were her savior. The policeman came inside barking, "What's all this about?" He scanned the room before his angry eyes settled on Byeong-hwa. The other two young men were relieved to see the Japanese officer, and, all of a sudden, they felt drunk again. In the policeman's eyes, they all were drunkards, so after hearing them out, he ordered all of them to follow him to the police station, including Gyeong-ae and the proprietor. The proprietor pleaded with him, saying that she couldn't leave her shop unattended, so only Gyeong-ae went. Assuring the officer she wouldn't press charges for the cost of the broken chair and other items, she begged him to send them all home without further incident.

Sang-hun had no choice but to go with them, though he was afraid he might meet someone he knew.

The crowd broke up but then tagged along behind them in twos and threes. Rather than attempt to control them, the policeman ignored them. The shops on both sides of the street were closed, but bright streetlights reflected off the snow onto their faces. Sang-hun doubted he would run into members of the congregation at this hour, but a chill ran down his spine whenever anyone's shadow appeared in the distance. He pulled up his coat collar and put on his thick-rimmed glasses.

Upon arriving at the station, the policeman who had brought them in became even more overbearing. He listened to what the two Japanese men had to say, but he addressed Byeong-hwa and Sang-hun in a menacing tone and refused to hear them out.

Another policeman noticed Gyeong-ae. "Isn't she the girl at Bacchus?" He smiled at her and said snidely, "You'd better be more careful when you fool around with men."

Gyeong-ae was furious. She didn't expect to be treated well in a place like this, but never before had she been shown such disrespect. It pained her to think how she had become the laughingstock of these policemen largely because she was Korean and worked at a bar. She knew, however, that this was no place for her to talk back.

The policeman who brought them in explained the situation to his colleague. The Japanese words *"koitsu to kissu wo! koitsu to kissu wo!"* came up several times. He was saying that the woman had kissed that bastard.

The young policeman continued to provoke Gyeong-ae, peering at the shabbily dressed Byeong-hwa. "Well, if you're going to go that far, wouldn't it be better to find a man with some money to kiss or to do whatever you do with him?"

"What business is that of yours! We need the police to catch thieves, but now I see that you've got plenty to keep your hands full! A kiss isn't a crime, you know!" Gyeong-ae couldn't help getting in one good line.

"Shut up, you arrogant bitch! Just where do you think you are?" roared the policeman who had arrested them.

"She's still drunk. We'd better take her down to headquarters and keep her there overnight," said the infuriated officer. Nevertheless, he kept his hands off Gyeong-ae, perhaps forgiving the beautiful woman for her drunken babble.

After learning how the fight had started, the policeman wrote down the names and addresses of the Japanese men and sent them on their way. They paid no attention to the three Koreans until they called headquarters and were told to release them as well. One of the policemen said, "But they haven't been very cooperative . . ."

After hanging up the phone, the policeman ordered his tactless colleague to take them down to headquarters.

"Who are you saying isn't cooperating? I'm not going anywhere, unless you take those other guys with us." Byeong-hwa's eyes were ablaze. Since he was hassled by cops all the time, he was rarely passive in a situation like this.

"I'm going home," said Gyeong-ae, spinning around and heading for the door.

The policeman quickly grabbed her by the collar.

Gyeong-ae stumbled and almost fell to the floor. She managed to regain her balance but then found herself in the policeman's firm grip. Stifled giggles came from the crowd of spectators, who had gathered to witness the excitement.

The policeman who was to take them away quickly attached a sword to his belt, letting it clang against him, and took his hat from the wall. Gyeong-ae brayed in protest, and Byeong-hwa stamped his feet and railed, but they were both drowned out by the policeman's sharp voice. Meanwhile, Sang-hun stood pleading with another policeman, half in Korean, half in Japanese. Provoked by Gyeong-ae, the policemen were not inclined to change their minds. Still, they couldn't simply tie these three together with a rope to lead them away, and they didn't seem eager to venture out on a snow-covered road with three uncooperative people in tow. Byeong-hwa was slapped on the face a couple of times, but he continued to put up a struggle. From the outset, the police had talked about taking them down to head-quarters only as a threat. After a policeman kicked Byeong-hwa in the shins, and the young man fell in a heap on the floor, things finally quieted down.

Sang-hun took this opportunity to plead with them again. Only then did the policemen tell him to write down his name, address, and occupation. When Sang-hun wrote down "teacher" as his occupation, they demanded to know which school he taught at and gave him a long-winded sermon.

"Isn't that a missionary school? As a teacher and a Christian you should know better than to go out drinking with young people and making trouble for us. You should be ashamed of yourself!" They scolded him as they would a dog, but Sang-hun nodded his head in agreement.

Sang-hun felt he couldn't leave by himself, but he knew he would have no influence on the release of the others. The policeman took Byeong-hwa into a back room, perhaps a detention room or a toilet.

As for Gyeong-ae, they escorted her to their tatami-floored night-duty room. "You stay here. If we put you two together, you'd probably start kissing him again!" Actually, they treated Gyeong-ae quite well. While it was ridiculous for them to put her in the very room where they slept, she figured it was better than standing out in the cold in full view of the spectators.

Sang-hun reluctantly headed back to Bacchus. With nothing left to watch, the spectators scattered.

"Teacher!" someone called out to Sang-hun as he walked away. Turning his head, he saw a young man clad in a Western suit and a hat. He didn't recognize the man because the lower half of his face was wrapped in a scarf. Sang-hun instantly broke out in a cold sweat.

"Where are you headed?" the young man asked without tipping his hat, but even when he pulled off his scarf, Sang-hun didn't recognize him. The young man smiled mischievously. He told Sang-hun his name and that he had graduated with Deok-gi.

Sang-hun acknowledged the young man with a grunt. The young man's breath smelled of alcohol.

"We went to school with that girl at the police station. What happened?"

"Well, I was just trying to break up a fight between a few young people who'd had too much to drink . . ." mumbled Sang-hun, trying to make his escape. But the young man hurried after him wanting to continue the conversation.

"You don't know me very well, Teacher, but I've never forgotten what you did for me. Please don't dismiss my sincerity."

Such banter from the mouth of drunk sounded like mockery. Sang-hun suppressed his anger and managed to send him away, only to run into the proprietor of Bacchus who was on her way to the station. Sang-hun thought this was a happy turn of events, and the two went to the station together, where they pleaded for almost an hour before managing to get the two detainees released.

The policemen had never forgotten that the proprietor hadn't treated them to free drinks when she first opened up the bar. They also resented that, unlike other café girls, Gyeong-ae hadn't fawned over them when they once visited the bar for an inspection.

The following day Sang-hun didn't have the energy to get up. He ended up sleeping in the same room as the mahjong players, because they had waited up for him until he returned at three in the morning. They woke late, like professional gamblers, and asked him where he had been the night before, but he gave no reply. The more he thought about it, the more his face burned in embarrassment. Nothing could have been more humiliating. Never mind that Gyeong-ae had taunted him about being a pathetic sight and that he had been chastised at the police station. The memory of it all — how Gyeong-ae had kissed Byeong-hwa, how he had run into a former student — enraged and worried him. It was all Byeong-hwa's fault, but he couldn't just leave things as they stood. Today was Saturday, so he thought he might meet Gyeong-ae on his way home from church. But there still remained the matter of the young man he'd run into. He was probably not a churchgoer, judging from how he'd been out on the town getting drunk, but Sang-hun still panicked that rumors might spread among his acquaintances and reach the ears of the congregation.

New Trouble

———

The old man's cold had worsened from the night before. When Sang-hun arrived at his father's house after a servant delivered a message, he found the doctor sitting at his father's bedside. The doctor said that his father's condition could easily develop into pneumonia and advised them to pay close attention to him for the next few days. Then he promptly took his leave.

The way Sang-hun saw it, his father's cold had begun the same day he had had his fall. Sang-hun thought a Chinese brew might make him feel better, but knowing his father wouldn't listen to the idea if he were to mention it, he told Secretary Ji to suggest it. His father refused it all the same. Perhaps his father had suddenly become enlightened, for he insisted that Western medicine was not only as good as Chinese medicine for the treatment of a cold, but better for the lungs.

Secretary Ji sat with the old man all day in order to change the hot packs on his back and chest. The one on his chest was added that day to ward off pneumonia.

Except for his limbs and head, the old man lay shrouded in warm, wet cotton, which made him feel as though he were lying in a puddle of his own urine. He had never experienced this sensation before, but he liked how it felt on his bony body. If he had been able to get up and move around a bit, he would have certainly gone to the main room to lie down comfortably under the Suwon woman's care. But because of his bad back he had been told not to move a muscle, and truth be told, he wouldn't have been able to even if he had tried. The old man thought that it would be all right for him to take the Chinese medicine if only he were able to lie down in the main room. He refused to take it not because he really preferred the Western sort, but because the Western medicine had a cork that could be sealed with paper. The bottle could be placed beside his pillow, where he could pour out a dose of it himself or watch someone else pour it. In the unlikely event that anyone had tampered with the bottle, he could immediately dispel his doubts by asking the doctor to examine what was left in the bottle. The doctor would be obliged to take the job of administering seriously.

It would be impossible to supervise all the steps in the preparation of Chinese medicine, however, from the initial brewing to its final delivery to the outer quarters, and the old man would not have peace of mind, knowing that it had passed through several pairs of hands before reaching him. If he had the medicine brewed in the outer quarters in front of him, everyone would consider it most bizarre, and his secret paranoia of being poisoned would be exposed. Furthermore, Chinese medicine, unlike Western elixirs, is not taken in several small doses. A Chinese brew had to be swallowed all at once, and that was that. If the brewing pot was washed out and the dregs disposed of, there wouldn't be a trace of evidence left to suggest foul play. The old man's hypersensitivity made him increasingly suspicious as the days went by. He grew even more paranoid after the Suwon woman whispered to him those disparaging remarks about his daughter-in-law. It was perfectly understandable for someone already frightened of dying to become even more afraid after being told that his children wanted him dead. These groundless suspicions had found a perfect breeding ground in the mind of this bedridden man, who normally didn't sleep much during the long nights. To make matters worse, he had plenty of assets that he knew his children coveted. So when he thought about it, he felt he could trust only the Suwon woman, the woman with whom he shared a bedroom. The others, he figured — the whole selfish lot of them — went around with greed-filled eyes and were only interested in wringing as much money out of him as they possibly could.

On his way to church after dinner, Sang-hun paid his father another visit. The patient would suffer chills toward the late afternoon and grow feverish, but Sang-hun still felt he couldn't bring up the subject of using Chinese medicine. His father fretted like a child, demanding to be moved to the inner quarters, and Sang-hun agreed to have him moved the next day after it had warmed up outside. After calming the old man as best as he could, Sang-hun left for church to pray for his father's quick recovery.

Sang-hun had to answer numerous inquiries from fellow churchgoers concerning his father's health. When the congregation prayed, they made sure to include a petition for the speedy recovery of the old man.

Saturday worship ended before the clock struck nine. The mahjong players then gathered around Sang-hun, trying to read his mind, hoping that he would suggest that they go off to have some fun, but he made an escape and got on a streetcar by himself. Since he was heading for Jingogae, he didn't have to take the streetcar but took this detour in order to distance himself from the group.

As Sang-hun passed Bacchus, he didn't feel like going inside. The place was quiet; there seemed to be no customers inside. Passing the police station, the scene of his humiliation, he instinctively turned his face away. He remembered how the police had dragged off Gyeong-ae and felt a pang. But his compassion gave way to anger when he recalled how she had kissed Byeong-hwa like a madwoman and how she had sung that mocking song.

It's been only two years! How could she have changed so much since then?

Sang-hun remembered how his son had mentioned his "responsibility."

Why should I be the only one who's responsible for the affair? He tried to come up with whatever excuse he could before finally confronting himself. *I'm not trying to get out of anything, but what else can I actually do to fulfill this responsibility of mine?*

He couldn't think of anything. Had he been addressing his responsibility by going to see Gyeong-ae the day before and hoping to see her today? No, that was not what he had in mind. It had been old memories that had tempted him to visit her, and today's visit was simply an extension of yesterday's. But it was more than mere curiosity, it was a matter of jealousy and of the inability to bear the fact that Gyeong-ae had insulted him in front of his son's friend.

Sang-hun entered the K Hotel and asked that a rickshaw be called so that he could send a note to Gyeong-ae. He hadn't been to this hotel for almost three years now; the maids were new, but nothing else had changed.

"It's been so long since we've seen you here. Your wife is well, I hope?" The Japanese clerk greeted him and started chatting away idly. Sang-hun whiled away a bit of time with the man while he was waiting for a reply from Gyeong-ae but eventually headed to a room in the back, the only room on the premises with an *ondol* floor.

The room was cozy and welcoming, but it was the impressions, memories, and associations it recalled that he found so pleasant. Five years ago— the first time he had been here—it had also been a winter's day. The mat and cushions, decorated in pure Korean style, had become somewhat soiled since then, and a new gas stove had been added, which was turned up high.

Sang-hun frowned as he caught a whiff of the gas. He asked the attendant to remove the stove and leave behind a brazier.

As Sang-hun sat on a mat, which was cold to the touch, loneliness landed on him, but his heart fluttered at the same time as if spring had arrived. He looked around the room and remembered the first time he had been there with Gyeong-ae. The memory transported him like a beautiful dream.

Wondering if Gyeong-ae would ever show up, he began to feel nervous. Many a time he had waited for her here as nervously as he did now. Oddly, he felt as if he had waited for her just yesterday or the day before. Today he was less nervous about her not showing up than he was of losing face in the eyes of the proprietor and the servants were he to be stood up.

A maid came and served him tea. The rickshaw driver hadn't come back yet. Sang-hun fumbled through his coat pockets for a pack of cigarettes and by mistake took out a small book, a Bible. Caught off guard, he stashed it away again, afraid that someone might catch sight of him holding it.

He remembered that he had no cigarettes on him because it was a church day. As he was about to press the buzzer to order some, he heard footsteps approaching. Sang-hun's heart lept. He quickly took off his coat and hung it up.

The footsteps belonged to only one person. The maid opened the door and said, "She'll be arriving in a little while." He asked whether they had received word by phone, and she replied that a message had been sent back with the rickshaw driver.

This was a good sign. It was almost ten o'clock, and Sang-hun thought that if Gyeong-ae arrived late, they might end up staying overnight. The floor below the mat had gradually warmed up, but the room was still chilly, and he was restless. What he wanted was a drink, but he knew he would lose his air of authority if she found him drunk. Besides, if he had a few drinks, he would most likely crack some silly jokes, as he had the day before, and let her go without saying what was on his mind. He decided to resist the temptation.

His teacup had been replaced twice already, and it was now cold again. Yet there was still no news from Gyeong-ae. Sang-hun curled up on the mat to wait some more, but he couldn't stand the chill, so he ended up ordering some booze. When he started drinking, it was almost eleven. Not even a maid wanted to linger in this isolated room. Not wanting to sit there and drink alone, he called for the clerk, who came in eagerly from the cold to share a drink.

"I suppose it's not the wife you're waiting for, but whoever it is, she's taking her time, isn't she?" the clerk said. Whenever Sang-hun offered him a drink, he bowed three times before accepting it. By "the wife," he meant Gyeong-ae. Sang-hun had told him that he'd set up house with her in Bungmi Changjeong.

"It's just someone I need to meet with briefly," said Sang-hun, smiling. He knew that Gyeong-ae would arrive soon, but he wanted to avoid uncomfortable small talk.

The clerk laughed aloud. "Will your wife turn a blind eye if you keep seeing other women? Aren't you going a bit too far when you have such a good wife?"

The clerk thought he knew what kind of woman was coming, and he was glad to have such customers, knowing that he'd be generously tipped in the morning—especially when business was as slow as it had been recently. Besides, he knew that Sang-hun was a lavish spender and therefore treated him with particular cordiality.

"Don't go around giving me a bad name," Sang-hun said as he chuckled. "I never have any luck with women."

"You'd better watch out if you keep up with these affairs. By the way, whatever happened to that young woman we last saw you with? I was sure you'd visit us again after that." The clerk was talking about an incident that had taken place two or three years earlier. When his affair with Gyeong-ae ended, Sang-hun had roamed the town as if in heat and happened to meet a modern girl supplied to him by the madam of a salon he frequented on the sly. Overcome with lust, he had brought her to this hotel and kept her there for several days. Later on, he came back with her a few more times to spend the night. By now, he had totally forgotten about this affair.

"It's been almost two years," the clerk continued, "but you stopped coming altogether. Have you been behaving yourself in the meantime? Or did you find another place? I don't remember doing anything to offend you." The clerk laughed; Sang-hun just smiled.

"I'm not as bad as you make me out to be!" Sang-hun laughed. "I think I'd better send the messenger out again."

"We can arrange that. Where would you like him to go?"

"The place is just around the corner." Sang-hun hesitated, feeling embarrassed about bringing in Gyeong-ae. For the sake of appearances, he explained to the clerk, as briefly as possible, that Gyeong-ae managed a bar and had asked him to send someone over there.

"Ah, yes, yes. In that case, it would be my pleasure to escort her here, if no one else is available." He bowed several times before he left.

Less than ten minutes had passed when Sang-hun heard approaching footsteps. The clerk couldn't have returned with her so quickly, he thought; she must have arrived on her own. The door flung open and there stood Gyeong-ae.

Wearing a derisive smile on her face, she was in no hurry to enter the room. Sang-hun looked up, thinking she was probably drunk, although she didn't act it.

Gyeong-ae had mixed feelings. The room looked familiar, yet utterly disgusted by it, she couldn't bring herself to step inside and felt a strong urge to turn around and leave. She had guessed that Sang-hun would come to see her again, at least once more. When she received Sang-hun's message, she was curious to hear what he had to say and eager to let out her own resentment and settle the matter of the child, but now, faced with this tipsy middle-aged man — in this room — she had a hard time holding back the fury within her.

Who can I blame? I was young and won over by his skill in seducing women. This was how she usually came to terms with her life whenever she was unhappy or wished she led a happy married life like other women.

Gyeong-ae came in and sat down at a distance from him, not facing him.

"It's so cold in here. Why not sit over here, a little closer to me?" Sang-hun's face revealed how happy he was to see her. Unlike yesterday, he spoke in a gentle, solemn manner, as if the Sang-hun whom Gyeong-ae used to worship had reappeared.

Gyeong-ae stared at him. "Why do you want to see me?"

Sang-hun had asked her to come because he had something to say to her, but now he wasn't sure what that was.

"Come now, there's no need for you to act so defensively. What happened between us is all my fault," he began, but the maid who had led Gyeong-ae to the room reappeared.

"Will you be staying overnight?" the maid asked. "If so, we'll go ahead and get the bedding ready."

Sang-hun had made up his mind to stay, but he made a show of looking down at his watch before he said to Gyeong-ae, "It's so late. Let's just stay."

Gyeong-ae turned to the maid and said, "I'm leaving soon, so don't lock the gate."

Sang-hun winked at the maid as he said, "Go ahead and do whatever you have to do."

The maid seemed to understand what was going on and left the room.

"You called me because you were afraid that I wouldn't have anywhere to sleep tonight, is that it? You're here because you were worried that I'd have to sleep at the police station again, huh?" Gyeong-ae sneered.

"Oh, stop it! I'm not going to try to talk you into staying. I've asked you to come here because I haven't spoken with you in a long time. If you're too busy to talk, then leave. We can arrange to meet some other time," Sang-hun spoke as if he had nothing personal at stake.

Gyeong-ae was softened by the man's apparent indifference. That was a tactic Sang-hun often used to steal a woman's heart, and this was indeed how Gyeong-ae had first fallen into his arms. The very first time he had held her hand — as they were strolling the streets one night — he dropped it without warning and ran away, as if he were absolutely insane or had all of a sudden regretted making an impulsive mistake. With this, Gyeong-ae's heart had taken one step backward but then two steps forward. When Sang-hun further stirred her curiosity and vague expectations by paying no attention to her after giving her a simple note of apology two days later at school, Gyeong-ae felt somewhat miffed and wrote him a reply, which sparked the events leading up to this day. Five years earlier, she hadn't quite understood her emotions and longed for someone of the opposite sex as if in a dream. Someone who approaches but then backs away only intensifies one's interest. Gyeong-ae responded to this more profoundly than most.

"What is this sudden interest of yours in me, yesterday and again today? Has God told you it's now okay to see a woman like me? Have all the whores at Maedang House run away?"

Maedang House was a high-end hostess bar where Sang-hun and his cohorts had frequented on the sly for the past several years. It also happened to be something of a hangout for pimps and women of a certain ilk. It came as a great surprise to Sang-hun that Gyeong-ae knew of it.

"Where's this Maedang House you're talking about?" Sang-hun asked, laughing. Could she have cultivated links with such establishments? Once again, he was astonished by how far she had fallen. His heart sank with a vague sense of disappointment as though she had deceived him.

It took him a while before he spoke again. "So is the child getting along well?"

"Why do you ask all of a sudden?" Her face became flushed — she looked like a totally different person — and she glared at him as if she were ready to fight. "She'll take leave of this world soon enough for the sake of Mr. Jo Sang-hun's honor, don't you worry!" She bit her lower lip and tears welled up in her eyes.

Was it because of her love for the child? Was it the affection she still had for Sang-hun? Was it the pent-up resentment she had harbored toward this man, who had said unimaginable things to her in the past? Something surged up from deep inside her and set her teeth grinding.

"Is the kid sick or something?" asked Sang-hun with a blank expression.

"Why would you care whether she's sick and fighting for her last breath? What more is there to say after you pronounced that she wasn't born of the Jo family seed?" Gyeong-ae leapt to her feet.

"Why are you so worked up? Sit down."

"Why should I? Why should I sit down with you? Whoever her father is, I'm the one who gave birth to her, and her head will be resting on my lap when she dies."

Although she confronted him defiantly, she still worried that he might remain indifferent to her plight and wash his hands of the child. He hadn't shown any interest in the child for the past three years, and that he had suddenly come looking for her now probably had something to do with what Deok-gi had said to him. In any case, it had been impossible for her to make a living in these confusing times—she couldn't earn a decent income by lounging around Bacchus day and night. She needed to settle the matter here and now.

"It's not that I haven't given it any thought. I'll do my best to discuss the matter with you and figure something out, so don't worry." Sang-hun tugged at her coat, coaxing her to sit down.

Gyeong-ae grew suspicious over his unexpected willingness to cooperate. What motivated this feline grace? Was he planning to toy with her out of boredom, only to toss her away again? She wasn't in the least afraid of being abandoned, but she wouldn't let him get away so easily this time. She was going to make him suffer—a lot.

"What are you planning to do then?" she asked, sitting down.

He had no ready reply. He had sought Gyeong-ae on impulse and hadn't yet thought of anything concrete that he could do for the child.

"Tell me, what would you like me to do?"

"She has the flu, and there's no knowing what might happen to her. I can't live without her. She could die at any moment."

Sang-hun thought it would be better if the child died, but if she did, his link to Gyeong-ae would be cut forever. He didn't want that to happen.

He said, "I don't mean to say that you should give up on her, but don't you think it would be good for her, too, if you put all the misunderstanding and bitterness behind you and tried to move on? I don't care either way, but it can be solved right now if you just change your mind, Gyeong-ae."

"What are you talking about? You can't deceive me with such superficial words—my situation doesn't permit it," she retorted, although she did think she could hem and haw to get what she wanted from him.

"What do you mean?"

Gyeong-ae's reply was totally unexpected. Sang-hun wondered if she had a man in her life. The young woman couldn't have been on her own all this time. How had she supported her family? It was too late to delve into the question, but who was the man? It couldn't possibly be Byeong-hwa. But then, judging from what happened yesterday, he just might be the one. Though penniless, he was young and personable. From his experience he knew that neither Gyeong-ae nor her mother was particularly obsessed with money. There was no reason Gyeong-ae shouldn't be able to get along with Byeong-hwa merely because he had no money.

If this were true, it was impossible to think that she kept company with those who frequented Maedang House. She had probably become a Marxist girl, playing the queen among the ideologists. If so, all the more reason for Sang-hun to do something about the situation.

"How long have you known Kim Byeong-hwa?"

"Why do you want to know?" Gyeong-ae knew what he had in mind, and a contemptuous sneer rippled across her face. Her smile fanned his fiery suspicions.

"I know you were drunk yesterday, but how could you act the way you did, knowing that he's a friend of my son?"

"Am I expected to keep track of who is friends with whom? It's your fault for going around drinking with friends of your son's."

"He spotted me in the street and dragged me along with him. He was drunk already, so there was nothing I could do," he replied. Then he added in a stern voice, "But what an ugly act you put on! We were dragged to the police station because of that kiss of yours."

"What 'ugly act' are you talking about? Who drove me to behave like that?" Gyeong-ae's words stung.

"Don't go on like this—just tell me clearly. Please don't embarrass me."

"What do you mean, tell you clearly? What embarrassment? You talk about embarrassment all the time, but why did you commit such acts yourself?" Sang-hun winced. His suspicions deepened.

"To speak frankly, do you mean . . ."

"What?" Gyeong-ae glared at him and then snickered. Her expression seemed to say, *What are you dying to know?*

"Not to beat around the bush—you seem to be living with someone. Do you mean that I should do something for the child because she's in the way?"

"Why so many 'do you means'?" Gyeong-ae retorted, lighting a cigarette. A calm discussion was out of the question.

"You've ignored me for years. Why are you now dying to know every single detail of my life? What do you care about me or how I live or whom I marry? Just put the child in your civil registry and set aside a portion of income for me, enough to raise her and last my lifetime. I'm not asking you to take her home with you and raise her."

"Is putting her in my civil registry that important?"

"If she's not in it, I wouldn't be able to bury her. If she survives and goes to school like other children, what can I do without her name in a registry?" Gyeong-ae stood her ground, seeing that the man was eager to hold on to her.

"Well, that's not difficult, but are you really planning to marry?"

"I am."

"Who's the man?"

"Why do you want to know?"

"Well, I just thought how thrilled you must be . . ." The words spilled out of him, with an idiotic smile in their wake.

Sang-hun figured they'd better say good-bye for now, realizing that they would be talking at cross-purposes no matter how long they were at it. But he wanted to find out whether she'd marry for sure and whether she was living with someone already. If there was no chance of winning her back, there was no need to make the effort. Desire raised its head again, although that hadn't been the case while she'd been out of sight. He knew that it would be difficult to find another woman of Gyeong-ae's caliber, though he hadn't had a lot of experience with women. There was no reconciling with his wife, and he couldn't lead a celibate life waiting for her death. If he wanted a woman, Gyeong-ae would be best, all things considered, and the matter of the child would be solved smoothly as well. But if there were another man behind the scenes, Sang-hun could get hurt by making a hasty overture. He could even end up worse off, with nothing but the child on his hands.

But there couldn't be a man in the picture; she was working at a bar. A man had probably just come into her life or was about to make an appearance. Was it Byeong-hwa? Even if she didn't care about money, it would be impossible for her to go out with him, a penniless loser.

"I'll accept the child," Sang-hun said firmly, as if his mind were made up.

"What do you plan to do after you take her to your house?"

"Whatever I do, isn't it natural that I take her in because she's mine? If things go the way I think they will, it won't be good for her, and she'd be in the way of the newlyweds."

"You're so considerate, aren't you?" Gyeong-ae didn't trust a word he said, for it was hard to believe that he suddenly considered the child important. However, it would be troublesome if he asserted his rights out of spite and didn't make concessions.

"If I do this, it will be good for all concerned, right?" he asked in an attempt to draw out her response.

"No. Where's the law that says that the child belongs only to the father and that the mother has no rights?"

"Of course children belong to their father! The law recognizes it, and ethics and custom dictate it. There's nothing to discuss."

"I don't care what the law and ethics say. I can't give up my child. Is your plan to take her and then ignore her?"

"You thought I'd offer you money if you gave up the child. You're playing a game, right?" Sang-hun was provoking her deliberately, though he bore no grudge against her.

"What nonsense is this? How much of your money did I spend? How dare you throw such insults at me? I would never make a living by sacrificing my child. Your money stinks! You've said all along that she's not yours. Why on earth would you try to claim her now?"

"Since you haven't gotten any money yet, you're clinging to the child in order to put your hands on some, right? You said you'd marry soon. What other reason is there to hold on to someone else's child with a new husband in the wings?"

"Stop it! Are you human at all? If I wanted money, do you think I have no other way to get it? I could sue you for violating my virginity. I could claim a settlement if I wanted to. I could seek patrimony. Do you think I care in the least if you tell me to give her up? Go ahead! Do as you please! I've put up with you long enough. I'm not going to sit back with my arms folded. I'll do everything in my power to stop you!"

The conversation escalated into a senseless quarrel. Gyeong-ae atremble, adjusted her hat to leave.

Sang-hun tried to calm her. "Do you think I batted an eye when you acted the way you did? I don't know who's behind all this, but stop talking nonsense. Let's discuss the matter and find a reasonable solution."

When she saw that he was backing down, Gyeong-ae sprang to her feet.

"I don't care. I thought you might have repented a little over what you had done to us and had come to your senses. They say you can never make a silk purse out of a sow's ear," she spat out before she left the room.

Sang-hun regretted having gone too far but made no attempt to keep her there. If he had held on to her, she would have found more fault with him. With her talk about the sow's ear, he was forced to make an outward show of outrage to save face, if nothing else.

Innocence or Ulterior Motive

———

The morning after the incident at the police station, Byeong-hwa discovered a letter from Deok-gi on his desk. When he learned that Deok-gi had come by the previous evening and written it in his room, Byeong-hwa realized that they must have just missed each other. He was happy to find a ten-won note inside the envelope but still felt a twinge of regret. Had he known that his friend would go out of his way to leave money for him right before his departure, he would have made a point of seeing him off at the station rather than idling at Hwagae-dong, gorging on Chinese food. Byeong-hwa hadn't made a special effort, though, because if he had shown up at the station under last night's heavy snowfall, Deok-gi would have thought that his friend had made the trip only to collect the money he had asked for.

Deok-gi wrote: *I dropped by to show you once and for all what a loyal friend I am, but the trip wasn't entirely futile because at least I got to see Miss Pil-sun. It's hard to write this letter with a smile on my face. I can never express myself lightly. When I'm gone, you'll miss having cigarettes, so I'm leaving you my lunch money . . . I said this casually the other day, but if Miss Pil-sun really would like to study, just let me know. Surely, I can find a way . . .*

At first, Byeong-hwa had no idea what his friend meant by the phrase that he could never express himself lightly. After rereading the note, though, he grasped its meaning by linking the part about Deok-gi's being glad to see Pil-sun with his reiterating the offer to help her with her studies.

Staring at the letter, Byeong-hwa didn't know whether to laugh or cry.

The spoiled child of a rich family, who had never known anything resembling Byeong-hwa's plight, Deok-gi might have developed a deep sense of sympathy, but would he have been this enthusiastic if Pil-sun hadn't been in the picture? Deok-gi's motives couldn't be entirely innocent; he'd met Pil-sun only once. It was hard to believe that he offered to help simply because he felt she deserved a better life or because he took pity on her circumstances. Could he be so innocent? One could say that Deok-gi was being honest and sympathetic, expressing his feelings boldly and frankly, but what was behind Deok-gi's fascination with Pil-sun? Was there some ulterior motive? He was, after all, a married man with a child.

It was possible that Deok-gi simply felt sorry for her, that his interest was prompted by nothing more than the sentimentality typical of a coddled child of a wealthy family. But Byeong-hwa felt he couldn't just sit by passively. He feared that something unfortunate might occur between Deok-gi and Pil-sun.

Suppose the two fell madly in love, and Pil-sun could enjoy a luxurious life and her parents wouldn't have to be hungry any more. What would this really mean? For Pil-sun's family, it would amount to bartering their daughter, compromising their principles, and selling out their comrades. For Deok-gi's wife and child, life would be hell. In short, nothing good would come of it. Byeong-hwa entertained such thoughts as if they were real, and soon his blood was boiling.

Still, the ten won left by Deok-gi was most welcome. More than anyone else, Pil-sun's mother was overjoyed and couldn't stop praising Deok-gi. *Never mind that he looks gentle and elegant. No one else in the world would have braved such heavy snow, even for a good friend, and come all this way right before his departure just to give money.* One would think the money were meant for her.

Byeong-hwa didn't mind that his friend was being praised, and he knew that their friendship went beyond Pil-sun. Nevertheless, he was rather put off, thinking that it was partly Deok-gi's vanity, his desire to show off to

Pil-sun, that motivated him. Byeong-hwa therefore didn't care to listen to the woman's boundless praise.

He also didn't feel like writing a thank-you postcard to Deok-gi; contrariness was the backbone of his character. He was grateful all right, but to write back promptly, as if swept by emotion, might come across as groveling. And as it was customary for someone who'd gone away to write that he had arrived safely, Byeong-hwa thought he'd write a reply then and take the opportunity to talk about his night out with Deok-gi's father.

As Byeong-hwa expected, a short postcard arrived several days later offering the standard greetings. Deok-gi explained that he couldn't write at length because he was busy preparing for his graduation exams. At the end, though, he asked Byeong-hwa to give his regards to Pil-sun and her parents.

Byeong-hwa smiled to himself—give his regards indeed! Deok-gi hadn't even properly met the landlord and his wife. It was natural for him to think of Pil-sun's parents when he was favorably inclined toward her, but Byeong-hwa didn't think the comment was made simply out of politeness. Still, it could be an expression of his genuine goodwill and sympathy for the family's extreme poverty. Viewing Deok-gi's comment in this light, Byeong-hwa immediately felt as if a burden of suspicion had been lifted.

Who can comprehend the heart? Sometimes you will feel unaccountable hostility toward a stranger on a streetcar, sometimes your heart will be softened by a familiar-looking soul that passes you in the street. Deok-gi's feelings toward Pil-sun's family were probably of the latter sort. They were practically strangers to him, and it wasn't by grace of Pil-sun's looks that their situation merited more sympathy than anyone else's. The recipient in these cases may or may not deign to accept such sympathy, but generating such goodwill in the first place is what people describe as being lucky with people in general. No one disliked Pil-sun's family, and in fact, it seemed to attract goodwill. They were good-hearted, decent folk.

Byeong-hwa's thoughts ambled along these lines as he reclined on the floor. Then he snapped up and went to the desk, which, like his hair, was coated with a thin gray layer of dust. He had the urge to write about how he had spent the evening with Deok-gi's father.

Hey, I couldn't make it to the train station to say good-bye because the Bacchus queen's shower of kisses (well, they might have been closer to a torrent) and the hot, wet blur of those kisses interfered with my intention to see you off. I'm not boasting or making excuses but just honestly confessing—reporting—that I was at the zenith of happiness that night, which I'd never before experienced. I've had butterflies in my stomach since—not that an earthquake has shaken up my convictions or my view of life, but a blush rises to my cheeks when I imagine going to that bar again. I think of getting a haircut, dusting off my clothes, and putting on face cream, if possible. Hey, are you laughing? Don't. It's true. You left cigarette money with that remarkable letter of yours the other day, but you may have to give me money for face cream, too. At least I got rid of that sorry overcoat. I'll explain the details later, but there's a saying that everyone has a place in which to be buried in one of the green mountains, so people can choose to live one way or another in this world. What I mean is that, fortunately, my coat was torn to shreds on a certain occasion. So your father—in the spirit of charity—gave me his spare overcoat. To my astonishment, I look like a neat gentleman in this royal hand-me-down, even in my eyes, the eyes of a nobody. I yearn for an audience with the Bacchus queen, sporting this overcoat, but I might embarrass myself because the coat is clearly secondhand, and besides, I also need cash for drinks. I'm entertaining the idea of going there after pawning the coat, but to do so, the weather must warm up. A rumpled jacket and pants won't do, like a bird with missing tail feathers. Even now, looking at the coat hanging on the wall, my mouth waters . . .

But do I really love this woman? If so, would I express it so hastily and flippantly, even to you? I'm not sure, but I believe you've never experienced real love in your life. I failed to keep my virginity, but I've never had the experience of loving a woman. People say that wasting one's youth and growing old without loving someone is a misfortune, but I don't agree. It has something to do with my cerebral, calculating character and with my environment since I graduated from secondary school, which has made me the way I am.

To this day, Pil-sun is the only woman I've known other than the ones I've paid to cool my lust, but she is more like a sister to me. I can't think of her as anything more than that. She has been the center of my life. Thanks to her, I have been spared the pain of starvation and inadequate clothing—well, at least much of the pain. Thanks to her, I have been able to keep my heart pure. But I've never thought of her as a love object or as my future spouse, even in my fantasies. She's too pure, too innocent, and has too many endearing qualities for me to entertain such thoughts. Does my emotion contradict this? I don't think so. Like all other girls, she may have absorbed all sorts of instinctive desires and fantasies from this society, but I pray that she never has a chance to fulfill them. When she chooses a husband in the future, a good-for-nothing like me won't do, but she should reject a young man like you, too. It is unfortunate that she works at a rubber factory, but it's better than becoming a daughter-in-law of a well-to-do family like yours. Working in factories, women have to fend for themselves, but in a middle-class family they become mere mannequins. If you were an impoverished student, I'd say you would be about thirty percent qualified to love Pil-sun.

I'm rambling, but what I want to know is the real intention behind your enthusiasm for offering Pil-sun an education. It may sound like I'm picking a fight with you, but where does this enthusiasm come from? Schooling is fine, but what about afterward? I suspect there is a touch of the petit-bourgeois in you. Without her monthly income of fifteen or sixteen won, her family would starve for days on end. There is no need to talk about a worthless person like me, who has installed himself amid such a family, but if you want to give her an education, you'd better be ready to cover her parents' living expenses as well. Does your financial situation and sincerity go that far? You may well feel sym-

pathy for her, but what would come of it — even if she received a thorough, modern education? Please forgive my bluntness.

Having written this much, I see that this is useless prattle. Let me talk more about our queen. Help me judge whether I'm qualified to love Hong Gyeong-ae. I am aware that I'm no more worthy of her than you are of Pil-sun, but to my eyes, Gyeong-ae doesn't look like an ordinary woman. Do you know her? Your father seems to, which strikes me as odd. I can't help but think that she showered special attention on me, a guy in whom she has no interest, just because she wanted to taunt my companion. And how does that make me look? When I think about it, her kisses did taste strange. Were they a special favor for me, or did she have some other purpose? Don't laugh over there, far away, as you imagine me delirious after having made a fool of myself . . .

Byeong-hwa couldn't bring himself to write about how he had been hauled off to the police station with Deok-gi's father. It would be unkind, and as a son, Deok-gi might not appreciate hearing about it, so he decided against it, though he had much to say about their adventures that night.

The day before, Byeong-hwa visited Deok-gi's father to see whether he was all right after all that had happened. It was then that Sang-hun gave him the coat, for which he was thankful, but he was irritated by Mr. Jo's probing questions.

"How could she possibly act that way toward someone she'd seen only a few times?" the older man kept saying, in a manner most undignified for his age.

After attempting to clarify the matter, Byeong-hwa tried to make light of it. Laughing, he said, "Oh, I'll step back if you like her so much."

Sang-hun was thrown. Growing more impatient, he said, "How can you be so flippant? Tell me the truth — I've guessed as much anyway."

"I *am* telling the truth, but I've guessed as much about you, too." A bluff.

"Do you mean that you know who her father is?"

"I have a pretty good idea."

"So you know Mr. Hong ____?"

Gyeong-ae is his daughter? Byeong-hwa swallowed his shock and said, "That's why I feel so bad for her."

Byeong-hwa knew the name very well because he'd heard about him after the 1919 Independence Movement.

Sang-hun said, "I met her when she was small but had no idea what had become of her since. I was surprised to find her there, but if you meet her again, give her some advice."

"Such as?"

"Tell her to quit working there and either find a proper job or get married."

"Well, other than becoming a rich man's concubine, she wouldn't be satisfied with anything mundane, and it's not easy to find a decent job in times like these. Why don't you help her out?" asked Byeong-hwa coyly.

"You're right—I can't ignore her, considering that her father was an acquaintance of mine, but I'm afraid my actions might be misconstrued," Sang-hun said with a laugh.

Although Sang-hun tried to learn what Gyeong-ae meant to Byeong-hwa, he ended up revealing his own feelings. He hoped his hint would prevent Byeong-hwa from pinning his hopes on her. But he didn't want to reveal everything from beginning to end. This young man, who couldn't afford even a haircut and who had to scrounge up money for cigarettes, could never keep company with such a high-collar modern girl, and Gyeong-ae herself would never take Byeong-hwa seriously.

Still, Sang-hun found it rather suspicious that Deok-gi had suddenly talked about the issue of the child. He imagined that Deok-gi couldn't bear to look on after learning of Byeong-hwa's relationship with Gyeong-ae. It was possible that he wanted his father to settle the matter and take the child into his care.

If Sang-hun did so, the future might prove extremely messy. It would be premature to inform Byeong-hwa of his personal history. He had all the more reason to wait and see how things worked out.

Still suspicious, Sang-hun reiterated his advice as Byeong-hwa took his leave. "I guess she knows what she's doing because she's no ordinary girl, but you should be careful. Don't do anything rash."

"There's no need for you to worry. I don't have a problem, but you do," Byeong-hwa said as he left, snorting to himself. He'd find out the truth from Gyeong-ae one of these days.

Sang-hun vowed to see Gyeong-ae as soon as possible to get her to promise that she would not reveal anything about their past to Byeong-hwa.

In his letter to Deok-gi, Byeong-hwa didn't say a word about how he had verbally sparred with Sang-hun the day before. No, he would wait to hear from Deok-gi—he'd reply one way or another, especially since Byeong-hwa had hinted at his suspicions about Sang-hun and Gyeong-ae.

Byeong-hwa finished writing but didn't have any postage. It had been a few days since he'd been given the ten won, and naturally not a coin was left in his pockets. The landlord's family might still have a coin or two, but Byeong-hwa couldn't bring himself to ask for one when they were scrimping as it was. Perhaps he could drop it in the mailbox without a stamp or get some money from a friend. He lay down, pulling the quilt over his head to keep himself warm.

Even on days when Byeong-hwa could have two meals, he had nothing else to do. The place where his comrades gathered was bleak, and the stove remained cold, so he wasn't in the mood to go there only to gaze at the dust. Since the beginning of winter, they had been getting together at an inn where a few of his friends stayed but had suspended their meetings after a comrade's arrest. For the time being, everyone was lying low, waiting to see how things developed. Byeong-hwa was bored by this forced hibernation, but he didn't want to be arrested before he did his share of work.

He had been taking a lot of naps recently, probably because his body and soul were comfortable with enough firewood to heat his room and enough food to fill his stomach. After one of these naps, he opened his eyes and found Pil-sun looking down at him. The electric lights, which came on after dusk, had already switched on. Her presence must have woken him.

"Why are you sleeping so much? It's dawn already," she teased him. "Why don't you get up and eat something?" Her sleeves were rolled up, her hands smudged. She must have been helping out in the kitchen after returning home from the factory.

"I'm sorry—I deserve your scolding. It's cold outside, isn't it? I'm sorry for sprawling out and snoring like this while others are working and trudging home in the cold." Byeong-hwa kicked away his quilt, sat up, and bowed.

"You must still be half asleep. Wake up."

"I'm wide awake, but . . ." Byeong-hwa was about to make a joke but stopped himself and smiled. "Why is the room so warm? Did you heat it? I'm so ashamed—why don't you eat my share of rice today? I wouldn't dare grumble about it." He stretched his arms out high and gave a big yawn. Byeong-hwa usually attended to the firewood for his own room, so he felt all the more ashamed that Pil-sun had taken care of it for him.

Like a mischievous child, Pil-sun pretended to press her fist into his yawning mouth. She giggled and said, "Look at this mouth! Look how it's unwilling to eat! It's all your fault, Mr. Lazybones, not your mouth's. What mistake did this mouth make to be denied food? Why don't you go over to the main room and eat?"

Pil-sun stopped short when she caught sight of the letter lying on the desk. "Are you going to mail a letter?"

"Yes, just leave it there."

"Did you write about how thankful we are?"

"Yes, I said everyone was thankful, but only Pil-sun . . ." He was going to joke that only Pil-sun failed to say thank you.

"Only Pil-sun what? What did you write?" Holding the letter, she shouted to Byeong-hwa, who had moved to the edge of the veranda. She wanted to know the rest and was somehow glad to see the four characters written on the envelope: Brother Jo Deok-gi.

"It's nothing important. I just wrote, 'Only Pil-sun badmouthed you.'"

"Why would I badmouth him? Why would I badmouth someone who has nothing to do with me?" She tried to sound flippant but sounded annoyed instead.

Byeong-hwa regretted his sillyness. "I was only joking." He entered his room again.

"Why haven't you mailed it?"

"I don't have a stamp. Just leave it there, won't you?" He snatched it away from her and put it in the pocket of his overcoat hanging on the wall.

"Shall I give you some money? I have three jeon."

"If you have three jeon, why don't you buy yourself some sweet potatoes?"

"Do you think I'm a child?"

"Grown-ups never eat sweet potatoes?" Byeong-hwa let out a giggle.

Byeong-hwa ate with the landlord. His wife had a meal tray taken to the room across from the main room, which she said was in disarray.

As they ate, Pil-sun's father talked about Deok-gi. He had overheard Byeong-hwa and his daughter from the main room.

"I don't say this because this food actually came from him, but he seems to be quite gentle and kind. I don't know about his politics, but there is no harm in taking advantage of his generosity. Whatever our own feelings, we have no choice but to accept money from those who have money to give."

Byeong-hwa made no reply and ate in silence.

Pil-sun's father looked almost fifty, much older than his actual age, with a bushy salt-and-pepper mustache. His gauntness gave an impression of rectitude, but in truth he was a middle-aged man, not very capable, though friendly enough. Taking Byeong-hwa's silence for disagreement, he elaborated.

"A while back, a wealthy man wanted to make a donation to a hospital for the poor in Japan. It was controversial. Some people didn't want to accept it while others did, and in the end the donor withdrew his offer. I thought it wouldn't have mattered if they'd taken the money. Regardless of whether or not the donor intended the gift as a means of appeasement, what is important is that you don't get wooed over to the other side, seduced by such gestures. Look at it this way: that means of appeasement is like jumping into a fire with hay strapped to your back. Nothing stops you from fighting your enemy while eating the provisions he supplies. Such scruples are signs of the petit bourgeois, nothing else."

"But when such a deed is known to the public," Byeong-hwa finally answered, "the childish consciousness of the general public will be swayed, and that's what the donor wants. It is therefore right, as a policy, not to accept it."

"True, but such scruples are unnecessary in the case of Korea, where there's no organizational base and where the use of illegitimate means is inevitable."

"But what's there to exploit in a young man like Deok-gi? His grandfather will die one of these days, and Deok-gi's father will inherit his assets. If we want to talk his family into giving, we'd better work on his father." Byeong-hwa said this as if he already had something in mind and added, "But will you make use of Deok-gi? Don't take this seriously, but after he met Pil-sun, he said that he'd like to pay for her education because it's a pity that she is wasting her time in a factory."

"Education?" Pil-sun's father raised his head but said nothing further.

"What do you think?"

"Well, I'd like to send her to school when we become a little better off, so that she can make a living. But how can we trust such a young man?"

"You sound different now than you did a moment ago, when you talked about taking advantage of them." Byeong-hwa smiled, but he wasn't unaware of his landlord's feelings.

The landlord was about to explain, but he stopped abruptly when he heard someone coming out of the main room, probably Pil-sun getting rice tea in the kitchen.

The landlord was not much of an activist nowadays, but seven or eight years ago he had been a member of the first group of dissidents who went to prison. Now, well over forty, he was, in a sense, over the hill. He was too impoverished to feed his family, and it was impossible for him to get a job given his background, so he idled away his time, living on what his daughter brought home. But he wasn't completely resigned. He didn't want his daughter to follow in his footsteps—he wanted her to have a decent life. After supporting her family for several years, as a son would, she would be married off to a good family. It would have been nice if he could have sent her to school like other girls, as she herself wanted, so that she could at least become an elementary school teacher, but she had to leave secondary school in her second year after her family's financial collapse. Being able to continue her studies would have brought Pil-sun great joy.

Overcoat

———

Byeong-hwa wolfed down the rest of his food and dashed out of the house, eager to see Gyeong-ae. Byeong-hwa didn't think he was in love with her, and it was impossible to think she loved him, but still, he was curious to know who she really was. He didn't lack passion, but as his situation wouldn't allow it, he didn't entertain any hopes.

Byeong-hwa set out for Sang-hun's house. He had been regretting leaving his torn coat there the day before. Walking against the chilly wind, Byeong-hwa passed the Six Boards buildings and climbed up the hill toward Samcheong-dong. When he arrived, Byeong-hwa was told that Sang-hun had gone out toward evening. Perhaps he had gone to meet Gyeong-ae. Once Byeong-hwa's thoughts headed in this direction, the more jealous he grew and the more he wanted to follow through on his plan to soften Sang-hun up for money. Letting the keeper of the outer quarters enter ahead of him, Byeong-hwa went inside, but his coat was not hanging there. As though he were a policeman with a police warrant, he ordered the keeper to open the wardrobe, but it was locked. Disappointed, Byeong-hwa stood motionless, and his mind went blank.

Only then did the keeper ask, "What overcoat are you looking for?"

"Well, I left it here yesterday, but . . ."

"The torn one?"

"Yes, that's the one." Byeong-hwa's face lit up.

"Oh, the master gave it to the manservant earlier today." He grinned.

"Manservant? The manservant?" Though chagrined, Byeong-hwa couldn't help laughing, but that wasn't going to get him his coat back. "That's my only overcoat. And, frayed as it is, it is a treasure in my family, handed down for three generations. I can't lose it. I came here to change into it . . ." Byeong-hwa made excuses.

"Why don't you keep what you're wearing now? I don't think my master will make you return it." The good-natured keeper continued to grin and offered his opinion as if he were solving a thorny problem for Byeong-hwa.

"No, that's not possible, though I'm embarrassed to say so." Byeong-hwa didn't think about saving face.

The keeper had been holding in a laugh, but now he guffawed. Moving to the edge of the veranda, he called out, "Hey! Won-sam!"

Instead of the manservant, his wife answered and after some time rattled open a door in the servants' quarters. "Are you looking for him?" she asked. "He went out to the avenue."

Thinking his efforts had been wasted, Byeong-hwa began to worry.

"Why don't you go and fetch him?"

The woman went out as directed. Could the manservant by any chance have left the overcoat hanging in his room to save for special occasions? Then, Byeong-hwa thought, it would be better if he took it now, rather than snatching it away from him in person.

"If he has left it in his room, I'll just take it." Quickly slipping his feet into his shoes and dragging them along, Byeong-hwa ran to the servants' quarters, though the keeper tried to stop him.

As Byeong-hwa emerged empty-handed, the manservant ambled in, clearing his throat. He looked warm, the collar of his overcoat pulled up, his head covered with a winter cap, and his hands buried deep in his pockets.

"Hey, take off that overcoat and give it to this gentleman," said the keeper.

"What?" The manservant was stunned.

"Don't ask me why. Just take it off and hand it over. The coat belongs to this gentleman." The keeper chuckled as if making fun of both of them.

The manservant was reluctant. "But my master gave it to me."

The keeper said, "But what are you doing with this coat anyway? Wearing it one day was more than enough for you." He burst out laughing.

The manservant still wasn't ready to hand it over. He looked himself up and down a few times and grunted in frustration. Finally, he tore it off and threw it at Byeong-hwa. "Take it!"

Byeong-hwa said, "I'm very sorry about doing this when it's so cold . . . I'll give it back to you in a few days when my situation improves."

"No, I don't want it," the manservant grumbled. As he walked out with shoulders hunched, he muttered, "I'll probably catch a cold now."

Byeong-hwa slipped into the old coat, then put the new one on over it before strutting out. The keeper followed him to lock the gate. "Looks like you're on your way to the pawn shop," and again he laughed heartily.

About an hour later, Byeong-hwa made it to Bacchus. The proprietor was not pleased to see him, but Gyeong-ae, seated in a chair next to the stove, beamed at him.

"What have you been up to?" A trace of scolding could be heard in her voice.

"What do you mean by that?" Byeong-hwa answered casually, though he was pleased with her more familiar manner of speaking.

"Well . . ." Gyeong-ae lowered her eyes. Byeong-hwa noticed she had been sitting dejectedly when he first walked in. He liked this Gyeong-ae much better than the one who talked and acted frivolously. Her demeanor today revealed more subtlety and depth.

"Why don't you have a seat?" Gyeong-ae said, coming out of her reverie. Byeong-hwa was warming himself by the fire next to her.

"Is something wrong?" Byeong-hwa asked, as he took out a cigarette and sat down.

Without answering, she touched the sleeve of Byeong-hwa's torn over-coat, its long tattered pieces barely holding together.

"Did it get this torn the other day? How can you wear this thing?"

Byeong-hwa was pleased, for she sounded like a concerned poverty-stricken wife worrying about her husband's clothes. *What would have happened if I had come in the overcoat Sang-hun gave me?* Even though she wouldn't have known that Sang-hun was the source of the new coat, she probably would have ridiculed Byeong-hwa, believing that he had worn it to put on airs. Even if she hadn't, she wouldn't have offered such solicitous words.

"Doesn't matter. Now I have a new overcoat thanks to it." Animated, Byeong-hwa began to tell his story, but Gyeong-ae had to serve a group that was sitting quietly in a corner. It was almost nine o'clock, but because of the cold weather, only one group of Korean customers occupied a table. They did not make a lot of noise or many demands on Gyeong-ae, though they kept a watchful eye on her, probably because they were new to this bar or perhaps because they were trying to behave in line with the Western suits they were wearing.

Gyeong-ae poured some alcohol for the customers, but soon returned to Byeong-hwa.

"So what did you do with it? Why didn't you wear it?" Gyeong-ae asked softly.

"I wore it for a day, but it didn't suit me, so I used it to get the money to come here today." Byeong-hwa laughed.

"Whose was it?"

"Whose was it? Think hard." Byeong-hwa smiled and studied Gyeong-ae's face triumphantly, anxiously awaiting her response.

"Did it belong to the man you came with?"

"Do you know who he is? It seemed that you knew each other, but why did you pretend that you'd never met him?"

"Well, I could say I know him, and at the same time I don't know him. Did he say anything to you?"

"Not much, but . . ."

Gyeong-ae didn't want to tell Byeong-hwa about her past with Sang-hun, but this didn't prevent her from admiring him for his frankness. Soberly looking back on the other night, she vaguely remembered kissing him and dancing with him, perhaps for the wrong reason yet without regret.

Byeong-hwa appeared personable enough at first glance, and she felt sympathy for him after Deok-gi told her that he was roaming around town after a clash with his father over a religious question.

As for Byeong-hwa, the main reason he felt so at ease with her was that she had kissed him. Although he suspected that she'd done it in the spirit of casual flirting or for some other purpose, he felt it rather odd that they had grown familiar enough to speak their minds.

"Aren't you having anything? After all, you did take the trouble to pawn the coat to come here," Gyeong-ae commented to break the lull in their conversation.

"Of course I will. It's my treat today."

"I can't drink today."

"Why?"

"I have to go somewhere."

"Where? If it's a nice place, can I come along?" Byeong-hwa's smile was disarming. Gyeong-ae returned the smile but shook her head regally.

His mind leapt to Sang-hun. To his astonishment, he was consumed with jealousy and was determined not to let her get away.

Gyeong-ae decided to sip a drink to kill time. Byeong-hwa didn't try to discourage her, hoping that she wouldn't leave if she got drunk.

Byeong-hwa told her how he'd made the manservant take off his coat, and they laughed together.

"Though threadbare, it must have brought honor to his entire clan. I did something inexcusable. He must have gone out to the avenue and shown it off to his friends. Maybe even danced around with joy. What a shame."

"Then why don't you recover the pawned coat and return this one to him? I'll buy you drinks, as many as you want."

"I've been thinking of doing just that, but actually I didn't come here because I was dying to drink."

"Then what are you dying for?"

Sensing he was being mocked, Byeong-hwa changed the subject and resumed questioning her about Deok-gi and his father.

She wouldn't offer any explanation and just said, "You'll know soon enough. I'll tell you when the time is right. I need to get to know you better first."

"What do you mean? Do you want to make sure I'm the kind of person who'd keep your secrets? Is that it?"

"That's part of it . . ."

This woman was a riddle. *Is she educated? Is her consciousness elevated enough to become my colleague? Is she merely interested in me sexually? Or does she want to use me as a way to get to Sang-hun, believing that I'm one of his or Deok-gi's lackeys? She has nothing to gain from me, so why is she acting this way? Most women would sulk after learning that I'm the kind of person who takes an overcoat off a manservant's back. She's so different from other women.*

"Don't you need to get going?" It was Byeong-hwa who finally brought it up.

"Eventually. But won't you come along with me?" Gyeong-ae seemed a bit inebriated now.

"Where? Count me in if it's a nice place."

"Why would I be going if it weren't a nice place?"

"Is it out of the way?" Byeong-hwa asked lightly.

"It's out of the way, all right." Gyeong-ae smiled.

"Only you and me?"

"Of course, only you and me."

"Who are you going to meet?"

"Whoever."

"This doesn't make any sense."

"Stop talking. You can tag along if you want to. It's a great place."

"Now that I've come to know you, I see you're quite a delinquent, aren't you?"

"Yes, yes, a delinquent. A serious delinquent." She laughed and disappeared into a back room.

All the guests had left the bar. Byeong-hwa poured himself a drink as if he were enjoying himself. Gyeong-ae took a long time to change her clothes before she reappeared.

She approached Byeong-hwa and sighed, "There's not a delinquent worse than me, going around drinking when her child has to fight for breath."

"Child? You have a child?"

"The Virgin Mary gave birth. Why shouldn't I have a child just because I'm single? It's more difficult and modern to make a baby alone than when two people do it together." Gyeong-ae loved to mock Christianity whenever she had the chance.

"It must be difficult, but if you want to be modern, the child's father should wash diapers, while the mother goes barhopping. That's the way it should be. But what was this about the child being ill?"

"Yes, she's ill." Gyeong-ae pulled out a Western medicine bag from her coat pocket, her face suddenly plaintive. "I carry this medicine with me."

"Where's the child? How can it be that you don't have time to give her medicine? Let's go to the child first thing. I'd like to take a look at the child's father, too."

Inwardly, Gyeong-ae was amused; Byeong-hwa had no idea they already were on their way to have a look at the child's father.

Out in the street, Byeong-hwa kept going on about the medicine, but Gyeong-ae sped ahead of him, and told him to shut up.

As he tagged along, his first thought was that she was on her way to meet Sang-hun. But then why would she want to drag him along? Had she made an appointment with Sang-hun while drunk? Following her might not be a good idea in that case.

When they arrived at K Hotel, Gyeong-ae told him to wait outside a minute and ran into the building.

Byeong-hwa wondered if she was pulling his leg. Were they actually there by themselves? In that case, he was ashamed to enter the hotel the way he looked. The thought that Gyeong-ae frequented a place like this filled him with contempt for her. Although he imagined that modern girls behaved this way, it was disenchanting to think that Gyeong-ae was no better than the average. But if there wasn't anyone waiting for her, Sang-hun or no Sang-hun, why had she been in such a hurry? Then again, why should he care? As he watched, Gyeong-ae, who had gone into the office, came out to the edge of the veranda with a maid and motioned to Byeong-hwa, who was standing in the dark, to come in.

As Byeong-hwa took off his worn-out shoes, he thought he should have shined them before leaving home. Like a hapless hick, he followed the two women into a secluded hallway with butterflies in his stomach.

The maid stopped in front of a Western-style door at the end of the hall. A pair of slippers was lined up neatly, toes facing them. It came as a surprise, as if he had been lied to. Byeong-hwa was about to say something to Gyeong-ae, but before he had a chance she turned the doorknob and flung open the door. He wasn't prepared to see a Korean wall screen in the room; it felt as though he had stepped into a strange dream.

As he peered into the room from behind Gyeong-ae, Sang-hun's flushed, smiling face came into view. His smile promptly dropped from his face, and his eyes flashed with menace, which he quickly masked with a wide smile.

"Welcome. Come in."

What humiliation! I shouldn't have come! thought Byeong-hwa. But he entered the room with his head held high and burst out laughing. *Why should I be humiliated? He's the one who should be ashamed of himself!*

Byeong-hwa said, "It's as if you duplicated your room at home. It's really cozy, and it looks like a perfect place to drink with a beautiful woman in your arms!"

"That's why I invited her." Choking down his embarrassment and fury, Sang-hun let out an empty laugh, steeped in bravado.

"Now that I've brought you a drinking companion, I'm leaving," said Gyeong-ae.

Sang-hun didn't know what was going on. Byeong-hwa found himself in an even more difficult position.

He said, "You brought me here without a word. What am I supposed to do if you leave? It was ridiculous of me to have followed you without know-ing that you two were meeting here. Please don't go. I'm going to leave soon." He held on to her.

"Who says I'm leaving because of you? I need to bring the medicine home." For the benefit of Sang-hun's ears, Gyeong-ae spat out, "Do you think I'd sit here with a drunk when my child is gasping for breath?"

"Then why *did* you bring me here? Please sit down. If you just tell me where you live, I'll deliver the medicine on my way home."

"Thank you, but why would you want to go there? You said you wanted to take a look at the child's father, didn't you? Then take a good look at him and keep him company for me while he drinks." A grin crept across her face; she seemed to be making fun of both men.

Byeong-hwa pretended not to be alarmed. "How can a drink taste good to him if my hand pours it?" Turning to Sang-hun, he added, "Please accept my apologies, sir. She told me that you had asked her to come with me, so I came along but had no idea that it would be a place like this. I'll take my leave. Please forgive me." He made a motion of getting up.

Sang-hun, flummoxed and angry, believing himself a laughingstock, nevertheless asked Byeong-hwa to stay. He vented his anger at Gyeong-ae, demanding to know why she hadn't left yet.

"Why are you angry at me? To you, the child may mean nothing, but not to me. You'd like it if I played the companion during your drinking binges, whether the child dies or not. Why do you pester me every day, asking me to come, asking me to go?" Gyeong-ae sat down as if she were determined to settle the matter once and for all.

Sang-hun had come to this hotel the past two days and sent for Gyeong-ae. She had ignored his summons the day before, but today she had debated whether to come or not and decided to accept his invitation only because Byeong-hwa had turned up unexpectedly.

Gyeong-ae hadn't really intended to shake them off and leave, and the men were relieved when they saw her take a seat.

Sang-hun thought he'd lose even more face if he replied to Gyeong-ae, so he pretended nothing was out of the ordinary and poured Byeong-hwa a drink. He hoped he could send the young man away after several cups in quick succession.

"Am I your family's grave keeper?" Byeong-hwa asked, watching Sang-hun pour him a brimming cup.

"How about you become our grave keeper, and I watch your family's grave?" Sang-hun laughed. He then caught sight of the overcoat for the first time. "What are you doing with that coat?"

"Why? It's mine."

"I gave it to my servant."

"Yes, and I took it back from him."

"That doesn't make any sense. What did you do with mine?"

"I drank it."

Sang-hun made a face. "Take it off. My servant has worn it. It must be crawling with lice."

"If I take it off, will you give me another? Every item has its owner. It was wrong of you to give it away without asking me first."

"You'd pawn it again if I gave you another one. If I had anything to give you, I'd rather give it to my servant. That's always the way it is with the poor. It's like pouring water into a bottomless jar."

Byeong-hwa was annoyed and was ready to contend with the older man but resisted out of consideration for Deok-gi.

Gyeong-ae cut in. "How can you say such things to this gentleman? What did you give him anyway?"

Byeong-hwa said, "Well, he's right, you know. Drinking really is like pouring water into a bottomless jar. I wouldn't have to listen to this if I hadn't gotten drunk off him. I'll return the overcoat tomorrow, sir. And I'm leaving. If I stayed any longer, you'd tell me to leave anyway." He snapped to his feet.

"I'm going, too. Let's leave together." Gyeong-ae stood up as well.

Byeong-hwa didn't want to stop her again, but he was baffled by the way things had turned out.

"Look, wait a minute." Sang-hun tried to hold Gyeong-ae back. "I have something to tell you."

Gyeong-ae began to walk away as she said, "I really have to take this medicine home. We can talk on the way." She couldn't bring herself to shake him off.

Byeong-hwa strode off without looking back. He was several meters ahead of Sang-hun and Gyeong-ae when they had no choice but to follow him out.

"Hey, Kim! Kim!" Sang-hun called out because he thought he'd lose face if he let the boy go off in anger.

"I'll get him," said Gyeong-ae.

When she caught up with him, she said, "Please don't be so mad. There's a reason why you shouldn't be, so please try to be on his good side. And come to the bar at three in the afternoon tomorrow."

She sent him off and waited for Sang-hun to catch up with her.

"He said he had to go because he's drunk. He asked for your forgiveness for the trouble he caused." Gyeong-ae sounded milder than she had a moment ago.

"What trouble?" Sang-hun trusted Gyeong-ae's words. "I said some hurtful things, but he took it too much to heart because he's poor."

The pair, in silence, passed the Bank of Korea and headed toward Namdaemun.

"Where are you going? Aren't you going home?" asked Gyeong-ae, stopping in her tracks. She hadn't spoken until Sang-hun followed her to the Jaedong Building.

"Come on, I'll take you home." He wanted to have a look at the sick child and clear up the long-standing resentment harbored by Gyeong-ae's mother. He figured he could learn in detail what Gyeong-ae's plans were.

When they reached the gate of her house, Gyeong-ae said, "It's too late. Why don't you go home? It's not right for you to come in now. Why don't you return in several days when the child gets better?"

Gyeong-ae walked through the gate, which the maid had opened, and blocked the entrance with her body.

He had no choice but to turn away. He couldn't help being disappointed, wondering whether she had behaved the way she did because there was a man in the house. It wasn't possible to force his way into her house after all these years.

The following day, Sang-hun woke up late. As he washed his face, he caught sight of the manservant trudging in wearing a dingy Korean coat. Sang-hun found it amusing. He said, "I heard he took the overcoat back."

"Yes, sir. It was a really good coat. What could I do, though, when he forced me to take it off? Where does that gentleman live?"

"Why? Do you want to go and ask him to give it back?"

"No . . ."

"Did you deliver that letter? Did you see her?"

"Yes, I did. But . . ." He hesitated, his eyes blank with helplessness.

"What is it?"

He came out with it, "Well, she wrote something."

"So? What did you do with it?" Sang-hun asked impatiently.

"I . . . have dropped it somewhere. I looked everywhere before breakfast, but I can't find it. I must have—I mean, I probably put it in the pocket of that overcoat . . ."

"What do you mean must have and probably? Go and get it back right away!" Sang-hun barked at his servant.

At first, the manservant had considered lying about the matter. He knew that his master would lash out at him because the lost letter was a reply from a woman, but if the owner of that overcoat showed up later and produced the letter, saying, "I found it in my pocket," he'd be guilty on not one but two counts in the eyes of his master.

"Yes, sir. If I really put it in that coat pocket, it would be still there, wouldn't it?"

"Enough! Go and get it right away, you bastard!"

"Yes, sir." He dashed out.

Sang-hun wasn't concerned about losing the letter—he was worried that Byeong-hwa might have opened it. Chances were, however, that it was still in Byeong-hwa's pocket if he had taken off the coat and hung it up in his room, given that he had been drunk the night before, and it was still early.

Sang-hun sat fretting before his breakfast tray, his appetite gone, when the manservant rushed in.

"Why haven't you gone? What are you doing here?" Sang-hun thundered, flinging open the sliding door.

"Uh, where does he live?"

"You're crazy! You act like a character in an old story. I thought you knew where he lived by the way you rushed out like that." He scolded the man but had to laugh to himself. The master and servant were equally nitwitted—Sang-hun himself had no idea where Byeong-hwa lived. He decided to give his servant directions to Gyeong-ae's house, so that she could point him in the right direction.

It was almost noon when the manservant returned empty-handed. Scratching his head, he reported, "People at that house say they don't know either."

Secret Talk

———

"A Jo family servant went to your house, didn't he?" Gyeong-ae asked as soon as she met Byeong-hwa.

"A servant? No . . ."

"He came to ask for directions to your house."

"He didn't come. Looks like both the master and the servant are vying for my royal robe."

"Ha, ha. I don't think so. Anyway, why haven't you reclaimed the over-coat? This one's horrible. How much do you need?"

"Can you help me get it back?"

"I can contribute a little."

"Don't worry about it." Overwhelmed by the kindness she showered on him—empty words though they may be—Byeong-hwa couldn't even joke about it. Suspicions, however, continued to gnaw at Byeong-hwa. He could understand Deok-gi's kindness since they were close friends, but it was hard to comprehend why Gyeong-ae was so nice to him, even if he was close to Deok-gi and his father. *Is it because I'm lucky, and people like helping me?*

Gyeong-ae pulled out a wallet from under her belt and took out a five-won note. "I guess this should be enough. If not, can you make up the rest from what you have left over?" Byeong-hwa flatly refused and told her to put it back. He just couldn't accept her money. Besides, he had pawned the coat for seven won, and after spending some of the money yesterday, he had given the rest, except for some change, to his landlord this morning.

"Don't be stubborn. Why don't you give me the pawn ticket?" She leapt to her feet and came closer.

Why is this woman so persistent? She was making him apprehensive.

"We can't talk here, so let's go somewhere else. I'd be ashamed if you came along in that coat," she explained frankly.

"Where are you planning to go? You don't think I could go anywhere at all? Not even a party?" He stood his ground, but Gyeong-ae grabbed him, put her hand in his coat pocket, and rummaged through it for the ticket.

"What's this?" Before Byeong-hwa had a chance to get away from her, she pulled out a letter and tried to see what was written on the envelope. When he attempted to grab it, she hid the letter behind her back and said, "Then give me your ticket. Let's exchange."

Byeong-hwa had no choice but to hold out the pawn ticket and swap it for the letter.

He had no intention of hiding the letter from her and had, in fact, been planning to show it to her, but only after teasing her and making her ache to see it.

"Why were you so startled? What is it? A love letter?" No name was written on the envelope.

"Yes, it's a love letter."

"Then let's have a look," said Gyeong-ae with a fierce look in her eyes.

"I'm not showing it to you precisely because it is a love letter. Why would anyone want to read someone else's love letter?"

"Then I'll reclaim the overcoat for you. Why don't you make yourself spiffy and go see your girlfriend? You won't get such a great deal anywhere else." Gyeong-ae seemed to laugh at herself as she went inside with the pawn ticket in hand.

In less than thirty minutes, one of the kitchen servants returned with the recovered overcoat.

"I'm so very obliged. Shall I show you something interesting?" Byeong-hwa asked lightly, as he changed into the new coat.

"Forget it, I'm not the sort of person who reads someone else's love letter. But I wouldn't mind seeing the woman who has fallen for you! There's no need, actually; it's so obvious." She turned to the young servant warming himself by the stove and, pointing to the old coat Byeong-hwa had tossed aside, told him, "Why don't you wear that?"

"Is it for me?" No sooner had she spoken than the youngster picked it up and put his arm through the sleeve.

Byeong-hwa was taken aback. "Whoa! That doesn't belong to you." But then he laughed and said, "Forget it! When it gets warm, I'll take off this one and give it to that manservant."

"Give me a minute," Gyeong-ae said. She ran inside and soon returned wearing a Western outfit.

"Where are we headed?"

"Siberia!" Gyeong-ae said as she strode out with Byeong-hwa in her wake.

The proprietor came out at that moment and pleaded with Gyeong-ae to return early.

Gyeong-ae said to Byeong-hwa, "Walk a little with me, will you?"

"Whatever you want."

It was almost four o'clock in the afternoon, but as it was warmer than the day before, their hands and feet didn't go numb. Gyeong-ae took the road to Namsan. Byeong-hwa followed her quietly.

"What are you doing these days?" she asked.

"I take naps and pick fights in bars." Byeong-hwa chuckled. "You have no idea what I do, but you'll hang around with me anyway, huh?"

Because they'd become friends overnight, he thought it was natural for her not to know what he was up to, but once she knew more about him, she'd be as shocked as a child who had discovered she was playing with dynamite. Then again, she might not mind. After all, she was no ordinary woman.

"How about getting a job somewhere? You wouldn't be able to find a position with the Government-General of Korea, but what about something along the lines of a clerk or some other position in a county?" Gyeong-ae asked, feigning ignorance.

"Did you drag me out in the cold just to tell me that?"

"Yes. I was thinking of introducing you to an official at the Government-General. That's why I had that coat recovered."

"That would be terrific! Is he willing to hire me?"

"Yes."

"Then what will you expect from me once I get a job? An evangelist woman in our neighborhood received a commission after arranging the delivery of Salvation Army rice for people living in hovels—you know how the Salvation Army distributes rice right before the New Year's celebration. Are you doing this thinking you'll get a commission if I get a job?"

"What are you talking about? An evangelist woman . . . living in hovels . . . the Salvation Army . . . rice—what a lot of rubbish! Wouldn't you like to get a job, get married, and sit in your warm house with your stomach full of hot food?"

"As the saying goes, everything's ready except one thing—the southeast wind. Anyway, I can't go along with the idea because I don't have a bride." Byeong-hwa laughed it off.

"It's not so difficult. If you can't find one, I'll play at being your bride," Gyeong-ae kidded him. "Listen"—she addressed him in a low voice and in a masculine manner suitable for bringing up something serious—"Please don't act as you did yesterday in front of Mr. Jo Sang-hun. It's natural for rich people to be high-handed. If you find fault with them every time, we'll get nowhere. I know he says annoying things, but try to brush them off."

"When will I see him again? If he's pleasant, I won't need to say a word. The other day I put up with him only because of Deok-gi," said Byeong-hwa, though he thought Gyeong-ae was right.

"That's not true. You can't get anywhere with such a confrontational attitude. Just do as I tell you."

Byeong-hwa perked up. "What do you intend to do?"

"Nothing right away. But having ended up like this because I was blinded by money, I'll have to get some cash and settle things one way or another. From now on we shouldn't give him the impression that you and I are on friendly terms. Please be careful."

"What did I do?" Byeong-hwa whined. "And just where are you taking me now? It's cold out here. Do we really have to climb against the brutal wind of the Namsan valley just to discuss such things?"

"There's something else. Would you like to go indoors?"

"As long as there's heat, any place will do."

They quickened their pace and passed the deserted front of the new Joseon Dynasty palace; and side by side, they descended the stone steps that are said to number more than 380.

It was already dusk by the time they reached the avenue with streetcar tracks, and Gyeong-ae suggested that they go to her house, only a stone's throw away, and have supper together. Byeong-hwa agreed to the idea.

He was curious to see how she lived and wanted to have a look at the child, but he still couldn't fathom why she was being kind enough to invite a virtual stranger to her house. She was impetuous, cheerful, nervous, and clever.

"Only three men have been to my house, including you. You may think I'd ask in anyone by the way I run around, but my house, whatever its reputation, is not a place for just anyone." She sounded like a famous *gisaeng* whose stock had gone through the roof, as they say.

"In that case, I'm honored by your kindness. Only three and I'm one of them! It's more difficult than winning a Chinese lottery, and I feel as distinguished as someone who's passed royal examinations. But who are the other two lucky men?"

Gyeong-ae cut in, "Don't make fun of me. Do you think I'm a *gisaeng*?"

"I'm thunderstruck. At any rate, who are the other two?"

"You've met one, and I'll show you the other some day if we have a chance."

"Who's the one I've met?" Byeong-hwa blinked his eyes, his face blank.

"The child's father. You've seen him," she said snidely.

"Then I'll have seen everyone if I get to see the second child's father. Am I the third child's father, then?"

"You have such a dirty mind!" Gyeong-ae drove her fist into his arm, not bothering to pay attention to passersby, though she wasn't completely oblivious of their reactions.

"What do you mean? I have a dirty mind?" He kept smiling insinuatingly.

"Think as you please."

"But what happened with her father? How did you get involved with him in the first place, and why, after ignoring his duties for so long, is he engaged in a comeback campaign? I don't get it. I feel as if I were looking at boxes within boxes."

"When a baby is born, the father plays his role. He stops playing that role if the child's mother treats him badly. If she has a change of heart, she lets him play father again. If she doesn't, he's banished. Isn't that clear enough?"

"You sound like a queen in her prime, so confident and powerful. But any child's father gets to eat rice-cake soup, right? Can I become a permanent fixture?"

"Stop joking," Gyeong-ae said mildly, but then a fierceness seemed to spread through her. "This is no time to kid. If you keep making such flippant remarks, you'll be slapped in the face and kicked out of the house, so be careful!"

Taken aback, Byeong-hwa took a sidelong glance at her, pretending not to be affected. "Where did that scolding come from? It sounds like you had it rehearsed!"

She didn't speak again. The more he thought about her behavior, the odder he found her. Judging from what she had said, she was no different from most young women, and it looked like she was simply encouraging him to satisfy her sexual appetite. For all Byeong-hwa knew, she could be a nymphomaniac—at the very least perverse—given the way she had taken Byeong-hwa to Sang-hun the night before or how she had kissed Byeong-hwa in front of Sang-hun several days earlier and from the things she said about arranging meetings with every man who had been involved with her. Her shouts and threats came from nowhere. She could easily pass as the boss of an unsavory gang of delinquent young women. She fit the description of the female counterpart of a bandit in old stories and detective novels. As they passed through the gloomy, dismal alley of Achanggol, lined with Chinese shops, opium addicts, and prostitutes loitering in droves, Byeong-hwa grew edgy but at the same time curious, as if he were being led into a den of sin.

When they reached Gyeong-ae's gate, Byeong-hwa laughed at his runaway imagination. It came as a surprise that the tile-roofed house was neat, clean, and well cared for out to the gateway. Near the middle gate, evenly cut firewood was piled high, and the platform holding a full range of condiment jars, seen at an angle from the middle gate, looked well tended even in winter. Far from a den of hooligans, it was by no means the household of a fast woman, where any kind of man could come and go.

My nerves must be frayed. Byeong-hwa laughed at himself for having been frightened for no reason.

Gyeong-ae led him to the main room and took off her overcoat and hat. She lowered herself carefully next to the sleeping child in the warmer part of the room. The child opened her eyes and began to whimper.

"All right, all right. Let Mommy warm herself first. Mommy's still too cold to hold you."

Byeong-hwa gazed at Gyeong-ae, awestruck.

The Gyeong-ae of Bacchus, the Gyeong-ae raging against Sang-hun, the Gyeong-ae outside the gate a little while ago, and the Gyeong-ae in this room. How could she have so many faces? Probably all women were like her, but he thought no other woman could play as many roles as easily as Gyeong-ae.

"She's almost recovered. Until three or four days ago, I thought she was going to die," said Gyeong-ae to Byeong-hwa sweetly, turning her head back toward him, while touching the child's forehead and comforting her. Now in her own home, she treated him kindly and her hard edge softened, as if she had forgotten that she'd both flirted with him and reprimanded him only minutes before. Now she was the hostess.

"Mother! Mother! Could you please come here?" Gyeong-ae called out. Her mother was cooking with the help of the maid. She gave her mother one won, asking her to prepare some special side dishes. "Please get some liquor, too," she added.

At last Gyeong-ae lifted the child to her lap and comforted her. She then asked Byeong-hwa, who was sitting quietly, to show her the letter. She was not particularly interested in it but wanted to break his stupefied silence.

He smiled at her. "Real love is a secret, not something to brag about. Love is all about pain, not happiness. You should know that much. It's pathetic that you keep asking to take a look at other people's secrets."

"Has someone like you ever had such an experience?"

"You're looking down on me. What was it like between the child's father and you?"

"That was my first love."

"If it really was first love, you'll end up going back to him."

"There was a huge gap in our ages, and it happened so suddenly that I could do nothing about it. Looking back, I can't believe it happened. What I know is that I feel half-affection, half-hatred toward him now."

"But you have a child, so you can't cut him off forever."

"I don't care if he's cut off or not." She sounded as if it were too trifling a matter to consider, and she changed the subject. "But you said you'd show me something interesting. Let me see it instead of the letter."

"Not so fast. I'll show you, but will you buy me something delicious in return?"

"Why have you changed your mind? You promised to show it to me in exchange for your reclaimed overcoat." She sounded like a little girl. Then she grew persistent. "If you show me, I'll buy you anything you feel like eating."

"How can I trust you? But all right, I'll do it anyway, even if I get nothing in the end." Byeong-hwa took out the letter and tossed it to her.

"Why are you making such a fuss?" She slowly pulled the letter of out the envelope and unfolded it.

I will use with gratitude what you have so considerately sent me, for I have been in urgent need. But why haven't I been able to see you for over ten days? Please stop by later today. If you hesitate and dawdle, I'm no better than dead. There's a commotion in my family every day. What is urgent is the matter of your officially divorcing your wife. My father is making a fuss every day, saying that he's going to go to Keijo City Hall and have a look at your civil registry. I will fill you in on the details when I see you, but I wouldn't lose face in the eyes of my relatives and friends if only you'd give me definite word. I am fretting every day. But that's not the only problem. Please think of the situation I can't talk about with others. I don't know if I'm making sense because I'm writing this in a hurry while your messenger waits. I will wait for you at six o'clock this evening at the place. The day before yesterday, I waited for you until eleven and came home only to get a scolding . . .

"You're surprised, right?" Byeong-hwa said before she finished reading, as if to provoke her.

"Why would I be surprised? You think I don't know that he's such a person? But where did you get it? In the overcoat?"

Instead of giving an affirmative answer, he snorted.

"That's why they were running around madly, trying to get it back, but who could it be?"

Byeong-hwa laughed aloud. "If you knew who she is, would you rush over and make a scene?" Then he made fun of her again. "Careful, now. Don't be regretful after your child's father is stolen."

Gyeong-ae remained unmoved.

"So the manservant ran an errand and brought the letter back but lost it after putting it in his pocket. How about taking it to the manservant and finding out who she is? I'll seal the envelope for you." She took out a glue dish from under the wardrobe, sealed it neatly, and gave it back to him.

Byeong-hwa said, "You're worried, aren't you? How about telling him that he should divorce his wife and kick this woman out, whoever she is? Tell him that only then would you let him play father."

"What's the use? Let him play with as many women as he wants. But we'd better teach him a lesson before he keeps on seducing the daughters of any number of families. If he does get a divorce, I won't sit back and suffer quietly. I admit I'd hoped that he'd do it at one point, but when I think of Deok-gi, I feel sorry for his mother."

Byeong-hwa thought Gyeong-ae's point of view was generous and far-sighted.

Gyeong-ae's mother, who had been busy preparing the meal, rattling pots and pans, called out, "Will you eat now or will you wait?"

From the way Gyeong-ae answered that they'd eat later, it seemed as if she were expecting someone.

"Is someone else coming? The child's father, maybe?" Byeong-hwa joked again.

Gyeong-ae glared at him and gently put down the sleeping child. She smoothed out the front of her wrinkled skirt and sat hunched over the brazier, pensive.

Finally she said, "How are the affairs of the alliance going?"

"Alliance?" Byeong-hwa's eyes widened at the unexpected question.

"Aren't you an executive member of the ____ Alliance?"

"What about it?" Byeong-hwa thought she could have easily heard about it from Deok-gi, but he didn't know why she mentioned it out of the blue. Besides, it was odd that she seemed tense as she said it.

"Why are you so surprised? I want to know how the alliance is doing."

Byeong-hwa's suspicions swelled. When she had talked about getting him a job or introducing him to someone at the Government-General, he had shrugged it off as a joke. Now he felt apprehensive. *Is she a spy?*

"Why do you ask?"

"No particular reason. Why weren't you involved in the latest incident?"

"What incident are you talking about?"

"The second ____ incident. Your alliance did not play a central role."

Gyeong-ae wasn't in the dark when it came to the activities of leftist groups, whatever her own political views. He stared at her in astonishment.

"Why? Were you frightened? I bet you were afraid that you'd be implicated, right?" She taunted him, then added seriously, "You should be careful. Before you leave this house, a group of detectives from police headquarters will arrive. You're like a mouse caught in a jar. What can you do? Don't humiliate yourself. Brace yourself and accept what is coming. In return, I'll treat you to anything you'd like to eat, so enjoy your last drink."

Byeong-hwa hadn't been involved in the latest incident but had lain low for several days to make sure that he wouldn't be implicated. Only when things had calmed down did he sneak into Pil-sun's house; he and several of his comrades could take care of the alliance later. Since he hadn't run away, the authorities wouldn't have had to resort to Gyeong-ae's help to arrest him. But if she were a spy, she might try to talk him into disclosing some of the alliance's internal workings.

"How much do you get paid when you snitch on a person?" he said with a laugh.

"What payment? Do you think they put up tens of thousands of won per head as they do in China?"

"Without any profit, why would you help catch someone, spending your own money to buy him drinks?"

"For fun. But you wouldn't think that it was unfair even if you were caught, right?"

"What does it matter?" he snorted. "I'm not guilty, and they'll release me."

"Not guilty? They clearly know that you have organized the third ____Party, carrying on the work of those in jail." Her eyes glinted.

"Does that mean there was a report that Kim Byeong-hwa is the alliance's chief secretary?"

"How could you be qualified to be a chief secretary? Whenever you see anything unusual, you turn your tail and run."

"If they know so much, what would they want to do with me after they arrest me?"

"When such a person is caught and interrogated, if he doesn't have a lot of backbone, he will spill the beans and tell even more than they want to know. He knows he'll be released as soon as he confesses, so he tries to save his own skin, even though dozens of his colleagues may be implicated and arrested."

"How do you know so much?"

She tried to goad him. "Why wouldn't I? I can't read minds, but common sense tells me that it was wrong for a person like you to get involved in such nonsense as social activism."

"Is that why you say I should become a county employee or a township clerk?"

"Why not?"

"Who told you about organizing the third ____ Party?"

"Forget it—do you think I'd tell you? For a week now, every police precinct in the city has been turned upside down. You had no idea what was going on, so you trailed behind Jo Sang-hun and wasted your time at Bacchus. What kind of activist are you? One kiss and you go limp. Looks like my spit is stronger than vinegar!"

Byeong-hwa couldn't tolerate such disdainful words. Whether or not she was telling the truth, he couldn't help feeling that the joke had gone too far. His face burning with fury and shame, he found his hat.

"Enough! Do you think I'm a child? Either play the spy or have me arrested!" He flung open the door and stepped out on the veranda.

All Byeong-hwa heard behind him was Gyeong-ae's snort of disgust. She didn't try to hold him back. To fan his anger, she spat out, "Let's see if you can leave my house. Just don't return before you reach the gate!"

"It was wrong of me to come all this way with you. No matter how debased you are, you should have at least some integrity."

Byeong-hwa wanted to pour out his resentment until he'd emptied himself of it, but he was too ashamed, for it was his own fault that he had been misled. At the same time, he was puzzled. Was she tricking him at this very moment? He couldn't say anything sharper.

Gyeong-ae's mother rushed out from the other room, her eyes wide with accusation, her anger palpable. "I don't know who you are, but what right do you have to call my daughter debased?"

Byeong-hwa didn't reply but sat hunched on the veranda, putting on his shoes. When the middle gate creaked open and someone stepped in, Byeong-hwa's heart sank.

A tall man, wearing a limp Western suit and a mocking smile, walked over and stood before Byeong-hwa. He stared at Byeong-hwa, his eyes huge behind his glasses, much to Byeong-hwa's embarrassment.

Is he an investigator?

Shock ripped through him, but strangely, Byeong-hwa soon felt calm. He decided to take his leave and briskly walked past the tall man.

The newcomer's shoes looked Western-made—a rare commodity in Korea, the kind worn by a friend of Byeong-hwa's who'd been to Shanghai. His Western suit fit him well, though it was not overly fashionable. Byeong-hwa had met enough police detectives to spot one right off, and he quickly shook off his knee-jerk fear.

Is he the second man who frequents this house, the would-be father of her second child?

Gyeong-ae's mother welcomed the man, saying, "You're just in time for dinner."

Gyeong-ae opened the door and came out, exchanging glances with the newcomer, though Byeong-hwa didn't notice.

"Hey, you," she called out, not wanting to call Byeong-hwa by name right after they had quarreled.

Byeong-hwa spun around in the yard. He wanted to keep going but was worried that he'd look ridiculous and didn't want her to think that he was fleeing.

"Have you been stung by bees? Why did you go away in the middle of a conversation?" Gyeong-ae stepped into the yard and pulled Byeong-hwa back.

The newcomer said, "Please come in. I'm sorry to see that you're leaving just as I'm arriving. It's like the old saying: A pear falls right after a crow flies away. It is only a coincidence, but it looks like you're leaving because I'm here." The man wore a cheery expression and sounded more down-to-earth than expected.

"As for the pear falling, that should be my line. I was on my way to turn myself in because I heard that a policeman in charge of this area is keeping an eye on this house. And then you walked in. If you're from the police, take me with you." Byeong-hwa sat on the veranda, facing him.

Gyeong-ae was all smiles. "You made the right decision. Remember what I said a little while ago? You knew you would come back before you reached our gate."

Gyeong-ae's mother was the only one not laughing. She stood in the middle of the veranda, baffled.

"Mother, please take the dinner tray to the other room," Gyeong-ae said, after ushering the two men into the main room.

"Let me introduce you. This is a relative of mine. He's recently arrived from the countryside. And this is an executive of the ____ Alliance. He's shortly going to get a job as a county employee or a township clerk. I'd like to offer you both some wine, to welcome one and say good-bye to the other." Gyeong-ae rattled on while the two men exchanged names.

When Byeong-hwa heard that he was Gyeong-ae's relative from the countryside, he studied the man's face closely. Byeong-hwa was disappointed that he was not the father of her unborn second child. Judging from his appearance and manner, he hardly seemed a newcomer to the city. Byeong-hwa found it impossible to believe that his name could be Pi-hyeok —both *pi* and *hyeok* meant leather. Did he run a leather shop? Did he attach leather to apparel? He didn't look shallow like leather, though. Let's say his surname was Pi, but how could a child be named Hyeok in that case? Byeong-hwa knew of people who'd been abroad as well as some young people these days who reversed or shortened their names when necessary and even when it was unnecessary, probably to be fashionable. Byeong-hwa didn't believe this man was a relative of Gyeong-ae's, and his name sounded phony, as well.

Byeong-hwa sat shyly, shifting back and forth between the two faces.

Pi-hyeok didn't say much after they moved to the other room and started eating. He studied Byeong-hwa furtively. With some hesitation, Pi-hyeok asked, "Do you think it will be easy to get a government job? Your situation is different from other people's, isn't it?"

"She was teasing me, just to see how I'd react." Byeong-hwa was still wary, but his anger seemed to have dissipated.

"A few drinks and you've changed your mind!" Gyeong-ae was playful again. "You looked like you were going to do something desperate. That's why you're cheap. If someone gave you a thousand won, or even only a hundred, your politics and philosophy would flit away like a feather in the autumn wind!"

"You'd find out for sure if you gave me the money."

"There's no need. You sound confident now, but let's see what happens if someone gives you a job as clerk at the Government-General. Not even a clerk. You'd make a perfect county employee!"

"Certainly, if they gave me a job. Anyway, how can you know what goes on in my mind? Can a narrow-minded woman know the heart of a big bird?" Byeong-hwa sat up straight and pulled his shoulders back slightly.

Pi-hyeok said, "You're right. Women—especially modern girls these days—are so greedy, and with their narrow-mindedness . . ." Laughing, he did not heed Gyeong-ae's fierce expression and changed the subject. "If you really want a secure job, how about coming to my town? It might sound as if I'm boasting, but it wouldn't be too difficult for me to find you a position in the county office." He looked squarely at Byeong-hwa.

"Why are you doing this to me, too?" Byeong-hwa laughed, but his suspicions ran high. *Why are they behaving this way?*

"What's the problem? These days well-known people change sides so easily—so easily that it would shame even the most promiscuous *gisaeng*. Who'd take Kim Byeong-hwa seriously?" Gyeong-ae commented.

"You've undermined me completely. What did I do to deserve such contempt?" Byeong-hwa lamented, almost to himself, as he moved away from the meal tray.

Pi-hyeok said, "There're too many temptations in the city. It's the center of politics, so they come your way all too easily. Even if you don't have enough money to feed yourself, your name is known. By contrast, regional youth are straightforward and enthusiastic, and local government offices have no tolerance for such high-handed policy and don't have the brains to play tricks. Plus, since they are constantly involved in confrontations, youngsters in the countryside are more alert and are given a bigger impetus for struggle."

Byeong-hwa thought he made sense. The man was no fool. "Where's your hometown? What do you do?" he asked him.

"Me? I live in the countryside in Hwanghae Province. There, I can feed myself, thanks to my ancestors." A self-deprecating chuckle came out.

Byeong-hwa wanted more details but bit his tongue since Pi-hyeok's answer was so perfunctory.

After the tray was taken away, Gyeong-ae went over to the main room and soon returned wearing a new outfit.

"I have to go earn money. Byeong-hwa, why don't you stay and talk some more?" she said, looking into the room where the men were sitting. Byeong-hwa stood up.

"Yes, please stay," Pi-hyeok said in a show of good manners, but he wasn't overly enthusiastic about convincing Byeong-hwa to stay. Pi-hyeok went out to the edge of the veranda and said good-bye to both Gyeong-ae and Byeong-hwa.

Gyeong-ae watched Pi-hyeok's expression from where she stood in the yard. She asked Byeong-hwa to wait outside the gate, took off her shoes, and went back inside to Pi-hyeok.

"What do you think? Is he all right?" she whispered impatiently.

"Yes. Make him visit often," Pi-hyeok whispered back.

Gyeong-ae left, smiling.

"Who is he?" Byeong-hwa asked as they walked in the dark. "Is he really a relative of yours?"

"Of course he's a real relative of mine. Is there such a thing as a fake relative?"

"But why did you two keep making fun of me?"

"What did we do?"

"Well . . ."

Gyeong-ae laughed aloud, saying, "You've been interviewed. That's why."

"What do you mean interviewed?" Byeong-hwa's eyes grew large.

"Oh, he's looking for a son-in-law. That's why I played go-between for you. He thinks everything about you is fine, except the fact that you're an activist and you drink too much. That's why he kept saying you should get a county job or become a township clerk."

"If the candidate is pretty, why wouldn't I play his son-in-law?"

"You'd have to abandon your ideology and stop drinking."

"Let me think about it," Byeong-hwa answered halfheartedly.

"What's there to think about? It's a done deal if you make money and stop drinking. She's the only daughter, there's no son in the family, and her dowry will be at least five hundred bags of rice."

"What a windfall! I thought I had a lucky dream last night."

"You're not listening to me."

"But does a man become impotent when he has an ideology?"

"What's the difference? He'll be in prison all the time."

"If I go to prison, I'll send a proxy to her," said Byeong-hwa, the humor leaving his voice. Abruptly, he changed the subject and asked, "But listen, when did he arrive?"

"What?"

"I mean, when did he get here?"

"You saw him when he got here, didn't you?"

"You've harassed me enough. You just wait. Soon the tables will be turned."

"What are you talking about? How about making a good impression so that I can eat your wedding noodles?"

"Look." Byeong-hwa softened.

"Yes?"

"I'm sorry to say this, but how about we let him eat our wedding noodles?

That's the way to go, don't you think?" Byeong-hwa drew his mouth, reeking of alcohol, close to Gyeong-ae's cheek.

"You should watch what you say!" Gyeong-ae recoiled, but she didn't look angry.

"I was wondering why you were so kind to me, and in effect . . ." Byeong-hwa stopped abruptly. He regretted being so frank.

"In effect what?"

"Well, in effect, the whole point of this evening was to introduce me to him, right?"

"What do you mean?" Gyeong-ae pretended she had no idea what he was talking about.

When they reached the avenue where the streetcar ran, they both stopped talking.

Who is Pi-hyeok, really? That he came to find a son-in-law is surely an excuse Gyeong-ae invented. Does he really have some other agenda? What group does he belong to?

Impatient by nature, Byeong-hwa wanted to rush back to the house and ask him point-blank. *If he really has snuck into Korea with a certain plan, what is it? Should I say yes or no? No matter what, it would take strong determination and resolve, but it would be good to catch a break when I'm twiddling my thumbs, and our movement is at a dead end. But what do I do with this woman? The more I get to know her, the more extraordinary she is. Could I really give her up at this point? Who cares whether she had a relationship with Sang-hun or that she's like a stepmother to Deok-gi?*

As long as he had already taken the first step, Byeong-hwa thought he'd go all the way. He didn't want to let this opportunity slip away. Even if Byeong-hwa ended up working with that man, it would be no fun if Gyeong-ae withdrew after arranging tonight's meeting.

One can't buy love in the name of work. Work is work and love is love, and Byeong-hwa wanted love as well.

"What made you think he's from abroad?" Gyeong-ae asked when they reached a dark street, where there weren't many passersby. She had been curious about it all along.

"I saw him during my Vladivostok days."

"Nonsense!" Her voice, though unruffled, was tinged with surprise. "When did you go to Vladivostok?"

"When I was in my mother's womb. But isn't it true that he's from somewhere over there?"

"What makes you think so?"

"Isn't it obvious from his shoes and the cut of his Western suit? If I noticed these telltale signs, tell him to be careful because there are sharper eyes out there."

Gyeong-ae was astonished. It was impressive that Byeong-hwa had been so observant; she'd better tell Pi-hyeok to change into something else.

"I'll have to say good-bye here," Gyeong-ae said in front of the Bank of Korea. She took off her gloves and extended her white hand for a handshake. She squeezed his hand firmly and said, "Please find out about that letter. Why don't you come by around the same time tomorrow?"

She walked away, taking brisk steps. Byeong-hwa smiled to himself—she hadn't forgotten about the letter. Rooted to the spot, he watched her back disappear into the night.

The Dream of Youth

———

"Don't worry about heating the rooms, Pil-sun. Just straighten them up a bit. Looks like he's drinking in town again."

Pil-sun's mother shooed her away from the kitchen when she tried to wash the dishes and told her to go inside and rest. Her mother was concerned about her, as she had returned home in the cold after a long day's work. In turn, Pil-sun was worried about her mother washing dishes with ice-cold water.

"I'm all right today because I took the streetcar," said Pil-sun as she started to feed some kindling into the furnace to heat the room across from the main one.

She put in a bunch of twigs and was about to add some paper from a heap nearby when her hand stopped in midair. There was a Western-style envelope, torn into three or four pieces with a letter still inside, in the pile of scrap paper. Pil-sun broke a twig with one hand while with the other she picked up the pieces of the envelope and held them near the fire. The address, a certain *chome* of Kami-gyou-ku, seemed to be Deok-gi's. Continuing to break twigs with one hand, she pulled out four folded sheets of paper.

She wanted to see what his handwriting was like.

"Not come . . . got to see Miss . . . wasn't entirely futile . . . said this lightly . . ."

She stared at the phrase "got to see Miss" again and again, and imagined that "Pil-sun" came after it. She realized her face was blushing with embarrassment.

As soon as she added twigs, the fire would leap up but then almost immediately die down into flickers. Distracted by the paper scraps she was fumbling through, she almost jumped when she realized that the fire was going out. She quickly broke more twigs and threw them into the furnace.

It wasn't easy to find more of the letter, most likely because Byeong-hwa had torn it up with others. Impatiently, she rummaged through the heap to locate the missing pieces and connect them to the parts she had already found. Though the meaning still wasn't clear, she could now piece together some phrases.

"I said this lightly the other day . . . really wants to study . . . find a way . . ."

"What are you searching for?" Pil-sun's mother shouted as she creaked shut the kitchen door. "It's so windy out here. Finish up quickly and go inside."

Pil-sun came to her senses. She pushed the heaps of paper into the fire, picked up a short broom to sweep the other bits in, and covered the furnace's opening with a roof tile.

"I'll clean up. Go and sit in the main room." The mother was reluctant to let her grown daughter clean a bachelor's room. Though Byeong-hwa was like a member of the family, Pil-sun's mother always felt uncomfortable and on the alert.

"It's all right. I'll clean it." Pil-sun picked up a broom and entered the room ahead of her mother. The room's male odor, its scent of stale sweat, assaulted her.

"Look at this mess!" she muttered to herself as she started sweeping. It wasn't that she suddenly felt an urge to clean Byeong-hwa's room—what she wanted was to rummage through the desk drawers.

After her mother left, Pil-sun dropped the broom and made a beeline for the desk. What she had spotted a minute ago was the first letter Byeong-hwa had received from Deok-gi after his arrival in Kyoto. Had there been others since?

Listening for telltale sounds as if she were a thief, afraid that Byeong-hwa might come home any minute, Pil-sun opened the desk drawers one by one. Though there weren't many letters in the drawers, she zeroed in on one in particular, in a Western-style envelope, torn in half atop some stray paper.

Why didn't he rip it up into smaller pieces? she wondered.

Her eyes slowly took in its shape, and her hand plucked it out furtively.

Pil-sun didn't stop to think whether she should read it. She simply had to know whom Deok-gi meant when he said "got to see Miss" and "really wants to study."

Why do you always have a chip on your shoulder? Can't you say anything that isn't cynical or angry? And about Miss Pil-sun, there's really no need for you to be so harsh, is there?

Pil-sun's eyes burned and she blushed down to the nape of her neck. She swallowed, feeling her throat tighten, and read on.

You actually desire a struggle—rather, your narrow-minded views, which have become rigidly fixed by force of habit, have imprisoned your body. I find it pathetic. There is a reason you've become so cynical, like a boy who grew up under the thumb of a stepmother, and I do sympathize. But I can't believe that you can become a great man and distinguish yourself when you hold such inflexible, narrow-minded views. That said, do you think it is right to deal with me, considering your so-called commitment to class struggle? You say that you're looking for a friendship between comrades—true comradeship, rather than an ordinary, social friendship. It's not that you're wrong to think the way you do—it's just that you can't tell the difference between public and private yearnings because you're adhering to a principle far too literally, don't you think? Such thinking has pushed you to rebel against your family and cut ties with your father, but if you were a married man and your wife supported you only to the extent of tacitly accepting your work, would you divorce her because she's not your comrade? Assuming that no greater happiness exists than brotherhood in society, you still need to pay attention to your private life, your day-to-day life. Struggle isn't the answer to everything. Generosity and persuasiveness have as much effect as stray bullets. If struggle is for the front line and the troops, then generosity and persuasiveness are the means reserved for prisoners of war. These two traits are as effective as struggle. You may think that you and your father are engaged in a prolonged battle, but in my opinion, you're the one who has beat a hasty retreat because of pettiness and your frustration at not being able to get your elder to budge. It is a great defeat. If your father heard me say this, he would be shocked, but don't you have the courage to meet him halfway in his fortress of religion—generously and persuasively? Likewise, if you seek my comradeship, you need to go beyond the thin motions of struggle. I'm not whimpering like a coward. What I'm trying to say is that you need to do something about your attitude. It wouldn't hurt to keep someone like me around. I'm not begging to be your friend. What I mean is that although my own path is different from yours, there will be times when I may be able to assist you and your friends. Laugh at me if you want. You may ask why I don't take the next step and join your cause, but I have my own opinions, and there is an unavoidable path for someone like me, so you mustn't think that I'm a coward. This letter may sound like a sermon, but it really isn't. I would like to hear your opinion, so . . .

Pil-sun tried to take in this avalanche of words, but it didn't interest her and she couldn't quite understand it. This wasn't what she had gone to so much trouble to get her hands on.

Looks like something's happening every day over there. Are you asking me to send money for your face cream? You're clamoring for your own now, but after a while, won't you demand money for Hong Gyeong-ae's face cream, too? More than that, you must be dying for some drinking money. I sympathize with you a great deal, but sympathy is all I can give you. The weather will soon get warmer, so why don't you dispose of that overcoat? When you're truly in love, you don't need food. How do I know this? That's what people say, so who cares if you go around naked, let alone without an overcoat? As long as Hong Gyeong-ae likes you! But seriously, you need to give the whole thing some thought.

Pil-sun bit her lower lip and stifled a laugh. The letter was getting more interesting. Who was this Hong Gyeong-ae? And Byeong-hwa in love? She couldn't picture it, no matter how hard she tried to imagine it.

You asked me if I know her. What does that have to do with your feelings for her? Can you get what you call comradeship from her? She may be attracted to you out of vanity and impulsiveness. There are some women, after all, who take pride in loving penniless men, and some will do anything to get their names in the papers, even if it means they have to kill themselves. But she's also very intelligent and calculating. She's the kind of person who can turn at the drop of a hat—even if she already has one foot in the door. When it comes to love or work, she's not going to involve herself too deeply. But why would you want her to? Unless she took the initiative, why would you impose a commitment on her that would be heavy even for a man? Not to mention that it involves illegal business. People often ask whether women are just supposed to cook and raise children, but what can we do when the world needs hands to do just that? Until men develop breasts, women's liberation is only a pipe dream. Why insist that women give up taking care of families? Mobilizing men to your cause will be more than enough.

Do you know why I say this? Because Hong Gyeong-ae has a young child (I don't know if you are aware of it, but the child is my half sister), and if she were to get involved in your affairs, she might not be able to raise her. Hong Gyeong-ae also has a mother. Who else would be able to take care of her in her old age?

Besides, it is anybody's guess whether the young woman would actually get involved in your group. Given that the proprietor of Bacchus is not an ordinary woman, however, Hong Gyeong-ae herself may not be a woman who only sells liquor, smiles, and even kisses. You may not know who the proprietor is, not even her name, but when I met Hong Gyeong-ae briefly on the day I left (I dropped by to inquire about the child's illness), she asked me to find out about O Jeong-ja, a student in the English Department of the women's division at Doshisha University. She told me that it was the proprietor's request. From her name, you probably think she's Korean, but she's the daughter of a Japanese judge or prosecutor who used to work in Korea. Anyway, since my arrival here, I've been so busy that I had forgotten all about it. Then, the day before yesterday, during a gathering of the Korean Students Association, I met a female student from Doshisha and inquired about O Jeong-ja. This may not come as a surprise to you, but I heard that she's in a detention cell! The case is still under wraps and can't be reported in the newspapers, but isn't this out of the ordinary for the daughter of a judge or prosecutor? After I learned this and received your account of how Hong Gyeong-ae poured a torrent of kisses on you, I suspect that the two cases are related. The proprietor and O Jeong-ja, however, haven't been in touch for quite a while, so perhaps they are just relatives or acquaintances.

Pil-sun's head was bursting—she had to get a look at this Hong Gyeong-ae!

I may regret saying this, and I may aggravate you, but I hope Hong Gyeong-ae quits Bacchus. Nothing good will come of it if she stays there. If you love her, tell her this. And the same is true with Miss Pil-sun's affair. I know you want to give her your guidance as a comrade, but would you give her the same advice if she were your sister or daughter?

Pil-sun's heart leapt. Her eyes caressed every word.

You said you thought of her as a sister. But there's a difference between as a *sister and* a *sister, isn't there? We should let her parents do with her as they wish. We shouldn't interfere in her life, except to help her find the path she wants to take. It's a sin to force a child who doesn't have much life experience to conform to someone else's experiences or thoughts, and to the habits they've picked up from the crazy world. I think all tragedies begin right there. Furthermore, should we feel contempt for a young person's dream just because it's a dream? It's wrong to think that you can stop her from dreaming because she'll wake up sooner or later anyway and will feel sad and disillusioned as a result. Why wake her prematurely from the dream of youth? Those who are older and wiser should let her dream as long as possible. Depriving someone of a dream is to take away an all-too-brief moment of happiness, for we have no other place to look for happiness than in a dream. Those who take no satisfaction in reality, or have no means to achieve satisfaction, are not happy. And even if they do find satisfaction in life, it's not happiness but only a jumping-off point for happiness on a higher level. Isn't hope—which aspires to greater happiness—a dream, too? It is a fantasy, a vision, a reverie. That's why I think happiness is never truly lasting but something we happen to taste amid our discontent, as we yearn and strive in real life. If we didn't taste it, how could we live in this troubled world?*

My sermon has grown long-winded again, but please don't disillusion a young woman who's not even twenty. Don't meddle with her destiny. If you're kind, you'll teach her to brace herself, you'll protect her from slipping into despair when she wakes up. By the way, I read in today's paper that a woman from a respectable Seoul family killed herself for love, creating a furor. It goes without saying that this isn't just some noble sacrifice by a woman transfigured by love. It may reflect some character defect on her part. Physiological conditions may have also been involved, along with the influence of climate. But more than that, older people sowed the seed of tragedy by confining younger generations to their own warped experiences, thoughts, and habits. And they got what they deserved because they made the mistake of turning a blind eye to young people's plights and didn't teach them how to think and behave when their dreams were shattered. Is this too simple a view, too unrealistic? If my opinion and observations are right and if you really love Miss Pil-sun like a sister, you shouldn't force her to come around to your view of society and live your way of life. If you do, it will be too extreme, too selfish an impulse, and it will negate her own existence. If she grows up and independently and voluntarily accompanies you on your path, fine — but how sad it would be if you hastily chilled a bud with frost and let it fall before it blooms! Let her dream on. Let her enjoy her youth naturally and peacefully. You might wonder why I'm so enthusiastic about Miss Pil-sun. It may be greedy for a traveler to pluck a lone flower blooming among rocks, but there's no reason why he shouldn't take note of its beauty. If he protected the roots of the flower with a handful of earth, onlookers might think that he has a dark design, that he'll come later with a flowerpot to transplant the grown flower and carry it off with him. But isn't this view too cruel?

By the time Pil-sun had read this far, her mother had twice shouted that she should finish up quickly and come to the main room. Pil-sun rushed through to the end of the letter.

It was difficult to read every page by assembling two ripped parts, but she understood what was being said about her.

In effect, Deok-gi offered to pay for her schooling, but rather than feeling glad, she was embarrassed. She was boundlessly thankful, of course, but she thought she was unworthy of such kindness. *What does he see in me? He hasn't known me long, so how can he be so kind?* She reread the part about the traveler who finds a blooming flower. She pictured her own face. *Am I a flower?* Without having to look in a mirror, she knew that her face was pale and narrow with a pointy chin. She imagined a withered wild chrysanthemum swaying on a deserted hill after the Harvest Moon Festival in the weak sunlight. She broke into a smile at this absurd image but soon blushed at the sight of her hands. Who knew how many thousands of strangers were wearing the rubber shoes made with these very hands? Her bones had thickened and her knuckles had knotted since she began working at the factory. Ashamed of her hands when she held the overhead straps on the streetcar, Pil-sun preferred to lean in the corner while riding. In any event, these hands were trustworthy workers. Thanks to them, four or five people could eat, though not very well.

If I study, who's going to make money and feed my family?

Dwelling on her shame over her hands, she grew frustrated with this reality.

"What're you doing? Sitting on the cold floor?" she heard her mother shout, followed by the sound of the door to the main room opening and shutting.

Pil-sun quickly placed the two halves of the envelope, into which she had returned the folded sheets, in the drawer and finished sweeping up trash into the dustpan.

Her mother opened the door and looked in. "What're you doing?"

"I was reading the newspapers."

As Pil-sun left the room with the broom and the dustpan, she worried that Byeong-hwa might find out that she had read the letter.

But why did he leave it there instead of ripping it up? Did he want to show it to me?

"Why is Father late?" Pil-sun muttered as she drew a sewing basket closer to her.

"He must be out drinking with Mr. Kim again," her mother said in a disapproving tone. They didn't have enough to eat, not even porridge, even though they had pushed their daughter of marriageable age into the world to make a living. And yet her husband spent his time doing idiotic things like following detectives around. When he was lying low, he stayed home all day or would come home late after drinking, always at someone else's expense, drunk and disorderly. Since her husband was almost fifty now, it would be difficult for him to land a job to his liking, but he should at least try to do something. Not a day passed without their having to worry about their livelihood. Whenever she imagined their future, she saw only darkness.

"Father's frustrated, so he drinks." Pil-sun sympathized with her mother, but she couldn't bear to be harsh with her father.

"However frustrated, does it make sense for him to drink while his family has nothing to eat?"

"He drinks when someone treats him."

"That's right. If someone offers to buy him drinks, he should ask them to give him the money instead. What prevents him from saying that he can't drink when his wife and daughter are starving?"

"*Egu*, Mother, how can he say that? That'd be too embarrassing." Pil-sun laughed off such an idea.

"I guess you're right. People don't mind buying drinks, but they scowl when they're asked to treat someone to a meal."

Pil-sun sat quietly as she stitched the hem of a pair of cotton-padded Korean socks to wear to work the next day. Phrase after phrase of the letter kept dancing around in her head. She couldn't gather her thoughts to decide what to do. Her chest swelled, though, as if an empty corner, one she'd never noticed, had been filled up. She realized that it had been empty only after something came along to fill it. How astounding, how mortifying and thrilling it was to imagine that someone faraway was wishing for her happiness!

The dream of youth.

The phrase hummed in Pil-sun's head. *But what was that dream?* she wondered, blissfully unaware that at that very moment she was dreaming the dream of youth.

Manservant

———

"Give me your report."

"What report?"

"This is too much," said Gyeong-ae, pretending to pout. "You're not taking the favor I asked you seriously."

"Ah, I forgot," Byeong-hwa said with a grin. "If you're so impatient, why don't you go to ____ Kindergarten?" He laughed.

"So she's someone in a place like that."

"Yeah, she's someone in a place like that," Byeong-hwa responded mimicking her, finding Gyeong-ae's contemptuous tone amusing.

"Her name?"

"I won't give it to you for free! I obtained it after spending quite a bit of secret funds and walking all over the city for half a day."

"Did you see her? Was she pretty?"

"Oh, yes — her beauty surpasses that of Lady Yang, the emperor's beautiful concubine of T'ang China."

Such exaggeration dampened Gyeong-ae's enthusiasm. On the other hand, that the woman was employed at _____ Kindergarten was believable. Gyeong-ae's guess — that she could be one of those who frequented Maedang House — proved wrong. An unexpected pang of jealousy surged through Gyeong-ae. If indeed it were true, the woman could be her competitor in a sense, unlike an easy woman with no family background to speak of. And if she were really stunning, Sang-hun's renewed interest in

Gyeong-ae could be a trick. What did he have in mind? Since the woman was pestering him about getting a divorce, he probably lied about his lawful wife. Did he intend to snatch Gyeong-ae's child and offer her up as evidence? Would he say, "See how I split with my wife and took on the responsibility of raising this child?" Gyeong-ae recalled how impatient he had been to take the child. It looked as if he were using this opportunity to put his affair with Gyeong-ae behind him and settle the matter of the child, she thought.

If that is what he has in mind, I'll make sure he loses not only his crabs but his fishnet, too, and winds up empty-handed! Gyeong-ae bit her lip.

"So the manservant told you that? I'd like to see her."

"If you just go to ____ Kindergarten and look for Kim Ui-gyeong, you can see for yourself."

After Byeong-hwa said good-bye to Gyeong-ae the night before, he felt like drinking some more but didn't want to go home and drag Pil-sun's father out to a bar, nor could he seek out his comrades, considering their situation these days. He wandered around Jongno and then went to Hwagae-dong to look for the manservant, remembering Gyeong-ae's request. His intention was to take the servant to a cheap bar as a gesture of good will, but before he made it to Jo Sang-hun's mansion, he ran into the manservant on the street in front of the grocery store at the far end of the district. Byeong-hwa accosted him right away.

"Hey, comrade! It's so cold today. Let's have a drink together."

The manservant was employed by Jo Sang-hun's family, but Byeong-hwa considered him a friend and actually preferred to spend time with someone of his ilk. The servant, however, was flabbergasted and gazed at Byeong-hwa, speechless. The affair of the previous day aside, by the way Byeong-hwa addressed him, the servant figured the young man was not right in the head.

"I don't want a drink or nothing. Just give me that letter, please. Today I ran all over town to get it, and my legs hurt a lot. I'm gonna lose my job. I'm in a jam here!" He didn't want to talk about anything else. He stretched out his hand.

"What letter?"

"That coat—my overcoat with a letter in it—don't tell me you threw it away."

"What overcoat and letter? Don't get upset. I'll find it for you later—let's go drink."

"You don't understand. Just hand over the coat or the letter. Why did you show up now—to make fun of me?" If the manservant were to really speak his mind and tell Byeong-hwa how he had been feeling since the day before, he'd be openly rude. Or he'd respond, "That's right, you buy the drinks." He'd make Byeong-hwa take off his overcoat, by force if necessary. But he had to suppress his temper, for he was dealing with a friend of his master's.

"I told you I'd find it for you, overcoat or letter. Why are you so impatient? If you're cold, wear the coat yourself." Byeong-hwa was about to take off his overcoat for the servant, momentarily forgetting that he'd freeze if he gave it away.

"I ain't gonna refuse it if you give it to me," the manservant responded roughly. "But if you're drunk, why don't you go home and sleep it off like a gentleman?" He looked around at his friends working in the shops, who gazed at the scene incredulously and muttered, "Now I've seen everything."

"Take it," a bystander goaded him on. "It's much newer than the one you had on yesterday."

Another said, "Just take it. Pretend you can't say no. You'll get free drinks, too. Someone's a lucky dog, ain't he?"

A third said, "How about I wear it instead? He's gonna buy you drinks just for accepting the overcoat. Is that so hard? Master, can I try it on?"

They all laughed raucously as if they were mocking a lunatic. Byeong-hwa ignored the uproar around him, tore off his overcoat, rolled it up, and held it out to the unwilling servant. "Wear it for now. The letter's in there, too. You'll go now, right? Why put up a fight when a friend asks you to share a drink?" He was pretending to be a little drunk already.

The manservant was stunned. His quarrelsome tone disappeared, and his voice turned apologetic. "I'll come, so please put it on. And it seems wrong to put my hand in your pockets. Would you take out the letter, please?"

"The letter can't jump out of the pocket. Let's go." Byeong-hwa strode off, still holding the rolled-up coat, while the servant cleared his throat and followed him.

The servant's friends, who worked in the shops lining the street, looked with envy at the backs of the two men as they slowly descended the slope. Arms folded, they called out after them, "Why don't you wear the overcoat now, Won-sam?"

"I never seen a guy who picks a fight because he wants to buy you drinks!"

"He's like the middle part of Buddha! He can't be more generous!"

"Hey, he didn't want to go to a bar with someone like us, looking like a day laborer. That's why he wanted to dress him up."

"Is he going to a marriage interview? What's the use of cleaning up?"

"What about his own appearance?"

"Anyway, the guy's incredibly lucky. How about I stand here all night? Who knows if such luck ain't gonna come my way?"

"You're right. Don't move, stand still. After you become a frozen fish, Keijo Mayoralty will come out early in the morning to take you out on a carrier. I promise I'll go out to the Gotaegol Cemetery and pour you a bowl of rice wine."

When they arrived at a bar, the manservant declined Byeong-hwa's offer to drink from the first cup. "I can't drink much. I can't drink much." For five or six rounds, he didn't say much else and tossed back what was offered to him.

"Let's get acquainted first," said Byeong-hwa as if it had just occurred to him.

"You're too kind. I'm Won-sam." The manservant made a bow.

"I'm Kim Byeong-hwa. But you don't have a surname. Or is Won your surname?"

The proprietor smiled to himself as he listened to their conversation. He had found them entertaining since they'd come in, for the Western-suited man had his overcoat folded up despite the cold weather, and the two kept pushing it back and forth, each insisting the other should wear it.

"My surname is also Kim. You can see where I am now, but I'm a Kim of Cheongpung," said Won-sam. His resentment had melted away after drinking a few rounds.

"We're of the same clan, then. But what do you mean by 'where you are now'? What's wrong with that, and what's it got to do with being a Cheongpung Kim?"

"I mean that I'm working in someone's servants' quarters, and I have no learning. I'm ignorant."

"When you're poor, you don't know how to read, and when you don't know how to read, you remain ignorant. Although being a Kim of Cheongpung is nothing to boast about, it's not shameful to be ignorant. You live in someone's servants' quarters, but you make a living by selling your services. What's wrong with that? It would be different if you didn't work and idled your time away." Though he wasn't saying anything profound, Byeong-hwa spoke firmly as if he were giving a lecture.

Won-sam was grateful for Byeong-hwa's kind tone, more than he was for what he actually said. "That's right, but . . ." He wanted to say something more, but he didn't know how to express his feelings.

"If you're concerned about your ignorance, I'll teach you. The old saying that one can learn how to read at the age of forty still applies today."

"That's only a saying. What can I achieve at my age? I manage to write my own name, and I'll grow old the way I am, but like any parent, I wish I could give my kid an education."

"You're right. As long as you know how to write your own name . . ."

"I learned up to book three of Beginning Readers when I was a boy, but what could still be in my head after I've lived like this for more than twenty years? I barely avoided being a complete illiterate." His words were a mixture of pride and lament.

"Then there's nothing to worry about. You know how to read, so next time I see you, I'll bring you some books. Are the Four Books and the Three Classics the only subjects of study? When you read books and magazines in your free time, your knowledge grows. You should know what's going on in the world, too, to teach your child, right?"

"That's so," Won-sam answered halfheartedly, because Byeong-hwa had shifted the direction of their conversation. He had wanted to boast that until his father's generation his family had produced some respected scholars.

"My real name is not Won-sam. My real name conforms to the family generational rule, but after we moved to Seoul and I fell to where I am now, I cut off ties with my relatives and lived apart from them." He still was looking for a way to speak of his respectable roots.

"You're talking about Cheongpung Kim again? You have a name by which people can call you. Names are not for genealogy books." Byeong-hwa spoke sharply, as if he were sick and tired of listening to such talk. All the same, he thought it odd but understandable that the son of a respectable family could have fallen so low that he now assumed the accent of a servant in his speech.

Byeong-hwa didn't think such a man would become his comrade, and he didn't want to draw him into his group, but it would satisfy him if the manservant came to acquire proletariat consciousness and communicated it to his friends. Then their children would be influenced, and Byeong-hwa could find real workers among this younger generation. He had a relatively grand vision. Instead of putting forth an infirm donkey because the situation was urgent and starving the donkey's offspring as a result, Byeong-hwa thought it more important to consider the offspring. He would be satisfied with influencing a father to raise his children well. This was one reason why Byeong-hwa was friendly with so many people working in the shops along the street.

Now that his first task was taken care of, Byeong-hwa decided to go on to the second one: finding out what Gyeong-ae had asked him.

Byeong-hwa took out the letter and asked a series of questions. At first, Won-sam just grinned, but he eventually told him everything he knew, partly because he had grown tipsy and partly because he wanted to repay Byeong-hwa's kindness. Besides, like most servants, he wanted to speak ill of his master.

"I think she's a concubine. Yesterday, I went to ____ Kindergarten to deliver her monthly payment and get this letter, but I still don't know where the lady lives."

"Why do you think she's a concubine?"

"One time, I took a letter to a house behind the detached palace at Anguk-dong, but the house didn't look like a regular house, and it didn't look like the lady's house either. I wasn't completely sure."

"What kind of a house was it?"

"Well, it looked like a house where someone's concubine lives or a drinking salon. The mistress was middle-aged, and there were many young women."

"Then it must be a bar or a whorehouse."

"It didn't look like one. But then, the guests were drinking."

Won-sam didn't know the address, but he gave Byeong-hwa detailed directions. He thought that "the place" the woman referred to in her letter was this very house.

"When you are sent out to deliver a letter again, will you let me know?"

"Sure I will. Just tell me where you live." Won-sam's mouth dropped open when he heard that Byeong-hwa lived outside Saemun.

"I'll give you drinking money, of course. Please just let me know." Byeong-hwa was hesitant to even make such a request, for he would look like a man who had nothing better to do, but he thought he'd better look into the matter quickly to gain Gyeong-ae's favor and to help her shake off Sang-hun.

Kim Ui-gyeong

———

That morning, Byeong-hwa went to see Kim Ui-gyeong at____ Kindergarten. He wanted to find out who she was, and it happened to be on his way downtown from his boardinghouse. He also enjoyed watching the children play whenever he had some spare time. As soon as he entered the school, however, he remembered it was a holiday.

Too bad I couldn't catch a glimpse of the bitch who plays with other people's angelic children and then sneaks into an unsavory house in Anguk-dong, Byeong-hwa thought. As he left, he came across an old man holding a tote bag that looked like it contained a Bible. He appeared to be a church guard because he had emerged from what looked like the servants' quarters next to the gate.

"Where does the teacher Kim Ui-gyeong live?" Byeong-hwa asked.

"Why do you want to know?" The old man looked Byeong-hwa up and down, and said, "If you need to see her, follow me to the church."

"I have no time for that. I just need to deliver a message to her house."

The old man told him that the church was around the corner and that Byeong-hwa should ask the lady herself. He probably didn't know where she lived.

Byeong-hwa followed the old man. At the church, it looked like Sunday school was in session.

Byeong-hwa was waiting outside when the old man came out of the building behind a wisp of a woman wearing gold-rimmed glasses. Everything about her was tiny, particularly her waist, and her hands and feet were as small as a child's. Her eyes, which resembled a Western doll's, bulged out, but her face was reminiscent of a beauty in Chinese paintings. Her cheeks were transparent; if pressed slightly, the flesh under them might get crushed. To Byeong-hwa, she looked like a girl of about fifteen or sixteen, but by the way she addressed him, he knew she was much older than she appeared.

When she saw that a shabbily dressed stranger was waiting for her, she stopped short at the top of the stairs and gazed down at him. After descending a few steps, she greeted him with a warm smile.

Byeong-hwa tipped his hat and spoke politely, "You don't know me, of course. Someone asked me to find out where you live, so I went to the school first and then was brought here."

"Who is it?"

"Me?"

"No, the . . . person who wants to find me." She seemed to be wary of something.

"A gentleman who'd like to visit the elder of your family."

"Number ____ at Gan-dong."

"Thank you." Byeong-hwa bowed and left without another word.

He stopped by the bookstore he frequented with his comrades and picked up a few volumes of the pamphlet they had published and then went to look for the house in Gan-dong.

Byeong-hwa paced in front of a large rising-roof gate at the entrance to Gan-dong. A big nameplate bore the name "Kim," but there were four or five other nameplates, and Kim was written on two of them. He had no idea which one belonged to Kim Ui-gyeong's family. Perhaps one of the smaller ones might be the one bearing her father's name. He entered the gate and found a maidservant washing clothes in the yard. "In which quarters does a female student named Kim Ui-gyeong live?" he asked.

"A female student? Do you mean the young lady of the family?"

This piece of information was new to Byeong-hwa. "No. Is there a kindergarten teacher among the tenants?"

"No one among the tenants."

"Then she must be the lady of the master's family. Is she at home?"

"No, she's not. She went to church. Where are you from?" The maid-servant's eyes grew large, for a man was asking to see the young lady.

"Is the master at home?"

"He's gone out."

"Where does he work?"

"He doesn't go to the office anymore." She didn't understand why he asked such questions. Turning away, she resumed rubbing the laundry on the washing rock.

"Are there any rooms for rent?" Byeong-hwa couldn't think of anything else to ask.

"No!" The woman wasn't pleased.

"I heard that a room has become vacant in the outer quarters."

"The larger room has been rented out for some time, and the smaller room that the master used was rented out several days ago. We're full now," she answered reluctantly and went in, water pail in hand.

Byeong-hwa left Gan-dong and went to find Won-sam to give him the books he'd promised. He didn't want to go to the outer quarters, so he walked back and forth outside the gate, until his eyes fell on a pair of man's rubber slippers placed in front of a room in the servants' quarters. When he knocked on the door, Won-sam flung it open from inside. Byeong-hwa walked outside with the servant in tow after he had given him the books.

"How about going to Anguk-dong today?" Won-sam had become quite friendly overnight.

"Why?"

Pleased, he told Byeong-hwa to go there around seven in the evening.

"You can take a look at the lady and drink there, too." He said that he'd been to the house in Anguk-dong earlier that day to deliver a message for his master. He remembered that he had promised to tell Byeong-hwa about the next message and had taken the letter to his room and opened it.

"What's the use of going all the way to your house? It's better that I open it here and tell you what's in it." Won-sam burst into laughter.

"So the message will be sent to the woman from the house in Anguk-dong." Byeong-hwa then added, "Today is Sunday, and it looks like they're going to have evening worship at the Anguk-dong house."

They exchanged a smile.

"What kind of service is that? Worshipping in front of a table laden with food and wine, and with women in their arms! Why don't you go yourself and have fun? They say you come to understand life only after seeing such things."

"Well, well! Our Won-sam is quite the playboy, I see!" Byeong-hwa slapped him on the shoulder and said, "This is all really very silly. Read the books I've brought you. Though we have no money, honor, position, or religion, nothing except our two fists, we can do anything as long as we join forces to live like real human beings and do our work. Those people are good-for-nothing. There is an expression, 'gisaeng's night blouse.' Though made from expensive silk, it is worn-out and torn, a useless rag. But us, we're like strong hemp thread. When it's woven, it looks clumsy and rough, but it's got its uses, right?"

"You're right," Won-sam concurred.

"I just went to the house of the woman in question for some business . . ."

"You know her?"

"I had no idea that she lives in a grand house and is the daughter of a respectable family. She is educated, too. Do you know why she runs around like that? In that fancy house, every room is rented out—even the master's room in the outer quarters. This tells me that they were once well-off but have now fallen on hard times. They make a living collecting rent from the only house in their possession, but how can they hold on to it? In several months — several years, perhaps — they'll be driven out to rent a place themselves somewhere else."

Won-sam gasped, "So she's the daughter of such a grand family?"

"Yes, but what's the good of it? She's used to living in luxury and what pittance she earns at the kindergarten isn't enough even for her face powder. She's really making her living from your master." Byeong-hwa beamed. "She's a concubine on a monthly basis, nothing more!"

"What's the difference? Ain't it okay if she enjoys her life this way?"

"Whether it's right or wrong, do you know what'll happen to the master who keeps paying her month after month? I can't guarantee it, but Kim Ui-gyeong's father may have been paying such monthly salaries for years. Judging from their appearance now, it's obvious what the future holds."

"But our master ain't gonna end up like that, is he?" Won-sam couldn't imagine it.

"Could be. Who would have dreamed that when they rebuilt Gyeongbok Palace, Gwanghwamun, its southern gate, would end up facing the east in less than a hundred years? In any event, read the books I gave you. You'll understand what I mean."

After they parted, Byeong-hwa walked around town for a while before going to visit Gyeong-ae. She was in a hurry, all dressed up and ready to leave.

"What will you do when you meet the witch?" Byeong-hwa asked Gyeong-ae.

"Never mind what I'll do. Let's go out," she urged him. Gyeong-ae wanted to leave before customers trickled in.

"It's useless to go to Gan-dong. Let's go have a meal, a combined lunch and supper."

Gyeong-ae just kept walking. She took a crowded alley and entered a restaurant whose magnificent gate was wide open, without so much as glancing back at Byeong-hwa.

"This is not Kim Ui-gyeong's house . . ." Byeong-hwa teased her as he took off his shoes.

"No more chatter. Did you think I'd chase after this Kim Ui-gyeong, whoever she is?" She sounded magnanimous, as though she'd never be jealous of the likes of Ui-gyeong.

"So you ordered Mr. Jo Sang-hun to come here?" Byeong-hwa kept cracking jokes as he sat down close to the brazier.

"Stop talking nonsense. When are you ever going to wise up?" Gyeong-ae asked, roaring with laughter.

"I'm so wise that I have nothing to eat. What'll I do if I become wiser than I am now?"

"That's enough of you! Today I'm treating you so you might not forget about me when you swagger around as the son-in-law of a wealthy family."

"No problem. But when a rich man pushes his daughter into the arms of a penniless man along with a bribe, what do you expect? It means that they assume that the husband-to-be will have concubines after the marriage. Why don't you play matchmaker and find me a real knockout when the time comes?" Byeong-hwa gleamed.

"When the time comes, if you decide I'm not too ugly, I can be your bedroom attendant," Gyeong-ae answered without missing a beat. Then she lowered her voice, and her expression changed. "Joking aside, Pi-hyeok seemed to like you a lot. Will you say yes?"

"I see that this matchmaker is truly inexperienced. Only after one is interviewed and hears all the details can one say yes or no," Byeong-hwa quipped — not sure exactly what she was after.

"You were interviewed yesterday. The details you can piece together for yourself." Gyeong-ae wondered if Byeong-hwa could be so stupid as to really believe that it was all about marriage, so she added, "The place for the new-lyweds has been prepared outside Seodaemun, off Independence Gate. Whether you'll be able to go there depends on how you behave." Through her bright expression, she studied him.

Byeong-hwa had guessed as much, but he realized now that he was in the thick of it, and though his hair stood up on end, he felt oddly relieved, like a traveler who finally encounters a dark shadow after fearing that he'd meet a thief or a wild animal on the night road.

His face turned red, his eyes widened, and a surprised laugh came out of his mouth. He himself didn't know what his laughter meant.

After being lost in thought for some time, he quietly asked, "But shouldn't I have more details? In the first place, I can't trust you, so how can I trust him?"

"You can't trust him? I'm worried that you're inexperienced, but hon-estly, it's no big deal for me—I'm just the matchmaker. If things go wrong, he's the one who'll be in trouble. I'm just concerned that I'll be ashamed for having recommended you."

"That's why you were toying with me all day yesterday, talking about making me a township clerk. Is this some kind of trick you two are playing on me?"

"Nonsense! What's so special about Kim Byeong-hwa that the whole world would want to set a trap for you? Don't worry, if you decide to take on the job and you have a firm resolve, go see him tonight. I've introduced you—you can get the details from him."

"Have you known him long?"

"He's a distant relative on my mother's side, the next generation after my mother."

Pi-hyeok had fled to Shanghai years earlier. There, he encountered a relative—Gyeong-ae's uncle, who had escaped to Shanghai with the money Gyong-ae's mother had entrusted him from the sale of her Suwon house. When Pi-hyeok returned to Seoul, he arrived with a letter from the uncle, in which he inquired about his family and enclosed one hundred won to contribute to their living expenses. After much effort, Pi-hyeok found that the uncle's wife had had to sell the family home after her husband had run off and that she and her children were living in Hyeonjeo-dong, outside Saemun, in a rented house. As the family had nowhere for Pi-hyeok to sleep, and as he was in no position to stay at an inn, where he would have to worry about the prying eyes of others, he was brought to Gyeong-ae's house, where he could stay for the time being.

Pi-hyeok kept an eye on what was going on in the outside world and studied Gyeong-ae's behavior. He asked her if she knew anyone in his field, but she couldn't think of anyone at first and paid little attention to his question. Soon after, she met Byeong-hwa and told Pi-hyeok about her new acquaintance.

Gyeong-ae admitted that she didn't know exactly what Pi-hyeok did, and she wasn't sure whether she would approve of his way of life, but he had taken the trouble of coming all the way from abroad. He asked her to find someone he could trust, telling her that he'd talk the matter over with the recruit and leave instructions with him before he went back home. Pi-hyeok would be impatient to get away as soon as possible after completing his mission, and Gyeong-ae would feel relieved only after he was gone. It frightened her to think that she might be implicated in Pi-hyeok's plans, but she couldn't just ignore him.

There's nothing I can do if something happens! she concluded. Still, she was carrying out the plan as intelligently as possible and in such a manner that she could easily extricate herself should the need arise.

She told Byeong-hwa that they should prepare a story in case something went wrong. "Just say that a relative on my mother's side wanted to find a son-in-law, and since I know Jo Deok-gi and his father very well, and you're a friend of Deok-gi's, I introduced the two of you. Otherwise, you can just say that Pi-hyeok came to see you and talked with you. We can say that was how you and I happened to meet."

"You're really scared, aren't you?" he needled. "I could say that you were annoyed with me because I was chasing you, so you hatched a scheme with Jo Sang-hun and dragged me into it."

"Stop talking nonsense! You should quit drinking and be careful from now on." Gyeong-ae seemed to think they had talked enough business. She poured another drink and handed it to Byeong-hwa, radiant.

"Like the ending of popular stories — all is illusion! Shouldn't the hostess pour me such a drink personally?" Byeong-hwa smiled and downed it before returning the cup to Gyeong-ae.

"You're acting silly again!" She cast him a reproachful glance and slapped the back of his hand.

It was almost seven o'clock when they finished supper under the electric lights.

"Will you go right away?" Gyeong-ae asked as they stood outside.

"I'll have to give it some more thought."

A surge of irritation shot through Gyeong-ae. "Why? You're scared, right?"

"Do you think I'm that helpless? Anyway, I have to sort out what kind of person he is and decide whether or not I can trust him. In the meantime, why don't you give me Pi-hyeok's real name?"

"You'll have to ask him that yourself."

"See? Even you don't trust me."

If Byeong-hwa had known Pi-hyeok's real identity, he would have realized that he was a person known both to activists and to the authorities.

"Think what you like, but he made me promise that I wouldn't tell anyone."

The two wanted to talk more, so they turned into a quiet alley leading to Myeongchijeong.

"If you gave him your word, then I don't want to know. But you don't think he'll keep it from me — someone he wants to involve in his work? You know, I can always ask around to find out whether it's all right for me to see him. What else do you expect me to do if you won't tell me?"

"I understand, but if you talk about it with everyone and spread the news that so-and-so has come to Korea, it may leak out, even if they're your comrades."

"You think I'd do such a foolish thing?"

"Of course not, but when three people talk about something, it leaks out the next morning. He told me that was the reason your group failed."

"Then even if I approach him, he won't tell me his name or background."

"I can't say." Gyeong-ae was pensive for a long time. She looked around and saw no one in sight. She put her mouth close to Byeong-hwa's ear and whispered, "Out there, he called himself Yi U-sam."

"What? What?" Byeong-hwa sounded impatient. Either he didn't hear what she said or he doubted his ears.

"Yi U-sam," Gyeong-ae whispered again.

Byeong-hwa fell silent.

"You know him?" Like a child, Gyeong-ae clung to him and looked up at his face, deciphering his expression.

Before Byeong-hwa could answer, they reached the avenue.

"Well, I'm off." Byeong-hwa walked away.

"Where to?" Gyeong-ae stopped in her tracks, but Byeong-hwa kept going. Then he turned around, rushed toward her, and grabbed her by the hand.

"You scared me! I could have lost my baby with such a start!"

"How far along are you? You should have told me," he said with a grin. "Does it belong to the second child's father?"

"No, no, it's just an expression."

"'Well, that's a relief. Shall we get together later?" he asked in a friendly tone.

"Where are you going now? Home?"

"Wherever. I'll come see you at ten or eleven." Byeong-hwa turned and walked away without waiting for her answer.

Watching him disappear, she wondered, *What kind of work can such a hasty character do?* His air of innocence, though, was lovable.

Gyeong-ae didn't have anything special to do, but she didn't feel like taking Byeong-hwa back to her house. Having introduced them the day before, she'd leave the matter to the two men. Though Byeong-hwa had left her for the moment, some part of him seemed to linger with her, both physically and spiritually. She'd shown him kindness for the sake of Pi-hyeok, but at the same time a corner of her heart seemed to be swept away by Byeong-hwa. She almost felt like the end of a skirt being dragged into a wheel. Although she could cut it off, she lacked the courage to do so.

When they were together, they would joke and make fun of each other. There were no romantic dreams or the exaggerated emotions a young couple normally feels, and they had not exchanged any words smacking of courtship, but there seemed to be something between them, however intangible. When they were apart, she didn't feel anything special for him, but the moment after he left, something seemed to be missing.

What do I see in him? she wondered. Love probably sprouts, she thought, when people least expect it. True, Byeong-hwa had faithfully found out about Kim Ui-gyeong and had done so to impress Gyeong-ae or to satisfy his own curiosity. Exposing the weaknesses of the man involved with the woman one loves is somewhat vulgar and awkward, yet it is an expression of affection all the same.

I don't have bad feelings about him, Gyeong-ae told herself, but if she really loved him, would she have coaxed him into such a dangerous scheme?

Actually, she had come to know Byeong-hwa while trying to bring him to Pi-hyeok. She tried to imagine Byeong-hwa without his work. He would be a nobody.

Now that that's done with, what should I do about Sang-hun tonight? Gyeong-ae thought. If she burst upon Anguk-dong, it would be embarrassing because she would look like a vigilant lawful wife, trying to catch her husband cheating on her, though she might get to see Kim Ui-gyeong in the process. But there was no satisfaction in ignoring Sang-hun's misdeed.

What should I do? She looked at her watch; it was not yet seven o'clock.

She didn't want to go to a place where drinking men gathered, and she thought of finding someone with whom she might take a stroll or listen to the radio while drinking tea together, but no one came to mind. She felt melancholy and lonely for the first time in ages.

Her child had recovered, and by the way Byeong-hwa had been so impatient, she supposed he had gone to see Pi-hyeok, so there was no need for her to go home. She thought of going to the cinema, also for the first time in ages, and turned toward Junganggwan from Hwanggeumjeong Street, where the streetcar was.

"Hello, madam. Going to the pictures?" She recognized the man. He was a driver who worked for the car service they would call for customers at Bacchus. Gyeong-ae often would use it herself. She greeted him and entered the movie house. While watching the film, thoughts of Anguk-dong filled her head, but she wasn't in the mood to run after Sang-hun. Perhaps she could send a rickshaw for him and wait to see whether he'd show up, but she wasn't sure a rickshaw driver would be able to find the place even if she gave him directions. It might be a wasted effort.

Should I take a taxi and pull him out? Remembering the driver she had just seen outside, she grew fidgety. She bided her time, though, deciding it would be better to drag Sang-hun out at the height of a party.

Maedang House

———

When the clock struck nine, Gyeong-ae left the cinema and hired a car.

She got out on the avenue at the entrance to Jae-dong and entered an alley accompanied by the driver. Following Byeong-hwa's directions, Gyeong-ae made her way carefully down the dark alley, but after a while, she became confused, for all the houses looked alike and there were no streetlights. Suddenly, a gate creaked open and whispers were heard.

Gyeong-ae motioned to the driver to stand still, as they overheard two shadowy forms.

"What should I do? What do I say to explain why I came here?" said a young woman's voice, filled with concern.

An older woman's soothing voice answered, "Don't worry about it. I blocked his view with my body. And he was drunk, so he couldn't have seen you clearly."

"I didn't know he went in just to relieve himself, and that's why I told you to come out," hissed another young voice.

"Don't worry. Make something up, like we've been friends for a long time, and you just dropped by to see me," said the older woman.

"Still, they'll blame me for going out at night when he's so sick." The woman, stepping out of the gate, kept fretting.

"Even so, he won't say anything. How can he talk? What about him, going out drinking when his father is sick! He'll pretend nothing happened."

"That's true, but what a coincidence!"

"It's because I had gone out. But go on now, before it gets too late."

"Yes, good-bye!"

"Good-bye, ma'am."

The voices were now loud enough to carry, and a small shadow darted out to the alley.

When their good-byes rang out, Gyeong-ae and the driver stepped aside and were partially hidden by the eaves. The woman momentarily stopped and stared at them, wondering if they might be acquaintances. She couldn't see well in the dark, though, so she went on. A cape was draped around her, and perched firmly on her head, buried deep in a black fur collar, was a traditional cap, decorated with golden butterflies and stripes that glittered even in the darkness.

That must be the Suwon woman! Gyeong-ae laughed to herself. Sang-hun must have unexpectedly shown up while she was there. She had hidden herself and was sneaking out while he went to the outhouse, but he had seen her. Gyeong-ae clucked her tongue, thinking, *What shameful behavior all around!* She asked the driver to go inside and call for Jo Sang-hun. If he was told that Sang-hun was not there, she instructed him to say that someone had been sent with a car from his father's house with an urgent message.

Gyeong-ae saw that the brand-new gate, with an overhead electric light, was now shut. The driver shook the gate and then stood quietly. Gyeong-ae hid herself in the shadows.

A murmur was heard, perhaps the buzz of an exchange with a female servant. The driver rushed over and said, "It's all right. Looks like he's coming out." He started to run off, intending to wait in the car to let them have a quiet rendezvous, but Gyeong-ae told him that she'd prefer to wait out on the avenue and asked him to lead Sang-hun to the car.

Sitting in the dark car, Gyeong-ae heard Sang-hun's angry, tipsy voice as he walked out of the alley. "Where? How can someone who's supposed to be waiting at the gate be this far away?"

The driver shepherded him to the car.

Sang-hun rushed over and looked inside. Gyeong-ae poked her head out.

"You tricked me!" It was not clear whether he was addressing Gyeong-ae or the driver as he stood there hesitantly.

"Please don't make a scene. Sit with me in here for a minute," Gyeong-ae said.

"How can I go anywhere dressed like this?" Sang-hun sounded uncertain but stepped into the car.

"Who said anything about going anywhere?" Gyeong-ae said as she winked at the driver.

The driver jumped in, turned on the headlights, and was about to turn the ignition.

"Wait! I don't even have my hat!" Confused, Sang-hun was trying to get out.

"Don't worry. I'll bring you back safely."

The car started right away.

"A car for prisoners is equipped with face covers that go all the way down to their chins, but here I am without even a hat!" Sang-hun was not very drunk, but he grew more and more outraged that he was being forcibly dragged off when he had momentarily stepped away from a table laden with food and alcohol.

"What a fabulous life! You have fun late into the night with oceans of wine and meat, surrounded by girls so lovely they could bring down an empire. And when you're a little bored, a modern girl like me comes around in the nick of time with a car for some fresh air."

"How did you know where I was?"

"I'm good at sniffing things out."

"I didn't know you were a hound dog." Sang-hun grinned sheepishly. "You're still seeing Kim Byeong-hwa, aren't you?" He remembered the letter in the overcoat. No one knew that he frequented Maedang House, except a few people in his clique and his manservant. *Byeong-hwa may have followed him there,* he considered. *Or perhaps Gyeong-ae had some connection with Maedang House. She could have easily fallen in with such a group.* In any event, he was not displeased that Gyeong-ae had come after him. She seemed eager to hold on to him, having learned that another woman was after him, though before she had shunned him. Now he felt inclined to keep her at arm's length.

"Your father is very ill, but even the Suwon woman doesn't seem to have the time to take care of him. She's far too busy staying up all night and having fun. He seems to be in such a sorry state that I came over personally to take you home. Shall I tell the driver to drop you at your father's house?" Gyeong-ae spoke in a teasing tone.

The car passed Changdeok Palace and was heading toward the residential area. Sang-hun was stunned by the mention of the Suwon woman and wondered if it had really been her who had flitted by in the yard of Maedang House. He scowled.

The driver was about to ask where he should take him when Sang-hun bellowed, "Hey, turn this car around!"

"Since it's on the way, why don't we go up to Namsan?" asked Gyeong-ae. Sang-hun figured she wanted to go to the hotel that had the *ondol* room with the wall screen. Sang-hun was silent. He snorted to himself, convinced that she was now taking the initiative out of jealousy, but he voiced no objection to her proposal.

When the car reached Yeongnakjeong, Gyeong-ae abruptly ordered the driver to turn toward Namdaemun.

"Why are you so impulsive? I should have at least taken my hat and overcoat," Sang-hun said sharply, even though he wasn't the least bit irritated. He didn't care about Kim Ui-gyeong, whom he had left behind at Maedang House. It wasn't so bad being spirited away like this, considering that Kim Ui-gyeong had lately been pressuring him with countless demands.

241

"What's wrong with wearing just your Korean coat? Your little concubine will take care of your hat and overcoat. At your father's house, the Suwon woman will have just arrived, so you needn't worry about him either. Can't you afford to give me one night out of your strict schedule?"

Sang-hun didn't appreciate her jeer but did nothing.

"Why do you keep talking about the Suwon woman?" Sang-hun asked, as if he had heard Gyeong-ae mention her for the first time.

"Don't pretend you don't know!" Gyeong-ae laughed and turned to take a good look at him. "You saw her a while ago when you went to the outhouse. I saw her from the car, but she was running off, looking over her shoulders, all bundled up in her cape."

"You've lost your mind! You've mistaken someone else for her. Anyway, how do you know the Suwon woman, and why would she go to a place like that?"

"Why wouldn't I know the Suwon woman? I'm a Suwon woman, too. I was born in Suwon, don't forget. Anyway, what could prevent her from going to such a place? Whether you go there or the Suwon woman does — Now, isn't that a nice arrangement?"

Sang-hun turned red and said in a tight voice, "Such nonsense — I don't believe it!"

"Don't vent your anger on me. If you want to scold someone, scold the Suwon woman."

Sang-hun thought this must all be some kind of trick. True, he *had* encountered the Suwon woman, but how did Gyeong-ae know that he had run into her in the yard as if she'd seen it with her own eyes? He couldn't understand it for the life of him.

When the car arrived at the entrance of Jingogae, Gyeong-ae told the driver to stop at Cheongmokdang and urged Sang-hun to get out. He didn't want to go anywhere without a hat and an overcoat, so he told her he'd wait in the car if she needed to buy something. He thought he'd take Gyeong-ae to her house before returning to Anguk-dong by the same car. But Gyeong-ae wouldn't listen. She asked him to buy her supper because she hadn't eaten yet.

"Forget about the hotel and please come with me for a minute. I won't keep you long."

Sang-hun couldn't insist on leaving when she said she hadn't eaten yet.

"If you miss Maedang House so much, I'll bring the girls over. So don't worry," Gyeong-ae said and got out of the car. Sang-hun had no choice but to follow her and dash into Cheongmokdang, as if he were guided by the old rule that men and women shouldn't be seen together in public. Gyeong-ae smiled, watching him sprint to the second floor. She didn't pay the driver but whispered something to him before sending him off. She then followed Sang-hun up the stairs.

Gyeong-ae observed Sang-hun's uneasiness with contempt. How on earth, she wondered, could she have once thought that "Mr. Jo" was admirable and remarkable?

She said, "Why are you behaving like this? Did you leave some taffy stuck to your brazier? There's a saying that a gentle scholar of Namjatgol can go all the way to Dongdaemun as long as he has some toilet paper and a smoking pipe, even if he's wearing clumsy wooden clogs. Do you honestly think anyone will care that you're not wearing a hat?" Then she shifted gears. "How about showing me the woman to whom you've lost your heart?"

"Who says I've lost my heart? At my age? I'm not young any more." He shook his head.

"When you get older, you may need a second Kim Ui-gyeong, or better yet, a third Hong Gyeong-ae," Gyeong-ae shot back.

Sang-hun made no reply.

"Let's have supper here and then go back to Maedang House."

"As you please," Sang-hun said. He didn't want to take issue with her cynical remarks. Maybe it wouldn't be so bad to take her there. In fact, he could even show her off. Kim Ui-gyeong might get angry, but he wouldn't mind if she turned her back on him. It looked as if Gyeong-ae had fallen into his hands, so he was relaxed. If he wanted to set up house with Gyeong-ae, he shouldn't lead her astray by taking her to a place like that, but by the way she had talked about the Suwon woman, he had a feeling she might know Maedang House even better than he did. In any event, he could take her there to see how the two women would react to each other.

Gyeong-ae had said she wanted supper, but now she claimed that she didn't want any food. She ordered a bottle of curaçao and sat drinking it.

Sang-hun told her they ought to leave if she wasn't interested in eating, but she rebuked him, asking how a gentleman could be so impatient.

Exhausted and resigned to the situation, Sang-hun changed the subject after ordering a drink, thinking he'd wait it out. "What's Byeong-hwa doing? When did you see him last?"

"You'd know if you went and asked him," Gyeong-ae answered sharply. Then without a trace of a smile, she said, "I haven't kissed him recently, and he has no overcoat to pawn, so he hasn't been around."

"Do you kiss people out of boredom? I thought there was a story behind it!" Sang-hun smiled as if relieved.

"Why? Are you jealous?"

While they were exchanging such trivialities, a waiter came in and announced, "The guests have arrived."

"Guests?" Sang-hun's eyes opened wide. Was Byeong-hwa here? He was afraid that Gyeong-ae had hatched a scheme with him.

"Please show them in," Gyeong-ae answered.

Sang-hun, glaring at the entrance, gasped and laughed out of sheer dismay.

Three Women

———

Her lush hair was parted in a neat straight line, not a strand out of place, and the skin on her face was tight and glowed in milky whiteness with few wrinkles, though she was over fifty. This middle-aged woman looked at least ten years younger than her age. She entered with dignity, a gray cape folded over her arm, followed by a slender female student wearing her hair bundled in a high, tight bun. At first glance, one might think them the mother and daughter of a rich, respectable family, but upon closer inspection, they felt more like a retired *gisaeng* or a court lady with her young companion in tow.

Ah, so this is Maedang herself, that celebrated woman of Seoul! Leaning back in her chair in a condescending posture, head tilted, lips curling at the corners, Gyeong-ae's gaze pierced the pair as they entered.

Sang-hun couldn't shed his sheepish smile.

"What wild-goose chase is this? If you intended to leave, at least . . ." Maedang spoke in a great admonishing voice, but her voice trailed off when her eyes met Gyeong-ae's mocking stare. The gold teeth of the female student in Maedang's shadow glittered briefly and then vanished, as the girl resumed a prim air.

After an instant assessment of Maedang, Gyeong-ae's eyes shifted to the "female student"—a label that would disappear in later years, but that was now laden with connotations, both positive and negative. Her deep-set eyes gave a somewhat doll-like impression when she blinked, and she struck

Gyeong-ae as a comely young woman. The young woman made a good first impression, and this made Gyeong-ae empathize with her, but her generous thoughts soon gave way to others—dance like an angel in kindergarten by day, and sit around drinking tables by night. Gyeong-ae didn't know whether she was clucking her tongue at Kim Ui-gyeong, lamenting the world, or simply feeling sorry for herself.

"Sit down," Gyeong-ae said, indicating the seat next to her. Ui-gyeong's mood soured at the sight of this unexpected beauty in Western dress. Though hesitant, she assumed a challenging attitude. Her eyes not meeting Gyeong-ae's, she bowed slightly and perched on the chair, still in her overcoat. Her refusal to take it off and exhibit good manners was taken as a deliberate slight by Gyeong-ae, who continued to look imperiously around the table from face to face.

Giving Maedang a sidelong glance as she exchanged whispers with Sang-hun, Gyeong-ae tossed back her curaçao and offered her empty glass to Ui-gyeong. *What a horror!* Gyeong-ae thought, as her first favorable impression of the young woman evaporated, and she wanted only to give her a hard time.

"*Egu*, I can't drink that!" Ui-gyeong recoiled. All her attention had been directed to what Sang-hun and Maedang were saying. She waved away Gyeong-ae's tactlessness.

"I've heard about *gisaeng* who can't sing and whores who can't have babies, but I've never seen a bar hostess who can't drink!" Offended by Ui-gyeong's scowl, Gyeong-ae burst out laughing. Maedang and Sang-hun abruptly cut off their conversation and looked over.

"Miss Kim Ui-gyeong! Have a drink. This is not kindergarten. Don't worry about it! Just drink! We're from the same school, aren't we?" Gyeong-ae was overcome with scorn for the rude young woman and felt a rash impulse to crush Maedang, no matter how seasoned the old woman might be.

Maedang blanched. Her cheeks fell, and her eyes danced with fury.

Ui-gyeong stared at Gyeong-ae, her face turning purple and her heart beating as fast as a frightened bird's. She didn't know who Gyeong-ae was but although she was angered only fleetingly by Gyeong-ae's insult, she was rendered speechless when Gyeong-ae called her by name and mentioned the kindergarten.

"I've been holding it so long, my arm might fall off. How can I put this glass down? My hand will be disgraced, won't it?" Gyeong-ae's will seemed to be softening, deliberately slurring her speech.

"Take it anyway," Maedang said in a persuasive tone. But a deep frown was etched between her eyes.

"I've heard people complain about no one buying them drinks, but why is it so difficult to offer someone a drink?" crowed Gyeong-ae as she poured more liqueur. Gyeong-ae jeered at them but at the same time felt elated, for Maedang—the supposedly powerful Maedang, whom the whole city knew—had arrived with Ui-gyeong in tow at Gyeong-ae's summons. However displeased she was, Maedang urged Ui-gyeong to accept the glass, and Gyeong-ae was confident that she had completely squashed Maedang's spirit.

"Let me introduce you two," Gyeong-ae said. "This is Lady Jang Maedang, one the most powerful women of Korea, and this is a modern woman of Seoul." Maedang nodded her head with a perceivable grimace. Gyeong-ae added, "I'm Hong Gyeong-ae, who sells alcohol. I've heard so much about you, but at last I have the pleasure of meeting you."

Maedang suspected Gyeong-ae's comment was tongue in cheek, but thinking that Gyeong-ae might prove useful in the future, she responded earnestly, "Why don't you come to see me at my house?"

"I was at your gate a little while ago, actually. Would you let someone like me in?" Gyeong-ae jeered.

"Where? At my house? You must have worn yourself out, running around to catch the playboy, but still, you should've come in."

247

"What use do I have for a man whose hair is turning gray? Could I use him as medicine? But I shouldn't say things like that in front of the young lady." Gyeong-ae addressed Ui-gyeong, "Don't worry about my stealing your man. Just put a name tag on him. He may get lost." She was lashing out in every direction.

"That's enough of your silly jokes!" Sang-hun jumped in. He had been curious about this for some time. "How long have you known about her?"

"What don't I know about affairs in the capital? I've seen her often. Didn't we pass each other all the time near Gan-dong?" Gyeong-ae snapped back.

Blushing, Ui-gyeong blinked her eyes and gazed at the glass in front of her, knowing that she'd lose if she argued with Gyeong-ae. She looked at her wristwatch and stood up.

Gyeong-ae also rose. "Are you leaving? You should empty your glass and return it to me first." Draping her arm over Ui-gyeong's shoulders in a friendly manner, Gyeong-ae sat her down, while Maedang quietly kept her seat with no intention of leaving. She didn't want to stay much longer, but she'd be damned if she had come all this way, marching to this bitch's tune, only to depart a laughingstock. Ui-gyeong resumed her seat helplessly, because neither Maedang nor her man showed any sign of leaving or excusing her to leave. Threatened by Gyeong-ae, she felt a tangible fear that Sang-hun might be lured away from her.

After Gyeong-ae urged her to drink more, Ui-gyeong listlessly pushed the glass toward her "mother." Maedang readily took it and gulped it down. She knew about brandy and whisky, but she'd never seen a bottle in the shape of a zebra's neck. She drank out of curiosity, but she felt she was losing ground by returning the glass to this impudent beauty in a Western suit. After their first exchanges, Maedang and Gyeong-ae faced each other squarely, offering and accepting shots of the liquor.

"Is this a competition between barmaids or a drinking party between alcohol-guzzling whales?" Sang-hun, who wasn't drinking much, thought he'd take a stab at humor. "Round one between Bacchus and Maedang, ladies and gentlemen. And Bacchus has taken the lead!" In a manner unbecoming for his age, Sang-hun cheered for Gyeong-ae, imagining he found himself in a drinking paradise surrounded by adoring women.

Gyeong-ae tossed Ui-gyeong a napkin. "Why don't you wave this, instead of a flag, to cheer on your mother?"

Maedang wanted to get Gyeong-ae dead drunk and take her to her house; she hoped to make her one of her girls. Although affronted by the young woman who treated her with such insolence, business came before saving face.

"*Egu,* it's almost midnight. We should go," Maedang said to Sang-hun after finishing off what remained in her glass. Amused, Gyeong-ae said, "You sound like you're talking to your husband. You're just like a married couple—with a daughter." She burst out laughing.

Gyeong-ae's footsteps were unsteady as she negotiated the stairs, but Maedang looked unfazed, though she had already drunk a considerable amount before coming to the restaurant. As they reached the door, four rickshaws waiting for them came into sight.

"Let's go share another drink," said Maedang as she helped Gyeong-ae aboard.

"Sounds good. Why don't we stay up all night drinking!"

The rickshaws crossed the avenue in a row, with Ui-gyeong's car in front and Gyeong-ae's directly behind. Suddenly, Gyeong-ae's car wheeled about, and Gyeong-ae shouted, "Good night and sleep tight! Thank you for allowing me a good look!"

In her rickshaw, Maedang snorted and clucked her tongue; her slight intoxication disappeared in the winter wind. She wasn't sure whether she was more infuriated over having been duped by Gyeong-ae's wiles or by the fact that a good piece of goods—by chance swept into her net—had slipped away. She would love to get her hands on such a bold and unusual girl, even though she knew she would have to pay a premium. Gyeong-ae was better than anyone else who frequented her house, on the basis of her looks, if nothing else.

"You've insulted me, Mr. Jo. You should bring that wildcat to me at least once. I'll teach her some manners," Maedang muttered sharply to Sang-hun when, later that night, they sat before a table laden with midnight snacks.

"You can try every trick you know, but I don't think you'll catch her." Sang-hun thought he'd better give up on Gyeong-ae, given what he'd seen that night.

Ui-gyeong spent the night at Maedang House. Several months had passed since she first began visiting the establishment, but never had she stayed the night. It was very late, but more than that, after meeting Gyeong-ae — such a powerful opponent — she grew more audacious. She threw herself at Sang-hun's feet more eagerly than ever before. Another worry stirred insider her — she was late that month. And the more anxious she grew, the deeper she felt she was slipping into an irreparable mess.

Slander and Schemes

———

Adviser Jo had a son, a grandson, and a great-grandson, but none was as important as one single person — the Suwon woman. He believed he'd get better if she just sat near him. But after being carried inside, despite the doctor's order to remain immobile, his limp noodle of a back was aggravated, though he was handled ever so gently. For several days, his back ached and the swelling worsened.

The room in the inner quarters was hot, for it was linked to the kitchen stove, which was in constant use. With characteristic impatience, the old man ordered his quilt removed time and again, which required that the door slide open and shut all the time. His cold improved one moment and then worsened the next, completely exhausting the old man. Meanwhile, pneumonia, which they had feared most, set in. Chinese and Western doctors came and went, and the entire house was in an uproar, abuzz with the preparation of medicine from early morning until well into the night.

The Suwon woman was losing weight. Many eyes were on her, and she was all the more resentful not being able to reveal her irritation.

It looked like the old man would be sick for a long time. Like a small child, he wouldn't let her out of his sight for a minute, and someone had to attend to his bedpan day and night. During the daytime, she could rely on others to empty it, but at night she had to do it herself. It was agonizing to be regularly wrenched from a sweet sleep, and to make matters worse, she wasn't able to air the room, which was permeated by a pungent odor.

———

She soon took to falling asleep with a perfumed silk handkerchief held to her nose. The old man grumbled about the handkerchief and wondered where the fragrant smell came from. He didn't mind the scent itself, but it irritated him to think they were trying to mask the stench of his body with perfume.

Still, the Suwon woman was most obliging. If she took this opportunity to pay extra attention to the old man, she could get more farmland—yielding two hundred bags of rice rather than a hundred, for example. She also went out of her way to cast aspersions on her stepgranddaughter-in-law. Now that the old man had become so estranged from his son and daughter-in-law, he might leave more assets to his grandson and granddaughter-in-law upon his death, and if the grandson's family was cut off, he'd leave more to her—such were the dark workings of her heart, even if it amounted to only a small patch of farmland.

"The young one's useless. She's so lazy." The Suwon woman blamed everything on the granddaughter-in-law whenever the old man appeared unhappy.

"It's no wonder. She's still young and has a child to raise. Maybe she's pregnant again." Even in his suffering, the old man found his granddaughter-in-law endearing, seeing her as a bud whose sap is rising.

The Suwon woman turned down the corners of her mouth. "What'll she do if she has another? She's struggling with just the one as it is."

"Still, it's better to have a second child when the time is right," the old man said, figuring that she could be pregnant after his grandson's recent visit. This prospect, however, was not as gratifying as the old man's dream of having another child with the Suwon woman. He was worried that the clan would end up with few descendants.

"Why do you worry about such things when you're not well?" The Suwon woman imagined the headache should the young one be pregnant again.

"Anyway, her mother-in-law spoils her. The young one's so coldhearted.

She separates everything—theirs and ours. She frowns at your chamber pot, as if it were contaminated. She doesn't touch it, of course, yet rinses out the one from her own room. Not that I expect her to wash ours." Her first salvo in the campaign to undermine the young one.

"Can't anyone else wash it? Why would we expect her to do it?" the old man said gently, though it was unpleasant to discuss these matters.

"That's what I mean. You can tell ten things from just one aspect of someone's behavior. She doesn't do anything about brewing medicine, leaving it all to the underlings. Couldn't she take a peek at the brew from time to time as she comes and goes? Apart from medicine, it's proper that she look in on things like the stew or the rice-boiled water if it's for one's elders. If she cared, that is."

The old man now remained quiet and attentive. When he didn't reply, the Suwon woman thought he was willing to listen, so her lips danced ever more busily and excitedly.

No one likes to take care of old people, and there is a saying that even the most devoted son cannot deal with a parent's long illness. The old man believed he had no one to rely on but the Suwon woman, who had joined his family without any roots of her own to speak of, though he had a son and a grandson and a considerable sum of money—enough to be talked about throughout the country. Even if the best medicines were brought in, a servant would brew it, and if it had simmered too long, the servant would just add water, diluting the medicine and reducing its effect. If too much medicine were left at the end of brewing, the servant would throw some away to make it look like a perfect concoction. The more he thought about it, the more admirable he found the Suwon woman and the more grateful he felt that she looked after him without a murmur of complaint. When he first took her in, the entire family had been against it, but what would have become of him without her? It would be the Suwon woman—no one else—who'd spoon him water on his deathbed.

"As for Deok-gi, he wrote to his wife, but he hasn't written you a line, has he?"

"He wrote as soon as he arrived. Did he write again?"

"A letter came yesterday, I think."

The old man called his granddaughter-in-law.

"Child, I heard your husband wrote a letter."

"Yes, sir."

"Then why didn't you show it to me?"

The old man's nerves were frayed. These days he felt the need to supervise everything, including things that had nothing to do with him. He easily lost his temper and grew even more irritable after listening to the Suwon woman.

"There's nothing special in it. He asks me to send a book that he left in his room, along with his necktie."

"Bring it to me anyway!"

The granddaughter-in-law didn't wonder about his behavior; she knew that it was another of the Suwon woman's ploys. She had no choice but to retrieve the letter and hand it over.

It contained nothing else of interest. Deok-gi simply asked whether his grandfather was better and went on and on about his child, telling his wife to be careful so that he wouldn't catch a cold and not to let him fall asleep at her breast — something he might have read in a women's magazine. The old man's feathers were ruffled.

Suddenly, the young one knows how precious his own child is! he thought. Then he asked, "So did you send him what he wanted?"

The granddaughter-in-law tried to read the expression on the grandfather's face, nervous over whether he'd throw a tantrum over something unexpected. "Not yet, sir."

"I don't have time to write a letter, so write him in detail. Tell him how sick I am and that this time I won't recover." That said, he ordered her to wrap up the things Deok-gi wanted and give them to Secretary Ji in the outer quarters to mail. He also told her that she'd better supervise what was going on inside the house.

"As for my medicine," he added, "if you can't be bothered to brew it yourself, how do you expect me to get better? Isn't it your duty?" He wanted to make himself perfectly clear without being too severe.

Nevertheless, the granddaughter-in-law found it unfair. Who else in the house paid more attention to brewing his medicine? The Suwon woman rattled on about it but never once brewed a single dose with her own hands! What could the young granddaughter-in-law do? She couldn't express her feelings to anyone in the family. She could only confide in her own parents.

"I'm doing the best I can, but . . ." She didn't continue, afraid that she might sound as if she were talking back.

"That's why I said you should pay more attention." He sent her away, still bruised by his grandson's apparent lack of concern over his illness.

After breakfast, Sang-hun visited his father to pay his respects. He had come by every morning and evening without fail since the old man had taken ill. His greeting consisted of no more than a few moments in the sick room, but these few moments were tedious for both men.

"Do you drink every morning?" The old man examined the color of Sang-hun's face.

Sang-hun hadn't drunk much, though he had gone from Cheongmokdang to Maedang House the night before, and his eyes were red from lack of sleep. He didn't normally overdo it, but recently he found he couldn't hold his alcohol very well.

"You didn't come here to see your father. You came to get rid of your hangover with some of your drinking buddies." The old man turned his face away.

Sang-hun stood silently before taking his leave.

"Don't come again! Even if I die, no one will bother to tell you! Go hole yourself up in a bar or some woman's house!" The old man barked at his son's back, like a splash of ice-cold water.

The father's outbursts always cut deeply. At such moments, Sang-hun was ashamed to be seen by the servants and his young daughter-in-law. He had made a vow to himself to be sincere with his father, for the old man's days seemed numbered, even if he couldn't act as his father wished. He became a sulking child.

I admit I'm not the most admirable son, but one can feel devotion only when the elder is willing to accept it, Sang-hun thought. Father and son had never exchanged kind words, but their relationship had grown much worse since the Suwon woman joined the family. Sang-hun couldn't blame his wife for this situation, though she was ready to pounce on the newcomer day and night. Recalling that the Suwon woman had been at Maedang House the day before, he thought that she shouldn't be allowed to remain in the house, but he couldn't do anything when it came to his father's affairs. Once his father died, she would no longer be part of the family, regardless of the fact that she had given birth to his father's child. In fact, she might be frequenting Maedang House with her future in mind. The biggest worry was that she'd take away hundreds of bags of rice. If she kept the assets and raised the child well, it would be a different story, but Sang-hun begrudged her even that much, believing that the rice would end up in some strange man's hands. Who knew whether someone hadn't already attached himself to her with an eye on the inheritance? She couldn't have told the old man that she'd met Sang-hun there, because it would reveal her own secret, but why did his father suddenly throw a fit, telling him to hole up in a bar or a woman's house? He'd never said that before. Had the Suwon woman been slandering him? That would be intolerable.

Sang-hun played for a while with his grandson, who was on his nanny's back. When he headed toward the outer quarters, he stumbled upon the Suwon woman at the outer gate.

"How long have you known Maedang?" Sang-hun asked quietly as she passed by. He brought it up as a warning that she shouldn't frequent the place, but he kept his voice hushed out of consideration for her.

"Maedang? I met her some time ago. I ran into her yesterday when I was getting something at Jongno. She urged me to stop by her house, so I went for a bit. Do you know her, too?"

Sang-hun was stunned that she spoke at full volume. She acted as if she wanted everyone to hear.

"Regardless of whether I know her, didn't we run into each other there yesterday?" A faint smile appeared on his lips, but his eyes scolded her.

The Suwon woman pretended to be astonished. "Did we? I wasn't sure that was you. Why do you drink there? Are you friends with the man of the house?"

"Yes, I know him . . . How long have you known Maedang?"

"We met at the Joseon Theater a while ago. The maid she'd brought with her was the daughter of a servant who grew up in my family. I got to know Maedang a little while talking with her maid, and yesterday she insisted that I visit her house. I don't have much leisure time right now, but I dropped by for a moment because I just couldn't keep refusing." The words rolled off her tongue like running water, seemingly without any effort.

"If that's the case, it's all right, I guess, but you shouldn't go there too often. Men go there to drink—it's something like a hostess bar." Thinking she could actually be telling the truth, Sang-hun offered advice, though he knew not to take everything she said at face value.

"Really? A place like that? I shouldn't have gone, then. She must be very well-off. Her house and furnishings looked expensive, and I've heard the master of the house is a gentleman. Why is she involved in such a business?" She cocked her head.

"Just don't go there again." Sang-hun stepped over the threshold of the outer-quarters' gate, where he found Clerk Choe pacing along the wall, his hands loosely linked behind him.

The man could have overheard them. The group of people who gathered every day hadn't arrived yet — who else could she have met other than Choe?

Choe had squandered his fortune on women. He was no different from the penniless men who talked about grand real-estate deals at Pagoda Park, but regardless of where he got his money, he was always decked out in gaudy clothes, and his brown shoes were always well polished. Dressed like that, he didn't have to go to Pagoda Park to kill time.

Choe had introduced the Suwon woman to her husband, so he had scored points with the old man. Whether selling spurious real estate was his main occupation and matchmaking was a side job, or the other way around, no-body knew for sure. He just pounced on whatever came along.

Sang-hun had heard that the maidservant, who had been hired recently, had come on Choe's recommendation. The three — Choe, the Suwon woman, and the maidservant — could be conspiring together. In fact, he had learned from his wife the morning after the ancestral ceremony that even on the day of the rites, the Suwon woman had been whispering with Choe at the gate and disappeared briefly. Sang-hun had heard a rumor that she had been intimate with Choe but had married Sang-hun's father because she and Choe couldn't make a living. Regardless of whether there was any truth to this gossip, whenever Sang-hun saw Choe, he found him detestable. Chang-hun, the cousin with whom he had quarreled on the evening of the rites, he also found despicable. Sang-hun vowed that he'd strip these two men of power when the time came. And the repugnance was mutual: the two reported Sang-hun's every move outside the house to the old man.

"How are you these days? You needn't sneak around by yourself. Bring me along — it couldn't hurt." Choe guffawed. He was older than Sang-hun by six or seven years but respectfully used a somewhat elevated form of speech.

Sang-hun snubbed him with a cold smile. It annoyed him to think that what had happened the previous night had already reached this man's ears. "Where? I hear you go to Maedang House often enough! We should go together."

"Sure! I've heard about Maedang, but I haven't been there."

"You mean you haven't been where the Suwon woman goes? You're not very up-to-date, not a real Seoul playboy, eh?"

"What kind of thing is that to say to an old man? Does the Suwon woman go to such a place? Who says so?" This pulled the rug out from under him, as if they were speaking of his own daughter.

"Didn't you just hear us?"

"What do you mean?"

"Never mind," Sang-hun replied as he strode off.

Choe looked at him with a smile and shouted, "Let's meet later! I never break a promise!"

In the main room, the old man wanted to know what the Suwon woman had talked about with Sang-hun.

"He says he is close to the master of that house I went to yesterday. I can't believe he's heard about my visit already!" Upon her arrival yesterday, she had recounted exactly the same story she had just fed Sang-hun.

"What does the master of that house do?" The old man was not suspicious, for had it been something fishy, she wouldn't have mentioned her visit there in the first place. He merely wondered if it was someone he knew, since his son was said to be close to him.

"I don't know. They probably go to the same church."

The Suwon woman spoke with caution. If Maedang really had a "husband," there wouldn't be one but many. Anyone she described wouldn't actually exist. She had concocted the story for Sang-hun and the old man.

"If he's Sang-hun's friend, he must be a disagreeable type," said the old man. "The importance of having respectable friends should never be underestimated. Nowadays, every woman who dishonors herself has been goaded on by some contemptible sidekick. And she doesn't end up humiliating just herself—she smears shit on her husband's face and sullies the clan—"

As the old man embarked on one of his long-winded sermons, the Suwon woman cut him short. "Are you worried because I'm such an innocent child? Well don't be. I will keep to myself. That'll make you happy, right?"

Activity

———

When Gyeong-ae returned home from Bacchus close to midnight, she was told that Byeong-hwa had left a while ago. Pi-hyeok's room was quiet, and his doors were firmly closed.

"Are you sleeping?" Gyeong-ae called out, but he didn't answer.

She wondered whether Byeong-hwa and Pi-hyeok had missed each other, but there was nothing she could do now, and she went to bed herself.

Early the next morning, someone shook the gate, which had yet to be opened for the day. Gyeong-ae's mother, who was stoking a fire in the kitchen, went out to see who it was. Holding a parcel at her side, a demure young woman entered without introducing herself.

"Is Miss Hong Gyeong-ae at home?"

The mother stared at the visitor before she answered, "Come in, won't you?" The old woman shut the gate and followed the visitor inside.

"Someone's here!" the mother called. The door of Pi-hyeok's room burst open, and he thrust out his tonsured head.

"Did you come from outside Saemun? That parcel is for me." He quickly took it from the young woman. "Thank you for coming all this way in the cold."

The visitor looked as if she wanted to meet the owner of the house by the way she planted herself, without acknowledging Pi-hyeok.

"Are you still sleeping? You have a guest!" the mother called out again.

Only then did Gyeong-ae slide open the door to the yard and peer out, her eyes still full of sleep. "Where did you come from?" she asked as she smoothed her hair into place.

"Outside Saemun . . . Kim Byeong-hwa . . ." Pil-sun stammered.

Gyeong-ae's face lit up as she slipped out of her bedding. "Ah, yes. Just a moment."

Pil-sun waited for Gyeong-ae to get dressed and open the door for her. She hadn't expected to meet Gyeong-ae so soon. Pil-sun thought she was pretty at first glance, but her overall impression of her wasn't particularly favorable. She realized that anyone who'd just woken up wouldn't look their best, but Gyeong-ae's unmade-up face was attractive. Pil-sun had the impression that she'd known her for some time. Upon entering the room, she stood dumbfounded for a brief second, for it was magnificently furnished, and Gyeong-ae was wearing Western pajamas that looked like a man's shirt or a Chinese jacket. Pil-sun thought Gyeong-ae looked beautiful in it, though she'd never before seen anyone in such an odd outfit.

Feeling a wave of resentment rise in her, she thought: *What's the point of living like this when you earn your money at a café? She's no different from a gisaeng.*

Pil-sun figured Gyeong-ae was promiscuous and began to feel contempt for her. Or, to be exact, she made an effort to hold Gyeong-ae in contempt in order to shake off her envy and feel better about herself.

"Did Mr. Kim arrive home safely and sleep well?" Gyeong-ae asked, thinking she came on an errand for Byeong-hwa.

"Yes, I brought Korean clothes."

Gyeong-ae didn't know what this meant. "What clothes? Where are they?"

"In the other room . . ."

Gyeong-ae nodded and seemed to mull something over before grabbing the overcoat hanging on the wall and draping it over her pajama shirt. "When did Mr. Kim say he'd come?"

"Shortly, I think."

Gyeong-ae excused herself, opened the door, and was about to leave when Pil-sun stood up and whispered, "If the overcoat is too short, I'll alter it here, so please tell him to try it on."

"Whose is it?"

"It's my father's, and he thinks it'll be too short. I was asked to make a rough guess and alter it, so please bring it back to me if it's too short."

Gyeong-ae nodded and went to the other room. When she saw Pi-hyeok, she laughed out loud and gave him a double take.

"What? Do I look really odd?" Pi-hyeok smiled and rubbed his smoothly shaved head.

"You look so young. I almost didn't recognize you."

"You think so?" He peered into the mirror.

"Where did you get the haircut?"

"I shaved my beard here, but then I wasn't sure what to do about my hair. So I wound up going to your uncle's house in Hyeonjeo-dong and asked the eldest there if he could get hair clippers. He ran over to his friend's house, borrowed some, and shaved my head. He did a decent job, don't you think? Is a one-won haircut on the expensive side?" He broke into a smile.

"Even ten won would have been a bargain. If you'd gone to a barbershop, where streams of people come and go, who knows who you might have run into? So what happened yesterday?"

"It went well," Pi-hyeok answered curtly and grew pensive for a spell. Finally, he said, "Give me some pocket change from that money and hand over the rest to him when he asks."

Gyeong-ae didn't ask for details.

"I'll leave later whenever the coast seems clear. I'll tell your mother that I'm going to the countryside, where my parents live. Be well. I don't know when we'll see each other again, but you must stop living the way you do and help that man out. You can't keep an eye on him every moment, but if he's aware that someone who knows the whole story is watching him, he'll take it more seriously. And if he happens to have a woman at his side encouraging him, he might feel inspired. In other words, it's not that I don't trust him, but half of my trust rests with you, Gyeong-ae, as I take my leave."

She nodded.

"But it won't do if you and Byeong-hwa become too close and spend your time out drinking. Such rumors travel fast, even abroad, so if something like that developed, we'd be in big trouble." Pi-hyeok's advice was lined with a subtle threat.

"Don't be so pessimistic!" sneered Gyeong-ae. "If you don't trust him, why did you approach him in the first place?"

"It's not that I don't trust him . . . I approached him precisely because he looked trustworthy, though it was a snap judgement. I'm leaving after entrusting everything to a fellow I've known just a day or two. Anyone would think I'm being rash; how can I say I'm not concerned at all?"

Gyeong-ae thought Pi-hyeok was sizing up the situation reasonably. "Anyway, he's not the kind of person who'd be swayed by such a trifling amount of money. As for me, do you think I have no other way to make money? Why would I try to ruin your work?"

Pi-hyeok smiled to himself; what she said sounded plausible.

When Byeong-hwa heard that Pi-hyeok was actually Yi U-sam, he immediately knew who he was. The name was on the police blacklist and had been found in court records of several people's trials. He was in charge of one of the groups working outside Korea, and his name was on many comrades' lips within the country. Byeong-hwa had absolute trust in Pi-hyeok and was willing to do anything for him.

Pi-hyeok was in no position to hesitate while vigilance was being stepped up all around him. He had entered the country with two missions. With the first one completed so easily, now he faced the second. The fact was that he was entrusting his projects to the same type of people in the same circles; if they were exposed later on, they'd be astonished. Pi-hyeok had to give them instructions separately, and even though they were in dangerous proximity of each other, they were expected to keep their missions to themselves.

Now that the work was proceeding smoothly, Pi-hyeok aimed to get away. He decided to wear Korean clothes on the road; Byeong-hwa had strongly recommended it, and he agreed that it was a good idea. The night before, Byeong-hwa had discussed the matter with Pil-sun's father and had made him hand over his sole garments for outings. Pil-sun's mother had stayed up all night to make padded socks, and Pil-sun did the legwork.

The overcoat was a bit small on Pi-hyeok. He could wear the trousers and jacket as they were, but it would attract attention to wear such a short coat. Pi-hyeok said it was all right, but Gyeong-ae took the coat into the main room.

"I think the length is okay," she told Pil-sun, "because people tend to wear their coats short in the country, almost halfway up to their knees. I think we should let out the sleeves, though. Leave the coat here. I'll ask my mother to mend it."

Pil-sun, however, insisted that it would be difficult to alter it at Gyeong-ae's house, since it would require space to spread everything out and tried to take it from Gyeong-ae, promising to bring it back after altering it at home. While they were wrangling, Byeong-hwa showed up.

With his nerves on tenterhooks, Pi-hyeok noticed that Byeong-hwa's face was unusually pale.

After whispering to Gyeong-ae in the main room, Byeong-hwa called in Pi-hyeok. A little later, Gyeong-ae came out and summoned the nanny to the back of the kitchen, where she told the girl to go to the uncle's house in Hyeonjeo-dong and inform the mistress of the house that she should come to Gyeong-ae's house. Gyeong-ae opened the back gate and sent her on her way. They used this gate only once or twice a year, when they would draw water from the well for spring cleanings. When a clinic was built behind the house, the well had been positioned behind its wall, and an alleyway as narrow as a wristband had been created between the clinic's wall and Gyeong-ae's house. Although it was often forgotten, there was one period when Gyeong-ae had put the gate to good use—during the months that she went around in a crazed state after parting with Sang-hun. It seemed like a long, long time ago now.

The nanny looked curiously at her employer. She'd never seen anyone use the back gate and had no idea why her mistress was leading her through it now, but she did as she was told. After the girl reached the avenue, she walked through meandering alleys toward Yeomcheongyo.

If anything happened, the young woman had to be kept out of sight. If the police took her, she'd certainly spill what she'd seen and heard as vividly as if she had drawn them a picture. If she'd gone through the front gate, they might have found themselves in serious trouble, for someone was pacing at the end of the alley, possibly a police inspector. All might be exposed with the simple query: "Who's in your house now?"

A short while later, Pi-hyeok also passed through the back gate. He had left at Byeong-hwa's urging, after having thrown on the overcoat and a pair of rubber shoes. Swaths of white jacket sleeves peeked out of his Korean overcoat. He had no particular destination in mind. With three hundred won as "pocket change," he was free to go where he pleased. But he felt that everyone's eyes were on him, no matter which way he turned.

Holding a parcel larger than the one she had brought, Pil-sun followed Pi-hyeok through the gate. Gyeong-ae and Byeong-hwa had wrapped the remaining two thousand won in a sheet of newspaper, rewrapped it tightly with Pi-hyeok's Western jacket, and gave it to Pil-sun to take to Bacchus. They asked Gyeong-ae's mother to hurry over to Hyeonjeo-dong and ask the nanny to stay there for the time being.

The mother didn't understand exactly what was going on, but she guessed that something must have happened to her visiting nephew. She quickly changed clothes and ventured out as directed but felt uneasy about leaving the two young people behind.

Gyeong-ae and Byeong-hwa were finally able to sit face-to-face. They had staggered everyone's departure by five or ten minutes and were relieved that the whole operation had gone smoothly. Worrying about one thing after another, their eyes darted frequently to the gate.

Gyeong-ae hadn't had time to change; she was still wearing her pajamas and overcoat, and she didn't feel like washing her face. Sitting across from Byeong-hwa, she smoked a cigarette, inhaling deeply. Neither said anything, but both were fraught with anxiety. A thought came to both of them: *We should give the same answers if interrogated.*

"I hope he makes it across the border. If he's caught, we'll be beaten to a pulp," Gyeong-ae considered calmly.

"We'll just have to wait and see. We'd better hurry over to Bacchus. Should I leave through the back gate, too?"

"What are you talking about? Use the front gate. That's our only option, even if it means getting caught."

He knew she was right. If the police noticed that he'd snuck out the back gate, they'd become more suspicious and would soon be in hot pursuit of Pi-hyeok.

"Do you really think the guy waiting down the alley is an inspector? You're probably scared of your own fart at this point."

"A very ladylike way of speaking you have," Byeong-hwa lamented. "Go and have a look yourself if you're so curious."

Gyeong-ae went out, pretending to shut the half-open gate, and caught sight of a Western-suited man leaning against the wall. Hearing the clatter of the gate, he looked her way and their eyes met, but he quickly turned back toward the alley as if he were waiting for someone.

"He's there! He's there! What do we do?"

"Now you're scared!"

"Why should I be scared? What did I do wrong? You're the one that needs to stay calm."

Fear was pressing down on them.

A little later, they heard the gate creak open and the sound of footsteps. "Is anyone home?" a voice called out. Gyeong-ae and Byeong-hwa froze, but as quickly as blood had rushed to their heads, it ebbed, and they regained their composure. Somewhere around the middle gate, they heard the clang of a sword. Again, someone called out, "Is anyone home?"

Gyeong-ae went out to the edge of the veranda.

"Household census. Who is Hong Gyeong-ae?" A policeman, holding an open ledger, approached the veranda, his eyes sweeping the entire house.

"I am."

"And Yi So-sa?"

"She's my mother."

"And Jeong-nye?"

"My daughter."

"Her father is not here?"

"No."

"Where is he?"

"He's dead."

"So you have only three family members?"

"Yes."

The policeman folded the ledger and looked around once again.

"Whose shoes are those?" He pointed to the shabby pair of shoes on the shoe ledge.

"A guest's."

"Open the door, will you?"

Gyeong-ae laughed in his face. "So, you take a look at guests when you take the census?" She flung open the door, revealing Byeong-hwa seated with his hat on. With a sheepish grin, he stood up and came out. The policeman stared at Byeong-hwa and made an excuse. "We're taking the census because of an epidemic," he said and then asked if he could open the door to the other room.

"No one's there. Open it yourself," Gyeong-ae said.

The policeman opened the window facing the yard and studied the interior carefully. There was only an old-fashioned two-tier cabinet and folded beddings, along with a neat display of personal items belonging to Gyeong-ae's mother, including a sewing basket, ironing paddles, and a chamber pot.

The policeman strode over to the kitchen and looked in.

"Isn't your mother home?" he asked.

"She went out to get something in town. So you keep an eye on contagious diseases like the flu in the winter?" She grinned as though they were involved in a delightful game.

"I don't know. I just do what I'm told. Doesn't anyone else live with you? A maid or a servant?" the policeman asked, his face finally brightening for some reason.

"No one."

"You're enjoying your peace and quiet, eh? Sorry to interrupt you," teased the policeman, tossing them another knowing smile before leaving.

The officer had been sent from a nearby police station by an inspector who had been pursuing Byeong-hwa. During his usual evening patrol of the area, the inspector had noticed Byeong-hwa passing the police station late the night before. When he saw Byeong-hwa again early that morning, he followed him, wondering if the den of those dubious characters had moved or if Byeong-hwa himself might have moved to his beat. After taking note that there was no official nameplate, only a makshift paper label bearing the name Yi So-sa posted during the previous national census, he had put the house under surveillance. The man at the end of the alley was not, in fact, an inspector. Gyeong-ae was the one, as it were, who had been frightened by her own fart.

Gyeong-ae and Byeong-hwa assumed as much. By the way a uniformed policeman had been sent in, it didn't look like they were after Pi-hyeok. If they had been, they could have surrounded the house early in the morning and entered while Pi-hyeok was sleeping.

In any event, a sense of danger was upon them. It was lucky for them that the police imagined the two to be lovers, though it meant that Gyeong-ae might have been placed on the watch list. At any time an inspector could burst upon them, and though they didn't talk about it, they were both on pins and needles.

They agreed that Byeong-hwa should leave the house first. Promising to meet Gyeong-ae later at Bacchus, Byeong-hwa went to meet Pil-sun, taking detours and choosing as many secluded paths as possible to determine whether he was being followed.

No one appeared to be trailing him. Still nervous, he looked around one last time before entering the bar.

Pil-sun, sitting in the dark, was clearly glad to see him. Her face was still flushed after her long walk in the biting cold.

"You've been waiting a long time."

"Did anything happen?"

"No. A uniformed bastard came, but it's all right. You can go home now. No, wait a minute." He took off his jacket, rolled it up, and wrapped it in the cloth that had held Pi-hyeok's clothes.

"On your way home, make a little detour to Jongno and find a tailor there and ask him to mend the tear. Even if it sounds rather expensive, leave it there. And get a receipt . . . If anyone's waiting at home and asks you where you've been, tell them you came back from the factory because your stomach hurt or something like that." Byeong-hwa opened the back door.

He was wearing Pi-hyeok's jacket, thinking it would be too dangerous to put it in his room in case the house were searched. He had made arrangements to dispose of his own jacket, for it would be risky if Pil-sun were caught taking it home.

The proprietor's room was quiet. Could she be sleeping this late? He called her to get newspapers to wrap up the overcoat, but there was no response. He knocked on the door when the proprietor entered from the back door with groceries in her hands.

"What's going on? Everyone's arriving so early—" She cut off her greeting and looked around. "Has the young woman left?"

"She's my sister. I asked her to bring this coat here. I'm sorry to bother you this early, but could you please keep it for me?" He handed it to her, with the two thousand won bundled inside.

She took the overcoat from him. "What's in here? A lunchbox? It's so heavy."

"Yes, just leave it in there." Byeong-hwa answered nonchalantly and asked her to warm up some liquor if she happened to have some heated water.

Byeong-hwa had second thoughts about leaving the overcoat there. He wanted to head for Hwagae-dong directly and give it to Won-sam, but he didn't want to take any chances. He decided to stay put and wait for Gyeong-ae.

More than two hours later, Gyeong-ae finally made an appearance. Her mother had returned and had prepared breakfast for her.

"Today things went all right, but let's be careful from now on. Since we have no good reason to meet, we'd better not see each other for some time," Gyeong-ae suggested.

"That sounds reasonable, but do you mean your business with me is over? That's a pretty heartless thing to say, you know. How will we be able to manage if we don't see each other at least once a day?" Byeong-hwa was relaxed again.

Radiant, Gyeong-ai said, "What good will come of it if we meet? To me, you'll look like an inspector and an inspector will look like you—"

Byeong-hwa cut in, "We're the only comrades, the only ones . . ."

Gyeong-ae's reproachful glance melted, and they laughed together. With their present worries behind them, Byeong-hwa felt they had become closer and a warm feeling of affection enveloped him. Gyeong-ae felt the same way.

"Anyway, let's hold discussion meetings in different places just two or three times a day," Byeong-hwa suggested.

"Forget about discussion meetings and you should stop drinking so much. Pi-hyeok expressed concern about that before he left."

"About my drinking?"

"Yes, and about your wasting money on unnecessary things; he was also worried that we'd become too close."

"What did he mean by 'too close'?"

Gyeong-ae studied his face for a long time before looking away. Byeong-hwa, whose youthful spirit remained a stranger to avarice, thought it impossible for greed to interfere with his mission.

"I just remembered something," said Byeong-hwa, who had been pensive for some time. "That Japanese woman, O Jeong-ja, is in prison. You know—the woman the proprietor wanted to know about before Jo left."

"I heard. Did Deok-gi tell you about her?"

"He was concerned about whether you'd become a Red." Byeong-hwa chuckled to himself but then asked, "The proprietor's a Red, isn't she?"

"She turns red after she has three or four drinks, but she rarely drinks."

"But she isn't being watched, is she?"

"No, why?"

"If she is, I can't come here, and you'd better quit working here as soon as possible. We should be very careful right now."

She knew he was right, but she couldn't just stop coming to Bacchus for no reason.

"And you should watch out because you may attract suspicion if you're seen spending money." Gyeong-ae warned him again for good measure, though she didn't think he was like so many other Marxist boys these days, who traded in their shabby clothes for crisp suits as soon as they happened to land some cash.

272

"Please, Gyeong-ae. Speaking of the money, where do you think is the safest place to keep it?"

"Give it to me. I'll take care of it and will report back to you. If you hold on to it, they'd find out about you right away."

"It's in the proprietor's room, in the overcoat. Do as you see fit."

"All right. Let's just leave it there. We can discuss the details later."

Byeong-hwa stayed a little longer, but not having slept well the night before, he couldn't stop yawning. Finally he decided to go home and get some sleep.

A Reply

———

"I pictured Hong Gyeong-ae to be a typical café girl, but she's actually quite modest and kind."

"What do you mean by 'kind'?"

"Well, she's a modern girl, but, at the same time, she's modest and friendly."

Byeong-hwa was glad that Pil-sun spoke highly of Gyeong-ae, but he felt it wasn't enough to praise Gyeong-ae for her friendliness and modesty. He would have preferred it if Pil-sun had lauded Gyeong-ae for her courage in assisting them in their work.

"Who told you that she was a café girl?"

Pil-sun was speechless. "Doesn't she work for that place in Jingogae? Anyway, you're lucky. Why rough it out here when such a nice set-up is waiting for you? Why don't you just go there?" Pil-sun asked him coyly.

"Don't be silly. Come, sit by me for a minute. I have something to tell you." Byeong-hwa waited until Pil-sun, who had been standing with her back to the wall, took a seat next to him and asked quietly, "Aren't you sick and tired of working at the factory?"

"I don't mind."

Byeong-hwa paused. "Lunar New Year's is several days away, so you'll be nineteen soon. Or is it twenty?"

"Why are you asking?" Pil-sun blushed slightly.

"I'm thinking of playing matchmaker. I know someone who's gentle and decent." Byeong-hwa shifted to his usual bantering tone.

"Don't make fun of me. Please don't," said Pil-sun as she stood up.

"I'm sorry. No more wisecracks, I promise. Please sit down."

"You can't start studying again, you can't work at the factory forever, and you're not interested in getting married. So what's your plan? Of course, even if I don't look after you, your parents are there for you, and you must have your own ideas, but . . ."

"What's there to worry about? If life becomes too much, I can just put an end to it. What in the world would I miss, anyway?" Pil-sun often talked this way.

Byeong-hwa imagined that girls her age uttered such sentiments casually, but he felt sorry for her all the same. He remembered the letter he had received from Deok-gi a while ago — *let her enjoy the beautiful dream of youth* — and inadvertently smirked.

Pil-sun asked, "What's so funny?"

"This talk about dying. Do you think it's easy to die? Don't be ridiculous. If you're not careful, you might develop the habit of talking about it all the time. Anyway, I was wondering, do you ever think of resuming your studies?" Although he brought up the matter, he had no intention of relaying Deok-gi's message.

"Do you think I could?" Pil-sun's face lit up in expectation.

"Would you study again if you could?"

"How can I? What about my family?" she asked, adding, "If I didn't have to worry about my family, nothing would prevent me from doing it even though I'm nineteen — or if I were twenty-nine, for that matter!" Pil-sun fantasized that Deok-gi had offered to take care of her family. She felt grateful, of course, but at the same time she wondered why he was so eager to give her such advantages.

"What would you like to study?"

"Anything." In fact, she had no idea what field she'd choose if she were given such an opportunity. Her first priority would be to choose a field that could help her find a good job.

"Then, what'll you do if you have to move far away in order to study?" Byeong-hwa asked after hesitating a little. His expression was resolute, having made up his mind. He studied Pil-sun closely.

"Where? Japan?" Pil-sun thought of Kyoto, where Deok-gi was.

"No, the place I have in mind is not so easy to get into."

Pil-sun's face fell when he mentioned Moscow, the capital of the Red country. "How could I go to such a place? I'm my parents' only child. If I left them behind, how could they manage?" Pil-sun felt like crying as she imagined such a scenario. She needed the warmth of her parents' love, regardless of whether she starved.

She remembered how the dog they had during their better days roamed about restlessly, refusing to eat after she had discovered that one of her litter was missing. The memory brought tears to Pil-sun's eyes. At the mention of Russia, her mind drifted straight to Siberia. She pictured a young woman seen from far away, the size of a dot, trudging through a vast field under the evening sky, her progress negligible. When she recognized herself in that field, her tears spilled over.

"Don't you like the idea? Is it that you can't pry yourself away from your mother's skirt? But what good is it if you're stuck here? Wouldn't it be better for you to study and see the world for a few years? I wouldn't like being confined to this small country. And I'll follow you soon, so you won't be lonely, and there will be nothing to worry about. How about it?"

Byeong-hwa's entreaties fell on deaf ears. This was completely opposed to what Deok-gi had asked his friend to do. She thought it was heartless of Byeong-hwa to encourage her when he was well aware of her family circumstances. But when he said he'd follow her abroad, her eyes opened wide.

Does he mean we'd go to Moscow, just the two of us, to make a private world of our own in addition to work? Does that mean he has special feelings for me? She hadn't considered it, but she was not shocked. Byeong-hwa and Pil-sun got along so well that they were like brother and sister, teacher and student.

Though Byeong-hwa said the contrary in his letter, does he have some other feelings for me? If so, what about his relationship with Hong Gyeong-ae? And why doesn't he bring up Deok-gi's offer to pay for my education, even in passing? Does Byeong-hwa mean for me to follow Pi-hyeok? Does he expect me to assist Pi-hyeok in his work? Didn't Byeong-hwa just say there was a candidate for my husband and talk about playing matchmaker? Is he thinking that I'd have the chance to study and to marry him, too, if I followed Pi-hyeok?

Pil-sun's imaginings had no end.

"If I had siblings, I'd be willing to go far away, but what would my father and mother do without me?" Pil-sun lamented.

"What if your parents gave you permission?"

"They never would, and I wouldn't want to study if I had to go to such lengths. If you need a woman like me, why don't you send Hong Gyeong-ae? I'm so ignorant that even if I went there, I wouldn't be of any use — studying or working."

Carrying the heavy burden of caring for her parents, Pil-sun couldn't even conceive of a vagabond life. Nor did she dream of leading a luxurious life as the daughter-in-law of a rich family. She had no ambition except to make money to take care of her parents and to get married if the opportunity arose. She saw study only as a steppingstone to a better-paying job. However influenced she was by her father and Byeong-hwa, she had no desire to leave her family behind to carry out some mission or other, and she didn't intend to sacrifice the possibility of marriage or happiness.

"You're right. It would be good for Gyeong-ae to go. Either she would follow you first or I would. How about we all leave the country and live in peace and quiet?"

His explanation made Pil-sun's mind spin again. He had no intention of going abroad with her alone. Rather, it sounded as if he had only work in mind.

Byeong-hwa, however, had no serious plans. One of the tasks Pi-hyeok had entrusted him with was the selection of three or four male and female students to send abroad. Though Byeong-hwa was aware of Pil-sun's circumstances, he had sounded her out because she seemed so eager to study. He thought she'd jump at the chance. But, sadly, it seemed that she was no different from other ordinary women who were focused on their families. He had said Gyeong-ae would go but hadn't yet raised the subject with her; with a child, it wouldn't be an easy matter for her. He knew of no other candidates among his female acquaintances. Byeong-hwa wanted to complete his duties in Korea and leave himself, but he needed to find others to send first. All things being equal, he would have preferred to send a woman he knew well, like Pil-sun or Gyeong-ae.

Byeong-hwa laughed and said, "You want to study, but you want to do it in a place like Japan, where you can live comfortably, and have someone pay your tuition. I doubt you'll find an opportunity perfect enough to suit your taste."

Pil-sun thought he was mocking her. Offended, her face turned red, but she didn't reply.

Byeong-hwa's rebellious spirit drove him to deliver another jab: "To find such an opportunity, you might as well consider becoming the concubine of a rich old man. How else in today's world . . ."

Now Pil-sun was angry. How low of him if perhaps he hadn't mentioned Deok-gi out of jealousy.

"Who says I'd sell my body for the sake of an education?" Pil-sun managed to say, as she fought down her tears.

"Calm down. I just meant that that's what the world is like these days. Education is considered a prerequisite for a good marriage—merely an adornment that makes women more attractive. That is how far the value of education has degenerated. It's not simply a means to land a good job. Lots of men are eager to marry female students, some even abandon their wives and children, don't they?"

"Some may, but others may not." Her contentiousness rose to meet his.

"Tell me who's not like that. Who? Would you be willing to study if such a person encouraged you?"

Pil-sun didn't respond. Her silence spoke for her.

"Deok-gi says he'd like to give you an education, but you should be wary of accepting favors from people. You are expected to give back as much as you get. How would you return such a favor? How many people in the world don't expect anything in return?"

He made sense.

"If he were single, I wouldn't oppose it, but he has a wife and a child. And he's young."

Pil-sun bowed her head.

Byeong-hwa stopped talking and let Pil-sun take her leave. He lounged on the floor for a while before shifting to his desk, intending to write a reply to Deok-gi's letter.

He opened the drawer and spotted the letter from Deok-gi that he had torn in half. Before he had gone to see Pi-hyeok, he had ripped up all his letters in case something happened to him. This one, however, he had wanted to respond to before getting rid of it.

Had Pil-sun read it? Reprimanding himself for having put it in such a noticeable place, he scanned the letter as he reassembled the torn halves. The pages of one half were in the correct order, but the sequence in the other half was wrong.

"She read it," Byeong-hwa muttered to himself.

Tedious days are dragging like thread spun from a silkworm. To talk about tedious days at my age—it's as if my life were not worth living and deserved to be thrown into the wastebasket, but will I ever be able to lead a disciplined life on a daily basis? I suppose prisoners live with a sense of tension while they await their release, so their lives must be much more worthwhile than mine, which goes on only because I can't bring myself to end it. To me, time and life seem inessential. What is there to do? Among Korean youth today, am I the only one who doesn't know what to do with his time and life? Not that it would comfort me to know that I'm not the only one . . .

Since Pi-hyeok's departure, Byeong-hwa's nerves had become frayed. He was more cautious when he went out, always looking over his shoulder, imagining that dark shadows were trailing him. Now that he was involved in a full-fledged mission, he was afraid that the police might even inspect his correspondence. With this fear in mind, he began composing his letter.

I write these letters because I don't have much to do. I write them to express my opinions, but I might as well stop writing. It's not that I've become busy, but what's the use when all is said and done? You and I are living in the same era, but sooner or later you will succumb to the values of the times, which your grandfather will hand down to you along with his fortune. You will hang onto these values and settle down with them. Wait until you get the key to his safe, until you get to manage his money. Now, you may think you'll get to ride the wave of the next generation, but you can't do that with a heavy safe clutched in your arms, so what else can you do but to hold onto the values of an earlier time as tightly as you can? You know that the unrealistic idea of holding onto a moribund epoch is not only conservative, but is also like a mantis trying to block the advance of a carriage with its arms open wide. Only that path will be open to you. I know you will turn a deaf ear to my sermons, so what's the use of toying with old sayings? I am disappointed in Pil-sun, whom I have cultivated for several years, but I'm afraid she will end up stagnating. Women are by nature conservative, so we can't expect them to be pioneers. Age and character may play a role, too, but when I think that I can't even coax Pil-sun to come along with me, what's the use of talking to you, even with a plea of a million words? Is it because I'm incompetent? Is it fundamentally wrong to preach or try to sway someone to become like me? You be the judge, but I still believe that a chicken that wanders will voluntarily return to its perch when the time comes. By that I mean that I believe I will end up meeting you and Pil-sun again some day, even though you two may make detours.

As you wished, Pil-sun is living the so-called dream of youth, but what is regrettable is that she has read your letter. This is why I say we should stop writing these silly notes. It is clear that your letters and your cheap sympathy encouraged her to hang onto the values of your epoch when she was actually coming toward mine. Now that things have turned out this way and though it is not unreasonable for someone her age, I wash my hands of the matter. You might as well take over as far as Pil-sun is concerned. Don't put me between you—do as you please, as much as your resources permit. But I believe that after she wakes up from her dream and returns to reality, she will seek me out again. As for you, you are likely to inherit soon all the customs and family rules maintained by your grandfather, along with his assets. You only desire land deeds, but a day will come when you will regard these deeds as insignificant as your family rules and manners. I know very well that you are conscientious and sensitive to changing times.

As a Christian, your father is a heretic in your grandfather's eyes, but he will be a heretic to you in terms of the zeitgeist. It would be preferable to leave him to his drink and in the lap of a nineteenth-century doll, but make sure he doesn't take opium.

And Hong Gyeong-ae? This woman is more likely to end up being mine than your father's, but she's a doll of the twentieth century, not the nineteenth. That's the extent to which I may love her. Enough for now. I have nothing more to write, and besides, I have no desire to write anymore. This has turned out to be a load of nonsense. But if I say something to the point, I may not be able to live out my share of life.

Telegrams

———

The old man's condition continued to grow worse, though at a barely perceptible rate, prompting Secretary Ji, Chang-hun, and Clerk Choe to stay in the main room deep into the night. As his health deteriorated, the old man didn't want to see his son, and for the sake of formality, Sang-hun came in the morning and left at night only to go to sleep, but he was reduced to loitering in the outer quarters.

The old man had his reasons for behaving this way. Believing that his final moments were drawing near, he ordered people to write letters and telegrams to Deok-gi, asking him to come home. As there was no reply, the old man was angry at his grandson, but still he awaited his arrival every morning and night around the time the train arrived.

Unaware of the old man's requests, Sang-hun volunteered a suggestion. "Your condition is not that grave, and Deok-gi has only several days remaining before his graduation exams. Why don't you let him stay there?" Naturally, he wanted to comfort his father, who seemed frightened by his condition, but, at the same time, he truly believed there was no need to bring Deok-gi home. His father's wrath erupted on the spot. He berated Sang-hun, complaining that Deok-gi hadn't replied to his grandfather's telegrams and letters because Sang-hun had discouraged him from coming home.

The old man wanted Deok-gi home as soon as possible mainly because he was anxious to settle the matter of his grandson's inheritance in his presence. Although he didn't intend to leave his son out in the cold, he preferred to deliver his final words to his grandson. He didn't believe he'd die from his illness, but there was no knowing when the end would come. Even if he had to repeat the performance after his recovery, he wanted to settle the matter, at least for now. He surmised that Sang-hun was preventing Deok-gi's arrival and raised hell, announcing that he was going to declare Sang-hun legally incompetent. Sang-hun had no inkling of his father's intentions. He offered to send a letter or a telegram, but Chang-hun advised against it strongly, insisting that three telegrams had already been sent. Sang-hun imagined his son might have left by now and anticipated his arrival. Several days passed, however, and still no news came. Chang-hun, impatient by now, composed a telegram in front of the old man and went out to send it personally. Again, no reply.

"Mother, I don't understand. Could he be sick? Is he on his way home? He would reply one way or another. Should we send another telegram?" Deok-gi's wife asked her mother-in-law. Deok-gi's mother visited every day now and sometimes stayed overnight, though she was permitted in the main room only once each day. Her father-in-law's anger had not abated, and he, in part, blamed her and his granddaughter-in-law for Deok-gi's failure to return home.

"I wonder, too," said the mother-in-law. "Nobody could be intercepting the telegrams, could they?"

"Who knows? How do we know what sly tricks they have up their sleeves?"

When Deok-hui came home from school, the two women asked her to go out and send a telegram to Kyoto.

A telegram saying that Deok-gi would leave Kyoto arrived at eleven that night. Since the last telegram had been sent over in Deok-hui's name, the reply in Japanese was addressed to her. The old man didn't know Japanese, but he could read katakana. He held the telegram his granddaughter-in-law had brought him, his face bright with relief. "Why didn't he . . ." He studied the address and the name a long time before he asked, "Who is this addressed to?"

"To his sister."

"His sister? Deok-hui?" The old man hadn't expected this. Deok-gi had the habit of addressing correspondence sent to the house to the "residence of Jo Deok-gi" or to the attention of his baby son.

"His sister sent a telegram earlier today," offered Deok-gi's wife.

"Why?" The old man's sunken eyes bulged.

The Suwon woman, sitting next to the old man, came forward to offer her opinion. "He didn't take our messages seriously, but he managed to get off his ass as soon as he got his sister's telegram."

"Who told Deok-hui to send a telegram?" The grandfather's tone revealed his displeasure.

"I was so frustrated that I told her to try reaching him one more time," said Deok-gi's wife.

"I'm glad to hear he's coming, but why did he think of coming only when he got a telegram sent by his sister?"

There was a simple explanation, but in the old man's eyes it was not so simple.

"Did we use the wrong address? Did he move to a new boardinghouse?"

"No. He is still at the same place."

"Then what was the matter? He couldn't have gone anywhere because he was busy with exams. Did you tell him to come home only when he hears from you?" The old man was losing his temper.

"That's not possible," Deok-gi's wife said, offering her opinion. "Other telegrams must not have reached him because of a wrong address or something."

This sounded plausible, but the old man was not willing to brush off the matter. "If the telegrams didn't arrive, they should have been returned, right? Oh, never mind. We'll find out when he gets here."

Deok-gi's mother and wife were more eager to get to the bottom of the matter than the old man was.

The following evening, Deok-gi sent a telegram from Busan. Though he had ignored previous summons, he now inquired about his grandfather's condition. The old man was pleased that his grandson sounded quite anxious.

Deok-gi arrived at daybreak.

Chang-hun and Secretary Chi went to the train station to meet him. Deok-gi was relieved to learn that his grandfather's condition was stable.

When Chang-hun heard that Deok-gi hadn't received any telegrams except for Deok-hui's the day before, he bristled and assumed that Deok-gi was lying.

Deok-gi said, "That's very strange, but how would I know what happened? It's probably because you wrote the address in your clumsy Japanese." He laughed it off, suspecting nothing.

In a taxi on the way home, Chang-hun said, "Look, if your grandfather asks, simply tell him you did get the telegrams. He'll scold us for being unable to do something as simple as send a wire. Tell him that you happened to read the telegrams after a school trip, and you were about to leave when you received Deok-hui's. Or something like that. You wouldn't believe the abuse we've taken because of all this . . ."

"Don't worry, and thank you for your efforts. It's good to hear that he's not any worse off, so we shouldn't squander this opportunity to find good medicine for him." Deok-gi was displeased that Chang-hun was harping about the telegrams instead of talking about his grandfather's illness.

As Deok-gi entered the sickroom, his grandfather wished to sit up. He was supported from the back and the front while receiving his grandson's bow. His back had gotten a little better, and he could move a bit. It was the superstition that only the dead receive bows lying down that had forced him to sit up. He shuddered whenever he heard the word *dead*, as if the messenger of death were standing in front of him.

A smile danced across the old man's mouth, but his bleary sunken eyes contained anger and suspicion.

"If you're a human being . . . how could you not . . . ?" The old man had to catch his breath three or four times to utter this phrase. By the time he could lie down again, he looked exhausted.

Deok-gi was happy to see that his grandfather's back was better and that he could sit up, but he had to avert his eyes from his grandfather's face as the old man lay down. He wondered how his grandfather's face, which used to glow with health, could have changed so much in less than a month. He looked seriously ill. The unhealthy color permeated his skin, and his face was sallow with thick, dark patches here and there. He looked as if he had been devastated after several years of internal ailments.

"You didn't even write a letter when we made such a racket, sending off one telegram after another. Were you dead? Or didn't you have thirty jeon?" Those listening to him were in agony, watching the old man pant as he tried to push his words out through gurgling phlegm.

"I didn't get the telegrams."

"What do you mean? Then how did you find the money to come home?"

"I borrowed it from my landlord." Deok-gi was about to continue, but he switched his story after noticing Chang-hun's frantic eye signals.

"I had been away skiing, but when I got back, I received all the telegrams together and left again at once." Deok-gi had been on the verge of telling the truth, for he didn't like Chang-hun and didn't want to deceive his grandfather with poor excuses. Prompted by Chang-hun's eyes, though, he changed his mind, thinking his grandfather would be worse off if his agitation increased.

"What is skiing?"

"It is sliding on the ice from the top of a mountain."

"Sliding on the ice on a mountain? Not in a river?"

"In Japan, it's on mountains."

"Japan or Korea, sliding on the ice must be the same. Stop it. I don't want to listen to such bare lies."

"So you didn't take exams but went sliding on the ice instead?" Chang-hun said provocatively, and the Suwon woman concurred with a sneer.

They were glad to see that the grandfather regarded Deok-gi's excuses as lies. Deok-gi wanted to pour out the truth, regardless of what would ensue. Hadn't he made up the story to help Chang-hun? How, then, could Chang-hun make such tactless remarks instead of supporting him? He refrained from lashing out, though, thinking it better not to make a scene.

"So what did you do with the money sent with the telegram?"

"I didn't get it." He could have made up a story, like he gave it to the landlord because he thought it was part of the money intended for his studies abroad, but soon asked the landlord to return some of it. But now he stuck to the truth, for he was annoyed.

"Why was that? Did you really send it?" the grandfather asked Chang-hun.

"Of course. I have the receipt. I forgot to give it to you, sir." Chang-hun took out his wallet and rummaged through it for a good while. "I must have left it at home. I couldn't send the money myself, so I asked my eldest to take care of it. Where else could it have gone if we have the receipt?"

"Then bring it to me later today." The old man wasn't satisfied unless he supervised everything himself. Already frustrated about having to stay in bed this long, he felt worse when he realized everything was going wrong.

"As long as you have a receipt, you can get the money back later. We'll be able to find out what went wrong," said Deok-gi, hoping to calm his grandfather.

The old man was even more irritated now; Deok-gi seemed to be hiding something. The grandfather managed to contain his anger, though, for Deok-gi was his beloved grandson, and he had come a long way.

Ring of Keys

———

Deok-gi stayed home all day with a splitting headache. Something strange was in the air. He felt infected by the mood, which was rife with jealousy and suspicion. Agitation was visible on everyone's face. His family had never exchanged frank opinions or laughed together and had never carried on conversations wearing placid expressions; yet this menacing pressure hanging heavily in the house was new. There's a saying that crows caw on the eve of someone's death. Was it because the dark spirit of death had risen up—was his grandfather really going to die? Was everyone gloomy because the family elder was in such bad shape? That couldn't be the case, for no loyal wife or daughters-in-law could be found in attendance. A huge storm must have rolled in while he was away. Was it because he had taken so long to come home? If so, Chang-hun was at fault. Why didn't the telegrams, allegedly sent on three occasions, reach him? Where had the money gone?

According to Deok-gi's wife, a group of conspirators huddled in the main room or in the outer quarters day and night, whispering among themselves. In her opinion, they were up to something, and trouble was brewing.

This sinister air wasn't confined to the main room alone. It seemed to emanate from wherever several men and women passed by, in the outer quarters and in the backyard. Maybe it was a whiff of copper coins, mixed with the scent of desire—an odor turning sour and fetid. What did they intend to do with the money?

The storm that seemed to be rising was the kind that blew through any house when the master who holds the keys is taking his last breaths. In this house it might be rising from behind the scenes, like a tendril of smoke from a fire started in dry weeds. Better keep his wits about him, Deok-gi thought.

The Suwon woman's behavior grew especially odd. Deok-gi watched her closely; she sat next to the old man all day, and she spoke to no one in Deok-gi's family. If Deok-gi's mother was the only one she didn't talk to, it wouldn't have seemed strange. In the past, she had been nice to Deok-gi, if only superficially, but now she was deaf to his questions. Only when he repeated his questions a few times did she reluctantly answer him. Even more unpleasant was the fact that she made it abundantly clear that she didn't like Deok-gi coming to the main room. When no one was around during the daytime or evening, Deok-gi would step briefly into the main room thinking his grandfather might like company or with something to tell his grandfather. On such occasions, the Suwon woman would wince. If she couldn't stand the sight of Deok-gi, she could have left the room, but she remained, cupping her chin with her hands. When she noticed that Deok-gi entered the room while she was outside, she dashed in from the veranda or the yard. His grandfather lay helpless, slowly blinking his frightfully sunken eyes. Deok-gi grew miserable, but he didn't dare show it or speak to the Suwon woman. Wasn't he the pillar of the household now? He tried to placate everyone, for they all seemed poised to lose their temper at the slightest provocation.

Deok-gi couldn't understand why those in the outer quarters frequently flocked into the main room. He didn't mind Secretary Ji—who was almost a member of the family and who prepared medicine for the old man with his own hands—but Clerk Choe and Chang-hun, on the other hand, were quite bothersome. At times, uncles—both older and younger brothers in the clan—gathered in the name of comforting the old man. They talked boisterously among themselves as if they were visiting a festive house, and the women in the inner quarters bustled around cooking lunch and keeping busy. Deok-gi's head ached so much from the racket they made as they swept into the sickroom in droves, as if they were conducting a clan conference, that his hair might have fallen out. He might not have minded so much if they had stayed in the outer quarters, but despite his irritation, he couldn't bring himself to object because his grandfather seemed to enjoy such lively visits.

These visitors spoke either in booming voices or whispered among themselves, as if they were helping out a great deal, though it was impossible to fathom what they really had in mind. No one took charge of the situation or gave intelligent instructions on the use of medicine. At such moments, Deok-gi wished that his father would exercise some authority and establish a somber tone in the house, but nothing could be done about it, and Deok-gi was too young to exercise any authority himself. On the rare occasions he tried to restore some order, visitors seemed to wonder what business a student had in such matters and would take control of the situation themselves.

"Uncle, did you bring the receipt?" Deok-gi pressured Chang-hun about the money transfer upon entering the main room, where Chang-hun was visiting after dinner. Deok-gi thought it odd that none of the three telegrams had reached him and wondered if the money had been embezzled somewhere along the way.

"Yes. I was waiting for my son Mun-gi to see whether he had made a mistake when he sent it, but he hasn't come home yet." Chang-hun took out his wallet slowly, eyes glazed over, and produced a neatly folded piece of orange-colored paper with letters printed on it.

Deok-gi unfolded it and laughed out loud.

"What's the matter?"

"This is the money order itself. You need to send it so the recipient can claim the money."

"Do you mean that he sent the receipt instead?"

"Possibly. But you sent a telegraphic transfer, didn't you? This is a postal money order."

"Postal money order? What's a postal money order?"

"A postal money order is what you enclose in a letter."

"Really?" Chang-hun's eyes widened as if he'd never heard of such a thing. "What a stupid boy! How could he be so backward?"

"Give . . . give me." The grandfather, who had been listening to the conversation, stretched out his hand and scolded Chang-hun. "Why, *eguegu*, why did you, *eguegu*, make the fool do it? Forget that fool, *eguegu*, but . . . you yourself still don't know what's what."

"Grandfather, you don't need to worry about the money because it's here. Please go to sleep. You're short of breath." Deok-gi found it torturous to listen to his grandfather's groans.

"I gave my son the money and the envelope from one of your letters," Chang-hun explained. "I told him to wire the money to the address on that envelope. It's clear he thought all money transfers were the same. He must have detached the receipt and put it in an envelope." Chang-hun laughed.

The old man would have given him a hard time if he hadn't been so sick. Without another word, he tossed the money order to Deok-gi and closed his eyes.

Seeing how debilitated his grandfather was, Deok-gi didn't have the heart to talk about such trifling matters. He silently put the money order in his pocket, signaled with his eyes for Chang-hun to leave the room, and then left quietly himself. At ten o'clock that evening, the doctor returned. He said the old man was neither better nor worse. His fever was due to the lack of good nutrition and the excitement of the day. Before the doctor left, he told them to let the old man sleep through the night.

The next morning, Mun-gi came. He dutifully visited the sick man in the main room, and when he noticed Deok-gi watching him from his room, he said, "My father says I made a mistake when I sent you money. The

Japanese guy made out a money order, and I didn't know what to do with it. I was in a hurry. I bought an envelope at the post office and sent it via registered mail." He handed over a receipt for the letter and smiled sheepishly.

"Doesn't matter," said Deok-gi mildly. Nevertheless, he didn't believe Mun-gi. Who—even a real country bumpkin—could possibly make such a stupid mistake?

Deok-gi remembered his grandfather's words, "Your father will be relieved when I die. To keep you from coming home, I think he must have stopped the telegrams from being sent."

Deok-gi didn't think his father would do anything like that, but now he began to wonder. It was possible that Chang-hun and Clerk Choe were plotting something, having latched on to his father.

But it was hard to accept that the relationship between Chang-hun and his father could have improved so quickly. It was also unreasonable to think that the Suwon woman had become an ally of his father's. Chances were, however, that she was responsible for devising one scheme or another.

"Whatever he does, I won't let him starve, but I won't give him more than that."

Deok-gi tried to calm him. "Why do you say such things? What are assets, anyway? You shouldn't worry while you're sick—it will just make you tired and nervous. Besides, you're going to get better soon."

The grandfather had banished even the Suwon woman from the room for this visit with Deok-gi. While they were alone, he asked his grandson to open a small safe behind his bedding and handed him a ring of keys. "If only you are right! But even if I get better, I'll be no better than a living corpse. Take these keys to the safe. I'm not going to listen to anyone. I called you home so urgently so that I could entrust these keys to you. Now that I've handed them over, I can close my eyes in peace. But don't open the safe as long as I'm alive. In the safe is your seal, but you mustn't use it until I'm gone. Take these keys, and if, by Heaven's will, I get better, return them to me."

"Why should I take them now? I should go back to school as soon as you get better, Grandfather. And how can I take these keys when my father is alive and well?" The propriety of according due respect to one's father notwithstanding, Deok-gi was in no position to give up his studies and install himself as the household's manager.

"Leaving again? No. You can't go even if I get better. Don't be silly and do as I tell you." The grandfather was adamant.

"How can I cut my studies short? I graduate in less than a month."

"What is more important, your studies or your family? It might be different if you weren't needed here, but though you're young, bear in mind what'll happen to this household as soon as I'm dead. Give up everything — graduation and whatever — and take the keys. I'm entrusting them and the ancestral shrine to you. The destiny of your life and the fortune of this family depend on those keys. You must hold onto them and safeguard the ancestral shrine. Apart from these two things, nothing is important, not my dying words, nothing else. I've educated you until now so that you can respect and carry on these two vital things. If you continue studying and refuse them, it's like having a funeral without a corpse. You've studied enough; you can function without shame, even in today's society, can't you?" This long speech exhausted him. His forehead broke out in a cold sweat, and he was short of breath, his chest heaving as he gasped for air.

"Why don't you entrust the household affairs to my father for now?" Deok-gi suggested once again.

"Stop that nonsense! If you don't like it, give me the keys. Do you think I can entrust them to no one else? I don't care if you choose to go from door to door begging for food." Despite his rage, the grandfather did not show any sign of reclaiming the keys.

Deok-gi didn't want to go against the wishes of his sick grandfather. He sat with his head bowed, determined to follow his grandfather's instructions for the moment, for he could do otherwise later. With her skirts rustling, the Suwon woman entered, her face red. She had been squatting below the window, straining to hear every word that escaped from the room.

When Deok-gi saw her, he quickly gathered up the keys lying in front of him and stood up.

With a murderous look on her face, the Suwon woman deterred Deok-gi from leaving. "Please stay for a minute."

She had intended to take the keys before she made her case but now that was impossible. If the old man had been much sicker and less conscious, or if Deok-gi had returned home after his grandfather had died and the household was in mourning, she could have gotten her hands on the keys. But Deok-gi had come. Did he come home too soon or had they acted too slowly? In any event, their scheme had failed.

As she suppressed her fury, her face turned pale, almost taking on a blue hue. "I don't care who takes charge of this household. But from what you said right now, you seem to have handed over management of the household to him. Given the way things are now, tell me what I should do."

Lying with his mouth agape and his chest in spasms, the old man managed to ask, "What do you want me to do for you?"

"If you told me to leave this house, I'd go without a murmur. I'm reluctant to say this, but no one knows what'll happen to you tomorrow. If you die before me, the family wouldn't let me stay a minute longer in this house. If I didn't have a child, I wouldn't mind dying with you. But who can I trust and what can I expect in this wretched world? Shouldn't you give consideration to my situation? What am I supposed to do?" She pleaded tearfully.

"Aren't you going too far?" Deok-gi rebuked her.

"Am I wrong? Think! Once your grandfather dies, who in this house will pay attention to me?" Wiping her tears, the Suwon woman spoke in a nasal voice, sniffling.

Deok-gi understood how she felt but wondered how she could shed tears on cue. She was not pretending to cry, however—she was shedding real tears, infuriated that the scheme had gone awry.

"Is my grandfather dying now? Am I taking over this household? You shouldn't say such things," Deok-gi said in a soothing tone.

"Stop talking nonsense," Deok-gi's grandfather scolded them gently. "Go away. What right do you have to prattle on so?" He was exhausted and felt bad for her.

"I know you think I was eavesdropping, but haven't you just entrusted household affairs to this young man? Shouldn't you tell me what's going to happen to me in his presence? In fact, shouldn't you summon everyone in the house and tell them?"

Deok-gi said, "Please calm down. Why are you worrying? Is my grandfather dying now? Even if he—" He couldn't bring himself to talk about death within earshot of his grandfather. Deok-gi said quietly, "My grandfather will make sure that you're taken care of. As for my father and myself, what reason would we have to shortchange you? Isn't it obvious whichever way you look at it? You should be able to understand that much—you've known us long enough."

"If I speak because I'm greedy, let me be struck by lightning right here; if I speak out of avarice, I am not my mother's daughter." She gestured to her sleeping daughter near the foot of the grandfather's bedding and said, "With her, I see only darkness in the future. That's why I'm acting this way."

The old man squirmed and opened his eyes, as if he had just managed to raise himself from a deep sleep into which he was slipping. Shifting his hollow eyes between Deok-gi and the Suwon woman, he said, "Are you still talking nonsense? Stop and go to bed now," he muttered weakly as if talking in his sleep. Then he opened his eyes again and continued speaking with all the strength he had. "Don't worry. I've already made preparations. I was concerned that I'd have to witness this scene while I was alive. I've divided my property fairly, like cutting cloth according to chalked lines. It's too late to argue about it now. Nothing can be done, even if my own father came back from the grave. You can't make a piece of cloth bigger or smaller when it's already cut to size. If any of you try to persuade me otherwise, I'm going to burn all the deeds before I die."

The old man heaved a long sigh. After Deok-gi left the room, the Suwon woman's shrill, endless whining filtered out of the room. She continued to plead with her husband, who was only the shell of a man; no one, as she herself put it, knew what would become of him the next day. She was tormenting a man on the threshold of death.

The Suwon woman would have liked it if she got half his estate. Deok-gi couldn't fathom how she could plead with her husband—regardless of whether she had any genuine affection for him—when he was struggling to breathe. She pleaded more fiercely than a debt collector or a bargain hunter. It had been said that good-for-nothing sons would frequently quarrel greedily among themselves, ignoring their dying father in his last days. Deok-gi wanted to run over to the main room and drag the Suwon woman out, but he suppressed the urge and left the house, asking his wife to keep an eye on the situation. It was his first venture outside since his arrival two days earlier.

A Changed Byeong-hwa

It had been dark for some time, but it was still early evening. The last day of the lunar year was drawing near. In this affluent neighborhood, the sound of rice being pounded for New Year's rice cakes drifted out here and there, and people in the streets appeared to be excited about the imminent festivities. Coming out of the dreary house, where no rice cakes were being beaten, as if New Year's had been forgotten, the outside world struck Deok-gi as utterly foreign. As soon as he had arrived in Seoul, he'd thought of sending Byeong-hwa a postcard but hadn't gotten around to it. Deok-gi might not have time for a leisurely chat even if Byeong-hwa were to pay his chaotic house a visit. Deok-gi would visit him when he had some spare time. As he boarded a streetcar, he wondered whether he should go outside Saemun or to Bacchus to look for Gyeong-ae.

When the streetcar reached the Bank of Korea, the Keijo post office came into view. Behind its windows, people moved around in the brightly lit room. After passengers streamed in and the car was about to move, he made his way to the door and got out.

Deok-gi looked up at the post office clock. It was only a few minutes past eight. He entered, resolved to find out whether Chang-hun had really sent those telegrams. The clerks he asked were a bit annoyed by his request, but since there weren't many customers, they rifled through their records of telegrams sent to Kyoto the preceding week. As he had guessed, the only telegram sent from the Keijo post office was Deok-hui's.

Deok-gi was determined to confront Chang-hun the next day; he would pressure him relentlessly as soon as he got hold of him. His grandfather suspected Deok-gi's father, but here was proof that Chang-hun was responsible and that Clerk Choe had urged the Suwon woman to join forces with them. Deok-gi felt for his wrongly accused father. He imagined him skirting around the family like an unwelcome visitor, without an inkling of what was going on. His grandfather must not pass away without learning the truth. Although Deok-gi had missed his exams, it was crucial that he had come to Seoul. His grandfather's actions were correct, though he didn't know how much was set aside for his father or the Suwon woman. He felt bad about his grandfather's refusal to bequeath everything to his father. But given how his father was behaving these days, it was a relief that Deok-gi could take charge of the family fortune. He would make sure that his father wouldn't lack for money.

Deok-gi didn't have enough time to go all the way outside Saemun to meet Byeong-hwa, for he wanted to return home by ten o'clock when the doctor was due. So instead, he made his way to the main avenue to stop by Bacchus.

Gyeong-ae was nowhere to be found. A new girl was there, who at first glance looked Japanese. The proprietor's face brightened at the sight of Deok-gi, and she asked him to come to the back room.

"Ai-san? She's rather unpredictable these days, but I expect she'll be here soon." The proprietor smiled in a friendly manner. Deok-gi was confused by her attitude, but he assumed she was being nice to him because he had found out about O Jeong-ja for her. According to the proprietor, Gyeong-ae didn't stick around the bar these days and went out frequently. The proprietor said Byeong-hwa came to the bar from time to time but not very often.

Deok-gi talked about O Jeong-ja and listened to what she had to say about O's past, while warming himself at the stove.

Gyeong-ae arrived before long. "Look who's here! When did you arrive in

Seoul?" Although she greeted him warmly, she didn't seem to be particularly glad to see him.

Gyeong-ae knew that Deok-gi wouldn't meddle in Byeong-hwa's work. Neither would he watch their actions closely, even if she became intimate with Byeong-hwa. Unlike last time, however, it would be rather disconcerting if Deok-gi hung around, now that Sang-hun was pursuing her.

Gyeong-ae was surprised to learn that Deok-gi's grandfather was so ill. *So that's why Sang-hun hasn't been around for some time.* She chortled to herself. *Well, I may have to let my hair down in mourning, then.*

Deok-gi changed the subject, trying to find out what was going on. "I'd like to see Byeong-hwa. Do you think he'll come tonight?"

"He's not very available these days. I wonder if he managed to get a nice haircut." Gyeong-ae actually had just seen Byeong-hwa.

"By the way, how's the child? How is she doing?"

"She's all right now."

Deok-gi's mind returned to his grandfather's safe. Though a Jo, Gyeong-ae's child wouldn't have a penny to her name; in comparison, the Suwon woman's child was much luckier. But regardless of what was in the safe, no one could be sure what would become of these girls.

The woman Deok-gi noticed when he arrived came over and whispered something in Gyeong-ae's ear. Cocking her head, Gyeong-ae exclaimed, "That's great! She says your friend has just arrived." She asked Deok-gi to go out first and greet Byeong-hwa.

Gyeong-ae was puzzled. Why did Byeong-hwa come when they had parted only minutes before? She smiled to herself, thinking that he must be in the mood for a drink. She couldn't blame him. He had grown so attached to her recently, like a toddler whose mother had just given birth to a new baby. She would have liked it if he could restrain himself a little. Boisterous greetings in the hall reached Gyeong-ae's ears.

"Hey!"

"Hey, you look the same!"

"I knew you'd be here." Byeong-hwa, in fact, had no idea that Deok-gi would be there.

"How did you know I was back? Did you stop by my house?"

"Look at my ears. Aren't they big enough to hear everything? But tell me, is your grandfather seriously ill?"

"It's not too serious, but I came home after I read your letter. What nonsense you wrote! You sounded as if you didn't want to see me ever again. I really shouldn't have made an effort to see you." Deok-gi avoided Pil-sun's name.

Byeong-hwa let out a snort but seemed to be preoccupied with something.

"What's going on? Did something good happen to you?"

"Why?" asked Byeong-hwa, smoothing down his hair.

"Your hair is neat, you're wearing a suit I haven't seen before, and it looks as if you might have even used some face cream!"

"Yes, I've used some all right. But what do you mean by a suit you've never seen? Are you implying that I bought it at a secondhand store?"

"Where did you get the money for the face cream?"

"Come on, why would anyone ask something like that?"

"Excuse me, Mr. Handsome!" he said to his friend in Japanese but then switched back to Korean. "I wish I had time to raise a toast to you, but I'd better go home now. I'm sorry I can't stay longer." Deok-gi made a motion to leave, without even having sat down. Although Byeong-hwa had no intention of holding him back, he urged him to linger for a minute.

Deok-gi had the feeling that Byeong-hwa had drifted far away from him, both in his feelings and in his attitude toward him. Deok-gi felt awkward, like a person meeting a friend for the first time in decades, one with whom he had studied under the same teacher. *What has happened?* Deok-gi had never seen Byeong-hwa so confident, probably because he now had a little money in his pocket, but his distant, distracted manner was inexplicable. The Byeong-hwa he had known was basically calm despite his constant grumbling. When a penniless person suddenly gets hold of some money, he frequently will take on an aloof pose, more than most affluent people. Still, this was not what Deok-gi sensed in Byeong-hwa. He seemed agitated. Gyeong-ae came out and didn't offer so much as a greeting to Byeong-hwa. A moment later, however, Deok-gi caught them exchanging glances. He sensed a difference here, too. Byeong-hwa's restlessness could be explained by his being in love, but was the money coming from Gyeong-ae? Deok-gi was tempted to attribute everything to Byeong-hwa's falling in love with Gyeong-ae.

If this were true, Deok-gi would be in an absurd situation. It was one thing to read about it in Kyoto in a joking letter and quite another to witness it. It was obvious that the two had grown close, and it made him ill at ease. But he knew there was nothing he could do if they liked each other. When Deok-gi considered his father — not to mention Gyeong-ae's daughter — he didn't know what to think. Perhaps it would be best for Deok-gi to turn a blind eye, to simply avoid being present when the two were together.

Conversation between Deok-gi and Byeong-hwa was strained, and it appeared that Byeong-hwa had actually come to the bar because he had something to discuss with Gyeong-ae. Deok-gi rose and said, "Come and visit me tomorrow if you can."

"All right. I'll come if I have time." Byeong-hwa's response sounded half-hearted. In the past, he would have replied earnestly, promising to come around at a certain time. Was it because Byeong-hwa was no longer short of change? In dismay, Deok-gi grinned sardonically.

Safe

———

The next day, Deok-gi's grandfather was admitted to the University Hospital. Deok-gi and his father were against the old man's hospitalization since his illness didn't call for surgery. The doctor appeared to share their doubts. The Suwon woman was more enthusiastic about the move, while the patient himself, though not entirely pleased with the idea, was of the opinion that it might be helpful.

Deok-gi and his father couldn't oppose it, though they were anxious about dragging the barely breathing old man to the hospital in such cold weather, and afraid that he might die there, away from home. The Suwon woman hurried home from the hospital and described to Deok-gi's wife what it was like there, with a sugary smile on her face. The lines deeply etched on her forehead for the past three months had disappeared.

"Why don't you go and see him sometime tomorrow morning?" she suggested.

"Yes, I will."

"As long as you're out of the house, take the opportunity to visit your parents and offer them a bow before New Year's."

Deok-gi's wife found the Suwon woman disgusting and wondered how she could change so suddenly now that her husband was out of the way. Still, the young woman couldn't object to the suggestion of visiting her parents.

Seeing the main room suddenly bright again enlivened the Suwon woman's face. Even her body seemed lighter. She picked up a broom and a mop, which she'd never done before, and gave the room a good cleaning.

"It is so much better for him there than in this gloomy room. Everything's so clean and quiet, and the room is kept warm with a burning steam stove, and pretty young women come and go," she explained to no one in particular.

The maidservant giggled and asked what use pretty young women were for an old patient. She was as happy as her mistress. But Deok-gi's wife couldn't help but furrow her brow, for it was clear what the Suwon woman and the servant had in mind.

The Suwon woman went on to say, "I think he's going to get better there in spite of himself. We wouldn't have been able to prepare food for New Year's while he was sick, so it'd be ideal if he gets better soon. That way, we can have a big feast before the fifteenth of the month."

Later that evening, the family gathered in the main room and ate dinner. The Suwon woman aside, the others in the house felt they could breathe again, as if a heavy burden had been lifted, and it truly seemed that the gloomy atmosphere had been dispelled. But how could the Suwon woman whirl around the house so, how could she act as if an aching tooth had been pulled out? One might think she'd dance for joy, not at the news that her husband might get better and come home before the first full moon of the year, but rather if the ritual wailing for the dead drifted out of the house and mourning lamps were hung at the gate.

After dinner, the Suwon woman went out with the maidservant in tow, saying she was on her way to the hospital. Around midnight, she came home with Deok-gi, leaving Chang-hun and a servant behind to keep an eye on the old man. Deok-gi had intended to remain overnight at the hospital, but there wasn't enough space for him to stay. According to him, the Suwon woman had arrived at the hospital around ten o'clock, though she'd left home at seven.

"Where had she been?" asked Deok-gi's wife.

"How would I know?" said Deok-gi. Clerk Choe had arrived at the hospital thirty minutes before the Suwon woman, and it looked like they had been busy hatching a plot or two.

At dawn, Deok-gi rushed back to the hospital; the Suwon woman soon followed him, saying that she'd return before breakfast. Before leaving, she said to Deok-gi's wife, "You'd better hurry up if you want to visit your parents. Clear away breakfast and get ready as soon as you can before I come home."

Deok-gi's wife began to make preparations for the outing, though she found the Suwon woman's sudden generosity suspect.

When the Suwon woman returned, she prompted Deok-gi's wife to take her leave right away, reminding her that she might not have enough time to visit her parents. "Your husband had his breakfast at the hospital. Hurry up. I heard your grandfather might have an operation this evening or tomorrow." Then she added, "With your grandfather not home, it doesn't look like we'll be able to hold the New Year's ancestral ceremony. I wouldn't mind if you returned from your parents' house after the New Year's celebration. Ask your husband how he feels about it when you see him at the hospital."

When Deok-gi's wife arrived at the hospital, she felt overwhelmed by all the visitors flocking in to pay their respects to the old man. They had been arriving since early morning. Although there wasn't much to do, she couldn't just leave while the elders were still around, so she sat with the guests until her husband arrived.

"Grandfather says we should go ahead with the New Year's ancestral ceremony. We'd better go home right away and prepare a simple offering," said Deok-gi. They decided to go home with Deok-gi's mother and gave some money to Secretary Ji to go shopping at the Baeugae Market for some bargains. Deok-gi looked for Uncle Chang-hun, hoping he could send him along with Secretary Ji, but he was nowhere to be found.

The sudden decision to hold the New Year's ancestral ceremony had been made on the arrival that morning of an uncle who had come to Seoul from the countryside. He thought it was not a good idea to have an operation on the last day of the year and advised that it be put off until two days after New Year's. When the patient heard that it was actually the last day of the year, he turned to his grandson and asked, "Is today already the last day of the year? Have you prepared for the ancestral ceremony tomorrow?"

"Would it matter if our ancestors didn't receive any offerings this year, in light of your illness?" asked Deok-gi.

The old man lost his temper. If they acted this way while he was still alive, what did they intend to do after his death? Deok-gi agreed to do as his grandfather wished and left.

When the three family members pushed open the gate of the house and entered behind the maid carrying Deok-gi's baby on her back, the maidservant rushed out from the servants' quarters and shouted, "Who's here? *Egu*, what brought you back so early? The mistress is getting ready to go out." Making this announcement as if she were obeying her mistress' order and anxious to prevent unwelcome guests from entering, the maidservant darted into the house ahead of them.

How dare she enter before us? they all thought, following her in. There was no movement inside, and no one seemed to be on the big veranda. The maidservant was nowhere in sight.

Nervously, like people who are aware that a burglar is sneaking around the house, they exchanged glances.

"Has everyone gone out?" Deok-gi spoke in a full voice, as if he had noticed nothing out of the ordinary, and climbed onto the veranda, worried that his mother and wife would sense his uneasiness.

As the women followed him, the Suwon woman entered from the outer quarters nonchalantly, softly scuffing her shoes. She addressed them in a composed tone. "Why have you all returned together?" Stepping onto the veranda, she stared at Deok-gi's wife, who had stiffened in her tracks. "Weren't you going to your parents'?"

What's going on?

Overcome with suspicion, everyone was rendered speechless.

"Is no one in the outer quarters?" asked Deok-gi, coming out of his room.

"No. I went out there to get something, but I couldn't find it. I wonder where your grandfather left it," the Suwon woman said calmly.

"What are you looking for?"

"Your grandfather's fur-lined Korean outer coat. I thought it might be hanging somewhere in the outer quarters, out of sight."

"Didn't he wear it to the hospital?" asked Deok-gi's wife.

"Ah, you're right! What was I thinking?" The Suwon woman laughed dejectedly.

When the old man was moved to the hospital in an ambulance, she was about to cover him with a blanket but then asked Deok-gi's wife to fetch the fur-lined coat. She placed it over her husband and spread the blanket on top of it. Had she completely forgotten? Even if they believed the Suwon woman, why had the maidservant rushed in so quickly? And where was she now?

Deok-gi went out to the outer quarters, where the safe was kept, but found no one there. But why was the outer gate pushed shut instead of locked?

When Deok-gi opened the front gate of the outer quarters and called out, the maidservant came through the gate from the inner quarters, answering in a long drawl, as if she were playing hide-and-seek.

"Why didn't you lock the gate? No one's around."

"I opened it just a moment ago to go to my room."

Deok-gi told her to lock it and went into the larger room of the outer quarters.

He unlocked the door to the loft; the safe came into view. More than a decade ago, when they had moved into this house, the original loft had been torn down and steel bars had been installed underneath the safe. Now, the keeper of the safe was about to take leave of this world. His grandfather had devoted his life to guarding it. Deok-gi remembered how, when he was seven or eight, his grandfather had joked as he jiggled open the safe: "Deok-gi, if you misbehave, I'll put you in the safe and lock the door."

Deok-gi's height had almost doubled since then, so he could never fit in it now, but soon his life as the safe's new keeper would begin. Why had he grown suspicious of the Suwon woman and the maidservant? Why had he been compelled to take a look at the safe?

The opening and shutting of this safe and the ancestral shrine door are now the two most crucial obligations in my life; I am like a prison guard manning the door to a cell.

Deok-gi didn't know what sort of shape the safe was in now, but even if someone had disturbed it, it would be in the same place. As long as he had the keys, no one could do much harm. He grew more curious about what was inside, and as it was not a Pandora's box, he wanted to take a quick peek, even though it meant disobeying his grandfather. In all the family, Deok-gi was the only one to whom his grandfather had entrusted the combination.

As Deok-gi turned the dial on the safe this way and that, shifting through his memory for the numbers, his eyes fell on some ash scattered on the loft's floor. He took a closer look. Though crushed when the door had been shut, it was clearly cigarette ash. His grandfather had been confined to bed for more than a month. Was the ash a month old? But his grandfather didn't smoke cigarettes; he preferred a long pipe. Did he open the door with his long pipe between his lips? Was this ash from a pipe?

He didn't think so. For one thing, the maidservant had behaved oddly. They must have been sneaking people out of the house, for it was strange that the nanny was nowhere in sight and that the gate of the outer quarters had been unlocked. Even if the maidservant's room were on fire, there was no need to unlock the outer quarters' gate. The Suwon woman's excuse was specious, but more than that, why had she, in a surprising show of generosity, encouraged Deok-gi's wife to visit her parents? Normally, she would have snubbed Deok-gi's wife if she had even intimated such a wish. The Suwon woman would have said that the young woman's hands were too full for her to leave the house. Obviously, the Suwon woman was planning something, pretending to keep an eye on the house, after driving everyone away. Deok-gi recalled Uncle Chang-hun's absence at the hospital a while back. Clerk Choe, who had appeared briefly in the morning, had vanished as well.

Do they think they can get away with something behind my back? They might be able to open the loft door by picking at the keyhole, but how can they open the safe? And even if they had opened it, what could they have done? They could have stolen whatever was inside, but they wouldn't dare do anything so obvious. If they took the bankbooks, they'd be caught immediately. Did they want to swap the land deeds with falsified ones? Perhaps they wanted to tamper with the will. If so, what would they do if his grandfather recovered his health?

Deok-gi studied the safe's door, shiny enough to reflect his face; there were fingerprint smudges on it.

Since the door to the outer quarters had remained open, someone might have snuck out, but on the other hand, someone could be watching him at this very moment from the corners of this vast space. If he charged toward Deok-gi from behind and gagged him, only the safe, standing immobile, would witness the attack. Deok-gi realized for the first time that money was frightening and sordid. When the safe door creaked open, Deok-gi began to examine its contents carefully.

The first thing he examined was a will or, rather, a list of names. Almost every family member's name was on the list. Each name was also written on more than ten well-sealed envelopes. Deok-gi scanned the list and found no one was missing. The Suwon woman's name was there, as was his own, and there was no indication that the envelopes had been opened. The envelope bearing the word *bankbooks* was there as well. The big seals belonging to Deok-gi and his grandfather were intact. They hadn't been able to open the safe.

Deok-gi was a little relieved, though still worried. He carefully went over the list.

Gwi-sun (the Suwon woman's daughter): fifty bags of rice per year
The Suwon woman: two hundred bags
Deok-hui: fifty bags
Deok-hui's mother: one hundred bags
Deok-gi's wife: fifty bags
Sang-hun: three hundred bags
Deok-gi: fifteen hundred bags
Chang-hun: five hundred won in cash
Secretary Ji: five hundred won in cash
Clerk Choe: three hundred won in cash

These are rough figures. The Suwon woman's two hundred bags were actually three times larger than Sang-hun's three hundred bags. And Deok-gi's fifteen hundred bags would reach seventeen or eighteen hundred, if not two thousand, because he was entitled to remainders as well.

Ten thousand won in bank deposits and the house were left to Deok-gi, the Suwon woman would receive a fifteen-*gan* house in Taepyeong-dong, and the Bungmi Changjeong house would go to Sang-hun in view of his illegitimate child. The old man specified that the money in the bankbook from which he withdrew living expenses was for the maintenance of the two Jo households, after paying for funeral expenses and granting bonuses to Chang-hun and Secretary Ji. Currently, it held almost ten thousand won. Oddly, there was no mention of the rice mill inside Namdaemun. Had the old man completely forgotten about it or did he simply have no intention of handing it down to any one individual? Perhaps he counted on its covering living expenses for the households dependent on him

The old man had written other instructions. Deok-gi was to supervise and safeguard the provisions for the underaged and the shares for his mother and his wife. For Gwi-sun and Deok-hui, he was to handle their shares until marriage, and for his mother and his wife, he would oversee their portions until his death. Evidently, the old man had entrusted Gwi-sun's future to Deok-gi, probably in the belief that the Suwon woman wouldn't remain with the family forever. He also made provisions for his daughter-in-law and granddaughter-in-law in case some future adversity, such as divorce, befell them. The will read:

Since the possession of assets may, in some cases, bring harm to the descendants that inherit them, I am dividing them as specified while I am alive. This is my absolute intention, and it shall not be changed. As the head of the Jo family household, I entrust to Deok-gi the means of life from one generation of the Jo family to the next. Deok-gi's portion is not for him alone, and he must ensure that he will never take even a penny of it without consideration.

The grandfather then went into details. The distribution of the assets was to be done openly after his burial. Specifically, the women would receive their shares after the three-year period of mourning, a stipulation seemingly made to bind the Suwon woman in particular. Even if she were to marry again, he wanted her to do so only after the grieving period for her husband was over, at which time the four-year-old Gwi-sun would be of school age—old enough to be raised by anyone.

The date on the will was only some ten days earlier, right before he had been moved to the main room. Imagining that his grandfather had woken up in the middle of the night and, though gravely ill, crawled to the safe and steadied himself by leaning against it as he took out the contents and then returned them, Deok-gi's heart went out to him, tears welling up in his eyes. Deok-gi disliked his grandfather's temper, his outdated ideas, and the hostility he bore toward his own son, but seeing the extent to which the old man was concerned about his descendants, Deok-gi was boundlessly grateful. His grandfather couldn't have arranged such a distribution overnight; he must have gone about it slowly from the time he was healthy. Deok-gi's eyes brimmed over with tears as he pictured how sad and lonely the old man must have felt as he made these preparations, without telling anyone. People had commented—even within earshot of Deok-gi's—that the old man's assets couldn't be safe, for in his old age he had become completely enraptured by the Suwon woman. Nevertheless, only two hundred fifty bags of rice were set aside for her and their daughter. Considering that Sang-hun was allotted three hundred bags, their share was quite big, but it was rather on the small side in the scheme of things. Sang-hun's paltry share was the result of the old man's obstinacy, a response to his son's Christianity, which prohibited its believers from performing ancestral ceremonies. In the end, the old man's feudal ideas prevailed. But would Deok-gi carry on his grandfather's dying wishes after he inherited his wealth? Would he maintain the ancestral shrine, as befitting his grandfather's trust, as faithfully as he would keep his grandfather's safe?

Clue

———

After putting the documents back in the safe, Deok-gi noticed that the Suwon woman, standing on the stone step, was peeking in through the tiny windowpane. How long had she been standing there?

She dashed up to the veranda, without properly taking off her curved-tip rubber shoes, and threw open the sliding door. Ill at ease and unable to get the thought of the safe out of her head, she had hurried into the outer quarters to see what was going on. When she noticed that the safe door was open, she jumped in, fury dancing in her eyes.

"I'm on my way to the hospital. Is there anything your grandfather wanted from home?"

Slamming the safe door shut, Deok-gi looked behind him. The Suwon woman appeared ready for a showdown, her hands buried deep in her gray coat pockets, her eyes blazing.

"You're having a grand time! Opening the safe whenever you please . . ." The Suwon woman stared at the bunch of keys as Deok-gi removed them from the keyhole.

Meeting her eyes, Deok-gi once again thought, *thanks to these keys, my own life might be cut short.* He dropped them into his pocket with a jangle and answered sardonically, "Is there something else to take to the hospital other than the fur-lined coat?"

The Suwon woman's expression changed, and a sly, ingratiating smile spread across her lips. "So what's inside?"

"What do you mean by that?" Deok-gi spat out disagreeably.

The Suwon woman regretted her awkward phrasing and began to pout. "How much has he set aside for me? That's what I want to know," she challenged.

"Do you really think now is the time to talk about that?"

"Did you take out the contents because it's time to do so? I'd like to find out what's there for me because I've got to make a living, you know. What's the use of doing nothing now and then harping about it after his death? What am I supposed to do if I'm shooed away empty-handed?"

"If you knew how big your share is, you'd go to my grandfather and make a fuss despite his upcoming operation, wouldn't you?"

"And why shouldn't I? He'd better give me at least five hundred bags. I have to support my baby! No one can imagine how I've suffered, coming here at a young age and taking all sorts of abuse, constantly looking over my shoulder..."

Secretary Ji, returning from the market, came in carrying something in a paper bag. Sending the manservant to the inner quarters with a bush-clover basket, he glanced at the scowling Suwon woman.

"Are you going to the hospital?" he asked her.

"Why do you want to know?" she snapped. It irritated her that Secretary Ji was not on her side; she had to be careful with everything she did around him.

"I found some plump, delicious-looking tangerines at the market, so I bought some for the master, but I have no time to visit him because of all I have to do here," he said, lifting the bag in his hand. Noticing Deok-gi, who was coming out to the veranda, he added, "I bought them with my own money."

"It doesn't matter whose money you used. I'm glad that you bought them," Deok-gi answered.

"Well, I like to be clear when it comes to money. Anyway, I don't know whether I can visit the master again today, so—"

"Don't worry," the Suwon woman said sharply, interrupting him. "If the master wants some tangerines, I'll pick some up for him on my way. Keep them a long, long time and eat them yourself!"

"It's not as if you're short of money, but I bought these especially for him!" barked Secretary Ji, usually so mild and polite. "I've served him for almost twenty years, and now that I see him hospitalized, I wish I could depart for the other world first." His eyes blinked behind his eyeglasses. "I'll wrap these up in a cloth. Peel some for him as soon as you arrive at the hospital. He must be thirsty." He entered the room without a second glance at the Suwon woman.

Deok-gi felt a pang of emotion. He was grateful to Secretary Ji and took pity on him, letting the words "especially for him" sink in. *What would it be like if my grandmother were still alive?* Deok-gi wondered.

From inside, standing at the window, Secretary Ji held out, instead of the bag of tangerines, a brownish scarf. "What is this doing here?" he muttered. "It looks like Chang-hun's scarf. Why would he leave it behind when it's freezing outside?"

The Suwon woman was stunned at the sight of the scarf. She shouted, "If you're going to give me the tangerines, wrap them up in a hurry!"

"Did Uncle come here?" Deok-gi asked, noticing how flustered the Suwon woman was, though the question was unnecessary because he had seen Chang-hun's face buried in the scarf during his visit to the hospital earlier that morning.

"I have no idea." As soon as she responded, the gate of the outer quarters creaked open, and Chang-hun entered as if on cue. No scarf was covering his frozen chin.

"What's going on?" he asked, facing the people standing around.

"Where have you been?" Deok-gi asked.

"We have to vacate our home, so I've been running all over town trying to find a place. No luck so far. It's hard to find a monthly rental, even with hundreds of won for a deposit. We're in big trouble."

This was news to Deok-gi. "Have you been renting a place?"

"What else can I afford? I wouldn't mind so much if we were kicked out after winter, but the landlord is a Japanese bastard. He couldn't care less that at this time of year Koreans face two major expenses—winter *kimchi*-making and the upcoming New Year's celebrations."

"But how can he evict his tenants on New Year's?" Deok-gi noticed that Chang-hun seemed to have his eyes glued on his grandfather's money.

"What do Japanese bastards care about our lunar New Year's?" Chang-hun's tone toward Deok-gi suddenly sweetened, probably because he remembered that Deok-gi would be the head of the household sooner or later. "I wish your grandfather would let me live in one of his houses. I don't expect much. If he let me live in a small hut, nothing more, he'd save my life," he muttered.

"I don't think my grandfather owns any extra houses."

"You're going a step further than your own grandfather. It's understandable because you'll soon assume control of the household, but your grandfather has at least five or six houses in Seoul. If you add this house, the Hwagae-dong house, the one at Bungmi Changjeong, and the house in Taepyeong-dong, they're more than ten. Do you think you know more about these matters than I do?"

Deok-gi brushed off Chang-hun's claim with a chuckle. "Whatever the case, were you really able to see any houses on the last day of the year?"

"Do you think I'm lying? Why would I? And why would I run around before breakfast in the cold, instead of staying with your grandfather at the hospital? I was going to ask you to take my case to your grandfather, but I can see now that it's hopeless."

For the life of him, Deok-gi couldn't believe a word of what he said.

"What nonsense is this?" Secretary Ji said sarcastically as he came outside with the bag of fruit tightly wrapped in a bundle. "Going around looking at houses on the last day of the year? Was that why you dropped your scarf here, because you had to run around for something so ridiculous?"

"Did I drop my scarf here?" Chang-hun looked uncomfortable.

"If you'd done any more house hunting, you'd have left behind your own neck, now wouldn't you?" Secretary Ji commented cynically as he stood waiting for the Suwon woman, who had retreated to the inner quarters.

Deok-gi was pleased to see that Secretary Ji had detected something odd as well and said to Chang-hun, "Anyway, please come in. I'd like to ask you to supervise tomorrow's ancestral ceremony."

Chang-hun, who had been cowed by Secretary Ji's sarcasm, seemed to recover his spirits. "You understand, don't you? Now that your grandfather isn't here, things have come to this. That's why you need older folks in the house." He spoke with confidence, as if he were given a responsibility only he could fulfill. As he entered, he quickly picked up the scarf Secretary Ji had dropped near the doorstep. Chang-hun put it around his neck and hung his hat on the nail in the wall.

When the Suwon woman reappeared, after having taken a look at the groceries brought home from the market for the ritual, Secretary Ji handed her the bag of fruit and sat down across from Chang-hun. He took out a flint pouch to stuff his pipe and was about to light it when he happened to glance outside through the large glass window in front of him. He put down his pipe and clucked his tongue. Deok-gi and Chang-hun turned to take a look and saw that the Suwon woman had torn open the bag of fruit and had given her daughter, who was riding on the nanny's back, two tangerines; the child had one in each of her hands. Now the Suwon woman was giving one to the nanny.

"Why get angry over such a trifle?" Chang-hun said to Secretary Ji. Chang-hun took out a pack of Pigeon cigarettes and lit one leisurely. Smoking cigarettes, rather than a traditional pipe, seemed incongruous in a man of his years.

"Young people these days don't know how to show respect for their elders. What's essential is sincerity." Secretary Ji hadn't taken a single tangerine for himself and had sent the entire batch to the old man with a devoted heart, though he had to swallow the water gathering in his mouth. The Suwon woman's behavior was unconscionable.

"Is it so wrong that the old man's precious daughter taste them before he does?" Chang-hun retorted.

Ji hid his displeasure, but when his eyes landed on the scarf, he brought up the matter again. "What made you lose that scarf of yours, the one you won't take off even now that you're inside?"

"Didn't I say I'm going to be kicked out of my house?" Chang-hun answered vaguely.

"It seems to me that the scarf has legs of its own, for I saw it a while ago at the hospital."

"If the scarf interests you so much, why didn't you just steal it? Do you want it for a New Year's present?"

"Steal it? I gather that's something you would say to your friends," Secretary Ji replied in a huff. As the saying goes, beggars don't go begging in a group. People who depend on others for their livelihood have the habit of cutting each other down. Besides, to Secretary Ji—who had devoted almost half his life to the master of the household and who couldn't be more loyal— Chang-hun and Clerk Choe were sorry excuses for human beings. Chang-hun, on the other hand, considered Ji no more than an old dog in a hole beneath the Jo family's veranda.

"Why do I have to be attacked like this today?" Chang-hun asked Deok-gi. "It was cold, so I had a quick drink standing up in a bar and stopped by here to take a nap. I left my scarf behind because I was a bit drunk."

Deok-gi changed the subject as though he wanted to cut their quarrel short, but he actually had something else in mind. "I've been meaning to ask you—who sent the telegrams for you? None reached me, you know."

"I asked my kids, and I sent one myself."

"Strange. The other day, as I passed by the Keijo post office, I remembered that you'd sent the telegrams from there. I went in and asked them. We searched everything but found no record."

"Is that possible? Aren't hundreds or thousands of telegrams sent from there each day?"

"All they have to do is check the ones that have been returned due to failed delivery. I'll check again when I arrive in Kyoto."

"I have no idea what could have happened." Chang-hun's expression didn't change.

Secretary Ji said, "Whether you're sending a telegram or wiring money, you'd better entrust it to someone who's smart enough to know what he's doing. Who knows, he could have put the telegram in an envelope and dropped it in a mailbox."

Deok-gi laughed in spite of himself.

Chang-hun shot him a reproachful glance as he stood up. "I'm going home, but I'll be back soon." He put his hat on and went out. He wanted to get away from them.

Secretary Ji sat quietly with his young master for some time. He must have been mulling something over because he finally ventured, "It's a good thing that you're here. But be careful. There's no one you can trust."

"What are they up to? The telegrams they claim to have sent didn't reach me."

"What do you think? Their mind is on one thing," said Secretary Ji, looking up toward the loft. "But what can they do? Their greed is futile, but they must have come here and concocted some scheme among themselves."

"Who do you mean by 'they'?"

"Isn't it obvious? Choe, Chang-hun, the Suwon woman, and the husband and wife in the servants' quarters. I'm a thorn in their side—they'd shoot me dead if they had a gun. I may be old, but I'm no fool." Secretary Ji sounded proud.

"Uncle Chang-hun, too?" Deok-gi feigned surprise to see how the secretary would react.

"His motive must be different from Choe's or the Suwon woman's. I hate to say it, but the most dangerous one of them all is the Suwon woman. Be careful."

"What do they intend to do?"

"If your grandfather had died before your arrival, they could have tampered with some document, though they couldn't switch everything in the safe or steal everything. It could have been disastrous. Your father seemed to be on to something, but who was there to help him? I was very worried."

"You've been through a lot."

"You know, before I went to the market, I came here to take the servant with me. The gate to the outer quarters was locked, and when I was trying to come in, the servant said there was no need for me to do so, that he'd be right out. I thought that was rather odd. I peeked in through a gap in the gate, and it looked as though someone were moving around in the room."

"Really? Were there shoes outside?"

"No, actually. There was no sound, but through the tiny windowpane I saw a shadow flitting near the loft. I thought it could be a burglar. The more I thought about it, the more anxious I felt. Anyway, when I returned, I found the scarf on the threshold. It's even more distasteful that Chang-hun is a part of the gang than Clerk Choe, isn't it?"

"I agree, but on the other hand, had there been a womanizer in the family, who knows what could have happened?" Deok-gi laughed.

Secretary Ji studied Deok-gi. "Well, well, I see now that I don't have to worry about the Jo family. I didn't know your potential!"

"Not at all—I'm confused about running this big household. Please help me as much as you can." To this old man, Deok-gi expressed all the loneliness and anxiety that he couldn't reveal to his own father.

"What more can I say when I owe your family so much?" Secretary Ji said with great modesty. "I'm ignorant, and I don't have enough energy left." He felt moved and was proud to have had a frank talk with the young master, with whom he would play a role in holding the household together—a household whose foundations were crumbling and whose divisions were growing deeper.

"What else have you heard?"

"All I know is that behind everything is a lousy woman who runs a place called Maedang House. Your father goes there for drinks, and once he ran into the Suwon woman there. Anyway, that louse's place seems to be the den where the scoundrels gather. When they aren't conspiring here, they go there whenever they can with their dirty schemes."

"Where is Maedang House? Does my father spend time with this group?" It made Deok-gi feel guilty to suspect his father, but he couldn't trust him.

"I don't think so. I'm not sure of the details, since I haven't seen the Maedang woman, but she's notorious for blackmailing people, and she rules with an iron fist the women who sell their bodies in secret. Looks like she's manipulating both your father and the Suwon woman. It may be that she hopes to squeeze something out of them—or, at least, from one of them."

This shocking news displaced all of Deok-gi's other preoccupations.

"Please keep it to yourself, but from the beginning, Clerk Choe cooked up a scheme to make the Suwon woman your grandfather's concubine, with the understanding that she would split the inheritance with him. Then Chang-hun got involved. One of these days those bastards will receive a blow when they least expect it and fall pretty hard." Secretary Ji, a man of principle, ground his teeth.

"If they were the ones who brewed my grandfather's medicine, how could he have gotten better?"

"Exactly!"

When Deok-gi heard that the medicine itself could have been tainted, he reeled. Although Secretary Ji was reluctant to go into details, Deok-gi remembered what his wife told him the day before, though he hadn't paid much attention to her words at the time. She complained that no one was allowed to touch the medicine other than the maidservant. Deok-gi's wife was always entrusted with taking it to the main room. The Suwon woman would nag her about how she didn't brew the medicine herself or how she didn't pay enough attention to the old man's illness, but she wasn't allowed to touch the medicine in the first place. Deok-gi's suspicions mounted.

Then there was the maidservant. At first, everyone liked her because she was friendly and accommodating and handled her duties promptly and expertly, but it became apparent that she was crafty and talkative, like the madam of a *gisaeng* establishment. Deok-gi's heart sank to think that this maidservant had been in charge of brewing his grandfather's medicine.

We'll know soon enough! However depressed he felt over his grandfather's hospitalization, Deok-gi resolved to get to the bottom of the matter.

Farewell to Grandfather

––––

The men gathered at the hospital to perform the New Year's ancestral ceremony. The patient was well enough during the day, but toward evening he lapsed into a coma and regained consciousness only at dawn.

The doctor felt that it would be better to put off the operation for several days to give the patient time to regain some strength. An operation in name only, the procedure amounted to draining liquid from both sides of the rib cage. The doctor explained that it would nevertheless be difficult to perform, given the patient's weakened state. He couldn't understand how the patient had become so enervated. He assumed that the old man had taken considerable amounts of invigorating medicine—he could certainly afford it.

The next three or four days passed without incident. Still, the doctor couldn't attempt the operation because the patient remained lethargic for no discernable reason. To make matters worse, the old man couldn't keep down solid food.

"This doesn't make sense. It looks like a toxic syndrome," speculated the doctor.

"What toxin would you say?" Deok-gi prompted.

"We'd better wait and see what symptoms he shows." That was all the doctor would say for the time being. Several times a day, injections were administered into the old man's hardened veins. Thanks to these injections, his only source of nourishment, he hung on to life.

––––

The Jo family doctor came to the hospital when he learned that the old man's condition was critical. Deok-gi arranged a meeting between him and the hospital doctor in the hope that together they could reach a diagnosis.

The two discussed the patient's condition, the care given him, and examined each other's prescriptions. The diagnosis could have been wrong, but there was no possibility that their own prescriptions could have been toxic. However, when the results of the stool analysis were brought to the family doctor, he gasped.

After extensive consultation, the two doctors asked Deok-gi to bring them the Chinese herbal prescriptions and whatever dregs of the medicine remained. Suspicion had now shifted to the Chinese medicine doctor. Deok-gi went to see him personally, hoping to find some sort of a clue.

The Chinese doctor accompanied Deok-gi to the hospital, explained his diagnosis to the family and other doctors and shared his prescriptions with them. He had been treating the patient for internal weakness due to a cold, but he hadn't been aware that pneumonia was the cause of the fever. In any event, there was no evidence of any toxic substance to be found in his prescription, and nothing remained of the medicine itself.

The patient was given an antidote, but it caused a kidney inflammation and stomach catarrh, and he began to lose his eyesight. In light of these symptoms, the diagnosis of arsenic poisoning became decisive, and the hospital doctor grew desperate.

Amid the commotion, the Suwon woman stayed in bed for three days, claiming that she had a cold and her body ached all over. On the day of the operation, though, she did visit but moaned and groaned so much it was embarrassing to hear her. From the sound of it, you'd have thought the young wife was going to die before the old man.

The women went so far as to poke fun at her. "You're exhausted because you had to take care of your sick husband for so long," they said. "We were afraid that you might die of exhaustion while taking care of him."

"What more could I wish for if I could die first?" said the Suwon woman between short breaths, prompting a peal of laughter from the women.

The operation finally took place, and the fever abated, but the ordeal pushed the patient into a coma. Without opening his eyes for two days, his breathing grew shallower until, at last, it stopped.

The doctor, afraid that the family wouldn't understand what had happened and blame him for hastening the patient's death with the operation, explained that arsenic poisoning was the cause, and everyone accepted it. No one in the family would speak their mind about the cause of the poisoning, yet they regarded it as a criminal case.

When the doctor raised the subject of performing an autopsy for research purposes, Sang-hun, the head mourner, expressed agreement before anyone else had a chance to offer an opinion. Deok-gi had actually wanted to suggest a postmortem, but he didn't dare open his mouth, afraid to provoke his relatives' complaints and accusations.

Sure enough, Sang-hun was showered with abuse.

"Are you crazy? Do you want to besmirch the Jo family name?" Chang-hun spewed accusations. And his weren't the only ones.

How can a fifty-year-old man have so little sense? What kind of bastard wants to rend his parent's body apart piece by piece, like a butcher slaughtering a cow? Who in the world would do such a thing? How could the body be brought to the coffin room at the funeral? The debates grew more vehement.

The old gentleman was his parent, not his enemy! Just because his father said some unpleasant things to him while he was alive, it doesn't justify his trying to humiliate him by hacking his dead body apart with a knife. If Sang-hun is sane, he should be killed and dismembered. If he's insane, he should be confined to an animal shed or else beaten to death by the Jo clan. Chang-hun freely encouraged such sentiments among the mourners.

No one would be surprised if such a man had given his father arsenic. He wants the corpse torn to pieces to get rid of the evidence because he's afraid his crime will be discovered. Then he'll either burn the pieces or leave them to float in bottles in some corner of the hospital and walk away from the matter. Clerk Choe and Chang-hun spread notions like these to anyone who would listen. Everyone thought it made sense. In the meantime, the Suwon woman bawled hysterically, and dozens of people spoke up to put in their two cents worth. A corner of the hospital might as well have been destroyed from the racket they made. Sang-hun ended up like a crushed horsehair hat and was forced to sit quietly for the time being. It was not that he had nothing to say or that he didn't have a mouth with which to say it, but as the blade of the attack was so sharp, he thought he'd better be cautious. If the key to the safe had fallen into Sang-hun's hands, they wouldn't have insulted him to such an extent. Rather, Chang-hun would have said, "I think it's strange, too. Let them do the autopsy." But in fact, Sang-hun didn't think that an autopsy was absolutely necessary. He agreed to the idea because he thought that if a vicious conspiracy existed, it should be uncovered. He changed his mind, however, telling himself that there was no need for an autopsy when two doctors had confirmed the cause of death. There would be other ways to make it an issue if necessary—after his father was buried. The truth was that even though he didn't subscribe to the traditional distaste for such things, Sang-hun was loath to see a knife cutting into his father's still-warm body. In the heat of the moment, Chang-hun made Sang-hun out to be the bad guy, and indeed his accusations sounded plausible, but Sang-hun decided to wait for the right time, convinced that a hideous crime couldn't be concealed forever.

I'll bide my time, Sang-hun thought. *How long will you bastards remain so confident?*

Before starting preparations for the funeral, the corpse was transferred to an ambulance and taken to the house, where it was laid out. When the funeral ritual began, Sang-hun didn't perform the ceremonial keening.

This became another point of contention, but Sang-hun stood his ground. His eyes were dry, and he felt no regret. Sang-hun believed his reaction was far more honest than that of the Suwon woman, who squeezed tears out until her eyes swelled and than that of Chang-hun, whose mournful wails struck a false note.

Sang-hun was completely ignored. Though Deok-gi didn't wear the mourning clothes of unbleached hemp reserved for the head mourner, his role was no different from that of a grieving grandson whose father had died before his grandfather. The visitors bowed once to Sang-hun to pay their condolences, then gathered around Deok-gi to chat with him. Chang-hun took charge of every decision, either by getting permission from Deok-gi or approval after the fact.

Sang-hun had no choice but to sit awkwardly, like a borrowed sack of barley, in the warmer part of the big room in the outer quarters. Deok-gi, sorry that his father was being shunned, took pains to consult him about everything. Deok-gi felt it was only right to ask his father's opinions. Deok-gi's solicitousness notwithstanding, Sang-hun remained aloof. Whatever was asked of him, he said, "Do as you see fit. You can discuss it with the others and find the right solution." Though he didn't show it, Sang-hun was deeply hurt.

It irritated Deok-gi to be caught in the middle. Things were so chaotic and money was snatched away ever so quickly by swooping relatives eager to take advantage of the situation and get their crumbs that soon the bickering and fighting began. This was the mood as the funeral procession began on the seventh day after the old man's death. No matter how one looked at it, this was a propitious mourning—a rich man dying at a ripe old age. People wondered if the head mourner would wear a frock coat, but he was dressed in traditional mourning garb and rode a reed palanquin, followed by more than two hundred rickshaws slithering like a snake's tail.

Bystanders gathered along the road from early morning without any food in their stomachs. *What a magnificent procession! What a lucky life he had! Life is so unfair. When I go to my grave, I bet I'll be carried in a twenty-two-handle bier, not one with just twelve handles like him.* Who could have fathomed how many vices, roars, and resentments would linger in the wake of this funeral procession?

It was in this way that the grandfather's life finally came to a close.

New Start

———

"Is the young master home?" Byeong-hwa called out from the edge of the outer quarters' veranda. When the young master, sitting in the warmer part of the large room, looked out through the tiny windowpane, Byeong-hwa gave a grand bow. At first Deok-gi didn't recognize the visitor, and a low thrum of conversation had resumed inside the room.

"I'm a grocer. Lemme deliver to your house."

"We're not interested," a voice, not Deok-gi's, replied.

"Whether large or small, we deliver quickly if you phone us, and we're gonna give you bargain prices, at almost no profits to us."

Deok-gi now thought the voice sounded familiar. "What store are you from?" he asked as he looked out again. He threw open the door, saying, "Hey! What the—You've got to be kidding!" Deok-gi rushed out wearing a wide grin and his white mourning coat.

"Far from it, sir. We have just opened today and hope that you'll give us some business." Grinning, Byeong-hwa kept bowing.

"You're really something . . ."

One by one, everyone in the room peered out through the windowpane, smiles pasted on their faces. Standing before the veranda, Byeong-hwa announced the opening of his store without the least embarrassment.

Where did he get those clothes? Is he rehearsing for something? Is he thinking of going somewhere in that outfit? Deok-gi raised an eyebrow. He had seen Byeong-hwa briefly five days ago, the day his grandfather was buried, returning home with the spirit tablet in hand. That day Byeong-hwa had been wearing a Western suit, as was his custom. Deok-gi was baffled at the sight of his friend, wondering what ill-conceived heroics prompted him to run around in that outlandish outfit.

"Come on in. What makes you so scarce these days?"

"Wait a minute, sir. Let me do what I have to do first." Byeong-hwa pulled out a handbill from under his clothes and gave it to Deok-gi.

"Is it true? Are you really running it?"

"If someone like the young master gave me seed money, it'd be different. But how can a man with nothing but his balls run a store? I'm just a humble deliveryman, sir."

"Lower your form of speech when you address me, sir," Deok-gi quipped.

"You are too generous, sir."

Deok-gi laughed. "I can see you've passed the order-taking test. Enough of this. Why don't you come in?"

"No time—too busy. Allow me to leave with you a credit booklet." The name Jo was written on the booklet and on the inside cover was a three-jeon revenue stamp, complete with two official-looking seals.

"I see that you're a seasoned hand. Where did you get so much experience?" Deok-gi smiled and examined Byeong-hwa's face with intense curiosity. After meeting him briefly at Bacchus, he had of late seen his friend only twice: once when Byeong-hwa came to pay his respects after the old man's death, and again when Deok-gi was coming home with the spirit tablet, and on both occasions they had just nodded to each other. Deok-gi hadn't had the time to hear about the details, but he could make neither heads nor tails of what his friend was up to. Did he open the store with Gyeong-ae? Did he get capital through her Bacchus connections?

"I can't believe a Japanese store owner would use someone as dangerous as you. Who do you work for?"

"I've got a high post, thanks to a policeman's guarantee, sir."

"I see that you know how to address your elders respectfully. You've turned out all right." Still, Deok-gi didn't like Byeong-hwa's deferential tone.

"There's a big gap between a millionaire and a grocer, so how can I forget my place? Young master, the Kim Byeong-hwa you see now is not the Kim Byeong-hwa of yesterday, but a deliveryman of the Sanhaejin Grocery. Please think of us kindly and patronize our store. This humble soul will take his leave now, sir." Byeong-hwa bowed, a grin fixed on his face.

"Yeah, good-bye, you clown," Deok-gi said with a smile, though he was still dazed by this latest turn of events. "Forget the comedy, and tell me the details. There's no need to run a Japanese grocery store to sell stuff to Koreans, but if you wanted to have Japanese customers, they wouldn't let a Red like you anywhere near them. How can it work?"

"A Red? We are not carrying any green peppers that are turning red, but we've got dry red peppers and red pepper strips. If you need other red produce, we've got carrots, hard persimmons, and good soft persimmons, too. I can bring along a police inspector to Japanese households and sell things on his guarantee, can't I?" Byeong-hwa recited all this without a hint of a smile.

"Really? What an excellent life you're leading! That's great. When you sell with a policeman in tow, you're untouchable, right?"

"Please visit our store one of these days. It's near the old Maedong School."

"All right, I will."

As Byeong-hwa left, he could hear Deok-gi's laughter. After making the rounds among his friends and acquaintances, he returned to the store, where Gyeong-ae was waiting for him.

"You look quite authentic. Please deliver one-jeon worth of bean sprouts and a basket of bean curd to my house."

"Right away, ma'am! Where do you live, ma'am?"

"In Namsangol, where pine cones are strewn. Don't forget to bring chopped green onions to decorate the food!" Gyeong-ae burst out laughing.

Pil-sun, standing by, threw in, "I don't know how you deliver groceries when you have to drag your bicycle alongside, rather than riding it." Flailing her arms, she mimicked Byeong-hwa's clumsy bicycling.

"His riding is not too bad for a young man who's done nothing but study. Do you happen to know how to use an abacus?" Gyeong-ae asked in a jesting tone.

"In the abacus department, allow me to introduce a star graduate." Byeong-hwa pointed to Pil-sun, who, smiling abashedly, turned away. She had been practicing all week.

Byeong-hwa said to Gyeong-ae, "How about taking off your coat and helping us out here? A girl decked out in Western garb lounging around like that won't be good for business."

"Business will be good when you have someone like me sitting here. The Japanese hire women for their cigarette kiosks and bathhouses to attract customers, don't they?"

"You might as well climb out on to our roof and sit there."

A Japanese maid from a boardinghouse several doors away came in with a credit booklet and bought a bunch of green onions and six hundred grams of dried anchovies. Soon after, an old Japanese woman bought three eggs and half a cup of red beans. Though not a rice store, they had put other grains on display, as Japanese grocers often did. Byeong-hwa measured the red beans, and Pil-sun handed over the eggs. The old woman gave them a won note, Pil-sun clicked the abacus beads, clanged open a small steel box, and returned her change.

"How much did you give back?" Byeong-hwa asked.

"Seventy-nine jeon. Nine jeon for red beans and twelve jeon for the eggs. They're four jeon each. Right?"

"Perfect!" Byeong-hwa smiled.

"You two are the very picture of a harmonious husband and wife. You're so good at it one would think you had years of experience!" Gyeong-ae roared.

Watching the two selling goods so amicably, Gyeong-ae felt a pang of jealousy, wondering whether their rapport would really last and they'd become inseparable. She felt for them, though, understanding their fear that their inexperience might lead to bungling. But observing Byeong-hwa's renaissance—his sleeves rolled up, eager to work—Gyeong-ae was secretly pleased. She figured he could do anything he put his mind to; he would never starve, even though this project was established for a purpose other than making money. There weren't many young men who had so much vitality, she reflected, who couldn't care less about money and household affairs, and yet had the willpower to do something grand and ambitious. Her trust and affection for him grew, and she found him endearing, as if he were a little brother. She could talk to him. All the same, a vague jealousy toward Pil-sun raised its ugly head, although she was usually able to drive away such idle notions with a smile.

Despite her concern, she had no desire to take control of the store. Though it was she who had been most enthusiastic and who wanted to hurry things along, she didn't have the courage to jump into it. It had all begun when they had the idea of opening a small cosmetics store or a general store, or maybe a fabric shop near a girls' school carrying mainly yarns and laces. She approached Sang-hun for capital, and he was for the idea, indicating he'd supply the money if Gyeong-ae were to manage the store. He half consented, believing that he would be able to get his hands on several thousand won if his father died, though the plan would fall through if the old man didn't pass away soon.

When they were heatedly debating what sort of establishment to open, the proprietor of Bacchus asked, in passing, if they'd be interested in buying a tidy grocery store, one that was run by a Japanese acquaintance of hers, who was thinking of selling it out of anger after her husband had gone bankrupt from gambling. The decision was made quickly. The asking price was two thousand won for the building, three hundred for the telephone, and five hundred for the inventory, but in the end they agreed to rent the house for forty won, buy the inventory for four hundred, and lease the phone.

They were far from being at a disadvantage, as the seller was eager to rid herself of the store. Both parties wanted to act as quickly as possible. The grocery was located in a quarter that was rapidly turning into a Japanese residential area. Byeong-hwa put down four hundred right away, but for the rest, Sang-hun had to get hold of his father's money. Now that the old man had finally succumbed, it seemed that they would be able to buy the building after all.

Byeong-hwa's four hundred had come from Pi-hyeok, but the store and the payment were in Gyeong-ae's name. Byeong-hwa should have been ashamed to open a grocery with Pi-hyeok's money if he possessed even a modicum of conscience. Pi-hyeok hadn't come such a long way and put himself at such risk to let a stranger become a businessman, lead a comfortable life, and get fat.

It had been a mistake on Pi-hyeok's part to give him the money through Gyeong-ae. If anyone else had been chosen to watch over Byeong-hwa, he would have been beaten to a pulp by now, and news of the betrayal would have spread far and wide. Byeong-hwa would be either in a hospital or at the police station, and the Sanhaejin Grocery's signboard would have been pulled down.

Actually, the signboard had not yet been put up. None of Byeong-hwa's comrades knew that he had opened a Japanese grocery store, nor would they be able to fathom how he had managed to do it. Byeong-hwa had firmly made up his mind to turn his back on all of his comrades, and if they ever came to see him, he'd make sure they wouldn't set foot in his store.

This attitude worried Pil-sun. "How can you banish your friends? They'll take it personally and make more of a nuisance of themselves, and there's no knowing what they'll say or how they might interfere." What's more, she was concerned that he would give the cold shoulder to her own acquaintances.

"Doesn't matter. How dare they come and interfere in my affairs?" Byeong-hwa's stubbornness evoked trust, but hadn't he encouraged Pil-sun to run away to Moscow less than a month ago? Instead of feeling relieved, she was frightened and even a little contemptuous.

Pil-sun's family had moved into the store. Although Byeong-hwa hadn't set up the business only to make it possible for Pil-sun to quit the factory or as a means for her family to make a living, Pil-sun's family nevertheless felt as if they had been given a second chance in life. And, indeed, they were ideal shopkeepers; Pil-sun watched over the store while her parents kept house behind the scenes. Gyeong-ae was against the idea at first, feeling that Pil-sun's family was too large, but she ended up agreeing, for it was better to use them than unknown hired hands.

Though it was the middle of winter, Pil-sun got up with the rattle of the first streetcar, and quietly removed the plank door and arranged the goods on display, making an effort not to wake Byeong-hwa, who slept in a room inside the store. But he also rose early and worked in tandem with Pil-sun, riding his bicycle in his usual clumsy way on the icy road to the Namdaemun Market to purchase goods. Pil-sun's father had decided that his Korean clothes didn't seem to go with the store, so he now wore a warm, if worn-out, Western jacket and pants obtained from a secondhand shop and sat beside the stove. Everything they did felt a bit awkward, like a trial run, but they were excited because it was peaceful, and a bright future seemed to beckon.

Pil-sun went to bed only after the last streetcar had passed. Though exhausted, she had a hard time falling asleep, her head full of the prices of the goods they carried and strategies for better ways to sell them. She had forgotten her desire to study. The thought of Deok-gi struck her from time to time, and she imagined how embarrassing it would be if he came to the store. At the same time, she wouldn't mind showing off how skillfully she could sell groceries in her pale blue uniform, if only he wouldn't catch sight of her red, frostbitten hands below her rolled-up sleeves.

Sea of Mud

—

Deok-gi headed out to take a look at Byeong-hwa's store. He had been in seclusion since his grandfather's funeral, and it had been quite a while since his last outing. In addition to having to serve as head mourner, he was busy examining household accounts and had had little opportunity for excursions during the first few days of the new year.

As his streetcar neared Hyoja-dong, he got up from his seat and studied the Japanese stores that had sprouted up along the street since the 1929 Joseon Fair. He got off the car and walked down the street, examining one store after another, but the Sanhaejin signboard was nowhere in sight. He peered through a glass door underneath a sign that read Satoh Store and caught sight of fruits, leeks, and watercress. They sold cigarettes, too. Figuring he'd ask for directions to Sanhaejin while buying a pack, he slid open the door, and a shop girl came out, beaming. Deok-gi, startled, almost took a step back. It was Pil-sun. The girl, her face blushing pink and heart pounding, didn't know what to do.

"I had no idea I'd find you here," said Deok-gi as he entered. "Is Kim here?"

"He's not, but please take a seat. I think he'll be back soon."

The creaky low desk Deok-gi had seen in Byeong-hwa's room and a cushion near a brazier were all the furnishings in the small back room covered with tatami mats.

Looking around the store from its threshold, Deok-gi asked, "Did he go out for a delivery?"

"No, he went to Seodaemun Prison. He should be back soon." Pil-sun scrambled to tidy the room and offered him a cushion to sit on.

"Why did he go there?"

"To see people who were imprisoned some time ago and to bring them meals. It's been a while since he left, so he really should be back soon."

Pil-sun was afraid that Deok-gi might decide to leave. She wanted to express her condolences but didn't know how.

Deok-gi was relieved that Byeong-hwa was doing well enough to provide meals for his friends in prison and thought it was generous of him to do so after his own situation had improved.

"Tell me about the signboard — 'Satoh.' Did he buy a Japanese store?"

The question took Pil-sun aback. Byeong-hwa had implied that the money for the store had come from Deok-gi, but he seemed to know nothing about it. She knew that Pi-hyeok had left behind a bundle of money that he entrusted to Byeong-hwa, and she had guessed that this was how Byeong-hwa could acquire the store, but he had denied it vehemently.

"It's the name of the former owner, but I'm told we'll keep it for a while so as not to lose the regular customers."

Deok-gi agreed that this was a good idea. *But where did the money come from?*

While they were talking, they noticed two young men in shabby Western suits peering into the store from a distance and then moving away, out of sight. A bit later, one of them, with sharp, darting eyes, barged in and asked roughly, "Is Satoh home?"

His ratty clothes and long hair, and his crude walking cane (thankfully, not a menacing cherry stick), did not give him the aura of a police inspector. Rather, he resembled the Byeong-hwa of old.

"Satoh has sold the business," Pil-sun replied.

"Who's the owner now?"

"Hong Gyeong-ae."

"Hong Gyeong-ae? A man or a woman?"

"A woman."

"Who's her husband? Does she have a husband?"

"There's an attendant."

"Who is he?"

"Kim Cheong."

"Where is this Kim Cheong fellow?"

"He's out."

"Who are you?"

"I'm an attendant, too."

"Are you Kim Cheong's wife?"

"No." Pil-sun frowned, a blush rising to her cheeks.

"Then when do you expect him to return?"

"I don't know."

The hostile young man left the store.

"Who are you? What do you want?" Pil-sun asked, following him outside, but the stranger strode away without answering.

"I'm not convinced that he was looking for the previous owner," Deok-gi commented. "At first glance, I'd say he looks pretty shady—one of those radicals looking for trouble."

"That's what I was thinking." Pil-sun was pensive, her face pale, her eyes blinking from fright.

"Do Byeong-hwa's old friends still come to see him?"

"Not really. He says he wants to stay away from them for a while."

"Is that why he's calling himself Kim Cheong? What about the police inspectors? Do they come?"

"Yes. They joke that they're like doctors who have nothing to do except swat flies after all their patients get better, and that they can't make a living since Byeong-hwa turned over a new leaf and is doing what's good for him.

They say they're thankful, anyway, and talk about opening accounts at our store for their families and maybe even bringing some of their friends to shop here. I guess they're satisfied."

"Oh, really! I bet they go around spreading the news that Kim has renounced his ideology and is now busy making money. His friends won't keep quiet about his betrayal."

"You've already guessed all that?"

"Well, yes." Deok-gi was afraid that Byeong-hwa might find himself in unexpected trouble. But had he really changed his way of thinking? Deok-gi just couldn't be sympathetic to Byeong-hwa if he had really turned his back on his comrades and was getting help from the police. It was possible that, having fallen head over heels in love with Gyeong-ae, he was now delivering groceries just to please her, like a bankrupt *yangban* playing both master and servant. He could have done pretty much anything in order to make a living. It could also be that Byeong-hwa hadn't intended to enlist the inspectors but realized that it wouldn't hurt to make use of them if he could. Those who were hostile to Byeong-hwa might actually have a bone to pick with him.

"Did Hong Gyeong-ae give him the money for this place?" Deok-gi asked, remembering that Pil-sun had said that Gyeong-ae was the owner.

"I guess so."

Though he didn't know how much it would cost to buy such a store, Deok-gi wondered if Gyeong-ae had enough money of her own to launch something on this scale. Had she gotten it from his father? If so, where did that leave Gyeong-ae's relationship with Byeong-hwa? Deok-gi couldn't bury this thought, as much as he'd prefer not to get involved in the affair.

"How is it for you?" Deok-gi asked. "It must be exhausting working here."

"Not really. I'm just a little nervous because I'm clumsy and inexperienced." Pil-sun was startled to realize that she and Deok-gi had grown familiar enough with each other to chat comfortably like this.

After a long pause, Deok-gi spoke again. "You know, I was considering helping you continue your studies. On the other hand, it wouldn't be bad for you to gain work experience, whatever it may be, but—" He stopped, remembering what Byeong-hwa had written—that Pil-sun should be allowed to decide for herself what she wanted. He didn't want to confuse her just when she had found something she liked.

Pil-sun hoped to draw him out, and said, "I'm in no position to study, and anyway, how can someone like me get an education?"

"You can always ask for my help if you need it. Let me be your sounding board if nothing else." Was he being too bold? Deok-gi was concerned that Pil-sun might misconstrue his intentions.

Pil-sun seemed to welcome his suggestion; blushing, she muttered something that Deok-gi didn't catch. It sounded like a thank you.

Parking his bicycle at the door, Byeong-hwa walked in and called out loudly, "I am so honored that you've come to grace our store with your presence!" He looked very clean-cut in his Western suit and overcoat.

"I see that you've abandoned a respectful form of speech, now that you're dressed as a gentleman."

"That'll change if you've come here to buy something."

"Then give me one-jeon worth of edamame beans," Deok-gi said as he took out his wallet.

"Thank you, sir, but we don't carry goods handled by tiny stores."

"By the way, a stranger came by a while ago. He was as rude as a police inspector. I have a feeling he'll come again."

Before Pil-sun had a chance to go into details, Byeong-hwa cut her short. "That's all right. Don't worry about it."

"Did you run into him on your way back?"

"No, I didn't, but it'll be all right." Byeong-hwa managed a feeble smile but seemed perturbed.

Lightheartedly, Deok-gi said, "He threatened to come back and beat you up and said that you opened the business with money from a Japanese detective or something."

Byeong-hwa smiled and said, "Bull's-eye!" Taking Deok-gi inside, he led him to a back room with an *ondol* floor. Pil-sun's mother's face lit up at the sight of Deok-gi. She scrambled to her feet, put down her sewing, and offered him a bow of condolence before taking her leave.

Why had Pil-sun's family moved here? Deok-gi wondered. Byeong-hwa was acting like the family's son-in-law.

"Where did you hear that rumor?" Byeong-hwa broached the subject after Pil-sun's mother left.

"So it's true?" Deok-gi asked with ill-concealed surprise.

"Far from it. But some people actually seem to think it is. I've just been to the prison, and the fellow I went to see already knew that I'd started this business."

"But Byeong-hwa, wasn't it wrong of you to drop your friends? You should have sought their understanding."

"How can I expect them to understand? And anyway, the ones that go around speaking ill of me without any grounds aren't even of my own group. They're just a bunch of blackmailers."

"Then what about your group?"

"There aren't many left, but the few that remain are saying nothing in my defense. They're passive, no one's said a word to me. For all I know, they're pleased to hear others bad-mouth me. Maybe they're cheering them on."

"Then why did you distance yourself from them all of a sudden? It's no surprise they suspect that policemen are helping you out."

"I don't care whether they suspect me or come and beat me up . . . Look, let's change the subject. I need to ask you a favor."

"What sort of favor?"

"I've already spent almost a thousand won since I started this business. It took only four hundred to acquire the store, but there wasn't any inventory to speak of, so we had to put in some five or six hundred to stock the shelves..."

Deok-gi debated whether he should hear him out or cut him short. "Where did the money come from?" he finally demanded.

"That doesn't matter. I told everyone it came from you. If something happens and you're questioned, or if they bring us face-to-face, just tell them you lent me a thousand because I had renounced my ideology and wanted to start a business. Tell them that you took it from your grand-father's money before he died and gave it to me at the hospital."

Deok-gi let out a belly laugh. "No problem. I'll give you as much as you need if we're talking about make-believe money, but where did that thousand actually come from that you have to be so circuitous?"

"If I could tell you that, why would I ask for such a stupid favor?"

"Is it true that it came from inspectors?"

"Are you crazy? Is that what you think?" Byeong-hwa jumped up. "Why don't you just leave?"

"You're dismissing your guest? Come on, let's talk a little more."

"They'll come again, and it wouldn't be good for them to see you here."

"All the more reason I should stay."

"You think so? A cowardly bourgeois gentleman like you giving me a hand? You'd have a hard time staying in one piece if they got their hands on you." Byeong-hwa went to his room, took off his Western jacket, and threw on a store uniform.

"Do you think the bourgeois have tofu for flesh and knitting needles for bones? Maybe you're looking to get involved in a gang fight." Smiling, Deok-gi put on his shoes and walked back into the store.

"To take on a gang *and* take care of business," Byeong-hwa said with a carefree laugh.

Deok-gi lingered, not having the heart to simply walk away. As he took a closer look around the store, the door to the shop creaked open. The young man who had been there earlier beckoned Byeong-hwa with a tilt of his head. As if he had been waiting for him, Byeong-hwa followed him out, saying to Deok-gi, "Go home. I'll see you in a day or two." Noticing muddy footprints on the floor, Byeong-hwa called out to Pil-sun, "What is this mud doing here? Sweep it up, will you?"

Outside, the ground had already started to freeze over, though it had thawed during the day. Byeong-hwa and his visitor walked side by side toward the streetcar terminus, bathed in a slant of sunshine. Pil-sun and Deok-gi followed Byeong-hwa's lonely back until he and the visitor disappeared past the terminus. Deok-gi told Pil-sun he'd be back soon and ran after them. She was afraid that Deok-gi might get involved in something dangerous, but she couldn't bring herself to discourage him.

As they reached Chuseongmun, Byeong-hwa turned around and saw Deok-gi following them. At first he stopped short and waved him away. From a distance, Pil-sun saw Deok-gi run toward the two men as Byeong-hwa stood waiting for his friend to catch up. They spoke briefly, and Deok-gi returned to the store.

"What did he say?" cried Pil-sun, who, with her mother, had watched the scene unfold.

"He says he's going to a friend's house at 110 Samcheong-dong through Chuseongmun. He says we shouldn't worry, that he'll be back in an hour. I didn't think I could do anything, even if I went along. Besides, I need to get home." Deok-gi knew that his family was waiting for him to oversee the evening mourning ritual. Missing one might not be a great offense, but it wouldn't have been proper to leave it to the women when the ceremony marking the first fortnight after his grandfather's death had not yet been held. Still, it was not easy to leave Pil-sun and her mother.

"Of course. I'm sure he'll be all right," Pil-sun's mother tried to assure him. She abruptly turned to Pil-sun. "Where did your father go? Why isn't he home yet?"

"When your father returns," Deok-gi advised Pil-sun, "tell him to go to Samcheong-dong to check on Byeong-hwa. I'll come back again right after the ritual." Deok-gi made a phone call to his house before leaving.

The electric lights came on after Pil-sun waited on a flurry of customers. Still no sign of Byeong-hwa, and her father hadn't yet returned. Once dinner was out of the way, her mother came out to the store again. Neither of them could do anything but worry about the men. Their mouths were dry.

From the store's glass door, Pil-sun frequently looked out in the direction Byeong-hwa had taken; Chuseongmun was bathed in hazy thirteenth-day moonlight. Her heart sank whenever a dark shadow approached, and her face lit up whenever she caught sight of a man in a passing streetcar who looked like Byeong-hwa, but it was never him. Deok-gi managed to phone around six o'clock. Hearing that they still had no news of Byeong-hwa, Deok-gi said that it would be a good idea to send someone to find him and that he would stop by after dinner.

Pil-sun couldn't wait for her father any longer; "Mother, I'd better go."

But her mother wasn't about to let her young daughter wander around Samcheong-dong after sundown. Pil-sun was also afraid that her mother, left alone in the store, would have difficulty selling even a pack of cigarettes. With her father still absent, she was scared that he, too, might be in trouble along with Byeong-hwa. She finally made up her mind and went out, her mother unable to hold her back any longer.

Pil-sun had hoped that Gyeong-ae would come by, but they'd seen nothing of her all day.

After Pil-sun left, the telephone rang. It was Deok-gi again. When he heard that Pil-sun had gone out, her mother was relieved to hear him say that he'd go to Samcheong-dong before coming to the store.

After quite some time, a rickshaw with a shade over the passengers' seat rolled into view, coming to a halt before the store. Hong Gyeong-ae stumbled out of it.

Pil-sun's mother was disgusted, thinking that Gyeong-ae was drunk again. Even so, she was glad to see the young woman.

"Where have you been?"

"Byeong-hwa — is Byeong-hwa home?"

The two spoke at once.

"Early this afternoon, he went . . ." Pil-sun's mother stopped short, shocked. "What's the matter?" she said, taking a closer look at Gyeong-ae's left cheek. It was swollen with a bluish bruise. Under the light she discovered that her eye over the swollen cheek was bloodshot and had closed into a narrow slit.

A chill shot down her spine as her daughter's face flashed through her mind.

"He hasn't come back? Did he leave with someone?" Gyeong-ae's voice was nasal and shaky, as if she were trying hard to hold back tears, but she was also somewhat drunk.

"Pil-sun went off to look for him. What happened to you?"

Tears welled up in Gyeong-ae's eyes, but she didn't reply. Collapsing in a heap by the doorway, Gyeong-ae said, "Please send the rickshaw away."

Pil-sun's mother asked the rickshaw driver where Gyeong-ae had boarded and was told that he'd picked her up in front of a Chinese restaurant in Hwagae-dong. After paying the eighty jeon he demanded without haggling, she rushed back in and asked who had been at the Chinese restaurant.

"Never mind. I was there by myself."

Pil-sun's mother was beside herself with worry; no one who had gone out tonight would come home safe and sound.

No matter how hard Pil-sun's mother tried to get the facts out of her, Gyeong-ae remained silent, deep in thought, tears rolling down her cheeks.

After a long silence Gyeong-ae asked, "So where did your daughter go to look for him?" Her voice had steadied.

"Samcheong-dong, I think. Number 110."

Gyeong-ae leapt to her feet and said she had to go look for them. The desire for vengeance took possession of her.

"Don't even think of it! You're not going anywhere in that condition. Let's wait a little longer because Jo Deok-gi said he'd go there, too."

Ignoring the older woman, Gyeong-ae flew out the door and headed toward the streetcar terminus in search of a rickshaw. Pil-sun's mother ran after her. Gyeong-ae carried herself briskly now, filled with purpose, not only to avenge the abuse she herself had suffered but also to defend Byeong-hwa.

Gyeong-ae was about to turn toward Jinmyeong Girls' School when she halted, her eyes fixed on something in the distance. Pil-sun's mother, startled, went out into the avenue and saw a group of dark shadows approaching in the hazy moonlight.

Pil-sun's mother never imagined that anyone would try to make their way through Chuseongmun at night, but when she saw Gyeong-ae sprinting toward them, she, too, broke into a run.

Pil-sun's mother couldn't believe her eyes. Her husband was at the front of the group, supported by two others. Behind him was Byeong-hwa, to whom Gyeong-ae clung.

"What happened? My God, how can they do this to an innocent man?" Pil-sun's mother whimpered, her voice breaking and her breath coming in short gasps.

"Stop talking . . . so loud . . ." her husband said, panting. He was supported by his daughter and Won-sam.

"How could someone do this to my husband? And Byeong-hwa? How is he?"

A rickshaw driver was supporting him, but his gait seemed steady.

Deok-gi, still in his mourning overcoat, told Pil-sun's mother to rush back to the store ahead of them to lay out the bedding. "Has the room been heated?"

Pil-sun's mother scurried away.

"Did they take you to the Chinese restaurant first?" asked Gyeong-ae.

"What Chinese restaurant?" Byeong-hwa replied in a nasal voice, for a torn handkerchief had been stuffed in his nostrils to stanch the bleeding.

"Then you didn't go to the Chinese restaurant. Those bastards!"

"What are you talking about?"

"Some bastard came to Bacchus and said you wanted to see me right away. I followed him, and there were three guys sitting there, bantering and eating and . . ." Gyeong-ae choked up with emotion.

Deok-gi cut in. "Why did they act the way they did?"

"I hope they didn't do anything to you." Byeong-hwa spoke in a measured voice.

"They're hoodlums." Gyeong-ae's voice was shrill.

"What did they do? Did they beat you, too?" He forgot about his own pain.

"I'll tell you the details later. Where does it hurt? Do you feel a throbbing or a dull pain?"

"No, I'm all right, except my nose bled some." Byeong-hwa seemed oddly indifferent.

"Why are you covered with mud? Where did you fight? How many people were there?"

"I think there were six drunks altogether—I'm sure I scared three of them out of their wits. They must have come from the Chinese restaurant."

When they finally reached the storefront and caught a glimpse of each other in the light, they were shocked; they looked as if they had tumbled into a sea of mud. A thin crust of ice coated the mud. Their suits were ruined, and their hands and faces were quite a sight. Luckily, there wasn't a single bruise on Pil-sun's father, who had difficulty standing on his own, but blood was running in scarlet rivulets over Byeong-hwa's muddied suit. His bloody mouth looked like that of a wild animal. Blood also streamed from a gaping wound on the back of his right hand; it looked like someone had bitten the flesh off. Afraid that onlookers might gather at the doorstep, they went into the store through a back alley. As they took off their clothes and cleaned themselves, Deok-gi tipped the rickshaw driver, who had accompanied them all the way from Suha-dong, and sent him on his way. The driver had left his gear at the stone steps on the Samcheong-dong side and now had to traipse through to Chuseongmun again to get it back.

Deok-gi had taken the rickshaw to Hwagae-dong in order to take Won-sam with him and had asked the driver to accompany them as backup, in anticipation of trouble.

Deok-gi ran to the telephone and called his family doctor to ask him to come over.

The gang had been seven in number; one had given orders to the other six. A pair of thugs had charged toward Byeong-hwa. Pil-sun's father, who had left the store ahead of Byeong-hwa, was dragged away by a man who had been waiting in the alley. The two that grabbed Byeong-hwa had missed him when he'd rushed out of the store and jumped onto a streetcar on his way to the prison. They had waited half a day for another chance.

Of the group, Gyeong-ae had had the roughest time. A stranger had come to Bacchus, insisting that Byeong-hwa was in trouble and needed her. He accompanied her to Anguk-dong and led her into a filthy little Chinese restaurant at the foot of the Hwagae-dong hill, where another man was waiting for them.

"Where's Byeong-hwa?" she demanded.

"Byeong-hwa? He's in hell. If you want to see him, you'll have to go look for him there yourself."

Gyeong-ae was overcome with fear. Trying to get out of there by any means possible, she made a fuss, argued, and even tried to win them over by drinking what they forced on her. But when she made a break for the door, one of them barred the way. She hated their disparaging remarks about Byeong-hwa. Their demand that she hand over the money, however, sent a chill through her.

The very sound of the word *money* made her dizzy. Had all her secrets been revealed? Had Byeong-hwa also been kidnapped? Were these men police snitches? Gyeong-ae was relieved when they insisted that she hand over the secret funds from the police.

"How long have you been frequenting the Police Affairs Bureau? We hear they gave you five thousand won. You gave two thousand to Byeong-hwa to open the business, so you've still got three. Give it to us, and we'll pretend we know nothing about it—we'll forget about the whole thing and let you go home. No one would know, not even our boss."

As they kept at her, threatening and coaxing, she laughed at them, careful not to show any fear.

"Let's go find Kim Byeong-hwa," Gyeong-ae said, as if willing to go along with their plan. "You can sort this out with him yourself."

They wouldn't hear of it, though. They continued to threaten her and started slapping her around. After two or three hours of abuse, they whispered to each other—most likely because they had run out of intimidation tactics—that they'd go fetch Byeong-hwa.

Then they began to quarrel: "You go!" "I'm not going." At last, the man who had lured Gyeong-ae to the restaurant went out tentatively, claiming that he was not as drunk as his partner. After a while, he came back with an older man. As the target of the drunkards' harassment, Gyeong-ae at first thought it was good that someone sober had been brought in, but then her heart lurched at the thought that perhaps this man was their boss.

When the older man, striding in, caught sight of the dishes and glasses strewn about on the table, he flew off the handle. "So you're rolling in money, aren't you? That's why you've been drinking so much? Get out of here!"

Watching the underlings slink away, retreating as if to the nearest hole, Gyeong-ae felt she could trust this newcomer.

The man told Gyeong-ae to sit down and asked, "When did you get here?"

In spite of Gyeong-ae's revulsion, there was something about his low-key manner that she found reassuring.

"Are you the one who made them lie to get me here? Who the hell are you?"

"A friend of Kim Byeong-hwa. I'm very sorry about all this, and I'll let you go if you give me a clear answer to one question: Where did Byeong-hwa's money come from?"

"How would I know? What do you hope to gain, dragging me here to ask such a stupid question?"

"It's far from stupid. I want to know the truth."

"I told you—I don't know."

"Then tell me this. The man who visited you a while ago—where is he now?"

Gyeong-ae's heart sank, and she broke out into a sweat. He interrogated her, first coaxing, then threatening. He slapped her several times and acted as if he might kill her on the spot. He shouted, "I'm not going to let a bitch like you seduce and corrupt Kim Byeong-hwa."

From the passion in his words, he could have been one of Byeong-hwa's comrades, but who knew whether he was just pretending to be a kindred spirit to get the information he wanted? She made up her mind not to breathe a word even if she were beaten to death.

The man continued to harass her for another hour, until a young man, whom she had not seen previously, looked in. Her interrogator told her to stay put and left the room. A moment later he returned. "I need to leave, but we'll see each other again soon. Think hard in the meantime. You will tell me the truth then!" He turned and went away, to her astonishment.

Perhaps he had received a message that Byeong-hwa had been brought in, Gyeong-ae wondered in hindsight.

Having listened quietly to Gyeong-ae's account while on his back, Byeong-hwa uttered quietly, "I'm sorry that you had to go through such a thing."

But Gyeong-ae's ordeal wasn't over—she had been captured by the drunken gang again. "Just as I was leaving, I saw the two guys jump out from nowhere—I couldn't do a thing. It was useless to provoke them, so I pleaded with them and was able to calm them a bit. Then I offered to pay the bill for their drinks. Only then did they loosen their grip on me."

"So they pummeled you and you bought them drinks," Pil-sun's mother commented, unable to suppress her outrage. She sat massaging her husband's lower back.

"Never mind about that." Stroking her swollen cheek, Gyeong-ae asked, "Why couldn't they agree on what they wanted to know, even among themselves?"

"You mean why were the two guys talking about secret funds while their boss had other ideas?" asked Byeong-hwa, who understood her right away. "Only a couple of people are privy to the whole story. The underlings will say anything that pops into their heads. Besides, those two were no comrades of mine. They're good-for-nothings who knock around and get themselves involved in a lot of bad business."

"I suspected as much. I wondered why they looked so uncertain when they badgered me about secret funds. They didn't know a thing." Gyeong-ae's eyes found Byeong-hwa's.

"How can those guys do anything right?" Deok-gi asked. "There must be professional brokers in their midst."

"They're not the brains of the outfit—they're the muscle," Byeong-hwa explained. "The bosses need guys like them. Nobody can do it alone. As for what happened today, they needed some young bait, a modern young man, somewhat rough, but with enough experience with women to be able to lure Gyeong-ae to the restaurant. If your goal is to spread the rumor that Kim Byeong-hwa has pocketed secret funds, using these fellows works better than running an ad in the papers. Those idiots have squandered all their family assets—they don't have enough money to buy a drink, let alone eat in restaurants. They get the cold shoulder at *gisaeng* houses, and even playing billiards is beyond their means. They can't stay home all day, so they run around Seoul as if it were their playground, sponging off whatever acquaintances they can. If you whisper something to them, it will spread immediately, faster than the morning headlines. And there's no better source of information than those guys when you want to gather rumors. I started this grocery business to feed and cultivate such people."

"I see that you're a generous Red," observed Deok-gi. "But there's a saying that your own trusted ax can chop off your foot. Looks like you'd better grow eyes in the back of your head."

"I intend to be careful. But if I manage to get through to these bastards, I might even be able to find a real comrade or two among the lot."

Jang Hun

———

Whenever Pil-sun's father let out a groan of pain, those sitting around him stopped talking and looked up at the clock, wondering why it was taking so long for the doctor to arrive.

Pil-sun's father had been taken hostage simply because Byeong-hwa had been late coming home. Unlike Gyeong-ae, he wasn't harassed at the house where he was held and had been treated as an elder, though he was considered incompetent among activist circles. When asked questions, he told them as much as he knew and defended Byeong-hwa. He told them he was helping the young man, though he was uncertain as to what his plans were. He claimed that he wasn't keeping an eye on Sanhaejin merely to stave off hunger, though as the saying goes, hunger is as scary as the Police Bureau. Meanwhile, Byeong-hwa had been brought in and had started arguing with the owner of the house. They were eventually released without further incident.

Nothing more would have happened had they taken the main road and made their way past the Government-General building. But since the incident had ended without mishap and night hadn't yet fallen, they let down their guard. Continuing past the Police Affairs Corps, they were about to climb the stone steps leading to Chuseongmun when Byeong-hwa was confronted by a man stumbling through the street. They bumped into each other, but Byeong-hwa said nothing in consideration of Pil-sun's father and kept climbing the steps, confident that the drunkard would be no match for him if he tried to pick a fight.

"You rude beggar!" the drunk cried, grabbing Byeong-hwa by the hair, just as he was about to walk past him. With the drunkards' words as a signal, several men swaggered out silently from the shadows. Byeong-hwa knew instinctively what was about to happen and shoved them away as they charged toward him. Pil-sun's father, however, was immediately thrown to the ground.

Passersby and people who lived in the area came to their aid. Fortunately, Pil-sun and Deok-gi arrived a few moments later, physically restrained the men, and brought Pil-sun's father and Byeong-hwa home.

Pil-sun had rushed off to find Byeong-hwa and managed to locate 110 Samcheong-dong, but she was told that the visitors had just left. Relieved but exhausted, she ran into Deok-gi. He had just stepped out of a rickshaw with Won-sam and was searching for the house with the help of the rickshaw driver, who held a lamp out in front of them.

Pil-sun had never felt so grateful for others' concern, nor had she ever trembled with the emotions that surged through her when she saw Deok-gi.

"Even if they were really drunk," Deok-gi speculated, "and had planned the whole thing in advance, how could they think they could get away with beating people up on such a busy street? Just across the bridge, neighbors were all around saying that they'd go fetch a policeman. What dimwits!"

When Deok-gi made this comment, Pil-sun looked up at him while kneading her father's shoulders. Her eyes grew brighter and a smile danced across her lips, but when her eyes found his, they immediately fell to the ground. She somehow knew to keep her emotion to herself.

At last, the doctor arrived. His eyes went first to the man lying in bed and then to Gyeong-ae's swollen cheek. A crowd had gathered around the store. The doctor tried to size up the situation as he approached the bedridden man: *Deok-gi, the millionaire's grandson, has summoned me. Would he pay for the treatment?*

"Two ribs have been fractured. How did this happen? He looks very weak, and the broken ribs are right over his left lung."

"Can we take him to your clinic?" Deok-gi asked, inching closer.

The room fell silent.

The doctor seemed to have gotten the answer to his question and said, "That would be helpful. But it would be better if I could take some X-rays first. Would you like me to call some people at the medical school nearby?"

"Please do everything in your power! As you see, it's cramped here, and the situation is dire."

Driven by Deok-gi's decisiveness, the doctor left to make the necessary phone calls.

"It's difficult to have X rays taken tonight, but we can at least take him to the hospital now. I can even operate if the situation warrants it. If we let him stay here, it'll certainly . . ." The doctor appeared genuinely concerned.

Once the doctor finished tending to the cuts on Byeong-hwa's chin and on the back of his hand, they took Pil-sun's father to the hospital. Though Deok-gi was young, he was now a thousand-rice-bag-a-year millionaire; his wealth made it impossible for the doctor to refuse him this favor.

Byeong-hwa wanted to accompany Pil-sun's father to the hospital, but everyone was against the idea and insisted that he stay behind. His body hurt all over, and with Pil-sun and her mother also going to the hospital, he couldn't leave Gyeong-ae behind by herself.

Deok-gi asserted, "I'll go with them on your behalf. You should lie down." Pil-sun and her mother nearly wept with gratitude. After everyone left in a taxi, Gyeong-ae took care of Byeong-hwa and prepared for her overnight stay. Now that all the commotion had passed, she realized for the first time that day how hungry she was. Pil-sun's mother had brought in a dinner tray earlier, but no one had touched it. No one had felt like picking up their chopsticks after such a night.

"I wonder what's going on at the hospital. I should call," Byeong-hwa said.

"Don't worry about it. I'll call. Eat your stew before it gets cold." Gyeong-ae stood up and walked toward the store, but Byeong-hwa held her back and went to the telephone himself. Gyeong-ae draped his overcoat over his shoulders and returned to put the stew on the brazier.

"They say he needs surgery right away. I'd better go." Byeong-hwa lost his appetite.

"Is it that serious?"

"They say he'll be all right after the operation, but how can I stay here when Deok-gi is staying there overnight? I should be there, too."

"You're right, but you're in no shape to leave the house. And even if you do go, how will your presence help the operation?"

"Yeah, but this is no way to behave."

"I'll go in your stead if you feel that way. Nevertheless, the rest of them should eat something, especially when it's so cold outside. Should we order something for them?"

"That sounds good, though they're probably too worried to eat."

Gyeong-ae went out to the store and called a *soba* restaurant. She then called the hospital and told Deok-gi that dinner would be arriving soon and that he should make sure that Pil-sun and her mother eat.

Byeong-hwa appreciated her efforts.

Gyeong-ae returned and sat across from Byeong-hwa with the meal tray between them. "He's already in surgery, and it'll be over in about thirty minutes. Deok-gi will come here when things calm down, so he says there's no need for you to go out on a cold night like this."

Tears gathered in Byeong-hwa's eyes as he listened to her quietly. He was touched by everyone's kindness and overwhelmed with conflicting emotions. He couldn't bear to think of what Gyeong-ae had suffered because of him. Now she was comforting *him* and worrying about Pil-sun and her mother.

It had been less than ten days since Pil-sun's family had escaped the hovel at the edge of Hyeonjeo-dong. Delighted over their unexpected good fortune, they no longer had to consider over breakfast whether they'd have something to eat come dinnertime. But their joy was short-lived. Pil-sun's father was now hovering between life and death. Imagining what Pil-sun and her mother must be going through—their uncertainty and despair for the fate of the household—Byeong-hwa couldn't help but weep for them. What about the man himself? Broken from years in prison, he had gone hungry day after day. Only recently had he begun to regain his confidence, learning the ins and outs of the grocery business, clinging to the hope that his wife and daughter wouldn't have to go hungry again. Now he had been beaten to a pulp for no reason at all. Pity pulled at Byeong-hwa's heart.

Deok-gi must have some worries of his own, now that he was the guardian of his family's safe. That he would become involved in this unpleasant business that had nothing to do with him impressed Byeong-hwa greatly. The affection he felt was not simply sentimentalism in the wake of a crisis.

"Chiang Kai-shek is not a bad guy after all. Not bad at all. His true colors came out today." Byeong-hwa muttered to himself as he picked up his chopsticks.

Gyeong-ae stared at him in bewilderment. Had he lost his mind? "What are you talking about? What about Chiang Kai-shek?"

Byeong-hwa laughed and said, "You don't know Chiang Kai-shek?"

"What's wrong with you? Why are you acting this way?"

"Chiang Kai-shek, who has given us such a hard time. You know, Jang Hun."

"So that guy is Jang Hun? You're calling him Chiang Kai-shek?" The two were complicit again. The leader of the aggressors had a "Jang" in his name, a Chinese character rare among Korean surnames, so the nickname Chiang Kai-shek caught on.

"Well, what about him?"

"He's more considerate than he looks," Byeong-hwa said as he began to eat his rice.

"Oh? What makes you think so?"

"We've been taken in by his tricks." Byeong-hwa was now shoveling food into his mouth. He told Gyeong-ae, who hadn't touched her chopsticks, to eat, while he continued devouring the food set before him.

"Slow down. Talk to me while you eat. You'll give yourself a stomachache, eating so fast. Go on with your story."

"Huh?"

"About that Chiang Kai-shek or Jang Hun."

"I've said enough."

"Are you making fun of me? If you can't talk about it, why did you bring it up in the first place?" It annoyed her that Byeong-hwa still didn't trust her.

Byeong-hwa sat smoking and then stretched out to rest. One of his arms throbbed with a dull pain, and his swollen hand was tingling.

"You don't trust me because I'm a woman. How old-fashioned and feudal! It's not that I'm dying to know, but after all I've gone through, I have the right to know. It'd be different if it had nothing to do with me." Pouting, Gyeong-ae pulled a Haetae cigarette from her pocket and lit it over the brazier.

Someone rapped on the front door. "Do you have any cigarettes?" A man's voice.

"Which brand?" Gyeong-ae shouted as she lifted the small bolt from the door. The tiny door flung open, a cold wind swept in, and a man clad in a Korean coat entered, ducking his head under the low doorframe.

Her hair stood up on end as she took a step back and stifled a shriek. This cheerful man was none other than the bastard who had given her such a hard time at the Chinese restaurant earlier. Chiang Kai-shek.

A dingy scarf was tied over the black overcoat, and by the way his Korean socks were pulled up over his trousers' ankle ties, he looked like a police inspector in disguise.

Still wearing a mocking smile, he signaled toward the room with his chin.

"Is Kim in?" He seemed eager to invite himself in.

Had he not done enough for one night? Was he alone? Gyeong-ae's mind was spinning, yet she remained calm.

Byeong-hwa appeared.

"Come on in." Byeong-hwa didn't seem surprised, nor did he seem particularly glad to see the visitor.

"Well, it's good to find you home. No need to invite me in. There's something I'd like to know." His eyes settled on Byeong-hwa's bandaged hand. Breezily, he asked, "We didn't hurt you too much, did we?"

Does anyone, after beating someone up, ask after his victim? Who's kinder—someone who checks in on a fellow he punched out, or someone who forces a friend to get drunk and then comes by the next day to buy him a chaser for his hangover?

Byeong-hwa's reply was no less absurd. "Somehow I survived, and Comrade Yi just has a broken rib." Byeong-hwa held up a finger.

Jang burst out laughing shamelessly and asked, "Is he in bed?"

"You can't ignore a broken rib. He went to have it removed."

At this, Jang laughed again.

"If you feel like some meat, stop by the medical-school hospital on your way home. They must've carved it out by now. Clamp your teeth around it and take it home. You can do whatever you want with it—tuck it away or barbeque it . . ." Byeong-hwa smiled.

Jang asked, "Are you angry?"

"What's there to be angry about? The only thing I don't understand is why that idiot gang of yours had to do that to an elderly man." Byeong-hwa raised his voice. "Besides, your guys used tools, like butchers!"

"Quiet down, the Police Bureau people may hear you! My people aren't the only ones who use tools to harm people. Anyway, I'm sorry. I told them not to go to such lengths. At least it's over and done with now. Well, I'm off. I just stopped by to see how you are. Please don't hold a grudge against me." With that, Jang Hun vanished.

Gyeong-ae was flabbergasted by this exchange. Had everyone lost their minds? Did they think what had happened was a joke? Her ears were ringing.

"Do you find it amusing when someone is on the threshold between life and death?" Gyeong-ae had made sure that the door was locked.

"He must have wanted to check up on me because he was nervous." Byeong-hwa laughed it off and lay down again.

"What a piece of work—the type of person who'd host a burial for a man he's killed. Is that his mission?"

"Of course not. Actually, he floated the rumor that I had pocketed secret funds. When the younger ones in the gang made such a big fuss, he allowed them to take it out on me. But I believe that he told them not to hurt me."

"And that makes sense to you? He could have told you that because he wants to save face or because he's afraid of reprisals. No one would ever admit responsibility for such an incident. As for the money, were secret funds from the Police Affairs Bureau the only thing he could come up with? If he really wanted to help you, he could have said that a friend had lent it to you. Why make up a story about secret funds?"

"That's not it. When Pi-hyeok was here, he met with Jang Hun before me. Jang knows everything—how much was given to whom and where it was given. Only two people know this, other than the ones who handled the money: you and Jang. When we used the money to open a grocery store, Jang Hun wanted to know if we thought we could get away with it. This was his first conundrum."

If Byeong-hwa had pocketed the money or opened the store with a lot of fanfare, the authorities and his comrades would both say that the money had to have come either from secret police funds or from abroad, an allegation that would interfere with other comrades' work. Furthermore, although police detectives were now praising Kim Byeong-hwa for renouncing his radicalism, they would eventually try to discover the truth. For all Jang Hun knew, they could've sniffed it out already. If Byeong-hwa were caught, Jang Hun's work would be put in jeopardy, and he would be in danger. And if Pi-hyeok's part in it came to light with Byeong-hwa's arrest, Jang Hun would be in trouble immediately. Jang Hun needed to prove to the authorities that his entourage and Byeong-hwa's were not one and the same. Like shutting off electricity with an insulator, no sparks could land on Jang Hun if he severed his ties with Byeong-hwa. Jang Hun intended to have an excuse in place even before one was needed.

Jang Hun had another purpose: to make Kim Byeong-hwa reflect on his misdeeds. Whether Byeong-hwa was blinded by a woman or dazzled by the money, Jang Hun intended to give him a jolt and to reignite his dulled ambition for the struggle. The attack was both a lesson and a warning to other comrades whose dedication might be wavering.

Such a clash between two groups might also deflect the police's suspicion of Byeong-hwa. Secret funds do not come from a single source, and even police agents themselves don't know exactly how these funds are relayed. As long as nothing wildly out of the ordinary happened, the police wouldn't do anything about it. They might even try to recruit the suspects. In fact, Jang Hun couldn't be sure that Byeong-hwa wasn't being used by the police, but even if he were, he knew that he could be trusted not to inform them about Pi-hyeok's visit. Byeong-hwa might be nonplussed to find himself the target of a temporary misunderstanding, but it was a move intended to provide him with an out, in case he needed one.

Jang Hun hadn't said a word about his plan when he had met with Byeong-hwa earlier that day. "Give me the money," he had said, as if it were his own.

"What are you talking about?"

"Don't waste your breath. Just give it to me. That money wasn't for you to open a grocery store or for Hong Gyeong-ae to use as pocket change."

"What are you talking about?"

Jang Hun tossed a rolled-up bundle to Byeong-hwa. "Then buy this!"

"What is it?"

"Just open it. It should be worth at least that much."

When Byeong-hwa failed to open the bundle, Jang Hun opened it himself. It contained a black Korean overcoat, a pair of shoes, and a small pistol.

"This coat looks familiar, doesn't it? And you've seen these shoes before, too, haven't you?" Jang pointed to the pistol and said, "I don't intend to aim it at you, but if you don't want to buy these things, I'll use them to buy your life. Then you can leave the money to Hong Gyeong-ae as an inheritance." A cold smile played over his lips.

"All right! But I can't buy them now. I don't have any cash on me."

"Then what will you use?"

"Why are you doing this?"

"To protect myself!"

"Then there's nothing more to say. This coat and these shoes are clear evidence that you helped Pi-hyeok disguise himself to get out of the country. You can't expose him. After all, it's not just you, but the owner of the coat, his daughter, his wife . . . many are involved. That's why I'm showing this to you as if I had all the time in the world."

"Put that stuff away. And get rid of it. You're taking a big risk by keeping it around."

This was as far as their talk had gone at Samcheong-dong earlier that day.

Gyeong-ae was digesting Byeong-hwa's story. "But why did Pi-hyeok take his coat off there before leaving?"

"It was so small that he and Jang Hun decided to swap coats. I had assumed he left Seoul right away, but apparently he met Jang Hun somewhere before leaving."

Gyeong-ae simply nodded.

When Pi-hyeok fled Gyeong-ae's house, the rubber shoes Byeong-hwa supplied were too cumbersome to walk in, so he went back to his Western shoes, which he eventually left with Jang Hun. And the six-chamber pistol? About that, Jang Hun was silent.

Not knowing when his house might be searched, Jang Hun took the coat and shoes home and used them himself, but the weapon he kept hidden somewhere.

"But why did he have to beat a person to the brink of death?" Gyeong-ae still had her doubts.

"Before I left, Jang Hun quietly warned me to watch my back because his men might get carried away."

"You're so naïve! He could've easily talked his underlings out of mugging you."

"And the others might have thought that the two of us had cooked up a scheme to share the funds. Jang Hun's influence over his subordinates only goes so far. Besides, he was itching to have a full-fledged fight with me so he could let the world know that we had parted ways once and for all. Only then could we carry out our work comfortably. Things could be worse. Of course, it wasn't so good for you and Pil-sun's father."

"Wasn't so good? Luckily for you, I'm not the one with the broken rib." An angry flame darted from Gyeong-ae's eyes. "I've never been handled so roughly in my life. But even so, what kind of fool would stroll down a pitch black road at night in such circumstances?"

"I was actually thinking of turning back when I stumbled upon those drunkards. I actually never imagined that Jang Hun had made them do it. Only later at Samcheong-dong did I discover that he was behind it!"

Gyeong-ae erupted. "I don't want to hear any more! Stop talking such nonsense and wake up! You've been tricked by Jang Hun once, but who's to say he won't deceive you again? Do you think you'll be so lucky the second time around?"

"Why?"

"What do you mean, why? It's clear that he's just making something up so he can get all the credit. Can't you see he wants to have his cake and eat it, too?"

"I don't think so." Byeong-hwa looked up at the ceiling.

"For all we know, Pi-hyeok could be half dead, lying in some jail cell groaning with pain. This Chiang Kai-shek could have pocketed a considerable amount by now."

"I don't believe it."

"Your not believing it might get you killed! Before the night is over, a motorcycle gang will burst in on us, trust me!"

"That won't happen," Byeong-hwa tried not to waver.

Gyeong-ae paid no attention. "Let's not stay here tonight."

"That's crazy. If you're so worried, why don't you just go home?"

"If we're in danger, at least we'd be together if I stay. We'd still be in danger if I went home." The telephone rang.

"It could be the hospital," Gyeong-ae said, but her heart shuddered, as if she were alone in the dark after listening to ghost stories.

"Is Kin-san there?" The caller sounded Japanese. Gyeong-ae blanched.

"Who is this? Why are you calling?" Gyeong-ae replied stiffly.

"This is Geumcheon." Gyeong-ae had met this man several times since the store opened. Lacking the composure to exchange greetings with him, she put down the receiver and rushed over to Byeong-hwa.

"Who? Geumcheon?" Byeong-hwa asked, still horizontal.

"What do you want me to say? Should I say you're not in?" Gyeong-ae tried to hide her fear.

"I'll take it." Byeong-hwa grunted with pain as he raised himself.

Gyeong-ae changed her mind and thought it would be useless to say Byeong-hwa was out.

"It's surprising you've already heard of—Yes, I have a little cut on the back of my hand . . . Well, they were drunk . . . If secret funds were so easy to come by, I'd be grateful for a small share of them."

Gyeong-ae, standing beside Byeong-hwa, could hear Geumcheon laughing along with Byeong-hwa. Her face brightened, and she smiled, too.

"At nine o'clock tomorrow morning? I'll be there. But there's no reason to make them sleep there, is there? Please send them home tonight . . . Yes, I'll see you tomorrow. Good night."

As soon as Byeong-hwa got off the phone, Gyeong-ae grabbed his good hand, and asked, "Do they want you to report there tomorrow?"

"Yes. The drunkards have been arrested."

"How?"

"I don't know. The guy was making fun of me. He said I should have thrown a party instead of pocketing all the money myself. He asked me why I beat them up, saying I behaved like someone who not only refuses to give a beggar money, but breaks his bowl as well."

"So they talked about the secret funds at the police station?"

"I'm not surprised. They could have said anything in their state. They're being kept there overnight."

"Good!" But Gyeong-ae wasn't as delighted as she sounded.

It was almost midnight when Deok-gi called from the hospital to say that the operation had gone well and that he had decided to go home. At dawn, Byeong-hwa went to the hospital, leaving Gyeong-ae alone at the store. He felt obliged to visit the patient, and the bandage on the back of his hand needed changing; more importantly, he had to be at the police station at nine o'clock.

They didn't open the store. Byeong-hwa wasn't able to remove the plank door by himself, for his hand was throbbing even more violently than the night before.

On his way to the hospital, Byeong-hwa ran into Pil-sun on the street and told her to take the day off, but she opened the store in a hurry as soon as she got there. She had agreed with her mother to take turns minding it. Gyeong-ae rolled up her sleeves and did her share.

"How can we not open? We have regular customers. We'd better do what we are supposed to do, especially at a time like this." Gyeong-ae cast a grateful, admiring glance toward Pil-sun.

"I can watch the store by myself if I can practice for an hour. Just tell me how much things cost and then go on to the hospital," Gyeong-ae offered.

"I don't know many of the prices myself."

The two women, their worries forgotten, worked together in easy companionship. After a while, Won-sam trudged in. Byeong-hwa had gone to see him on his way to the hospital and had asked him to help out for the day. As soon as he arrived, he got straight down to business.

"You might not guess it from looking at me, but I can do anything. I can cook rice, I can boil soup, and I can even ride a bike if you want me to make deliveries. But I don't know how to go around beating people up, like the master does." Amid the young women's laughter, Won-sam picked up a broom and busied himself.

One Girl's Sorrow

———

After a flurry of morning customers, Gyeong-ae briefly left the store to check on her daughter and mother at home. As soon as she returned, Pil-sun rushed over to the hospital to relieve her mother.

Byeong-hwa still hadn't returned from the police station.

At the hospital, Pil-sun stayed by her father's bed until he fell into a deep slumber. Only then did she slip quietly from the room and gaze at the streets through the picture window in the corridor. Gwanghwamun loomed in front of her, standing tall in the mist of the field on the other side of the stream. The overcast day weighed heavily on Pil-sun, making her feel even more exhausted than she already was.

She noticed a few people flying kites on the frozen stream. Young children frolicked around them.

Today was still part of the long New Year's holidays, Pil-sun realized. *Until tomorrow they'll be flying kites and bouncing on seesaws.* She couldn't remember the last time she had heard the creak of a seesaw. Unlike most young women her age, she'd grown up totally isolated from other girls and had never worn a New Year's outfit or gone out to play during the first two weeks of the new year. For a long time, she stood listlessly at the window, melancholy rising within her. Sadness held a part of her while anticipation tugged at another. Her moods fluctuated like passing shadows or the drowsiness that invades you on a warm spring day. She felt like crying and laughing at once, as if she had just set her wedding date. Drifting through a fog, no particular thought remained in her head for long.

Wondering if Deok-gi would come, she began to watch the people approaching the hospital. He had called the store earlier that morning, inquiring after Pil-sun's father. He promised to stop by the hospital later.

I'm not going to wait for him. If he comes, I wouldn't know what to do. Pil-sun made excuses to herself and tried to shake off the thought of him. Deok-gi's sister came to mind. Though Pil-sun had never seen her, she imagined that she was a pretty girl who dressed in finery and who whirled around her big house, giggling happily.

Some people have no worries. Ashamed of having such a thought, Pil-sun tried to push it away. She could hear her father and Byeong-hwa chastising her. She turned around suddenly, thinking she had heard her father's voice. But when she silently pushed the door open, she could see her father sleeping in the bed by the window. The other patients turned their pale countenences toward her. Gently, she closed the door and returned to her post.

The hospital stay costs three won a day, which comes to ninety won a month. We make only five won a day at the shop, perhaps because we've just started, and we depend on the store for our living. After paying the hospital bill, we may even go through all that we have.

Pil-sun tormented herself with these worries. Also she couldn't bear to see her father lying under nothing but a dingy, paper-thin sheet with which he had covered himself three winters in a row. Her cheeks burned, imagining what others might think of the grimy sheet. At the hospital, they talked about providing a blanket but claimed it hadn't yet been returned from the wash. The other patients in the room had been placed in better beds, while her father was exposed to a draft from the window. Byeong-hwa had offered his own quilt in the morning, but that seemed out of the question. Pil-sun didn't have the heart to soil his new Japanese quilt that he had recently bought to sleep on the tatami floor at the store. What would he cover himself with at night?

She worked herself into a frenzy, until she could picture herself following a funeral bier. But then, from out of the blur came a familiar Western suit, about to cross Jongchinbu Bridge stretching out below her.

Managing to compose herself as blood rushed to her head, Pil-sun wiped away her tears. Deok-gi had already crossed the bridge. How delightful it would be if she could open the window and welcome him with a graceful wave. Pil-sun swallowed her excitement; her pride wouldn't allow it. She fully understood the tacit constraints of her position. His education, wealth, and class were vastly different from hers, and she would appear a flirtatious, loose woman if she weren't careful. But nevertheless, she was simply happy to see him. He was so elegant and pleasing to look at. Whenever a welcoming, joyful smile bloomed from her eyes and mouth, however, she did her best to disguise it. Her hidden joy would linger like fog hanging low on a cloudy day.

When Deok-gi reached the hospital gate, he caught sight of Pil-sun and smiled. She returned the smile and withdrew from the window.

Pil-sun met Deok-gi at the front door. The rattle of a bicycle being parked outside made them notice Won-sam. "Master! You walked over so fast." He bowed and brought over a bulky package.

Deok-gi thanked him. Pil-sun hurriedly intercepted it, preventing him from carrying the bundle himself.

Holding a fruit basket in one hand and a pale brown blanket, tied with a leather strap like a traveler's pack, in the other, she blushed and said, "You're so generous."

"Miss, I'm running two errands today—as a deliveryman for Sanhaejin and as the master's servant." Won-sam laughed as he turned away.

"You should take a break to thaw yourself out. Are you returning to the store?" Pil-sun called after Won-sam.

"It's all right. I'd better hurry back. Your mother says she'll be here soon, so I expect you'll come afterward, right?" Won-sam jumped on his bicycle and pedaled away powerfully. Deok-gi and Pil-sun watched him go, exchanging glances and smiling.

"I see that he's good-hearted, though I've known him only a few days."

"If he's useful, why don't you keep him as a helper?"

"I don't know whether he wants to or if the Hwagae-dong family will let him."

"It can be arranged one way or another." They walked down the long corridor together. "That blanket, you won't mind? It was my grandfather's. He wasn't covered with it when he died, though."

"Of course not. I don't know how to express my gratitude for your constant—"

"Please don't mention it. Your father looked so cold yesterday . . . But some people don't like using things that belonged to the dead."

"Do only the living use hospital beds and quilts? I'll cover my father with it, but you really didn't have to . . ." Pil-sun was so moved that her throat tightened and she couldn't finish her sentence.

When she spread the blanket over her father, he seemed pleased but was too weak to express his thanks.

Deok-gi sat briefly by the bed before beckoning Pil-sun to the corridor. Deok-gi lit a cigarette and spoke slowly. "You haven't heard from Kim, have you?"

"Not yet. Why? Has something happened?"

"They searched the house a while ago."

"What? The store?"

"They were looking for Gyeong-ae. She had gone out to take a bath, but your mother told them that she had gone home. Someone is still waiting there. Won-sam was waiting outside when I got there and told me what was going on, and your mother gave me a signal with her eyes, so I pretended that I was a costumer and bought some fruit. Otherwise, I don't know how long I would have been detained."

"Then my mother can't come, can she?" Pil-sun was anxious about what would happen at the hospital if she went home and was held there, and her mother was not allowed to leave, either. She still couldn't entrust the store to her mother, who knew only that a pack of Pigeons was ten jeon and Maekos five jeon. She didn't even know how much she should ask for Haetaes.

"Shall I go and make a phone call?"

"To ask your mother to come?"

"I can't leave here until she arrives," said Pil-sun as she headed downstairs. After a while, she came back accompanied by a man in a Western suit. Deok-gi immediately understood the nature of the visit.

Pil-sun seemed flustered; she shot a quick warning glance to Deok-gi.

Studying the stranger's face, Deok-gi could see that the man wasn't there to take Pil-sun away, but his heart was still pounding.

The man doffed his hat and said, "You must be Mr. Jo Deok-gi." He grinned unpleasantly while remaining perfectly polite.

Whatever the detective inwardly thought of Deok-gi, he bowed deeply, though to his seasoned eye, Deok-gi, clad in a student uniform with gold buttons, couldn't possibly amount to much; yet, he was the Jo family heir.

"I was told that you'd be here. I'm sorry, but will you please come with me?"

"What is this all about? Is it because I gave Kim Byeong-hwa some money?" Deok-gi laughed and added, "Let's go. But why make life difficult for someone who's trying to clean up his act and support himself?"

"I don't think this is anything serious. We just need to get some information because a few guys are making some noise." The detective had underestimated Deok-gi—the young man was unexpectedly firm and confident.

Pil-sun handed Deok-gi's hat to him, whispering, "They've taken Gyeong-ae. The detectives are still there."

Several of them must be surrounding the store, Deok-gi thought. The news gave Deok-gi a jolt.

"Can you stay here? Did your mother say she'd come?" Deok-gi asked as he followed the detective out.

"She can't. I'll wait here." Resigned, Pil-sun watched him disappear, wondering whether or not she'd see him again.

If Pi-hyeok's plot were exposed, she'd be taken away, too. But perhaps things hadn't gotten that bad yet. Pil-sun thought she wouldn't mind being taken to the police, along with everyone else. Nothing frightened her except her mother being left all alone. She knew that Deok-gi was innocent, and even if he weren't allowed home this evening, he'd be released soon enough, perhaps with Byeong-hwa.

Once she had regained her calm, Pil-sun sat down in the hospital room, which was dark enough to make her feel drowsy, when her mother rushed in.

"Mother! They let you leave?" Pil-sun ran to her.

"Go quickly. I asked Won-sam to keep an eye on the store. Neither of us knows how to make a phone call —"

"Has the detective left?"

"Yes, just now. Where's Mr. Jo?"

"They took him from here."

"That's terrible. He will have another sleepless night." She spoke of Deok-gi as if he were her own son. Stroking the blanket now draped over her husband, she asked quietly, "And how can we repay him?"

Pil-sun went back to the store. People were constantly coming and going. Their prices were lower than most of other stores and they were generous with their portions, even if it amounted to only a few extra stalks of green onions. Their circle of customers was growing.

Whenever there was a lull, Pil-sun leaned against the doorframe and gazed listlessly at the mountains in the distance.

When she spotted Deok-gi arriving in a rickshaw, her heart leapt. If she didn't have to worry about what he might think of her, she would have run out and grasped his hand.

"They asked me to give them proof that I had given Byeong-hwa a thousand won. I had to take a detective home and then go back to the police station."

"What did you show them?"

"I happened to have a check drawn in the amount of a thousand won dated two days before my grandfather's death, so I gave them that." Pil-sun was relieved.

"Even so, they refused to release Byeong-hwa and Gyeong-ae, so I stopped by Gyeong-ae's house to fetch a quilt and warm clothes, but the police wouldn't allow them in. Gyeong-ae's mother is still waiting there. Maybe they'll be released soon."

Deok-gi called out to Won-sam, "Is there a beef-soup restaurant around here? I haven't eaten yet."

"You haven't eaten! We have some rice but nothing to go with it." Pil-sun was at a loss. "I can't believe they dragged you all over town and didn't even give you a moment to sit down for dinner."

As Won-sam was stepping out, he remembered Pil-sun. "You haven't eaten yet, either. Should I order for two?"

"I don't want anything. I don't feel like eating."

"Then order for three people, Won-sam. You should eat, too."

"No, thank you, sir. I already ate."

After Won-sam left, Pil-sun went to the kitchen and set a tray. She brought it out and put it aside in a corner, to await the soup.

"I don't know what to say," Pil-sun said, as she stood by the stove with her head bowed.

"Why?"

"I had no idea that you went to such trouble, going from one place to another without pausing to have dinner. I was actually upset that you didn't phone me. It was wrong of me to be angry with you."

"Not at all! It wasn't wrong of you. I knew that you'd be anxious waiting all by yourself, but I thought I could come sooner. I'm sorry."

"Your apologizing makes me feel even worse. You've had such bad luck since yesterday, all because of us."

"Please don't mention it." Deok-gi was touched by this young woman's unadorned, frank words. No one would ever guess that she had worked at a rubber factory until recently. He wished she could always retain her natural innocence.

Deok-gi hesitated a moment before asking, "Do you have any idea how Byeong-hwa was able to buy the store?" He feared his question might have come too abruptly, but it was what he most wanted to know.

"I don't know. Did someone say something?" The look on her face told him that it was a difficult subject for her.

"No. I haven't heard anything except that that man Jang Hun made a terrible scene. Byeong-hwa asked me to pretend I supplied a thousand won in seed money. The whole thing is suspicious any way you look at it."

Deok-gi waited for Pil-sun's reply, but she hesitated, wondering whether she should reveal everything she knew. Won-sam's arrival with the beef soup put their conversation on hold.

Pil-sun asked Deok-gi to go sit in the back room and took the tray to him. Her cheeks burned at the thought that Gyeong-ae must have served Byeong-hwa in this manner the night before.

"Bring your soup, too, so that we can eat together."

"No, thank you. I'll eat later."

"The soup is getting cold. Come on, eat here at the stove." Won-sam put a bowl of soup on the stove.

"Here, Won-sam, take the change and get some rice wine for yourself. It's so cold today."

Won-sam dashed out to get some.

"That fellow, Jang Hun, why hasn't he been arrested?" Pil-sun felt bad deceiving Deok-gi, pretending she knew nothing when actually she knew quite a lot.

"Well, his name wasn't mentioned at the police station . . . perhaps they haven't gotten around to him yet. The focus of their questions was the thousand won, but Jang Hun couldn't have given it to Byeong-hwa, could he?"

Seeing that Deok-gi was slurping his soup with gusto, Pil-sun brought the earthenware pot from the stove and refilled his bowl.

"Someone . . . was here. From abroad," Pil-sun volunteered. She couldn't deceive him any longer.

"From abroad?"

"He gave money to Mr. Kim to do something, and that guy Jang Hun didn't like it, saying that Mr. Kim opened the store with the money he was given." Pil-sun was reluctant to say anything more.

"But what difference does it make to Jang what Kim does with the money?" Deok-gi asked.

"Because if he were arrested, the incident might escalate further. They might even take me in, too," Pil-sun explained as she took away the tray.

At that point, muffled voices were heard from outside. Gyeong-ae and her mother entered the store behind a rickshaw driver, who was carrying a bundle of quilts.

Parents

——

Gyeong-ae's mother had waited at the police station. When Gyeong-ae was finally released, she insisted on stopping by the store. Her mother came along, thinking she might as well have a look at the place.

Her mother had frowned on the idea of Gyeong-ae opening a store with Byeong-hwa, worrying that they might grow intimate. She was not at all pleased to learn that Gyeong-ae had slept at the store the night before to take care of Byeong-hwa. Earlier that day, Deok-gi had mentioned that Pil-sun's entire family had been out and that Byeong-hwa and Gyeong-ae had stood vigil at the store alone; Gyeong-ae's mother could no longer ignore the situation.

Without any knowledge of Pi-hyeok's bundle, she took it for granted that the money for the grocery had come from Sang-hun. She was familiar with their former benefactor's ways. She suspected that the two would reunite someday, even though they had been estranged for a few years. So when her daughter opened the store as soon as Sang-hun's father died, it pleased her to imagine that they were getting back together, which was the right course for them.

If Sang-hun and Gyeong-ae could just get along without too much trouble, she believed that she could spend her remaining days in comfort. What did it matter whether Deok-gi or Sang-hun was the heir? Weren't their pockets interchangeable? Gyeong-ae's association with Byeong-hwa at such a crucial time—that was reckless of her. Though Gyeong-ae had become friendly with Byeong-hwa through Pi-hyeok, her mother nevertheless remained uneasy. Sang-hun must have approved of Byeong-hwa's involvement in the store, and Byeong-hwa seemed to have a woman of his own, yet if something went wrong and aroused Sang-hun's suspicions, things might get ugly. Now that Gyeong-ae had been dragged into trouble because of Byeong-hwa, and with Sang-hun nowhere to be seen, the mother couldn't make heads or tails of the affair.

Looking right through Pil-sun, Gyeong-ae's mother greeted Deok-gi warmly. "Why are you still out on a cold day like this?" Her eyes fell on the empty beef-soup bowl. "Is that soup all you've eaten?"

Deok-gi smiled.

Gyeong-ae's mother bustled from one corner of the room to another, even swinging open the door to the toilet. "I could possibly live here in the summer, but never in the winter!"

Who asked her to come and live here? Gyeong-ae thought. Conscious of Pil-sun's presence, she was mortified by her mother's presumptuousness.

"Mother, please go home."

"Aren't you coming, too? Let's go together."

"I'll come later. Don't worry about me. Go home and get a good night's sleep. What if the baby wakes up?"

"You should come home now, eat something hot, and get some rest yourself."

While the mother and daughter were arguing, Byeong-hwa appeared, trailed by Won-sam's wife. They all stood up to welcome the newcomers.

"I'm sorry that all of you had to go through such trouble, especially Deok-gi." Byeong-hwa didn't show a trace of fatigue.

"Lie down on the *ondol* floor. You need to thaw yourself," Gyeong-ae urged.

Gyeong-ae's mother averted her eyes.

"Yes, she's right. Come on, let's go to the other room," Deok-gi suggested.

"No, I'm not cold or hungry because I ate what you sent me. But leave the talk for some other time. Let's drink tonight to celebrate the opening of the store. It's too bad that Pil-sun's father is not with us, but since the rest of us are here . . ." Byeong-hwa seemed to be in high spirits, having forgotten the pain in his hand.

Won-sam's wife, standing in the corner next to Won-sam, urged her husband to go now. "The master is angry. He asks where my husband has been all day."

By the way in which Won-sam was being summoned, Sang-hun's discontent was palpable. Gyeong-ae's mother found Byeong-hwa all the more detestable and scowled at her daughter, who was hovering over him. Gyeong-ae brushed off Sang-hun's irritation.

Let him be angry if he wants to! Let him do as he pleases—buy this house or hold his money tight in his fist. Bastard! If he wants to wreak havoc, let him take my baby! There's no guarantee that my mother will do a good job raising her. And what business does she have trying to supervise my affairs all of a sudden? She may be my mother, but what right does she have to oppose Byeong-hwa just because he has no money?

Gyeong-ae believed that her relationship with Sang-hun had started because her mother had whispered encouragement, tempted by Sang-hun's wealth. If her mother had instead scolded her and married her off to someone else, Gyeong-ae would have never ended up where she was. She particularly resented her mother's distaste for Byeong-hwa while she was growing increasingly attached to him, a rare sensation for her. After Won-sam and his wife left, Gyeong-ae nagged her mother to go home. Gyeong-ae felt she had to remain for Byeong-hwa's sake. He was not in good shape, and someone needed to tend the store. Though her mother insisted on taking the bundle of clothes and the quilt she had brought to the police station, Gyeong-ae wrangled them away from her. Her mother felt like storming out but somehow couldn't bring herself to leave. She pulled her daughter over to the doorstep.

"What are you thinking?" she scolded her, standing in the dark.

"What?" Gyeong-ae wore a pout.

"What do you mean, 'what'? He's finally changed his mind and opened a store for you. If you don't acknowledge that and act accordingly, he'll get angry. Anybody in his situation would lose their temper."

"What did I do wrong?"

"Isn't it obvious? Why else would he lose his temper over Won-sam working here, when the store is practically his? It's because of Byeong-hwa, isn't it? You should kick him out. What good will it do if you keep him and feed him? You will only be taken to the police station or get beaten."

"Will you mind your own business and go home?" Gyeong-ae tried to suppress her rising anger, hoping to avoid a scene.

"How can I mind my own business? If you hang around with Byeong-hwa, you'll lose the store and starve. Come to your senses! It would be better to mind your manners and talk Sang-hun into paying for this house, even if you end up parting. After that, you can do whatever you want."

Gyeong-ae finally exploded. "Do you think I'm the sort who goes around squeezing money out of people?"

"Then what is this about? What is it that you're doing?"

"What am I doing? Do you know who opened this store? Do you think I should kick out the owner? Do you think even a penny came from the Jo family?" Gyeong-ae said more than she had intended.

"Then whose money is it? Were you lying to me all along?"

"Why do you need to know? What can I expect from a guy who lost his father's trust because he's a womanizer and ended up inheriting only a few rice paddies? Sang-hun is mad about that, so he's trying to cut ties with his own son."

Gyeong-ae's mother was aghast.

"If you don't know what's going on, just keep quiet. He's trying to drive out his wife of thirty years, though together they raised a decent son. He hasn't come to his senses in spite of his years, and he brings home a girl still fragrant with her mother's milk and raises the roof . . . and you think he's a respectable man?"

Gyeong-ae's mother was dumbfounded, but when she asked for details, her daughter waved her away.

Later, on the streetcar, the mother wondered how much truth was in her daughter's words. When the car reached the front of the Government-General building, she got off in a huff, intending to pay Sang-hun a visit. It was late, almost nine o'clock, but he would surely be at home, and she wanted to see for herself the young thing he'd taken in to drive away his wife. She wanted to vent her anger, and while she was at it, perhaps secure some kind of support for her, even if it amounted to just a few dozen sacks of rice a year.

I've got to get Byeong-hwa away from my daughter.

When she arrived at Sang-hun's house, the gate was locked but when she shook it, a bellow came from the servants' quarters, "Who is it?" Won-sam rushed out.

"What brings you here?"

"The master is in, isn't he?" she hissed as she followed him inside.

"He's just left."

"That can't be true! You just don't want to wake him, but tell him I'm here because I have something important to say."

"No, ma'am. He's gone out."

"This late?"

"This is early evening for my master," Won-sam laughed.

"Then the young woman must be here."

Won-sam laughed again. "What young woman?"

"Open the gate to the outer quarters," Gyeong-ae's mother demanded, annoyed to be speaking with a male servant in the dark.

379

"Even if you go in, you ain't gonna find anyone there. The young woman came two days ago — maybe three — but left again."

So it was true. "Then who's inside?"

"The mistress. What's this about?" Won-sam had no idea why this woman was so agitated.

"So you're sure that the young one isn't here?"

"If you don't believe me, go in and look for yourself. She's not here now, but he may bring her later. The first night he brought her here there was a big fight, so now he brings her home very late."

So there had been a scene.

"If you want to see her, come early tomorrow morning."

That made sense, she thought. "What sort of fight did they have?"

"The mistress can't tolerate the situation silently, right? So she made a scene and told him to leave with her. She said he'd sullied her home, and she couldn't raise her children in it. She's right, but the master is no pushover, you know. He shouted back at her, saying she's the one who should leave. I don't know what'll happen to this family. Before, when the master had a drink, it was in private. If he had affairs, nobody knew about them. But these days, he does it in the open, day and night. Is it because it's time for him to follow his father to the other world? Or because he was pushed away? I don't know."

"In other words, that young woman intends to take over this house."

"I think so. The lady is pregnant, I hear. Besides, she is an adopted daughter of the madam at Maedang House, over in Anguk-dong. That madam is pretty tough — she's taken matters into her own hands and pushes the master around. He doesn't seem to know what to do." In his excitement, Won-sam volunteered more information than she had asked for.

Gyeong-ae's mother withdrew, saying, "I'll be back tomorrow, but don't warn your master."

Sang-hun was not thrilled that Gyeong-ae was running Sanhaejin with

Byeong-hwa's help. He had agreed to buy the building after she had pleaded with him, but he had no intention of doing so as long as she was with Byeong-hwa, regardless of what their connection might be.

He heard that Deok-gi had been taken to the police station. Out in the street, he phoned Gyeong-ae and asked to see her. She responded coldly but, after some wrangling, gave in. "If it's so urgent, I'll stop by your house tomorrow morning," she said and hung up. Gyeong-ae wanted to take a look at how he lived with Ui-gyeong, and Sang-hun didn't try to discourage her.

Sang-hun imagined he might be able to separate Gyeong-ae and Byeong-hwa if he bought the store for her. He wanted to hear how she'd react before he set up house with Ui-gyeong someplace or let her live with him after forcing his wife to live with their son. He was reluctant to cut Gyeong-ae off, but he couldn't just get rid of Ui-gyeong, who was pregnant. Ui-gyeong had left home, quit her job at the kindergarten, and made a new place for herself in his quarters, determined to let his wife's nagging go in one ear and out the other. What was fortunate was that Sang-hun's father had died in the meantime.

The old gentleman couldn't have lived much longer. Maedang and her entourage had been advancing hungrily, like a swarm of ants toward a dead fly. Even Ui-gyeong was angling for an opportunity to get something from the Jo family. Maedang was the queen ant reigning over her colony.

"How much did you get, little sis?"

"Only two hundred bags of rice! And another fifty for Gwi-sun."

"What can you do? Accept it for the time being."

So went the conversation between Maedang and the Suwon woman during Maedang's condolence visit after the funeral.

"My niece has stumbled into good fortune!" the Suwon woman said cynically.

"She certainly has! A son is a son, good or bad. No matter what they say, the old man couldn't have left everything to Deok-gi." Maedang's mouth split into a greedy grin, as if her own husband had become a millionaire overnight.

The Suwon woman grimaced. "Do you think he'll give you a penny even if he gets a thousand bags of rice a year? He only got three hundred bags! And he couldn't have gotten more than two or three thousand won in cash."

"What? Only three hundred bags?"

"You should look into the rice refinery. The old man, who was so thorough and precise about everything, didn't mention it in his will. We didn't think it was anything of exceptional value, but according to the old man's account book, it is worth more than roughly twenty or thirty thousand won in cash, and there's a house and a store connected to it, so it's worth getting your hands on!" Maedang's mouth watered; she seemed more heartened than the Suwon woman herself.

"What if the person in charge of the refinery takes over, now that the owner is gone?"

"Don't worry. The account book is there for everyone to see. I just wish I knew why the old man forgot to include it."

Maedang decided to involve herself more aggressively. To firm up Ui-gyeong's status, Maedang took her to the outer quarters of the Hwagae-dong house and talked her into installing herself there. Actually, it was the Suwon woman who had given her the idea. "If you don't hurry, Hong Gyeong-ae might take Ui-gyeong's place."

The Suwon woman didn't like the idea of mourning for three years, which was accepted practice during the Confucian era. She intended to choose a new husband and insist on dividing the rice refinery in three parts. It would be difficult to engage in a fight while living in the same house with the family. However, if the Hwagae-dong house were turned upside down and Deok-gi's mother came to live with her son, it would look like the Suwon woman was being forced out and her reputation would remain unsullied.

The stars seemed to align themselves in the Suwon woman's favor. The day after Ui-gyeong's arrival, Deok-gi's mother ran to her son and complained to him, and the son listened with sympathy. The Suwon woman smiled inwardly and decided to bide her time. She was confident that her plan would work, and perhaps even earlier than expected. Ui-gyeong, after the first day, however, didn't feel like returning to Sang-hun's house. The Suwon woman and Maedang had to coax her and, in the end, sent her back to Hwagae-dong to turn up the pressure on Sang-hun's wife. Though she had vowed to stay put for several days, Ui-gyeong had come back to Maedang on a whim.

"You can't behave like this," the Suwon woman scolded the pouting young woman. "Just consider it your house and don't budge. Our plan won't work if you scamper back the first moment something doesn't go your way."

The next morning, Sang-hun hoped to send Ui-gyeong away to Maedang's house in order to avoid a confrontation with Gyeong-ae. Gyeong-ae arrived well before ten o'clock—given the short winter days, the sun hadn't been up for very long. Although exhausted, she decided to pay him a visit. She would be careful not to give the impression that she was ready to break off ties with Sang-hun. If she did, she'd certainly come away with nothing and wouldn't be able to save face. It would be wiser to make it seem that she had distanced herself because of Ui-gyeong.

Gyeong-ae went straight to the inner quarters. The face of the mistress flashed in the tiny windowpane of the main room. Won-sam's wife, who was setting a breakfast tray in the kitchen, welcomed her. "What brings you here?"

Sang-hun's wife bawled, "Mind your own business!" Still bilious, she refused to greet Gyeong-ae. To see this woman when her husband's new mistress was at this very moment in the outer quarters added insult to injury. She didn't want her daughter to lay eyes on either of them.

"I'm sorry to hear about the trouble you're having. I happened to be in the neighborhood, so I stopped by to give your husband some advice." Leaving her sympathetic words hanging in the air, Gyeong-ae breezed out to the veranda and tapped on the door. A hush fell, and Sang-hun came out. Standing before her, he was visibly embarrassed. With her back to the door, Ui-gyeong was parting her hair in front of a mirror, with a washbasin beside her. Sang-hun seemed groggy. Ui-gyeong's startled expression shifted rapidly to one of feigned indifference. With a wooden smile on her lips, she continued to comb her hair.

"Are you enjoying your honeymoon? But what's this? Bringing some good family's precious daughter and making her live in a back room like this?" Gyeong-ae took a joking tone with him, and Sang-hun, without thinking, burst out laughing. Infected by the mood, Ui-gyeong turned around with a grin and nodded to Gyeong-ae.

Sang-hun was oddly taken aback that Gyeong-ae didn't lash out at them. His wife's incessant nagging was becoming unbearable, but Gyeong-ae's glee, on the other hand, was evidence of her heartlessness.

"You shouldn't have asked me to come until you had set up house properly. Or is it that you want to show off how much fun you're having?" Gyeong-ae asked.

"Who says I'm going to set up house?" Sang-hun smiled sheepishly.

"There you go again, toying with people." She turned toward Ui-gyeong. "Make sure you hold on to him tight. He often pretends he's crazy when he does something stupid. Both you and I ended up like this out of bad luck, but you should live well, with no regrets and a strong heart." She spoke earnestly, as if she were Sang-hun's lawful wife.

Ui-gyeong pinned her hair up.

Gyeong-ae addressed Sang-hun, "Look at your gray hair in the mirror. You're not getting any younger. Besides, whenever you spend money, it doesn't just disappear. It comes back to you with the curses of others. Don't you know that if you spend a hundred won, you earn a hundred curses, and if you spend a thousand won, you earn a thousand curses? Are you planning to go to the gates of Paradise and beg God to pull you up?"

"Will he even be able to make it that far when his sins are so heavy?" Ui-gyeong cut in, and they laughed together.

Sang-hun was miffed. Gyeong-ae's attitude didn't permit serious talk of any kind. *I'd better give her up*, he resolved. The more firmly he tried to cling to his decision, however, the more alluring he found her.

Ui-gyeong did nothing all day except eat, change clothes, and buy whatever frivolous thing that caught her fancy. When her indulgences were denied, her irritation was unremitting, and she took a sharp tone all day long. Sang-hun knew his interest in her would wane. Gyeong-ae, on the other hand, who was mature enough to supervise a household, seemed right for him, especially now that he was older. He sensed, though, that she belonged to someone else.

"Why was Byeong-hwa taken to the police yesterday?" Sang-hun finally managed to ask.

"Why are you so concerned about other people?" Gyeong-ae couldn't stand to hear Byeong-hwa's name uttered by Sang-hun. "Are you in any position to worry about others?"

"I'm not worrying about others. I'm just not sure whether someone is dragging him down or he's dragging someone down with him. Either way, they'll be in a hell of a mess one of these days."

"It's not that simple. But you know I could take over the shop fully if I return his money and send him away."

"How much do you need?" Sang-hun perked up.

Ui-gyeong blinked her eyes several times.

"Between twenty-five hundred and three thousand won."

Gyeong-ae and Sang-hun spoke no more.

The maidservant brought in a meal tray set for two.

"I haven't even washed my face yet. What's the hurry?"

As Gyeong-ae was about to leave, he asked her to stay, saying that the two women should eat together, that he'd eat later.

"Don't you think someone will pout if I eat a meal reserved for the two of you?" Gyeong-ae was saying when the gate of the outer quarters rattled.

The maid went out to open it. Like an evangelical woman, Gyeong-ae's mother held a black velvet bag, and a purple wool scarf covered her face up to her nose. The mother and daughter were startled to see each other, and Sang-hun looked on with an awkward smile.

Gyeong-ae tried to hasten her mother's departure to prevent her from making a scene. If Sang-hun were provoked, he'd lose face and would likely change his mind about giving Gyeong-ae the money.

Despite Gyeong-ae's calming efforts, the older woman poured out a stream of complaints and railed that if Sang-hun was unwilling to take in Gyeong-ae and his child, he'd better provide them with enough to last their lifetime. Otherwise, she'd drag him to court.

"I've heard of people sueing their own children, so what can prevent me from taking him to court, Gyeong-ae? Why are you following this lowlife around like a spineless fool? Are there no other men left in the world?"

Sang-hun was shocked; since when had this gentle woman's mouth begun to spew such venom? Yet, he had to admit that he had also changed considerably since their church days.

There was a rumor going around that if Deok-gi didn't quietly hand the rice refinery over to his father, Sang-hun would bring a lawsuit against his own son. The spinners of this rumor were Chang-hun and Clerk Choe; they felt there was nothing to gain from loyalty to Deok-gi, who lived by the book. When they sensed that Sang-hun was disgruntled at the frosty treatment he had received during the funeral, they whipped up the story, both to egg Sang-hun on and to flatter him. While they were at it, they also insinuated that Deok-gi should give up the house where he lived. They couldn't touch the rice paddies and fields because the old man had transferred the deeds to Deok-gi, but the big house still had the same owner; the grand-father had merely written in the will that Deok-gi should stay there. If Sang-hun, the inheritor in the eyes of the law, claimed the house as his own, he might well be able to obtain it.

Gyeong-ae's mother hadn't meant to unleash such an outpouring of invective, but the sight of Ui-gyeong made her blood boil and her maternal instincts took over. Back in the street, she immediately regretted the out-burst and tried to persuade her daughter to remain on Sang-hun's good side. "I said what I said, but how can we cut ties with him when there's your child to think of? That young thing he's fooling around with—it can't last long, can it?"

Gyeong-ae stared at her mother in profound disbelief.

Later that day, Deok-gi's mother stormed out of her house, asking the servant to pack up the furniture and appliances and send them to the big house. Her husband was defying all decency and speaking with him was like reading a Buddhist scripture to an ox. She couldn't stand the sight of the tarts—young and old—who flocked to her house at the crack of dawn, turn-ing it into a marketplace. Although Sang-hun did what he could to ignore the commotion, his wife's relocation to the big house provided no great relief.

It was noisy for a while, with Deok-gi coming and going, but two days later, the mother and daughter had moved. Won-sam and his wife didn't feel like staying on, and when Maedang asked them to vacate the servants' quarters to make room for her people, they jumped at the chance and found a rented room near Hyoja-dong with the thought of helping out at Sanhaejin.

The Suwon woman gave up the main room when Deok-gi's mother arrived with her furnishings, but she tried to hold her ground for the sake of appearances, saying that she could leave only after three years' mourning. Before long, though, she said she wouldn't mind going as long as they kept a room ready for her, even if they needed to keep her things in storage. She then went to Hwagae-dong, the house in which her "niece," Ui-gyeong, was now settling. She no longer bickered with Sang-hun or concealed anything from him. Sang-hun, for his part, got along with her well enough, perhaps because of their shared resentment for Deok-gi.

Maedang was charged up, as if she were helping her own daughter set up house. Flanked by the sisterhood, she made a majestic entrance even before the lawful wife's furniture had moved an inch. Maedang's contribution to the new household amounted to nothing more than a box of matches, but after ripping apart the house, she was enthroned in the main room and took control of everything. Accustomed to living well, she had in mind a complete list of essentials for a household, all of which materialized as soon as she gave the word. Chang-hun and Clerk Choe were her devoted runners. Regularly furnishing houses for her adopted kin, she was a seasoned hand, and so was Clerk Choe by now. Shops on Jongno supplied the items on Maedang's wishlist without hesitation.

This woman's credo was "buy the very best, for money is no object." The buyer naturally thinks this way when paying with someone else's money, but this woman's credibility and prowess were held in high esteem by the tradesmen; she paid in full, without haggling, as soon as they delivered her order.

Word was sent to a furniture store for a three-tiered chest of red sandal-wood, a wardrobe with a glittering full-length mirror, another in which to keep bedding—though no bedding had been prepared yet—a display for ceramic wares, a chamber-pot rest, another full-length mirror, a decorative day mattress with a long, squat armrest; there seemed to be no end.

A cabinet and a rice chest were brought to the kitchen annex, and the center veranda was to be furnished like a Western-style reception room. To the brassware store, to the porcelain store, to the fabric store Choe was sent.

She seemed to expect that Sang-hun would sell his rice paddy to pay for all these items. The commotion continued for several days, not unlike a house on the eve of a wedding. In a fit of anger, Sang-hun's wife had removed all the pots from their cradles on the stove and had whisked them away with her. New pots were being fitted in the kitchen, while seamstresses, brought in from several households, were seated together making new bedding. Won-sam's friends stood outside the gate and whispered among themselves whenever new furnishings were taken in, for they didn't see a penny being spent in their shops.

"How long will she last here?"

"Who does she think she is? Does she think her luck will last, hauling in such a load on the same day the legal wife was kicked out?"

"If I had a pretty daughter, I'd become a queen's father."

"I'll send my Eon-nyeon to a *gisaeng* house when the girl turns twelve."

"Then?"

"After five years, she'll become the youngest concubine of some important master."

"Sure, dream on."

Standing in the sun cracking jokes, they seemed to have forgotten how hungry they were.

"I don't need to listen to your story. When you get rich, I'm gonna get a high-interest loan and buy you a couple drinks. So why don't you borrow some money now and buy me one?"

"Sounds good. But how about you borrow money and buy me one of those drinks of yours first? We can toast to what's just around the corner anyway, right?"

"What was I thinking? We should hurry up and give birth to Eon-nyeon first."

They burst out laughing—jokes were their trusted friends.

Five or six days after moving in, Maedang assembled the bills and gave them to Sang-hun. Without even looking at them, Sang-hun told Clerk Choe to take them to Deok-gi.

Leafing through them, Deok-gi shook his head when his eyes settled on the grand total, more than fourteen hundred won.

"After the funeral expenses, there was over four thousand won in the bankbook my father took a while ago. What did he do with all that money and what does he expect me to do with these bills?" His father, who hadn't touched the land deeds, had taken the bank records with him after the will was read.

"One bag of rice fetches only fourteen won these days. I would need to sell a hundred bags to come up with this amount." Deok-gi muttered to himself as he folded up the bills and pushed them toward Choe.

"Well, I can't help you here, but your father asked me to bring them over, so I guess you'll do what's right."

Deok-gi sat quietly for a moment before placing the bills in a drawer.

The next day, Deok-gi went to Hwagae-dong.

Boisterous voices were drifting from the main room, knives clacked against chopping boards in a corner of the veranda, and meal trays were being piled in another corner. A festive house, it seemed. Everything looked so new that Deok-gi thought he must have come to the wrong house. Catching sight of a long white row of women's shoes lined up below the veranda, he hesitated. The women preparing food eyed the unfamiliar young man before the main room was informed that a visitor had arrived. The hubbub quieted briefly before Clerk Choe looked out.

"Come in. Your father is here."

The group of women in the main room leapt up as if someone had barked out an order. Deok-gi's face burned when the constellation of young women's eyes twinkled at him. He could discern neither their faces nor

390

their outfits, but as they filed out to the veranda, they looked like *gisaeng* going home after a voice lesson.

What kind of a party are they throwing? A house-warming party?

Deok-gi was greeted by the Suwon woman clad in a white mourning dress, who rose along with his father's concubine. The well-fed, imposing woman seated beside them had to be Maedang. His father, sitting on the new day mattress in the warmest part of the room, seemed to shrink sheepishly.

Clerk Choe was planted near the door, while Chang-hun was nowhere to be seen.

"Did you sleep here last night?" Deok-gi asked the Suwon woman.

"Yes. So, what do you think? Quite a different place with all this grandeur, isn't it?" said the Suwon woman mischievously, looking around the room.

Deok-gi was silent.

What astonished Deok-gi most were the reflected faces in the mirrors everywhere he turned. Even his own face jumped out at him through a bright array of women's overcoats, hats, and scarves hanging on the wall. The mirrors opposite each other reflected the objects in the room several times over. This mirror chamber must have been Maedang's idea, and he couldn't help but wince at her taste. The room was incomprehensibly stifling.

"Son, did you take a look at what I sent you yesterday?" Deok-gi didn't respond. "If you can't pay, just leave the bills here." Sang-hun wasn't in any mood to fight over bills in the presence of the gaggle of young ladies.

"It's not that I don't mean to pay them, but . . ." Deok-gi's heart was pounding with rage so it was almost impossible to go on. "Isn't all this a little extravagant, considering our situation? Wouldn't it have been enough if you had simply brought the furniture from the other house?"

Deok-gi felt it was utterly wasteful to shell out more than a thousand won merely to decorate the main room. It would be no easy feat to come up with the money to pay for it.

"What situation are you talking about? If you are going to speak with such arrogance, just leave the bills here and get out. As for the things that are lying around in the other house, you can use them yourself."

"If you stop and think of how you used to oppose my grandfather's spending on the ancestors' graves . . ."

"Who asked you to support me? This is disgusting—are you my supervisor? Send me the rice-refinery ledger today." Sang-hun was intentionally unpleasant.

"If you told me to hand over other things, not just the refinery, I'd do so willingly. But if you keep spending money like water, how can I hand the reins to you?"

"I'm claiming what is mine, whether you agree to it or not."

"Will it disappear if you let me take care of it?"

"You talk like a thief. You're saying you can't pay a thousand won, aren't you?"

Writhing with rage, the father approached his son and was about slap him on the face, but Deok-gi stood up and his father's palm struck his shoulder. Deok-gi wasn't sure whether his father was sick or going senile, but he quickly went out to the veranda, thinking that he shouldn't fan his father's agitation. His affection for his father was draining away; he now felt as if they came from different worlds. Deok-gi's heart went out to him, though, understanding that a person who loses his faith often will lead a chaotic life after his ambitions and hopes are dashed. On the other hand, without faith, his father was free to be himself and break loose from the constraints that had been imposed on him. But how could he have fallen so far, so late in life? Instead of feeling antagonism toward his father, Deok-gi merely felt sad.

When he returned home, Deok-gi wrote a dozen checks and gave them to Secretary Ji with the bills from the stores.

Sang-hun had set up house with his concubine, but Deok-gi still had to decide what to do with the Suwon woman. The situation was a headache. She had left Deok-gi's house with the child, telling him that they were going to stay at Sang-hun's. Deok-gi had asked the tenants at the Taepyeong-dong house to move out as soon as possible, but the Suwon woman wasn't interested. She stretched out her hand and demanded that he give her her due. She wanted it now and not—as her late husband's will specified—after the three-year mourning period was over.

"Do you think your share will shrink if you don't take it now? Will you need spending money for the next three years? It's not as if I won't provide you with food and other necessities. How can you go against my grandfather's wishes when it's been only a month since his death?"

"He could have made such a provision because he was afraid that I might not respect the three-year mourning period. Can't you trust me?"

"*You* are talking about trust? You're the one who trusts no one—that's why you're demanding your portion now."

"Well, as they say, if your knife is mixed in with the knives from other households, it'll be difficult to find it later. Family assets are strange. Who knows what may happen?"

They argued for two days. Deok-gi's father came over the day the Suwon woman moved and ordered his son to open the safe. "Give what has to be given as soon as possible. There's no use holding on to it. If she wants to go, she'll go. If she cares enough, she'll stay with our family for three years."

And so the Suwon woman and her daughter received their shares. Deok-gi's father took this opportunity to get his share of three hundred bags as well. After this was done, Deok-gi gave five hundred won to Secretary Ji, who asked if he could keep it for him. He wanted the money to be used for his own funeral and if anything was left over, he asked that it be given to his only daughter. Deok-gi told him not to worry about his funeral expenses and urged him to take the money and use it as he saw fit. Ji declined the offer and told Deok-gi to hold onto it, because he had nowhere to spend it and his daughter was not exactly starving.

Tongues wagged about how Deok-gi's father splurged on setting up house with his concubine, how he drove out his lawful wife, and how abominably the Suwon woman behaved. But now that Deok-gi had put the matter to rest — now that his mother was living with him and his father and the Suwon woman had settled down as they wished — things appeared to take a quieter course.

Wistful Affection

———

With the renewed calm, Deok-gi began to think of resuming his studies, and he soon made plans to leave for Kyoto after the coming month's first-day rite. He hadn't prepared for his examinations and would probably have to sit for a makeup test, but he was hoping to graduate and enter Keijo Imperial University. It would take only two months, including travel. When the time came and he was ready to leave, he came down with a fever. He wasn't sick enough to stay in bed, so he took a couple of doses of Secretary Ji's Chinese medicine, which Ji had concocted for him with the skills he had honed while caring for Deok-gi's grandfather. Deok-gi's fever, however, didn't subside. His body ached all over from exhaustion, which wasn't surprising, given the pressure of the funeral, his late-night outings to help Byeong-hwa, and the stress of settling various household affairs. Several days had passed since the evening he began to feel ill, but he hadn't gotten any better. Byeong-hwa learned that Deok-gi was sick and came by to see how his friend was feeling. Although trembling with a high fever, Deok-gi was full of questions: "How's business? Are detectives still on your case? Is Pil-sun's father doing all right?"

When Byeong-hwa returned to the store, he told Pil-sun that Deok-gi had asked after her father. Though pleased, she said with some anxiety, "He's done so much for us, and I can't even go see him!"

Byeong-hwa didn't encourage her to visit him. Byeong-hwa and Won-sam took turns visiting Deok-gi every morning and evening, but Pil-sun couldn't muster the nerve to join them, though her heart ached for him.

Several days later, after returning from a visit to Deok-gi, Byeong-hwa said, "How about taking him a fruit basket, Pil-sun?"

Pil-sun's face lit up but she was hesitant. First of all, what should she wear? It would be different if she were seeing him in a hospital, but how could she go to such a grand house?

Byeong-hwa said, "There's nothing to worry about. People live there, too. Go on. He asked me to send some fruit, and I said I would." He began to fill a basket with tangerines, apples, and pears.

"He asked for some fruit?"

"Yes."

"Then let's ask Won-sam to take it over when he comes back from his delivery."

"It doesn't make a difference who takes it. But if you go, it'd give you a chance to express your thanks." Deok-gi had actually said that he'd like to see Pil-sun, but Byeong-hwa was reluctant to tell her that. He didn't mean to prevent her from getting close to Deok-gi, but he was afraid that Deok-gi might stir her young heart.

"You're worrying about your clothes, aren't you? Don't be ridiculous. Is there a rule that you have to wear a silk skirt to go to a rich man's house? Actually, people would think it odd if a grocer showed up in such finery."

Though it embarrassed Pil-sun that Byeong-hwa knew what she was thinking, she set her fears aside. She figured the right thing to do was pay her respects, and she set off.

Following Byeong-hwa's directions, she got off the streetcar on Hwang-geumjeong at the intersection of Gurigae, turned toward Suhajeong, and soon arrived at the magnificent gate with a curved roof. With her heart thumping and her neck drawn taut, she dawdled, unable to find the courage to call out or enter the house. Eventually the maidservant emerged with what looked like a bowl of rice under her apron. Noticing Pil-sun, she asked, "What do you want?"

Pil-sun was relieved to be rescued from her dilemma—there was no way she could run away now. "I brought some fruit from Sanhaejin—from Hyoja-dong." Unexpectedly, her words came out confidently, for she was telling herself that she had come on Byeong-hwa's behalf, not to pay a visit to her acquaintance.

"Take it inside, please." The maid began to walk away.

"Excuse me, but could you take it in for me?" The maid was eager to get back into her room and out of the bitter cold.

Pil-sun figured that if she could just leave it behind, Deok-gi would know that she had come to pay her respects. That would be better than having to face him. The maid went inside with the basket, and although Pil-sun wanted to hear what Deok-gi would say, she ran off as if someone were chasing her.

It didn't seem possible that Deok-gi could be the owner of such a grand mansion. Hadn't he come to the store without pomp, wearing a student uniform decorated with gold-plated buttons, and eaten beef soup from a chipped tray? She wished that Deok-gi had no money. She couldn't understand why such a fortunate young man from a rich family would fraternize with Byeong-hwa and deign to befriend someone like her. This young woman found nothing remarkable about wishing Deok-gi were penniless. What she did find remarkable was that Deok-gi was so down-to-earth.

Pil-sun hastened her step, suppressing the temptation to look back.

"Hey! Wait a minute!" the maidservant called out breathlessly from behind. Pil-sun spun around.

"You, student, are you deaf? Do you have to walk so fast?" The maid addressed her as "student," reluctant to accord Pil-sun a higher level of respect. Sensing that Pil-sun wasn't someone to whom she had to defer, judging from the way she was dressed, the maid didn't think twice about criticizing her for her pace. "The master wants you to come in." She sounded as if she were blaming Pil-sun for the invitation.

"But I have nothing special to tell him." Pil-sun's face flushed.

"You can't leave. It doesn't matter whether you have something to tell him or not. Don't get me into trouble."

Pil-sun sensed that the maid was making fun of her. As she stood with her head bowed, the maid said, "It's freezing out here. You can't just stand there. Nobody's asking you to kneel before him. What's there to be embarrassed about? You can stand outside his window and listen to what he has to say."

Pil-sun followed the maid in silence. It would be foolish to leave when she was there to pay her respects to a sick man. The truth was she was eager to see him, and though she was ashamed to admit it, she was curious to see the grand house.

Pil-sun stopped at the high stone step before the veranda, unsure which room she should enter. It was fortunate that the big house was as quiet as a Buddhist temple and that no eyes were on her. She had imagined that it would be bustling with people.

"Come in, please." Deok-gi saw her from the main-room window.

Flustered, she stepped up to the veranda and entered the room. Had she haphazardly flung off her shoes on the shoe ledge instead of lining them up neatly?

"It's cold out, isn't it? Have a seat." Deok-gi was cheerful, his face bright.

"Are you feeling better now?" Pil-sun sat hunched next to the door. She felt her face burning, though it could have been that her ears were starting to thaw.

"You shouldn't have brought the fruit in this cold," Deok-gi said, glancing at the basket placed on the colder side of the room.

"I heard your father is doing better."

"He is, thank you."

Pil-sun found it more and more difficult to sit across from this young man, who spoke so gently and was cozily dressed in warm silk, with an elegant quilt pushed away behind him. To be addressed with such politeness by the master, after the maid had been so rude, made her feel abashed.

"You must be having a hard time in this cold weather, taking care of your father and tending the shop."

"These days I'm able to spend almost the whole day in the hospital because Gyeong-ae and Won-sam watch the shop for us." Pil-sun looked down at her hands; her hospital stay had healed the unseemly frostbite, but she immediately hid them anyway.

"So Gyeong-ae is helping out these days?"

"Yes. She comes every morning, as if reporting to work, and stays all day."

"I see she's serious now," Deok-gi laughed.

"It's not as if she hadn't been serious before, but now she works all day wearing Japanese shoes and an apron, like a devoted housewife." She flashed a smile.

In this brightly lit room, her pale skin took on a bluish hue, and her thin face, the result of bad nutrition, had a fresh, languid air, the kind you might glimpse in a girl recovering from a long illness.

"I'd better go now."

"Wait a moment. If you're on your way to the hospital, why don't you have lunch here?" Deok-gi's attitude was as natural as if he were talking to his best friend's sister.

"I can't. My mother's waiting. I'd better go."

Ignoring that Pil-sun had stood up, Deok-gi called his wife. It would have been rude to leave while Deok-gi's wife was crossing the veranda toward the main room, so Pil-sun waited.

Deok-gi's wife's face was open and kind. "Going already? You haven't even had time to warm yourself." Pil-sun bowed her head. The woman seemed good-natured. Though she was the daughter-in-law of a rich family, she didn't strike Pil-sun as all that different.

In the eyes of Deok-gi's wife, Pil-sun looked like a friendly and docile young woman. Though Pil-sun hadn't fully blossomed yet, she was neat and pretty. Her outfit was nothing much to look at, but Deok-gi's wife, who was plump, envied Pil-sun's thin shoulders and good figure. The thought of her husband spending time with a woman like Pil-sun didn't please her.

She guessed who Pil-sun was, but the young woman didn't look like somebody who'd work at a grocer's. Byeong-hwa came every day. Deok-gi's wife wondered why this girl had to come at all. She was not Byeong-hwa's wife. She took another look at Pil-sun; was something already going on between her husband and this woman?

"We should serve lunch. It is so cold today that some beef soup would taste good."

Despite the grandeur of this household (though it was not clear how things would change in Deok-gi's generation), a good welcome amounted to simple meals, such as rice cake soup during the first months of the year. A meal was reserved for special guests, while cakes and tea were served for most of Deok-gi's visitors. After all, they couldn't feed everyone when a dozen or so guests streamed in every day, both in the men's quarters and the inner quarters. The grandfather had economized this way.

Deok-gi's wife left, wondering. Already ill at ease, Pil-sun knew that a nerve-racking ordeal lay ahead of her. Couldn't he just let her go? She had wanted to see Deok-gi, but sitting face-to-face with him now, it became clear that the Deok-gi she'd seen outside and the Deok-gi in his own home were two different people. Though the kindness he showed her was no different from before, an invisible barrier had arisen between them. The yearning had left her. Pil-sun stood up.

"Why do you keep trying to run away? My sister will come home from school soon, and there's something I'd like to talk to you about as well."

But he didn't bring up what was on his mind. Instead, he asked, "Was your father a trader?"

"No, a schoolteacher."

"Really? Why did he quit?"

"He quit after the March 1, 1919 incident, and he's been jobless since."

"He must have suffered."

"He was in prison for a year and half at the time. Then afterward, he was imprisoned again for four years."

"Where were you living?" Deok-gi was particularly curious about her father's life.

"Inside Yeongseongmun. We lived next door to Yeongseongmun School. Everything happened when I was about to start the second grade." Caught up in the conversation, Pil-sun shed her awkwardness.

"Then you must have been about nine years old." Deok-gi imagined the young Pil-sun.

"I don't remember it very well, but my mother was as staunch as my father." She grinned, probably because she had used the word "staunch," for she couldn't bring herself to say "fervent."

Deok-gi smiled, too.

"Our family's luck went downhill from that point on. My mother was teaching at Yeongseongmun School at the time, and when I think about it now, she must have gone through so much." The painful memories came back to her in waves, as she remembered the ordeals of the past ten years, the journey from the house in Yeongseongmun to Sanhaejin. Deok-gi lowered his eyes and wondered if a revolutionary's blood ran in this girl's veins.

"I'm sure she did," Deok-gi agreed.

With the father in prison and the mother fired from the school, there might have been no other way but to sell the house and send the child to work in a factory to make a living for the family. Pil-sun's family hadn't been the only one to have undergone such hardship.

"My mother hasn't changed much since then. But my father has. Though it doesn't mean that he and Byeong-hwa share the same views."

"It sounds like your father is straddling the fence. So whose side are you on?"

"I'm also on the fence," she said with a grin.

"A moderate? You're an opportunist," Deok-gi laughed.

"There can be a meeting point," Pil-sun said. "We pity each other because we're poor. We have no energy to argue about why the other side is wrong when all of us, in both camps, have had to tighten our belts. That's how we can understand each other. That would be the picture of our families and society in broad strokes."

Deok-gi thought Pil-sun's words, though casually phrased, made sense. "That's true. There's definitely a meeting point, whether it's a social movement or a national movement."

"That's why my mother—who doesn't share Byeong-hwa's convictions, and says cynical things behind his back—is the first to come to the rescue when there's an emergency," Pil-sun said, remembering how her mother had helped Byeong-hwa with Pi-hyeok's escape.

Deok-gi nodded. "I'm sure she does."

"From what you are doing for Byeong-hwa, I'd say there is some similarity between you and my mother."

"You hit the nail right on the head!" Deok-gi laughed, impressed with her insight.

A low table was brought in. Pil-sun was astonished at the array of dishes —sliced boiled beef, pan-fried skewered strips of beef and colorful vegetables, and dried fruit that she had eaten only at weddings and sixtieth-birthday parties she had attended as a child. She was equally surprised that it was Won-sam's wife who brought in the table, whom she saw every day at the store.

"When I heard you were here, I hurried over. Take your time and enjoy the food," the woman told her, as if Pil-sun were a member of her own family, and left the room without another word.

Won-sam's wife came to the house during the daytime to help out, hoping to move in when the current servants quit and the servants' quarters in the Suwon woman's new house became vacant. Her life was much less arduous since she had been living in a rented room, and it did her good to receive better treatment from other people, but she couldn't support herself with the paltry sum her husband made at Sanhaejin. She also didn't feel like breaking away from such a grand household. She had grown attached to her mistress and was nervous about making ends meet on her own. Also, she wouldn't be able to eat as well as she was accustomed to. Hearing about Won-sam and his wife, Deok-gi thought they were no different from some liberated black slaves in America.

"Why aren't you eating?" Pil-sun asked him.

"I have no appetite. I'll just have some tangerines. But you should eat before the food gets cold."

Watching Deok-gi peel a tangerine, she lifted the lid off a bowl and discovered rice-cake soup inside.

Well, when I first met him, I slurped noodles he had bought me with my lunch box on my lap! Encouraged by this thought, she picked up the chopsticks. Her throat tightened, though, at the thought of her parents at the hospital. If she could have, she would have wrapped up everything on the table and taken it to them.

She managed to eat a few morsels when Deok-gi's wife joined them with her baby. Pil-sun felt blood rush to her face again.

"I'm not sure if our food is to your liking, but please enjoy it," urged Deok-gi's wife, seeing that Pil-sun hadn't touched anything but the noodles. She put down the child, went out, and returned with a bowl of rice-cake soup. "Let's eat together," she said, sitting across from Pil-sun.

Deok-gi smiled with gratitude at his wife's kindness.

"It's been a while since we made the rice cake, so it's grown rather dry," she muttered, picking up some beef slices and placing them in Pil-sun's soup. She had more favorable feelings toward their guest now, having heard Won-sam's wife praise her in the kitchen.

Now feeling more comfortable, Pil-sun tried various dishes. The sliced beef was tasty; it brought memories of better days when she had been able to sneak slices off the chopping board as her mother prepared her father's drinking snack, which she would do a few times a year at most. And the egg-coated fried fish delighted her, for her family hadn't been able to afford it for such a long time, even on New Year's. She could polish off an entire bowl of rice with just the *kimchi*, made with seasoned whole cabbage. Something she hadn't eaten all winter long. How fresh it tasted!

After the meal, Deok-gi's wife removed the table. After encouraging her to have some fruit, Deok-gi opened the loft door and fumbled inside, his back to her. She wondered whether he was going to give her some food for her father. It would embarrass her to be carrying anything in full view of others when she walked out of the house. Worried, she sat with her head bowed. When Deok-gi was seated in front of her again, she said, "I should take my leave. I'm sorry for making a nuisance of myself." She bowed.

"Hurry on to the hospital, then. And please give this to your father." He pulled out an envelope from under the bedding.

"What is it?" Realizing what it was, Pil-sun's face burned.

"I had meant to visit him before my departure, but I got so sick that I haven't been able to see him, and since you're here..."

"Please don't—"

"We know each other's situation well. It won't even cover his daily expenses."

Pil-sun stood up, but Deok-gi seemed reluctant to let her go. "When will you come again? Come if you're free tomorrow or the day after. Actually, I didn't get to talk to you about what I intended to, and I feel so trapped here, having to stay in bed like this."

Hearing the man's tender, pleading tone, Pil-sun blushed and felt as frightened as if he were holding her tightly from behind. She worried that someone might have overheard his words.

"I will, if I can," she told him, wishing she could come every day. But she thought, *I'd be crazy if I came again!* She couldn't understand why he was so kind to her.

Why should he feel trapped when he has such a good wife and child?

She made fun of herself for having been so easily excited by his words. She had never pictured Deok-gi as a bachelor or imagined that he lived by himself, but her heart had taken a sharp turn upon seeing for herself his comfortable family life. She had almost been swept away by his tender words and generous attitude, but she believed she would be better off not seeing him. Was Deok-gi's kindness merely a trait of the cultivated class or was it how he seduced women? What if she ended up like Gyeong-ae? Though still quite innocent, she was bright and had heard and seen her share during her years working at the factory.

Arriving at the hospital, Pil-sun said, "Mother, I've just come from Mr. Jo's house." Smiling as if she had done something forbidden, she tried to read her mother's reaction.

"Oh? It was the right thing to do, but . . ." Her emotions played tug-of-war on her face.

"Byeong-hwa asked me to take some fruit to his house . . . He insisted that I come in."

"You did the right thing to go in and see him."

"And he gave me this."

"He shouldn't have." She opened it.

A hundred won! Her mother's face was strained. When Pil-sun worked at the factory, it would take her three months to earn a hundred won. Deok-gi might be kind and gentle to everyone and might even pity them, but she didn't want to owe him too much.

The father, who had been looking on, heaved a sigh, his face devoid of expression.

Seeing that her parents were troubled, Pil-sun couldn't bring herself to tell them about the lavish lunch she had been served. She had never hidden anything, however trivial, from her parents, and there had never before been anything she couldn't discuss with them. It felt odd not to tell them that she had been treated to rice-cake soup and that Deok-gi had asked her to come again.

The next day, when there was a lull at the store, Pil-sun sat by the stove with Gyeong-ae.

"I would have never guessed it, but Auntie Pil-sun is not shy at all, sitting in the main room of a house she's never visited before, devouring a whole bowl of rice-cake soup," said Gyeong-ae in a teasing tone.

"What could I do? They told me to eat and I wanted to eat. What would you have done in a situation like that, Big Sister?"

"I'd have asked for food if I had been hungry."

"Do you think I'm too shy to do that? The first time I met Deok-gi, I went to a restaurant and slurped my noodles without thinking twice."

"How interesting to learn that Auntie Pil-sun has no shame!"

"You can say that again. After three years at a factory, I have none at all."

Gyeong-ae had never heard Pil-sun talk back, even jokingly. Pil-sun couldn't stand being teased about what she had kept from her own mother and guessed that the information had come from Won-sam's wife. Pil-sun was on edge. True, she usually didn't get enough sleep while staying overnight at the hospital, but she had had even less sleep the night before, managing to doze off for a few hours at best.

Gyeong-ae continued to tease her. "You're too young. If you want a man in your life, I'll find you a good bridegroom. But you'd better treat me to wedding noodles when the time comes!"

"What? Who said I'm looking for a man, now or ever?" Though Pil-sun knew that Gyeong-ae was just joking, she didn't like to hear her friendship with Deok-gi branded "a man in her life."

"I know better than anyone else, you know," Gyeong-ae said with a sisterly air. Her words seemed to contain a stern message: "Listen well, for I'm older than you, even if only a touch. Look at what I have become."

"It's nothing. I just took some fruit because Mr. Kim asked me to."

"You know I am kidding, but be careful anyway. Deok-gi is a good man, there's no doubt about it, and I know him well. But I've been where you are now, and you should take care. I can't just look on and say nothing, like a stranger. If you don't want my advice, I won't repeat it."

The two fell silent, as if they had had an argument. Pil-sun knew that Gyeong-ae was not wrong, but she couldn't bear to hear her speak this way.

What does he want to talk to me about? Pil-sun's mind strayed back to Deok-gi. *Is he going to ask me to go study with him in Japan?* This flight of fancy brought color to her cheeks, and she quickly mocked herself. *Why would he take someone like me with him, if not to keep his house?*

The third day after her visit to Deok-gi's, Won-sam said quietly to her, "The master wants you to come by tomorrow."

Her heart sank. She had a premonition that some kind of change was about to happen to her. She didn't know why, but the idea of going there weighed heavily on her. She decided not to go: he'd come to the store after he recovered, and she would see him then.

The next day, Won-sam reminded her of Deok-gi's request. "Aren't you going today?"

"I'm too busy. I just don't have the time." Pil-sun pushed away her complicated feelings.

She felt no relief, however, at her decision not to see him. Dazed, she was unable to concentrate on her work. But no matter how many times she reconsidered, she just couldn't bring herself to visit him.

Rumor

———

"Hey, Deok-gi, have you forgotten about that thousand won—you know, the money you told everyone you gave me?"

"Didn't I give it to you? It's recorded in the police report. What better proof do you want?"

Byeong-hwa egged his friend on. "So how about making good on your pledge?"

"I have no such intention."

"Maybe I should show you a pistol."

"Haven't you decided not to use Korean money—white money, that is—in the first place? Aren't you an international trader who sells food with red money from abroad?" Deok-gi laughed.

"Do you call nickels white money and copper coins red money?" Although Byeong-hwa laughed at the joke, he was startled by Deok-gi's comment. He must have heard something from Pil-sun—you couldn't trust women with their loose tongues. It would have been better if he had told Deok-gi himself.

"Look at you! You're really frightened! You couldn't have used up all your capital already. If I'd really given you a thousand, I might have to go to jail with you."

"A three-year jail sentence comes to more than a thousand days. If you were to pay one won a day, you'd have paid a thousand won by the end of your sentence. How about you just give me a thousand now?"

"No, no, how about *you* pay it back daily for a thousand days, with interest?"

"Since when did you open a debt-collection business? Or is that among your inherited assets, too?"

If it came to light that the thousand won was indeed "red money," Deok-gi might find himself in trouble.

"I know that you're skilled at manipulating people, but how can you cause trouble for me and then blame it all on me like this?" Deok-gi was willing to help Byeong-hwa, but a thousand won was out of the question.

"You're being very stingy. Okay, I'll pay you back daily for a thousand days, with interest."

At last, Deok-gi agreed that after he got better, he'd go to the rice refinery and try to find the money to lend Byeong-hwa.

"There's a strange rumor going around these days," Byeong-hwa said as he was hurrying to take off, now that he had accomplished what he came for.

"What's that?"

"I'm warning you, it's going to sound nasty. Did you bribe the doctors?"

"What did you say?" Deok-gi sat up straight.

"They say your grandfather died because the wrong medicine was used and that you bribed the doctors after the funeral."

"Who said that?"

"There's no need to name names . . ."

"Tell me exactly what you heard."

"Was the wrong medicine really used? Did you actually bribe the doctors?"

"What crazy bastard is saying this?"

"Won-sam heard it from his friends and was so shocked that he rushed over last night to tell me."

"Who did he hear it from?" Deok-gi wondered why Won-sam hadn't come to him directly but realized, after a moment, that it would have been difficult for his servant to do so.

"It wouldn't be good if the rumor spread."

"Who'd go around talking such nonsense? Tell Won-sam to come see me."

Byeong-hwa was about to leave, but Deok-gi held him back.

"I have a question."

"What?"

"How long will you be in business?"

"As long as possible. Why? Is there a deadline? If business is good, I'd like to entrust it to Pil-sun's family."

"You're beginning to see profits, I gather?"

Deok-gi now sounded more willing to provide capital, and Byeong-hwa answered eagerly, "It's doing pretty well. It's been less than a month, but all of us are making a living from it, and I'm sure we won't lose money."

"That's actually why I'm bringing this up; shouldn't you find a trustworthy person to settle down with?"

"What do you mean? All of us working at the store are trustworthy."

"I mean how about taking this opportunity to get married?"

"Don't be ridiculous! I didn't start this business to have children and rub my fat belly flaunting how well-off I've become. This is not private property. I'm planning to turn the store into a source of livelihood for my comrades. Whatever you do, you have to eat. I went into business to prevent Pil-sun's family from starving, as well as to use it as temporary protection for myself, but I'm also hoping to build it up as an organization of our own as it grows. Anyone can come in and take turns tending the store, but beyond feeding ourselves, we are not going to hoard the profits. No one is going to take away even a penny. That's the kind of group I'm in."

"Don't you have to resolve your personal situation first?"

"What personal situation? Nothing is wrong with my lifestyle. Even if I'm not bound by marriage, I still have a number of responsibilities. Look at Pil-sun's father. When a person marries, whoever he is, he expects his family to make sacrifices and ends up becoming useless himself."

"You may think so now, but that's not necessarily the case when you think in terms of a lifetime. What are you going to do with Pil-sun?"

"Now I get it." Byeong-hwa snorted. "I'll take care of Pil-sun's material needs until she marries. Her parents are the ones who have to deal with the matter. If I intervene in her life beyond that, it wouldn't be good for her. I also intend to keep up my relations with Gyeong-ae, even though I doubt it'll last very long." With such haughty words, he dismissed his friend's concern.

"But is there any guarantee that things will go the way you expect? If you have a child, could the situation be handled so simply? You should marry her."

"Who? Gyeong-ae?"

"How can it work with Gyeong-ae? Given your way of life and our family's reputation . . ."

"So that's how it is . . . You're telling me to give up Gyeong-ae and marry Pil-sun for your sake. This is a wild guess, but could it be that you want me to marry Pil-sun so you can forget your attraction to her? But, really, why are you bringing this up? I'll manage somehow. As for you, just do what you're supposed to. I don't want to have anything to do with it!" Byeong-hwa was unexpectedly inflexible.

"What do you mean, 'do what I'm supposed to'?"

"I'm talking about Pil-sun. It's not that I think you should ask her to live with you. But she's not interested in me. With me, she would suffer all her life. But don't worry about it—she'll go where she is destined to go. As for Gyeong-ae, what's so wrong about her living with me? Anyway, whatever happens, there's no need for me to rack my brain over it. Things will straighten themselves out one way or another." With that, Byeong-hwa stood up.

"What will you do if one of them makes a demand?"

"Who, Pil-sun? She wouldn't do that, and even if she did, I'd flatly refuse. Pil-sun is not the kind of person who'd become a comrade, and becoming a comrade will not make her happy, as you once said. Whoever she marries, her husband will have to be affluent enough to take on her parents as well."

Deok-gi knew Byeong-hwa was right, and he feared for Pil-sun's future. *It is probably useless for me to meddle in her affairs*, thought Deok-gi. Still, he would ask Pil-sun what she thought and try again to convince Byeong-hwa to come around to his idea.

Impatient, Deok-gi went out to the outer quarters to call Pil-sun. He disregarded his mother's gripe that he was exposing himself to the cold just when he was on the verge of getting better.

Pil-sun answered the phone herself, and Deok-gi was glad to hear her voice. She sounded well enough, but her voice didn't convey a hint of a smile as it had in the past. He suspected that she was trying to suppress her feelings, just as he was.

She apologized for not coming to see him, and said she had been busy. When Deok-gi asked her if she'd visit the next day, she reluctantly answered that she would. After hanging up, Deok-gi stood by the telephone, his mind a blank. He was ashamed of himself for having been so happy to hear her voice. He didn't recognize himself.

Until this moment, he'd had nothing to be ashamed of. But hadn't a false note crept into his attitude? Would he really bless a marriage between Byeong-hwa and Pil-sun from the bottom of his heart? Did he feel the same degree of sincerity in his concern for Byeong-hwa's well-being as he did for Pil-sun's future? If Pil-sun and Byeong-hwa were happily engaged, how would that make him feel? Could he bury his broken heart and live out the rest of his life?

No one realizes it, but I'm a hypocrite.

If Pil-sun became someone's wife, Deok-gi would distance himself rather than remain involved with her and her family. It was painful but sobering to reflect on his intentions and on what Byeong-hwa called his "attraction" to her. His effort to free himself from his temptations was selfish—it was not for Pil-sun's sake. He was an egoist.

Deok-gi was quick to criticize and reflect, and the more objective and unsparing he was in his self-criticism, the clearer Pil-sun's image was etched into his heart. The torment was unbearable.

Won-sam arrived by bicycle less than thirty minutes later. The telltale signs of a servant were gradually fading; nowadays, he didn't go about town on foot, and he sported an overcoat and a winter hat pressed down to his ears.

As he recounted it, Won-sam had heard the rumor from one of his friends who hung around the streets of Hwagae-dong, who had overheard it in a neighborhood bar. Picking up the gist of it, he had asked Won-sam to fill in the details. Won-sam knew nothing except that one of the drinkers was a young man in a Western suit.

As much as Deok-gi racked his brain, he couldn't think of any Western-suited young man among those who frequented his house or the Hwagae-dong house. His current buddies were all Koreans studying in Kyoto, and those living in Seoul were friends from his secondary school days or from the church, and not likely to go to a cheap bar. And other acquaintances of his would not talk about Deok-gi's household affairs.

"It sounds serious, like someone's trying to blackmail you." Secretary Ji, who was sitting next to Deok-gi, clucked his tongue.

"You're right. It must have come from someone who knows the inner workings of our household. It's like thieves talking about a robbery they committed because they just can't keep quiet about what they did. If this continues, I won't remain idle." Deok-gi sounded determined.

"It would be one thing if the thief merely pretended that he was innocent by yelling, 'Thief!' But it's quite another if he then goes behind your back and tries to steal from you again."

"That's exactly what they're trying to do."

"Did you give something to the doctors?"

"I sent them gifts. Aren't we expected to? I gave some pocket money to our family doctors, and I was generous with the Japanese doctor at the hospital since he worked so hard. I also had to take into consideration that he holds a doctorate."

"How much?"

"I was going to send gifts, but his assistant said cash would probably be better, so I sent three hundred won, thinking a hundred or two would be rather small."

"Three hundred!"

"It seems like a lot to us, but it is less than a month's salary for them." It was rather extravagant that he had sent four hundred won to the hospital doctors—a hundred for the Korean assistant and three hundred for the Japanese doctor—while he had sent a small fraction of that to the other doctors.

Even Secretary Ji, who had known the Jo family for many years, found it suspicious. Was three hundred won a reward for keeping quiet about something? Had Deok-gi covered up for the conspirators, though he was sickened by them, in order to protect his family name? Had he been driven into a corner because Sang-hun had masterminded some evil act?

The following day, when Deok-gi's family was in the middle of a late breakfast, Pil-sun hesitantly approached the veranda. She heard the maid mutter in the kitchen, "Did she come this early to beg for breakfast?" Pil-sun's cheeks burned. The Suwon woman had engaged this maid, and she seemed antagonistic to Pil-sun.

A long time passed before Deok-gi's wife looked out. She didn't seem overjoyed at the sight of their visitor. As Pil-sun stepped up to the veranda and approached the main room, a voice like that of Deok-gi's mother wafted out of the other room. "Why did she come again? As if she didn't stay long enough the other day . . ."

Pil-sun slid open the door and rushed into the room, as if someone had shoved her from behind. She was furious, wondering how those women could act the way they did, even if only out of concern for their reputations.

Deok-gi's drowsy eyes brightened, and a smile spread across his face. Pil-sun found more relief in being able to escape the chiding eyes than in Deok-gi's smile.

"Are you feeling better today?" asked Pil-sun, seating herself in a corner.

"I'm much better now, but I'm worried about your father. How is he doing?"

Deok-gi was unaware how rudely Pil-sun had been greeted, and he studied her countenance carefully.

"He's no worse, at least. My mother says I should express our thanks for your generosity." Pil-sun herself invented the message.

"Oh, it was nothing." Deok-gi sat quietly, struck by the unhappy air coming from the precious guest he had managed to bring over with such difficulty.

What happened? Has there been a misunderstanding because of something Byeong-hwa said to her? Regardless of Byeong-hwa's tendency to speak his mind, he wouldn't have said to her, *He asked me to marry you.*

"Are you on your way to the hospital?" Deok-gi asked, unable to think of anything else to say.

Pil-sun embraced his question as an excuse and hurriedly stood up, saying, "Yes, I'd better go right away."

"Why are you so intent on leaving when you just got here? Please forgive me if I did something wrong," Deok-gi said in a joking tone.

Only then did she flash a smile. "Oh, no, it's not that!" Once again, Pil-sun regretted venturing into a place she shouldn't have. Her anger had dissipated and, in despair, she was afraid of the humiliation she would have to endure if she wanted to maintain a friendship with this man.

"It will take only ten minutes. Please, sit down." Deok-gi decided to forgo any more preambles and get to the point. "I heard things are going well at the store."

"Yes. We're doing quite well," said Pil-sun as she sat down, her shoulders hunched.

"Do you enjoy selling things? Do you want to become a real business-woman?"

Pil-sun gazed at him for a long time, perhaps because the question was difficult to answer. She managed to smile. Was this what he intended to talk about? Crestfallen, she felt like a fool now that her fantasy about going with him to Japan had vanished.

"It must be challenging work for you. You're not a born businesswoman and . . . What I'm trying to say is that women—well, not only women—have an especially difficult time living alone. Our society is like that, you know."

Pil-sun grew tense.

"To put it bluntly, I think it would be better if you could find someone who could be entrusted with your care. You're going to get married eventually, so it'd be best if you decided, sooner rather than later, to settle down . . ."

Shocked, Pil-sun dropped her head without even realizing it. Who did he think would marry her? Instinctively, she thought, *If he had a really good potential bridegroom in mind, he'd want his sister to marry him.*

When Deok-gi mentioned Byeong-hwa, Pil-sun felt as if she had been hit on the head. She grew dizzy as Deok-gi went on and on about something she couldn't take in, until she heard him say, "Anyway, if it happens, it'd be satisfactory for Kim, and I'm sure you have no complaints, right?"

She wondered if he could be joking in order to gauge her feelings. She could never marry Byeong-hwa. And what about Gyeong-ae? She wanted to cut his excruciating counsel short. Pil-sun had never felt like marrying any-one, let alone Byeong-hwa, for whom she felt nothing, not even in her dreams, so the matter was not worth discussing. Byeong-hwa was no more than a friend to her, though Deok-gi may have been a better friend to him than she was. She also knew that Byeong-hwa didn't have any special feelings for her.

"I don't know what you think of Gyeong-ae," Deok-gi rattled on, "but Byeong-hwa has become close with her simply because they work together. There's nothing more to it. I don't think she's the type of person who'd be satisfied with quiet work in a shop or at home. On the other hand, if you consider Kim's future and are willing to rescue him from the hard life he's leading now, I think marrying him is the only way."

Pil-sun just sat there, her head bowed.

"Of course, your parents must have their say, and perhaps it isn't something I should get involved in, but I'm in a position to look at the possibilities from both sides, so I thought I'd ask your opinion first."

"I don't know," Pil-sun managed to answer.

"Then I should approach your parents?"

Pil-sun made no reply. He didn't think it meant that she was against the idea, so he took it up again from a different angle. "I'm not talking about this matter only for Kim's benefit. I see that the shop is doing quite well, and I thought that if the two of you, well, not just the two of you, but your whole family joined forces, it could guarantee a good living."

She didn't say whether she liked the idea or not, though she now understood Deok-gi's good intentions. He was concerned about his friend as well as her family's livelihood. But there was no need to set Byeong-hwa up as her prospective husband, and besides, it was impossible to just ignore Gyeong-ae.

When a brief silence descended upon them, Pil-sun took the opportunity to take her leave. Nodding her head slightly she said, "I'd better go. Please don't talk about it any more. I'll . . ." She couldn't continue, her eyes welling up.

She was going to say that she'd take care of herself, but she couldn't speak as she fought to suppress her sudden tears. From all that Deok-gi had said, one thing was clear: he had no romantic feelings for her, and it angered her to think that she had even entertained the idea. But she had no one to whom she could pour out her sorrow, and she was sure that this man had no idea how she felt about him.

Deok-gi was astonished by Pil-sun's angry voice and tear-filled eyes. Knowing little about the psychology of young women, he was anxious. What had he said to offend her so?

"Please don't take it the wrong way if I didn't express myself well. I hope you'll give my advice serious thought," Deok-gi said, rising to his feet.

Pil-sun grew more frustrated and resentful. How could he not know how she felt? Perhaps he was feigning ignorance so that she would give up on him.

Pil-sun turned around to pick up her scarf, which she had almost forgotten, and was about to leave when the door suddenly flew open. Deok-gi's mother blocked the way, though Pil-sun hadn't heard her approach the room. Pil-sun felt her blood run cold. She stepped aside, closer to Deok-gi.

"After you take your medicine, you'd better lie down and look after yourself." His mother seemed to be saying this for Pil-sun's benefit, looking her up and down. Pil-sun was completely embarrassed. Moments ago, she was worried about crossing the veranda and walking through the yard under scrutiny. Now she didn't know where to stand. Had there been a mouse hole, she would have scurried into it.

"What are you doing, Mother? Please go back to your room." Deok-gi stood beside the humiliated young woman as if he were physically protecting her. He seemed prepared to shove his own mother aside if necessary.

"There's no reason for you to go out. It's cold outside. I'll show your guest to the door. You should lie down." She stepped aside for Pil-sun, saying, "I'm sorry, but please go. Come again after he gets better if you must."

Pil-sun didn't remember how she fled the house. She regained her wits only after having walked for some time. All that Deok-gi had said and witnessed was a haze. What was clear as she came to the edge of the veranda was the door of the other room opening a crack, and the face of a pretty girl peering out. She must have been the sister Deok-gi had talked about. Pil-sun was convinced that she must have struck the girl as a loose woman.

After Pil-sun left, the house was thrown into an uproar.

Still standing on the veranda, Deok-gi's mother spewed words like daggers toward the main room. "Is that tramp married? What does she think she's doing—coming here every day? Does she think she lives here?"

Deok-gi stroked his beardless chin, trying to contain his fury. He replied, "Please go to your room. It's cold outside."

"You should have more dignity. Or are you repeating your father's history? Why do you invite a grocer's daughter into the main room and chat away like that? You should bear in mind your status—you're the head of the family now!"

Deok-gi sat silently; his mother was being hysterical again. Her mention of his father's indiscretions stung him, and he felt a surge of rebelliousness. He was his father's son all right, but he didn't want to hear that he was like his father. He was nowhere near being the womanizer that his father was.

"Do you know how Gyeong-ae started coming to our house? Your father was sorry for her father after he was released from prison. The man didn't have any money to buy medicine. Then that whole family latched onto your father, as if he were a money-bearing tree."

Deok-gi's blood ran cold.

"The father of the tramp who just left spent years in prison, and now he's in the hospital, all beaten up, I hear. How long have you known them? Why did you call a doctor for them and take them a blanket? Now you're inviting her into our home. You're going to pay for his medicine, you're going to pay for his hospital fees, you're going to pay for everything, right? If she's not just like that leach Hong Gyeong-ae—they're all the same: the Suwon woman, Gyeong-ae, Ui-gyeong, and . . . What's this grocery girl's name

419

again? Why is this happening to us? Why are you trying to follow in your father's footsteps? Is it because your ancestors' gravesites are inauspicious?"

Deok-gi wanted to stuff his fingers into his ears.

"Why are you paying attention to other women? Whose feelings are you going to hurt? Who are you going to abandon and starve?" Her daughter-in-law was attempting to lead her by the arm to her room. "Please go inside. You might catch a cold."

The mother lashed out at her, too. "And what's wrong with you? Why don't you do anything? What are you made of? You treated her the other day to a table full of food, waited on her, and even ate with her. You have no guts!"

"What can I do? Let him take a concubine if he wants to. I don't care." The daughter-in-law smiled.

"This is ridiculous! Who said I was going to take a concubine?" Deok-gi yelled to his wife from the main room. "Just take Mother to her room."

"You act as if this doesn't bother you because you're so young," the mother-in-law said to her daughter-in-law. "It's not a matter concerning you only. Both you and I came into the Jo clan with the responsibility of making it grow and prosper. It was my fate to end up like this, but think what would happen to the Jo family if the same thing happens to you!"

Since Pil-sun's previous visit, the mother-in-law had been nagging her daughter-in-law, displeased that the young woman took things so calmly. The truth was she didn't want to see her son and his wife on truly good terms. The old woman had recently developed the habit of aggravating everyone around her and making scenes; she seemed to have nothing better to do. She was in a phase of life in which women tend to grow cranky anyway, but her inclination toward hysteria had become second nature for her in recent years. It was a tendency she had acquired while quarreling with her husband over the years, and perhaps was somewhat understandable, as she had lived like a widow since the whole Gyeong-ae affair.

"Plenty of men take concubines. If my husband finds one for himself, I'm not at fault, am I? I'll just take it easy," Deok-gi's wife said with a grin. Though easygoing by nature, she was now intentionally provoking her mother-in-law, sick and tired of her nagging.

"Don't tell me you're praying that your husband will take a concubine. This is beyond me. What kind of woman are you? You must have something else in mind."

The daughter-in-law was speechless. Deok-hui came out and tugged her mother away by the arm. "Mother, please come in. What's wrong with you? Why are you involving Sister in your tirade when she's done nothing?"

Her mother refused to budge. "Your sister should know that we ended up like this because of generations of concubine tramps!"

"What are you talking about? Who's talking about getting a concubine? I don't know what you're worrying about. You know that my brother isn't like that!"

"How do you know he wouldn't do it? I need to prevent it from happening."

"Just worry about yourself, Mother. You're upset over a concubine that doesn't exist. And it's none of your business!"

"Watch your mouth!" her mother exploded.

The daughter-in-law tried to shoo Deok-hui away.

"Do you think I act like this because I'm jealous of those tramps?" the mother continued. "Your father took a wrong turn when he seduced Gyeong-ae, and now he's driven away his wife and children and has taken a second one. They're kicking up a storm over there, turning the house into a free-for-all everyday, gambling. How long do you think his three hundred bags of rice will last? And that's not all. I hear your father isn't drinking much these days since he has another hobby."

"What are you saying?" Deok-hui cried in distaste.

"You want to know what I mean? That one of these days, he'll crawl back, right before my eyes, with only a thatched mat covering his body," she hissed.

Deok-gi was determined to ignore his mother's words, but, in spite of himself, a frowning furrow stretched between his eyes.

"Stop it right now and go inside! How can you say such things in front of us, no matter how you feel about him?" Deok-gi was unable to stand it any longer.

"Children are always on their father's side, you won't listen to me. But you wait and see if I'm wrong. The guys walking up and down Jongno—drooling, dozing, and keeping their bodies warm with thatched mats—do you think they got like that because they don't have families or money or because they're uneducated?"

A chill went down Deok-gi's spine. When he received Byeong-hwa's letter in Kyoto, he had brushed off his friend's outrageous notion that he should make sure his father wasn't smoking opium. Deok-gi was afraid that his mother's insinuation could be true. Suppressing his desire to question her about it, he opened the door and said, "Won't you please go inside now, Mother? You'll catch a cold."

"All right. Don't come out. I'm going inside." Though still unsatisfied, she turned around and went to her room, trailed by her daughter and daughter-in-law.

"Brother, why didn't you come out sooner?" Deok-hui called out, smiling, as she followed her mother into the room.

Lying on his bed, Deok-gi felt overwhelmed by life. Until the age of twenty-three, he had grasped the meaning of hardship only through novels and from Byeong-hwa. This was possibly the first time that his own affairs seemed to press down on him. Suddenly, he was at the center of things and was held accountable for his family's every move. Although he had accepted the responsibility, he was burdened with the understanding that nothing could be solved on its own.

The more he considered his mother's near-pathological laments, the more he pitied her. His wife seemed indifferent to the idea of his having a concubine, and she found her mother-in-law's rants amusing. Although Deok-gi was unhappy about the way his mother had disparaged Pil-sun and drove her away—shocked, really, that a gentlewoman of her station could behave the way she did—he tried to sympathize with her. There is a saying: once burned, doubly reticent. He knew it was impossible, however, to rectify her situation.

His father was just as pitiable. He had been born at the wrong time, in the wrong era. His fate actually had a lot to do with his personality. Perhaps it all began with Deok-gi's grandfather's persona. Though Byeong-hwa's father and Pil-sun's father both lived in the same era as his own father—in the same environment and under the same conditions—the path of Deok-gi's father was entirely different from theirs. Ultimately, one's personality was the deciding factor: not every rich man's son lived like his father.

Deok-gi sighed at his own fatalism. He wondered what would have happened had the management of his household been entrusted to Byeong-hwa. Byeong-hwa wouldn't have met Pi-hyeok or opened a grocery, but he would have supported Pil-sun's family all the same, made sure that Jang Hun always had some pocket money, and set up Gyeong-ae as proprietress of Bacchus. Byeong-hwa wouldn't have been strangled by household affairs or burdened as keeper of the safe. Deok-gi had no desire to live his father's life, but it seemed he might be able to relax and enjoy life better, to move about more freely, if he swapped his two thousand bags of rice for his father's three hundred. To be entrusted with the management of such a big household at such a young age, especially when he had no practical experience beyond his studies, was a staggering onus. Deok-gi was envious of Byeong-hwa, who had created a love nest at the back of a grocery store, and of his father, who had splurged and furnished a house for his concubine. They seemed to be better off than Deok-gi himself, the so-called master of this chaotic household, who had to worry about losing the keys and about even one missing rice bag out of two thousand.

If only my grandfather had lived longer! If only I had an older brother who could take on the household affairs!

Less than a month into his new responsibilities, Deok-gi was already utterly alone and despairing. Above all else, Deok-gi was horrified by the way Pil-sun had been shown the door. Recalling her tearful and enraged expression and his mother's tirade, he was deeply disturbed.

Deok-gi tried to forget Pil-sun. He took pains to push her to the back of his mind. It frightened him to think of her.

His manipulations and questioning had pushed the young woman's innocent heart into despair. At the very least, he had made the mistake of upsetting her.

But what could he do now? There didn't seem to be a solution.

Why are you trying to follow in your father's footsteps? You're going to pay for his medicine, you're going to pay for his hospital fees, and you're going to pay for everything. His mother's words cut to the heart of him. Deok-gi was taken aback by the similarities between his father's situation and his own. He felt as if his life were merely a dark tangle of fateful events.

I can't turn Pil-sun into another Gyeong-ae, he kept telling himself as he tried to hold back the tears that filled his eyes. He loved Pil-sun too much for that.

Sweeping Roundup

Deok-gi grew bored in the main room, so he asked that his bedding be folded up before he went to the outer quarters. Secretary Ji and the older guests had moved to another room, keeping their distance from the new young master. Sitting alone in the large room, he imagined that he would enjoy studying there. He felt ill at ease about sitting in his grandfather's place; everything in the room reminded him of him. Various relics he had used — the cabinet, the low desk holding the ink stone, the table — might have value as antiques and would be handed down from generation to generation, but they weren't suitable for him.

Deok-gi was worried that he might have missed the opportunity to take a make-up exam and figured he'd better leave for Kyoto as soon as possible. Realistically, he couldn't attend Keijo Imperial University while playing the master of his household. He might be able to finish studying in Japan if he delegated the household's external affairs to Secretary Ji and the manager of the rice refinery, while letting his mother take over internal affairs and money matters. Actually, this arrangement would be good for his mother; her hysteria might subside if she were occupied with the household accounts.

Although Pil-sun wouldn't accept his help willingly, Deok-gi couldn't turn a blind eye to her situation, no matter how hard he tried. She stole her way into his heart, unbidden, and he couldn't help but pity her. He didn't want to make her his concubine, but again he wondered why they should deceive themselves and conceal their feelings.

A couple of days passed. Deok-gi was thinking of going out for fresh air one afternoon when the phone rang. It was Byeong-hwa. He hadn't been in touch since he had pressed Deok-gi for the thousand won.

"Won-sam was taken away a while ago. Is everything all right over there?"

"Where was he taken?"

Immediately, Deok-gi remembered the rumor he had heard. Someone must have tipped off the police. Deok-gi knew that nothing would come of it, but it irritated him that his departure for Kyoto would have to be put off once again.

He found it odd that it wasn't the Jongno Police Station that had taken Won-sam but the Police Division. Byeong-hwa advised Deok-gi to stay put, because it looked like the store was under surveillance; he would keep Deok-gi informed by phone. At dusk, Byeong-hwa called again. Won-sam's wife had been trailed and had been arrested along with Pil-sun. Gyeong-ae hadn't come to the store that day; it appeared she had been taken in for questioning as well. Clearly, more was going on than an investigation into Deok-gi's household.

"Was it the High Police or the Judicial Police? If it's the High Police, I know someone who can get me information."

"It's not clear."

As he hung up the phone, Deok-gi wondered whether he should go see Kimura, the chief of the High Police. Deok-gi knew Kimura from his Jongno Police Station days. He used to see him from time to time when Deok-gi had acted as his grandfather's Japanese interpreter; as a wealthy, influential figure, his grandfather had been a representative of an organization of land overseers and a member of a poverty-relief committee.

If word had gotten out that an investigation was in progress because of the rumor concerning his grandfather's death, Deok-gi would be obliged to see Kimura. It pained him that Pil-sun should suffer in a cold cell. Mulling over the various ways he could help, Deok-gi went to see Byeong-hwa after dinner.

———

As Deok-gi had surmised, both the Judiciary and High Police were involved.

"It had happened the day before in the late afternoon. High Police Chief Kimura had been smoking near the stove in his office, idly thinking that it was time to go home, when Geumcheon, a section chief, came in and urged him to make a final decision.

"Chief, how about we begin rounding them up this evening?"

"What did the guys say?" Kimura sounded reluctant.

"What do they really know? What matters is that we're sure, and since we've already put our hands on it, we'd better go all the way."

Section Chief Geumcheon was dissatisfied with the High Police chief's casual attitude toward the case. It wasn't that he was unaware of his boss's reasons; when Kimura was head of the Jongno Police Station, he was rather close to Jo Deok-gi's grandfather. They couldn't treat the rich in such a cavalier manner. The chief's ambivalence made Geumcheon even more eager to take action. Unwilling to soft-pedal his suspicions, he was sure that his hunch was correct.

Of course, the situation concerning Deok-gi and his family was another matter and could be handed over to the Judiciary Police depending on what developed, but Geumcheon, as an inspector of the High Police, had another goal. If Deok-gi's grandfather had in fact been poisoned and the main culprit was Jo Deok-gi, Geumcheon was certain that Kim Byeong-hwa was behind it. When a rich man's son and a communist are so close, it isn't merely a friendship between old schoolmates. The Kyoto Police Division's investigation, conducted at the request of the Keijo police, showed that although Deok-gi had not acted in a particularly suspicious manner, the bookcase in his boardinghouse was noticeably ridden with books on Marx and Lenin. Furthermore, Deok-gi had given Byeong-hwa a thousand won to help him open a business—this after the two young men had been frequenting Bacchus throughout the winter, a bar whose proprietress was suspected of communist inclinations. Based on these facts, it looked like Jo Deok-gi could be what they called a sympathizer. And when one considered that the Jo family assets, for no apparent reason, had been passed over Jo Sang-hun, the legal inheritor, and given to the grandson, it certainly seemed that Byeong-hwa had to have played a role in some kind of conspiracy. The situation had already lent itself to such speculations, but the rumor that the old man had been poisoned and that the doctors had been bribed fanned the flames of Geumcheon's suspicions. It was time to take matters into his own hands.

The police chief had kept Geumcheon at bay for several days, insisting that they wait until they had obtained solid evidence, but he finally gave in to his subordinate's conviction.

The police chief, wary of his underling's ambitious zeal, had another goal in mind. Two or three months had passed since the winter roundup, and it stood to reason that the remaining agitators would be engaged in something or other, though everything appeared calm on the surface. Kim Byeong-hwa had, out of the blue, started a grocery business—a Japanese-style grocery at that. Numerous pieces of intelligence poured in from overseas but only one or two out of ten were useful. No matter how many of his informants he tapped, he wasn't able to get any further details on the activities of the agitators still at large. At present, the leaders in Seoul had more or less been rounded up in one big sweep, and of the moderates, Kim Byeong-hwa and Jang Hun were the principal figures. But no one knew what might lurk beneath the tag "moderate." The chief had to admit that Geumcheon was on the right track.

In any event, after the police chief consented, Geumcheon mobilized his subordinates and began rounding up the suspects, starting at the bottom of the ladder.

———

When Deok-gi arrived at Sanhaejin, the doors were tightly shut. He feared the worst. As he was turning away from the store, dejected, Pil-sun's mother approached him from out of the darkness.

"It's you!" she cried out. "What brings you here this late?"

"I heard your daughter was taken away. You must be so anxious!"

"I don't know what to do. Byeong-hwa was arrested a while ago. He called me at the hospital and told me to meet him in front of the Gyeonggi Provincial Government Office to give me the keys to the store and the money. They dragged him off right away. I don't know what's going on. What should I do?" The woman was on the verge of tears.

"How is your husband doing?"

"I can't believe this is happening. My husband's pneumonia is getting worse, and we've ended up making trouble for other people. I see nothing but darkness." She fumbled with the keys as she let them in. There was a chill in the air. The neat rows of groceries on the shelves were untouched by the recent turbulence.

While Pil-sun's mother tidied up, Deok-gi called Bacchus and learned that Gyeong-ae's mother had been taken to the Police Division as well.

"How can they sweep them all up like that?" There would be no one left to care for her sick husband if they brought her in as well.

"Try not to worry too much. I'll do my best to get them released soon." To calm her, he told her that he'd visit the High Police chief the next day. After she brought in the items that would freeze, Deok-gi accompanied her to the hospital on his way to Hwagae-dong. He wanted to see his father, now that he was up and about, and was curious to know whether the rapacious hands of the police had reached his father's house.

As Deok-gi entered the house, a game of mahjong was in full swing in the outer quarters, with the doors tightly locked. "I'm glad you're here," said Deok-gi's father. "I heard that the Police Division took Won-sam."

Deok-gi nodded.

"What's going on? They came for Clerk Choe while he was visiting."

"Clerk Choe, too? I had no idea."

"I hear they inquired about Chang-hun as well. Isn't that odd?" Deok-gi's father, in the middle of heavy gambling, sounded extremely nervous.

"I think I may be able to find out what's going on tomorrow," Deok-gi answered vaguely, before he left. Without knowing precisely what was going on in the inner quarters, his heart sank. He couldn't stand watching his father fritter away good money.

As soon as he got home, Deok-gi heard that Secretary Ji was the latest to be arrested. It troubled him deeply that old Ji would have to stay in jail in this cold. Knowing that the authorities were approaching, a wave of anxiety swept over him, though in his heart he knew nothing would come of it.

Sleeping in fits and starts, Deok-gi managed to get through the night and went to the Police Division early the next morning. Aware that he would be taken away eventually, he wanted to see the High Police chief as soon as possible. But the chief wouldn't see him. Instead, Geumcheon called him in. The detective was delighted that Deok-gi had come in of his own accord. Preventing Deok-gi from seeing the chief had been Geumcheon's doing.

The case was being investigated by two different police branches. Pil-sun, Gyeong-ae, and her mother, along with Byeong-hwa and Jang Hun, were to answer to the High Police, while Secretary Ji, the Chinese doctor, and Clerk Choe were being questioned by the Judiciary Police. Won-sam and his wife, and now Deok-gi, were in the spotlight of both branches.

They were trying to discover why the majority of the Jo family assets were left to Deok-gi. Why did he oppose the performance of a postmortem on his grandfather, and why did he pay the doctors excessive gratuities? Why did he help Byeong-hwa? How many left-wing books did he read? Deok-gi answered these questions as clearly as possible.

His grandfather had disliked his own son and hadn't trusted him, having clung to the conviction, verging on superstition, that his son would squander the family's wealth during his own lifetime. It was not for Deok-gi himself, but for the sake of the Jo descendants, that the grandfather had entrusted Deok-gi with roughly five times that which he had left to his son. As for the postmortem, he opposed it for two reasons: he shared the reluctance many people have about cremating their parents' bodies, and he didn't want to sully his family name by doing something dishonorable. Deok-gi simply could not accept the notion that his grandfather had been poisoned. He did not consider the gifts he offered the doctors to be excessive in light of his name and social position. They were tokens of gratitude. Perhaps the strongest evidence of Deok-gi's innocence was the fact that his grandfather had entrusted him with the key to the family safe while he was still alive. Even the Suwon woman, who was summoned the next day, had to attest that she had seen the old man give Deok-gi a ring of keys after his arrival from Kyoto.

As for his relationship with Byeong-hwa, Deok-gi reiterated what he had stated from the start. He said frankly that his actions were based on friendship; he wanted to help his longtime friend, who'd been hungry and roaming around town after leaving his parents' house. Deok-gi also had hoped to draw Byeong-hwa away from his radicalism. But the detectives weren't ready to accept his explanation, given the plethora of leftist literature found in his Kyoto boardinghouse. They wouldn't swallow his explanation that he had read them as part of his economics studies. That day, they didn't pay much attention to Deok-gi, who lay down in the duty room and fell asleep.

Geumcheon believed that the way to get to the bottom of the poisoning case was to hand over the Suwon woman and her cohorts to the Judiciary Police for further questioning. As for the matter of Byeong-hwa and Gyeong-ae, he was sure that something was bound to come out if he pressed Gyeong-ae's mother.

"My daughter must have met Byeong-hwa at the bar. I'm disgusted that he dragged me into all this. Do you think my daughter is stupid enough to get involved with someone of his ilk? He's so full of himself! Please release my daughter and lock him up for ten years." As Geumcheon proceeded, he grew more skeptical when he learned that her husband had been a notorious independence movement leader. Besides, she was Christian, not an old-fashioned woman who couldn't comprehend his questions. Geumcheon braced himself for more denials.

When the conversation shifted to her family, she mentioned that her brother had fled to Shanghai and hadn't been heard from since, which increased the detective's doubts. He was circling, waiting for his chance to pounce.

"What's your brother's name?"

"K___. He deserves to be killed."

Geumcheon's eyes bulged out of their sockets. He hadn't given Gyeong-ae a thorough going-over yet. He had been so busy asking about her relationship with Byeong-hwa that he had no idea what her family background was. He felt sure that it had influenced her actions.

"What about the individual who visited a while ago? Is this person still staying with you?" asked Geumcheon, assuming a sweet expression, as if he were inquiring about a friend of his.

"Who? My sister-in-law? She's still with us." It was true that one of the cousins on her husband's side had been staying with her for some time.

"No, the fellow your brother sent."

"Do you expect a thief to suddenly change his mind and send someone?

He earned money and used it just for himself. He hasn't sent a penny in ten years, even while his family was starving. He's a good-for-nothing who ran away with my money, the money I got from selling my house." She feigned absolute ignorance.

He, of course, had phrased his questions to see how she would react, but his suspicions grew when she sounded too collected, though her reply was plausible enough.

"Where's your brother's family?"

"They live in Hyeonjeo-dong, but I've never been there."

"I don't know how much of your money he took, but a brother and sister shouldn't cut ties because of that, should they?" Geumcheon surmised in his impeccable Korean, grinning.

"So you must have nephews."

"Two."

"Are they old enough to make a living?" One might think he was genuinely concerned.

"Yes. The older one is already nineteen, and the younger one is sixteen or seventeen."

Detective Geumcheon would bring them in for questioning.

A man, clad in Korean clothes and a winter hat, interrupted them. "Are you busy? It's rather urgent."

"I took them to three different places for appraisals, and they all had exactly the same response."

"Yes?"

"That they're foreign made, but are neither from Shanghai nor from the United States."

"Then where are they from?"

"From Russia, of course."

"Where did you put them?"

"Here." The man glanced at Gyeong-ae's mother, seated across from Geumcheon. She could see that the newcomer was concealing something beneath his overcoat, but she was unable to follow their Japanese.

Geumcheon felt no need to keep it under wraps. "Let me take a look." Extending his hand, he shot Gyeong-ae's mother a quick glance. When Gyeong-ae's mother saw the pair of worn-out shoes he pulled out, her head jolted back in astonishment. The detectives exchanged a glance, overjoyed. Gyeong-ae's mother now knew that they had her cornered. She felt dizzy but fought to stay alert.

"You recognize these shoes." Geumcheon took on a menacing expression. "Whose are they?"

"What are you talking about?"

The underling charged toward her and grabbed her by the shoulders. She was thrown to the floor, moaning; he kicked her a few times for good measure.

Jang Hun had been under surveillance, and as he was higher in the group's hierarchy, he was brought to the station a day after Byeong-hwa. After the recent melee between Jang Hun and Byeong-hwa, Geumcheon had noticed an unfamiliar pair of shoes under the outer quarters' side veranda at Jang Hun's. He had been visiting the house frequently, as part of his rounds, so it was strange to find these old shoes lying around, though there hadn't been any recent visitors. Furthermore, Jang Hun was never seen wearing them. Soon after his arrest, the shoes were taken to several haberdasheries for examination.

———

The detective had already searched the house. Ready to charge both Chiang Kai-shek's and Kim Byeong-hwa's factions with anything he could come up with, he knew that he must seize this opportunity to root out both bands of radicals. Geumcheon found it odd that in the aftermath of the recent fight, the two groups showed no outward signs of hostility. They do say that people grow closer after a quarrel.

"You called Jang Hun and Kim Byeong-hwa to your house so they could meet the visitor from Russia, didn't you?"

"I don't know what you're talking about. Why are you doing this to a foolish old woman? I know nothing." Gyeong-ae's mother pleaded desperately.

"I don't mean that *you* did," he thundered. "Your daughter did!"

"My daughter wears makeup and perfume and wanders around at night as if it's broad daylight. That's all she ever does." Gyeong-ae's mother was used to these investigations because of her husband, and she deliberately made her voice shake. She wasn't actually ruffled, but those damn shoes had made her flinch.

That fool! Why didn't he just put them in the trash if he didn't want to wear them? Why did he have to bring us all this grief?

"Then why does your daughter live with someone like Kim Byeong-hwa? Does he sell face powder? Or perfume?"

"How would I know? She must have followed him around blindly because he's handsome and tall. How would I know if that good-for-nothing is made of horse bones or ox bones?"

"You're quite the orator, aren't you? You must have learned that from your husband, the esteemed Mr. Hong, no?" But then Geumcheon lost his mocking tone: "You recognize these shoes, don't you?"

"If I did, I would tell you. Why would I lie?"

"Perhaps you're right." Geumcheon looked to his subordinate, who barked, "Stand up!"

Gyeong-ae's mother sprang to her feet, trembling all over.

"You'd better confess the truth if you want to be treated well," said the underling under his breath.

Ten years ago, she had suffered such indignities several times because of her husband. Now her knees buckled and her legs trembled violently with the sudden fear that she was being dragged away to undergo the same humiliation. But what could she do? If she told them what she knew, her daughter would fall into a living hell. The mother braced herself, vowing that she would never allow her Gyeong-ae to wither away in prison for years, even if she had to die on the spot.

After almost an hour of brutality, Gyeong-ae's mother fumbled around in the dark to find her clothes, sobbing and wiping the tears away with stiff, rubbery hands. She followed the detective out to a brightly lit room. Her molars clattering against each other, she couldn't shut her mouth; she didn't even possess the energy to sit down. Her hands and feet felt as if they had been cut away from her body.

"There's just one thing you need to say. This ranting and raving will get you nowhere, and your daughter will have to go through the same thing. If you love her at all, you'd better tell us what we want to know. We know everything, so don't pull any tricks," coaxed the detective.

No, she would endure it, for if she didn't, she knew her daughter and Byeong-hwa would be subject to treatment several times harsher than hers.

Senility of a Middle-Aged Man

———

When Sang-hun heard that his son had been arrested, he quietly stopped by the big house. It had been a while since his last visit. He knew that his son wasn't guilty and that he'd be out after a few months in a detention cell. It might even be good for him. Sang-hun took the news lightly, figuring that it wouldn't be inconvenient for him if his son were out of sight for a while. He would be able to do as he pleased.

Sang-hun's wife refused to greet him, but his daughter-in-law welcomed him in.

"How's the baby? Where is he?"

"He's sleeping in the main room."

Sang-hun's wife wondered what had sparked the sudden interest in his grandson. Her husband went into the empty main room and remained quiet for a long time. *Has he been watching his sleeping grandson all this time?* "Go and see what he's up to," Sang-hun's wife told her daughter-in-law.

In spite of the resentment San-hun felt for his own son, it was possible that he loved his grandson. The two women, however, didn't trust his sudden devotion. They had found it hard to look him in the face that afternoon; his expression was oddly distorted, and his eyes wandered wildly. Was he now in dire need of money after inviting his concubine to live with him? Was he under the influence of opium?

The daughter-in-law hesitated before the door, made rustling sounds, and opened it a crack. "Is the baby still asleep?"

Sang-hun was fumbling in his son's desk at the far end of the room. Startled, he looked toward the door. "Yes. Child, why don't you come in for a minute?"

"Are you looking for something, sir?"

The desk drawers were all open.

"Do you know where he put the key to the cabinet in the outer quarters?"

"I don't know. It should be there somewhere." She knew that the keys were kept in the small safe at the front of the loft, and Deok-gi always carried the key to the small safe in his wallet.

"It's just that during the funeral I left one of my documents in the cabinet, and I think the police would release Deok-gi if I could show it to them." His eyes took on a faraway look, as if he were indeed in deep trouble. "Are you sure you don't know?" he studied her face.

She didn't like to deceive her elder, even if, admittedly, he behaved more like a young playboy. Now he had whirled into the house and had begun to ransack it for its valuables.

"Child, where is the small safe the grandfather used?"

The daughter-in-law opened the loft, took out the safe, and brought it to him.

His face brightened. "Bring me the key."

"Your son always carries it with him."

Sang-hun grew despondent again. Like a child playing with a toy, he tried to open it with other keys. By no means did he fit the picture of a dignified elder.

The daughter-in-law was about to leave when she asked, "Since the police want it, maybe we could send a messenger over to retrieve the key from my husband." She didn't know what he was after, but the possibility of her husband's release tempted her.

"Forget it. We'll open it some other way."

The daughter-in-law went over to the other room and recounted the conversation to her mother-in-law. The old woman was furious. "That's ridiculous! He's making up stories to steal the key to the main safe — he knows it's on the same key ring."

She flung the door open. The daughter-in-law feared that there was going to be a scene and stayed put. She could hear the ruckus in the main room and the thump of the iron safe landing on the veranda.

Deok-gi's wife could hear her mother-in-law bawling, "Do you want to see us kicked out on the street with a beggar's bowl in our hands? Why are you here, making a fuss about small and big keys? You're like a burglar in broad daylight! You might as well carry the safe away on your back. You put your son in that miserable place just to try to get your hands on it! You're the one who should be locked up!"

Without replying, Sang-hun came out with his hat in hand. He told his daughter-in-law, "I wash my hands of it. Let the inspectors come for it themselves."

Deok-hui arrived home from school shortly after he left. When she saw the disarray and everyone standing around unsure of what to do next, she flinched, imagining the scene that she must have just missed. Moments before, when she stepped off the streetcar, she caught sight of her father in the distance, but his eyes darted away from hers, and he walked off briskly. His indifference hurt her, and she turned around several times to watch him go.

At school and when she visited her friends' houses, she talked freely and laughed as other girls did, but once in her own home, she felt stifled, as if something heavy weighed her down. She wanted to remove herself from all of them. It was enough to make her not want to come home.

Deok-hui didn't get along very well with her mother, and even less so with her father. It frustrated her that her mother didn't seem to care what was going on at school, and her constant complaints and frequent outbursts drove her to despair. She felt close to only one person in her family, her brother; he took the trouble to try to understand her. They were close in age, and he treated her with affection. But now he was in jail.

"Was Father here?" Deok-hui asked her sister-in-law. "What's the matter? Did they fight?"

"No. He came to get the key to the safe."

"My father's pathetic," Deok-hui sighed. "Deok-gi is in real trouble, but he can't stop thinking about the safe. He's losing his mind—he must be senile," Deok-hui said under her breath as she entered her study room.

"Senile? How can he be senile when he's not even fifty?" The mother resumed her harangue, sitting on the edge of the veranda. "He's an overgrown child. You'd think he's a man in his twenties by the way he falls over women."

Deok-hui shut the door to her room. *Other parents are not like this. Why do mine have to be so infuriating?* Deok-hui envied her friend whose family ran a grocery. Both brother and sister lamented their lot of being born into a rich family.

As they were about to sit down for dinner, the old man watching the outer quarters in lieu of Secretary Ji came in, followed by Sang-hun, and two men clad in Western suits. There was no need to ask who they were.

"Where is it?" The detective was impatient.

Sang-hun scrambled up to the veranda and opened the door to the main room, obedient as a puppy. The detectives went in, saying that they would allow the inhabitant of the room to be present. Deok-gi's wife stood closely behind her father-in-law. Her mother-in-law, Deok-hui, and the helpers stood on the veranda in mortified silence.

The detectives opened all the wardrobe doors, ransacked the desk drawers, opened the bookcase, and quickly searched the loft. Then, they took out the steel box, which had been returned to its place, and attempted to open it.

"We don't have the key," the daughter-in-law spoke up to discourage them.

"They got it from your husband," her father-in-law whispered.

"We've got the key, don't you get it?" the older detective growled, pointing to the younger man, who inserted the key, while entering the combination. The safe clanged open. The gruff detective found the ring of keys, and asked Sang-hun, "Is this the right one?"

"Yes, yes."

Sang-hun's wife, standing on the veranda, was unable to understand why her husband was so ill at ease and submissive before the younger man.

They tramped out to the outer quarters. Sang-hun's wife and daughter-in-law followed. "Are they really detectives?" Sang-hun's wife asked the keeper of the outer quarters.

He answered dismissively, "Don't you see how the master is being dragged around? I've got their card right here."

Why should she doubt them when it was all to get her son home? The two women stood on the stone ledge, peering into the room flooded with electric light. The detectives opened the cabinet first, then the main safe, shutting it securely before coming out to the veranda.

"What are you doing out here? Go inside," Sang-hun scolded the women.

"What happened?" the daughter-in-law asked, knowing that her mother-in-law wouldn't want to talk to him.

"Well, he'll be out by tomorrow, I think. Don't worry. Go on inside." As he took his leave, surrounded by the detectives, he told a young servant to secure the gates of the house.

———

"Master, are you going straight home?"

"Yes. Let's get a taxi."

The three flagged down a taxi when they reached Hwanggeumjeong.

"We'll disappear this evening. You should pay us now."

"Relax. You'll get paid when we get there."

"If things go wrong, we'll land in prison for three years — maybe even five or six. A thousand is nothing. We should get enough so that our family doesn't go hungry for however long we're on the run."

The other one agreed. "Don't worry. It's gone so well that I'm sure the master will give us an ample reward."

"You won't be sorry if you give us a big one each."

"Why are you guys so impatient? Wait a minute—" Sang-hun was alarmed.

"What?"

"The detective's card you gave to the keeper. We left it somewhere on the cabinet. What a stupid mistake!"

They had acquired the card from the detective who had taken in Clerk Choe. Sang-hun had insisted that it'd be better if they didn't use it, unless it were absolutely necessary.

"There's no need for you to worry. *Our* necks are on the line here."

"But that card can cause serious problems. It's like using a stolen official seal or a forged document."

"If you're so worried, we'll go snatch it back. How much is it worth to you?"

"You sound like a broken record. I'll give you as much as you want. Just get it back."

"How much?"

"How will you get it back?"

"Don't you worry about that. Just tell us how much."

"I'll give you a hundred won."

"That's it? If something goes wrong, it could cost a person's life."

"You're crazy! I'll give you a hundred, that's all."

"Put it in writing."

"A note?"

"No, a check."

"All right. Wait! You took the card back and put it in your pocket, didn't you?"

"Write the check, then hand over the rest of our money."

"I can't. I don't have that much cash with me."

Sang-hun wrote a check in the taxi parked in the front of his gate. The older man chuckled as he snapped up the check with one hand and brought out the card from his coat pocket with the other.

———

There was still no news of Deok-gi, who was supposed to be released the next day. Deok-gi's mother worried that her husband had been arrested as well. She sent a maidservant to Hwagae-dong to see if he had returned home. The servant reported that they were waiting for news from Deok-gi's house. Early the previous evening, two detectives had arrived with the master in a car and taken Ui-gyeong away with them.

Deok-gi's mother wouldn't have minded if the whore stayed in prison for ten years, but when she imagined her husband in jail, she felt a twinge of pity for him. Her thoughts weren't as generous, however, when they turned to Ui-gyeong and Gyeong-ae. She entertained all sorts of fantasies as she tried to fall asleep.

There was no one to take care of her husband now that he was in jail. What did he eat and how had he spent the two nights he had been there without anything to cover himself? Perhaps she'd take him a quilt the next day when she delivered her son's food.

She suddenly felt close to her husband, who had drifted so far away from her. The idea of looking after him while he was in jail wasn't completely altruistic though, for she was hoping her show of concern might change her husband's heart.

As soon as day broke, she pulled out her husband's quilt and assembled a selection of cotton-padded clothes. She made a fuss, telling servants to go buy new towels and to bring soap and tooth-cleaning powder. She packed everything up, then carefully made up her face. Dressing warmly enough to withstand the cold for the entire day, she left in a car with the boy who delivered Deok-gi's meals. No one in the house laughed at her for having had such a dramatic change of heart. In fact, everyone believed it was the best thing she could have done.

Those remaining at home weren't sure if the detectives would let her deliver the care package for Sang-hun since they had refused Deok-gi's quilt at first, relenting only after learning that Deok-gi had recently been seriously ill. Around noon, when they were still waiting for news from the mistress, a car stopped outside the house. Deok-gi stepped out of the car.

The family ran out and embraced him as if he'd risen from the dead while two Western-suited men peered in at them from behind the middle gate.

They've come again!

Deok-gi put up his hand and beckoned the strangers inside. As they stepped up to the veranda, he asked his wife to bring out the small safe.

"The safe? Didn't the police take the keys with them the day before yesterday?"

"What?" Deok-gi grew pale as he turned toward the stunned detectives.

"But isn't your father at the police station? Mother went some time ago."

Deok-gi spoke to the detectives in Japanese.

The detectives shook their heads, their faces falling.

"When did they take it? Who did they say they were? They must have shown you some identification," Deok-gi demanded.

"Didn't you send the key to the small safe? They might have left their card in the outer quarters."

"The key to the small safe is right here!"

"So your father was with them?" a detective asked.

"Yes, at first he came and searched for the keys, saying that there was something he needed from the cabinet. Then he returned at dusk with two men, one of whom had the key. He took something out of the safe in the outer quarters."

"There was nothing your family could have done, but people should know that we don't search houses after dark." Resigned to the situation, the detectives moved to the outer quarters. One question remained: Had his father been deceived by the phony detectives, or had he conspired with them? Deok-gi didn't want to believe that his father could be behind this.

The detectives called Geumcheon to report the incident and searched for the business card, but it was nowhere to be found. They had brought Deok-gi home so they could examine his grandfather's will. If it checked out the suspects would be released, but this turn of events made that impossible now. After asking a few more questions, the officers went away with Deok-gi in tow.

Deok-gi's mother soon returned, despondent, followed by the servant with the bundle on his back. At the police station, she had been told that they knew nothing about her husband. Then she was shunted to the Jongno Police Station, where she was directed back to the Judiciary Department of the Police Division. But she got nowhere. The family couldn't bear to see her disappointment when she learned what had happened.

Bloody Lips

Hasty footsteps could be heard amid whispers in the deserted corridor under the dim electric light. Doors burst open here and there, as heads poked out, asking, "What's going on here?" Bloodshot eyes glinted in the dark. The answers didn't seem to shock them, but every eye grew colder and each face sterner. Each day around this time, an interrogation began in every room and stretched through the night.

Geumcheon heard what had happened from his subordinates. He directed one of them to call a doctor immediately. Outside, he had a policeman stationed before each interrogation room to bar people from going in and out. A bit later, several policemen without swords brought in what looked like a corpse, covered with a black overcoat.

Slippered feet crossed the corridor solemnly. No one uttered a word. They were trying to keep this latest development sub rosa. When the policeman posted in Geumcheon's room opened the door, light streamed into the corridor. The body disappeared into the room without a sound, and the policeman pushed the door shut. The policemen standing guard at other doors stepped away in a wave, resembling the wake of a motorcade.

In Geumcheon's room, the policemen dropped the body they were carrying onto the dirty wooden floor. The body began to squirm and moan in agony. As Geumcheon drew near, an underling pulled aside the overcoat covering the body. The man's chest heaved and bloody foam gathered on his lips. He looked awful even to the untrained eye, and Geumcheon feared that he'd die before the doctor arrived.

The man's face didn't resemble a face—it was a dark mass of blood. Nose, mouth, eyes—everything was a bloody mess, like a lump of fermented beans molded during a moonless night. It was unclear where his mouth was, but one could see that his eyes were open and gleaming.

"What a pointless thing you've done. How can a man with such great ambition die this way—a coward? Who would have thought that Jang Hun would be so feeble." Geumcheon frowned as he stared down at the bloodied face. His words could be construed as mockery: "A patriot lives by the spirit of a warrior. And a warrior must end his life gracefully. What ugliness is this? If you have to die, it would have been more dignified if you had killed yourself with that pistol." He nodded to the gun on his desk. "Take it, Jang Hun. End your life in a manly manner. You must know that it's over for you. You couldn't accomplish what you set out to do in this era of impossible conditions, but before you die, you'd better tell the whole world what you intended to do. For the sake of your honor, and as a way to recruit comrades to your cause so they might carry on what you set out to do. Answer just three questions: Was that pistol left behind by Pi-hyeok or did it come from someone else? What did you plan to do with it? What orders did you receive from Pi-hyeok? Just tell me these things. Share this with us for Kim Byeong-hwa's sake. If you refuse to take responsibility, thinking everything will be finished once you're gone, remember that the people you leave behind will have an even harder time."

Geumcheon hoped he could get the man to spill something in his vulnerable state. Yet, if he had been willing to answer their questions, he wouldn't have swallowed the drugs and severed his tongue with his own teeth in the first place. Jang Hun had uttered nothing but "I don't know" during the past three days. The detectives shook their heads, saying they'd never seen such a stubborn devil since the foundation of the Police Division. Even if he hadn't drugged himself, Jang Hun wouldn't have gotten out of there in one piece. He looked so broken that it seemed as if his bones were hanging loose in the sack of his body.

On the verge of losing consciousness, Jang Hun blinked while listening to Geumcheon. When he heard the word pistol, he opened his eyes and stared at the detective, as if he had come to, and then spat something out. Blood sprayed from his mouth, and although Geumcheon leapt away, blood spattered his face and chest, like stray bullets.

The underling standing beside him shouted, "You bastard!" and kicked Jang Hun in the side. Jang Hun closed his eyes and let out several painful moans, which sounded as though they emanated from the bottom of a deep barrel.

The doctor arrived. Geumcheon had had hot water brought in and had taken off his shirt to wash it. In his undershirt, he wiped his face and greeted the doctor. "Take a look at him. We must revive him, no matter what." There was a sense of urgency in Geumcheon's voice. The doctor was used to such cases. He presumed the prisoner had been pummeled to the brink of death by Judo experts. He felt for a pulse and was stunned to learn that the man had taken poison.

"How long ago was that? Has he been spitting blood because of the poison?"

"No, he bit his own tongue."

Ignoring the prisoner's muffled moans, the doctor cradled the man's blood-drenched head as if it were the head of a cow that had just been slaughtered and forced his mouth open. He pulled out his tongue. Jang Hun merely groaned, having no energy left to scream.

The doctor muttered, "It's been torn in three or four places, but it's not totally severed."

The police had obtained a clue from Gyeong-ae's cousin. When they learned that Pi-hyeok had come to see him, and that he had helped shave Pi-hyeok's head before his departure, they began to torture Gyeong-ae and Byeong-hwa, who blamed everything on Jang Hun. Gyeong-ae insisted that she had introduced Pi-hyeok to Byeong-hwa only because he'd threatened her. She didn't like the idea of Byeong-hwa getting involved with him because they were falling in love, and Byeong-hwa was about to distance himself from the movement anyway. She asserted that after consulting with Byeong-hwa, she also introduced Pi-hyeok to Jang Hun. Byeong-hwa in turn claimed that he and Pil-sun's father had been beaten because Jang Hun had been angry that Byeong-hwa and Gyeong-ae had backed off from the movement. He insisted that the beating had also been a warning against revealing Pi-hyeok's secret. Gyeong-ae and Byeong-hwa knew their story would not contradict Jang Hun's. After Jang Hun beat up Byeong-hwa, the two had become close again. At one point, Jang Hun had said, "If anything happens, just say whatever is best for you. I'll keep silent no matter what, and if it gets really bad, I'll—" He gestured with his hand that he would cut his throat. Byeong-hwa and Gyeong-ae had worked out their story in advance and had full confidence in Jang Hun.

Jang Hun did as he said he would. However, he had no idea that it would be a dose of cocaine—which he had obtained on a lark from a friend visiting from Manchuria—that would end his life. He had put the cocaine in his vest pocket. It had slipped through a hole in the seam and had lodged at the bottom of his vest.

When Jang Hun was thrown into jail, the policeman on duty had cleaned out his pockets but missed the cocaine. Jang Hun himself had forgotten all about it. After suffering through three days and nights, he wanted to die. He remembered his promise to Byeong-hwa, and he suddenly thought of the cocaine, as if someone had whispered the word in his ear. He couldn't remember what had become of it but checked in his vest and felt something at the bottom of it. He was as happy as a jail breaker who had discovered an iron pick.

Jang Hun tore the worn-out lining and a small paper bag fell into his hand. Yet now that the cocaine was in his possession, his courage faltered. Despair and fear made him dizzy.

Should I die now? But what then? He scolded himself for being so cowardly. *If I die now, it's not because I can't endure the pain. Nor does it make sense that I'll be dying on behalf of dozens of my comrades. I just don't have the sacrificial spirit to rescue them and their families from pain and misfortune. With my death I'll protect a small incubator that will determine the fate of our cause. Several gifted comrades with superior scientific intelligence are gathering together to perform important research—research that may provide breakthroughs in the near future. For now, it's my responsibility to protect these scientists at all costs, even though by doing so I will never see the fruits of their efforts. My death is worthwhile—for this, if nothing else.*

As he drank some water after dinner, Jang Hun tossed the cocaine into his mouth as if he were taking an aspirin. He did it mechanically, in a daze. Now well past his fear of death, he paid close attention to how the drug moved through his system. When he cut his tongue, he was barely aware of what had happened; the poison had advanced too far.

And so, one daybreak, Jang Hun's life ended at the age of twenty-seven.

Father's Case

"Father, where is Grandfather's will? We've got to have it if we're ever going to get out of here . . . You're letting me go now, but Pil-sun, Yi Pil-sun, did you release her? Let me see her. Don't beat her. I know that she's innocent . . . Pistol? I don't know . . . I'm sorry. Thank you. Can I go home when I get better?"

In his delirium, Deok-gi rattled on, opening his eyes wide and shutting them again.

Deok-gi hadn't completely recovered from the flu when he was taken into custody, but he decided to conceal his condition. Actually, he was so weighed down with worries that he had little time to think about his fever.

After having been escorted to his house, he spent two more nights in a cell that was as cold as it was outside. His temperature rose, and it was difficult for him to sit up straight. The next morning, as he was being taken out, he collapsed at the threshold of his cell. They dragged him into an interrogation room, but fortunately, it was the High Police chief who had summoned him. Seeing how Deok-gi's eyes flickered and how he stammered, the chief hurriedly called the doctor, exchanged opinions with his staff, and had Deok-gi confined to the medical-school hospital with the understanding that he would take responsibility for this measure. They wouldn't allow Deok-gi to go home, and a brawny policeman stood guard at his bed at all hours. His mother and wife took turns taking care of him, but no one else was allowed access. Pil-sun's father was in the same hospital, and Pil-sun's mother had come as soon as she heard the news, but she was not permitted to see Deok-gi. For the first time, Deok-gi's mother and wife were grateful for the detective's actions.

"What a relief that all my assets are gone. Don't worry, Mother. I'm not going to let them kick you all into the street." He talked in his sleep and opened his eyes as if he were fully conscious. His mother's eyes were wet with tears.

Deok-gi's wife nursed him for three days without budging from her place near his bed. She didn't bother about her appearance and didn't even wash her face properly. Though her mother-in-law had urged her to take a nap, she didn't lie down once. She would doze off in her chair, using her arm as a pillow. Now that the baby was weaned, she had left him at home to be fed thin gruel. Not allowing herself to think about the child, she devoted all her energy to caring for her husband. That day her mother-in-law went home to rest, and her own mother would come to keep her company that night.

She felt a sharp pain when Deok-gi mentioned Pil-sun in his delirium. What deep feelings did he have for her that he would call out her name even in his confused state? How could he utter Pil-sun's name with such yearning if it were not etched in his heart? Was he repeating his pleas to the detectives? At times she couldn't bear the sight of him. The family's wealth was gone now, and her husband might soon have a concubine. If she had to endure poverty or tolerate a concubine or both, she would bear it all with a smile on her face, but what if he divorced her? But these were all just conjectures. She tried to calm herself. It was senseless to think such thoughts when her husband was hovering between life and death.

No. My husband wouldn't do it. Isn't he the eldest son of a yangban *family?* The thought comforted her.

A few days later, Deok-gi's temperature chart, drawn on a graph hanging at the foot of the bed, began to show a gradual drop, and the sharp ups and downs of his fever leveled out. He could now sit up and swallow some milk.

His family was thankful for his recovery, but they didn't want him to get better too quickly. They were afraid that the detective, who was standing watch at the head of the bed like a messenger of death, would snatch him away as soon as he improved.

Deok-gi's mother pleaded with the detectives. "We're relieved, but please put in a good word for us so they won't touch him until he makes a complete recovery." It might have helped if she had pressed a ten-won bill into their hands to pay for cigarettes. But she feared and despised them, not to mention she didn't know the ways of the world. The next afternoon Deok-gi was yanked from his bed and escorted back to the police station, although he couldn't stand on his own.

Amid the chaos, Deok-gi asked to see Pil-sun's father, but the detectives wouldn't hear of it. A nurse was sent to bring out Pil-sun's mother, and Deok-gi saw her in the lobby. She wept when saw him. Witnesses to the emotional scene, Deok-gi's wife and mother were perturbed.

At the station, the Judiciary Section chief greeted him with, "What was written about the rice refinery in your grandfather's will?" Deok-gi wondered whether his father had been caught. Or could it be that his father's whereabouts were still unknown, but someone else had raised the subject? He didn't know what answer would be helpful to his father, but he told the truth—that there had been no mention of the refinery.

"Then did he leave any oral instructions before his death?"

"He didn't have the time to do so."

"Then who's managing it?"

"I am."

"Would you give it to your father if he demanded it?"

"I thought I'd give it to him when the time is right."

"Did you know anything about a separate will, stating that he'd leave the refinery to your father?"

Deok-gi was astonished. It dawned on him that his father may have made such a fuss in order to take the rice refinery, by stealing his grandfather's seal and forging a will.

Deok-gi shrugged.

"Did you arrest the imposters? Did you find the keys?" Deok-gi asked.

The chief smirked. "What imposters? Do you mean your father? We've recovered half of your assets, money that would have been gambled away. You young people shouldn't resent the police. You ought to thank us."

When Deok-gi's grandfather was still alive, Sang-hun had used the deeds of the Hwagae-dong house as collateral and had left a trail of considerable debts. Sang-hun was being bombarded with demands for payment but didn't have the cash. Deok-gi had just spent two thousand won installing his father's concubine, and Sang-hun himself had squandered his father's bank deposit of four or five thousand. He had also used the land deed in his name to secure a loan of a thousand won at a gaming parlor but had lost it all that same night. While he was being pressured for the money, he was approached about taking over a stock trading shop. Sang-hun thought it might be the only way to recover his money, but at that point, as if heaven were on his side, Deok-gi was taken away by the police. Sang-hun thought that with his son in jail, depending on how long it took the police to discover that he was innocent—he could resort to an emergency measure.

On the day he went to the house to see if he could get the key to the safe, his wife had ruined everything when she threw the safe out onto the veranda. If she hadn't aggravated him, he could have easily opened the small safe himself. But instead he decided to use an old guy who had swindled money in mahjong parlors to pose as a detective. Though this lowlife was eager to be part of the action, he knew nothing about opening safes and recommended a retired office worker he knew, who used to oversee company safes.

While Deok-gi was asking in his feverish delirium whether his father had the will, land deeds were being converted into cash and a contract for the agent's office was signed. The father's luck ended with his arrest, while Deok-gi's turned with it. If Deok-gi were cleared of all misdeeds, suspicion would shift to Sang-hun or the Suwon woman, but Sang-hun hadn't thought this through. His theft of the documents was not linked to the Jang Hun case or to the poisoning and seemed to be of little importance. The police intended to conclude the matter quickly.

Seated across from Deok-gi, the chief took out a document from his briefcase.

"Whose writing is this?"

It was his grandfather's will.

Then he took out another one. It was his grandfather's will with the same date as the first one, instructing that the rice refinery be given to Sang-hun. The handwriting was identical. "What about this one?"

"It's my grandfather's."

"If you make a false statement, you'll be committing perjury, so be careful what you say. Where was your grandfather's seal?"

"It was in the safe, but my father asked for it."

"When?"

Anxious that his words might contradict his father's, Deok-gi remembered that he'd last used the seal when he gave the Suwon woman the deed for the Taepyeong-dong house. "I think it was last month." Deok-gi tried to read the chief's mind.

The detective asked nothing further. He simply told the assistant beside him to fetch Sang-hun.

Deok-gi was afraid of what might ensue. Within five minutes, his father entered the room, followed by a policeman. Deok-gi's head dropped as if a knife had landed on the nape of his neck.

How can this be? Deok-gi couldn't lift his bowed head. The police had removed anything that could be used as rope. His father's Korean jacket was missing its frontal ties, and his ankle ties were nowhere in sight; his trousers, too, must have been without a belt, as they were rolled up high to prevent him from tripping. It was possible they were treating his father more roughly than they were treating him.

The chief looked Sang-hun up and down, a mocking smile on his lips. He waited until Sang-hun sat down before he placed several documents before the father and son. The father sat with his head bowed, while Deok-gi took his time sorting through them.

The papers made up about half of what had been in the safe. What could Deok-gi do if he found that some were missing? He counted them, unsure how many his father had taken with him. Only several small deeds remained.

"One of your mother's and one of yours are gone. The others are still in the safe," Deok-gi's father uttered.

The chief made Deok-gi write a list of the documents that were on the table and asked Sang-hun when he received the will that granted him ownership of the rice refinery.

"Right before my father passed away. Through him." He thought it would be advantageous to make it sound as if Deok-gi knew about it.

The chief then asked Deok-gi, "Didn't you say you'd changed the name on the deed last month when you handed over the seal?"

Sang-hun had thought it was fortunate that the chief had questioned him first. Regardless of how angry his son might be, he wouldn't send his father to prison. Even if Sang-hun told outright lies, his son would not expose him. Knowing had eased his mind. But their stories didn't match. Sang-hun felt dizzy, thinking there was no way out for him now and that at his age he'd be in grave trouble.

The chief stared at the father and son, red-faced and stupefied before him, and burst out laughing. He was eager to make a laughingstock out of Sang-hun. The chief held a deep antipathy toward Christians, and he had long ago taken a dislike to Sang-hun. The detective couldn't resist this opportunity to humiliate him.

The chief ordered that the concubine be brought in. Ui-gyeong's stilettos clicked loudly. She wasn't handcuffed. Deok-gi hadn't expected to see her.

The detective separated Ui-gyeong from Sang-hun. Deok-gi didn't even look at her.

"How much is in there?" the chief asked, pushing a small suitcase toward Deok-gi.

"Two thousand three hundred won," Ui-gyeong answered, without a trace of hesitation or fear.

Given the small sum, Deok-gi surmised that the land had been used as collateral.

"Didn't you say you got three thousand five hundred in collateral?"

"Yes, but fifty won was deducted as interest in advance, and we spent some in Pyeongyang."

The chief took out a ring of keys from the suitcase and tossed it toward Deok-gi. "We're supposed to keep this here for now, but the safekeeping procedures are complicated. That's why we're giving everything back to you." He asked Deok-gi to sign a receipt and then directed his attention to Ui-gyeong.

"Your man was all the more lovable when he pressed a large wad of cash in your hand, wasn't he?"

Without any trace of concern, she smiled and said, "I had no objections, but I just kept it temporarily. He didn't want me to use it all."

Deok-gi couldn't bear to listen.

"Did you talk him into doing this?"

"What's there to talk him into? Did I know whether his wife owned a piece of land or part of the sky? I just went along with him. He told me we'd have fun."

"Then out of all the deeds why did you make him liquidate his wife's? You made him do it, didn't you? You told him to get rid of that one first because it was too small for you to swallow but too big to ignore, right?"

"I had no idea what was going on. He said it was hard to find a lender or a buyer for the big ones."

The chief laughed at her and said, "As long as you were at it, you should have taken a big one. You missed a good chance. As you see, they're now going back where they belong."

"Who wants to go to prison?"

"Do you think you won't end up there anyway?"

"Why should I? What did I do wrong? Women follow men, I just did what I was told. Is that a crime?"

"Quite correct. Since women follow men, the wife should follow her husband right to prison."

The word prison startled everyone.

The chief looked at Sang-hun and thundered at him, "How old are you? You've got to be at least fifty. Aren't you well over the 'age of doubts'? Was your learning useless? Aren't you ashamed to look your own son in the eye?"

The detective resented that he, a man much younger than Sang-hun, didn't enjoy the pleasures of a woman like Ui-gyeong. Deok-gi, on the other hand, pitied and scorned his father for sitting there and allowing himself to be humiliated by a callow young man just over thirty—a man almost young enough to be his son.

"If someone like me, who's just of the 'age of setting goals' . . ." The chief kept using classical allusions in his flawless Korean. With no consideration for Deok-gi's presence, the chief continued, "If someone my age sleeps around, it would be frowned upon but forgiven, for he still has time to grow up. But as the saying goes, a burglar who begins his career late in life doesn't know when day breaks. Will you ever clean up your act?"

Deok-gi wished he could hide.

Sang-hun felt that merely being alive was itself a humiliation.

"Normally, it's the wanton life of playboy son that prompts his father's premature death. You masterminded your father's poisoning, didn't you?" The chief harangued Sang-hun, though he suspected the Suwon woman and her group and had obtained almost all the evidence he needed.

"It's only natural that you suspect me of this, too, but I am innocent." Sang-hun bowed over and over again and pleaded with the detective in the humblest of tones.

"You mean to say that you committed this shameless crime when your son inherited the assets that should have been yours?"

Sang-hun hung his head.

"You stole your family's estate, then sold and borrowed on parts of it. You were ready to flee all the way to Manchuria."

Although Sang-hun had explained what had happened during his previous interrogation, which had lasted several days, he was now being threatened with a new account of the events. He sat and said nothing. Deok-gi couldn't keep quiet. "That's not true. I was going to give him some cash because he was being harassed by collectors, but then I was suddenly dragged in here. My father just meant to take the bankbook to get some money, but things got out of hand. If I had left the key to the small safe at home or left the bankbook in that safe, things wouldn't have come to this." Deok-gi did the best he could.

The section chief didn't silence him, probably because he found Deok-gi's explanation credible. He asked a detective to take Deok-gi to the High Police. Deok-gi was reluctant to leave his father behind but had no choice. After gathering up the keys, the land deeds, and the money, he was led away.

Acquittal

———

Deok-gi was released that very evening thanks to the efforts of the High Police chief. Actually, he had little to do with it; there was simply no reason to hold Deok-gi any longer. Deok-gi was relieved but kept looking back over his shoulder, not eager to walk away while his father was still detained.

A great flurry ensued at home, for everyone was euphoric to see him and doting over his health. Deok-gi himself was in even greater turmoil.

"How long do you think your father will be locked up? Ten years or so?"

"Don't worry, Mother. He'll get out tomorrow or the day after."

"You think I'm worried about him?"

That bitter morning she had run around preparing a care package had been the first time since they'd become estranged that she had felt some affection for her husband. Since then she had been embarrassed in front of her daughter-in-law and her servants, and any lingering feelings of warmth for her husband had vanished. She no longer considered him her husband.

After dinner Deok-gi went out. He was planning to visit High Police Chief Kimura's house.

I should have brought some ginseng with me, Deok-gi thought, already in a rickshaw. *No, perhaps it's better to arrive empty-handed; I will have to send something substantial soon.* Reconsidering, he made a detour to Hwanggeum-jeong and picked up eight hundred grams of ginseng at a pharmacy he knew well.

After returning home from Kimura's, Deok-gi seemed satisfied with what he had heard there. The Japanese chief didn't say that he'd grant Deok-gi any favors, but Deok-gi felt it was a good visit because he was able to talk freely with the inspector about his situation.

Two days later, on Sunday, he visited the homes of the division head and two section chiefs to pay his respects. Was this, he wondered, his first taste of hobnobbing? He wrote three significant checks without reluctance; he felt an obligation to express his appreciation for the recovery of his assets.

On his way home, he stopped off at the hospital to pay his respects to Pil-sun's father for the first time since he was released. Now he was confident that he could use his influence to hasten Pil-sun's release. Kimura had urged him to stay for lunch, probably in consideration of his ties with Deok-gi's grandfather. Geumcheon, who was also present, followed him to the foyer and said, "It'll be settled one way or another. Don't worry too much."

Deok-gi had never heard more welcome news in his life.

At the hospital, Pil-sun's mother tearfully welcomed Deok-gi. "You didn't have to come all this way! Are you feeling better?"

Deok-gi, too, felt like sobbing but responded with exaggerated confidence: "Your daughter will be out tomorrow or the day after, rest assured."

"What happened?"

"Do you remember Jang Hun? He killed himself in there." He had heard about it from Kimura only two days earlier.

"My goodness!" Pil-sun's mother seemed to momentarily forget that Jang Hun was the man who had put her husband in the hospital.

"It's not easy to say this, but he took all the blame before he died, so now it might be easier for some of the others."

Pil-sun's mother bowed her head. She couldn't help but feel sorry for Jang, who had become the sacrificial lamb.

Though Pil-sun's father was so weak he appeared almost lifeless in the hospital bed, he managed to open his eyes when his wife shook him. It wasn't clear whether he was conscious; he didn't even have enough energy to let out a groan.

"I'm so sorry," Deok-gi said.

"I just hope Pil-sun will be released before he dies." The energy seemed to have been drained from her as well.

"Don't be afraid, she'll be out soon. I visited the police chief and section chiefs twice, asking for their help." Deok-gi spoke with confidence, to make the woman feel better, if nothing else.

And in fact, Pil-sun was released the following day. Soon after Deok-gi had heard Pil-sun's exuberant voice on the phone, Won-sam and his wife appeared. Won-sam was half-dazed, his face gaunt and his eyes unfocused. His wife's face was pale, her lips completely drained of blood. They had suffered for nearly twenty days.

"You've gone through so much. It's a good thing that you don't have young children to take care of," Deok-gi said. He wondered about Gyeong-ae and the Suwon woman.

"It was quite an experience," Won-sam said. "Like visiting hell while you're still alive," he laughed.

"Has my father been released, too?" Deok-gi asked.

"Your father? Did he know Pi-hyeok? . . . Are you all right, sir?"

Won-sam and his wife were shocked yet somehow comforted to discover that no one had escaped the sweep. They had resented that fate had dragged them into an affair they had nothing to do with. Learning that even Deok-gi had been jailed despite his fragile health, they now felt fortunate to have gotten out in one piece.

"Why did all this happen?" Won-sam's wife asked. Had the old man's death triggered some curse? Had that been the case, the curse should have landed on the servants who'd been brought in by the Suwon woman, not on the two of them.

"It could have been the curse of money, the curse of a hard life, or a curse of anything . . ." Deok-gi let the query bounce off him.

Snorting, Won-sam added, "Or the curse of trying to escape our fate as servants."

After Won-sam and his wife went to the inner quarters, Deok-gi changed his clothes and went out again, this time to Hwagae-dong. His father might have been released as well, and it wouldn't do to sit back and wait for his call.

With all the doors firmly shut in the outer quarters, he reluctantly entered the yard through the women's quarters. A gaggle of young and old women bustled about.

The questioning young faces were all unfamiliar. If he hadn't run into the young woman who babysat the Suwon woman's child, he might have thought he'd come to the wrong house. After the Suwon woman's arrest, the child must have been sent here. He couldn't believe that this was the same house he'd grown up in.

"Hello there! I didn't recognize you."

Deok-gi stopped in his tracks. An old *gisaeng* rushed out of the main room and animatedly greeted him.

He had no idea who she was.

"The girls didn't recognize the young master. I'm so sorry! Please come in."

As he looked more closely, he realized that it was the woman he had seen a month earlier in the main room, Maedang.

"You have gone through so much, haven't you? Such calamity!" A stream of verbiage flowed from the woman.

"I came because I thought my father was released today."

"Is he coming home? I thought the world was turned upside down, because the old gentleman was taken in, and his son was released instead." Was she trying to be witty, or was she completely in the dark about what had happened? With a laugh she said, "Then the mistress of this house will be released along with him, right? But will the mistress of Taepyeong-dong get out, too?"

"I think so," Deok-gi said and left abruptly. Disgusted that the main room once inhabited by his mother had become this woman's playground, he couldn't bear another minute of Maedang's chatter.

It's been only two months since my grandfather died! Byeong-hwa said that the person who has to die must die soon and that a new era will emerge . . . Deok-gi knew that his grandfather's death would usher in a new era, but it hadn't been defined, and he understood that it wouldn't materialize overnight.

He took the Sogyeok-dong road to the hospital to see Pil-sun.

My grandfather was more than seventy when he passed away, so his death wasn't premature. But because we were not prepared, things have degenerated to this level of decadence in just two months!

What would Byeong-hwa have done in my place? There was not much his friend could have done; he might have thrown money here and there, knowing his generous temperament, but most likely a similar sort of confusion would have ensued.

As he approached the hospital entrance, his eyes rose to the second floor. Upstairs, he knocked and pushed the door open. Pil-sun stopped short when she saw him. Her face turned pale, then crimson. Only then did she seem to regain her composure. She bowed her head lightly and looked around for her mother. Her mother's presence would help contain her emotions.

Her eyes radiated in her wan, gaunt face.

"You've had such a hard time." Deok-gi's voice caressed her.

Pil-sun's smile was tinged with sorrow.

Her mother broke the silence. "They hung her upside down, twice, and beat her."

Not knowing how to comfort her, Deok-gi heaved a sigh.

"They didn't ask about that Korean overcoat. If they had, it could have been worse. Thank you for putting in a good word for her with the police chief and the section chief so that she could be released sooner." She turned to her daughter and said, "This gentleman has suffered, too. And he did all that was possible to get you released."

Pil-sun's face reddened again as she bowed her head shyly.

"I didn't do that much. It's good, though, that they didn't find out about the Korean coat."

"Has your father been released, too?"

"I think so. Won-sam and his wife are also back home."

Both mother and daughter were ebullient.

Won-sam and his wife entered just then, as if they'd been summoned.

After exchanging greetings with Pil-sun and her mother, Won-sam announced that Secretary Ji and Chang-hun had been let go.

"The outer quarters' man is out?" Deok-gi asked. "How's his health?"

"Well, he is one strong man. He said there wasn't much difference between jail and the outer quarters, except it was a little colder in jail," Won-sam chortled.

"Perhaps he was treated better because of his age," Pil-sun's mother said, gazing at her daughter. She herself had been tortured during the March 1, 1919 incident.

"What's going on with the shop?" Won-sam asked.

"I went there a few times. I brought back some vegetables to eat, but it's still shut down."

"Should I open it tomorrow?"

"Well . . ." Pil-sun's mother looked to Deok-gi. She wasn't sure what to do, with Byeong-hwa not there and her husband seriously ill.

"Can you manage it yourself?" Deok-gi asked Won-sam.

"Anyone can go to the market to pick out items and sell them as long as there's money. I have enough experience by now."

"How about letting him open the store tomorrow?" Deok-gi asked Pil-sun's mother.

"That'd be splendid. My daughter can't rest well here anyway . . ." She seemed pleased and informed Deok-gi that she had been keeping Byeong-hwa's money.

"Then you and your wife can look after Pil-sun until her father is discharged from the hospital," Deok-gi said to Won-sam. "In fact, why don't you move into the back of the store?"

"What do you mean, 'look after me'?" Pil-sun objected.

Won-sam felt flattered to be entrusted with the responsibility, while his wife's mind leapt to the possibility that Pil-sun might become Deok-gi's concubine. She cared for the young lady as if she were her own daughter, so she had no objection to minding her until she recovered from her recent ordeal.

Deok-gi thought he would ask Kimura to arrange a meeting with the Judiciary Police chief. Deok-gi visited the Judiciary Police chief's house three times over the next few days, but the chief gave no reassurance, saying only, "The problem lies in the seriousness of impersonating police officers . . ." And Sang-hun was their mastermind.

Nevertheless, Sang-hun was released several days later.

Sang-hun came alone to receive bows from his children, since he realized it would be awkward for them to visit the Hwagae-dong house.

Deok-gi was in the main room when his father arrived. He rushed down to the yard and prostrated himself in a bow, as Sang-hun's daughter-in-law, daughter, and others hurried into the yard, too. His wife remained in the main room with her grandson on her lap. She was still furious at her husband's deception and at herself for having expressed concern for him. She could barely contain her wrath. *How can he be so brazen as to come here to see his children? Does he still think he is the family elder?*

466

Sang-hun's children urged him to enter the main room, but he preferred to sit on the veranda. "I can't stay long."

"Your mother says I was wrong, but you realize that you neglected me more than your grandfather did, not letting me spend a penny as I wished. They attacked me for coming over here with phony police officers, but the actual police wouldn't grant me an interview with you when I needed the key, and it was impossible to know when you'd be released. I was in a bind. Why shouldn't I use the family money? Everything would've been fine if the rice refinery would have paid up, but the bastards made one excuse after another and wouldn't let me touch even a hundred won. Then, I came here, but your mother wouldn't let me near the small safe. So I brought someone who could open it. I didn't invite a thief into the house. The bankbooks were nowhere to be found. But I wasn't going to spend all the money. I'd honed in on a good business opportunity; the seed money would be recovered in a month or two if I bought into it, and the next day I had to sign a contract, so what else could I do? If your mother had behaved like a decent wife, I wouldn't have had to go through this humiliation."

An audible snort came from the main room. "Now I've heard everything! You were thrown in the slammer because I'm an awful wife. You don't have the slightest that you're out of prison thanks to your son. Without him, you'd still be locked up tight with all the other jailbirds—and I bet you'd have your new wife to thank for that!"

"Mother, please stop." Deok-gi tried leading his father to the outer quarters. He asked his wife to bring out a wine tray right away, hoping to prevent a scene any way he could. He grieved for his father and did not want him to feel more humiliated than he already was.

"I'll go. I just hope you'll take good care of everything from now on!" His father rose despondently.

"It's so cold. Please stay a moment more."

Without another word, the father turned to leave.

"Go and call a rickshaw," Deok-gi ordered a servant.

"I'll just catch one on my way out."

Deok-gi watched his father walk away, shoulders hunched, deflated.

The next day, a Sunday, Deok-gi called on Kimura to express his gratitude for releasing his father and to inquire about the release of the Suwon woman, Byeong-hwa, Gyeong-ae, and her mother. His exams were over and graduation was around the corner, but he thought he'd better wrap up affairs at home before leaving.

"That'll be difficult," Kimura explained when Byeong-hwa's name was raised. "Hong Gyeong-ae and her mother can be released, but the situation has become worse for Byeong-hwa because of what happened to Jang Hun." Then he added, "If it were proved that he has nothing to do with Jang Hun's faction, he wouldn't be prosecuted."

Deok-gi insisted that Byeong-hwa had nothing to do with Jang Hun and explained that Pil-sun's father, beaten by Jang Hun's followers, was hovering between life and death at the hospital. He then went on to describe Byeong-hwa's relationship with Pil-sun's family. Kimura seemed to take what Deok-gi said seriously.

When the Suwon woman's name came up, however, he was dismissive. "Her case is not in my jurisdiction, but from what I've heard, she's trouble. When she first came to live at your house, she was part of a conspiracy with that Choe fellow."

Kimura knew everything. Deok-gi was speechless. But out of respect for his grandfather, Deok-gi felt responsible for her, even if it might require some money to free her.

After he said good-bye to Kimura, Deok-gi went to Hyoja-dong to relay the good news and to see Pil-sun. Pil-sun greeted him near the shop. She appeared stronger, walking more steadily than she had a few days earlier, but was on the verge of tears.

"What's wrong? Is your father worse?"

"They just called. He's taken a turn for the worse." Tears welled up in her eyes.

"Let's go quickly." Deok-gi led the way.

"Please don't come with me. You must be busy. I'll go by myself."

They passed Chuseongmun on their way toward Samcheong-dong.

"My father spent half of his life in prison and then was nearly beaten to death. Why is life so unfair?" asked Pil-sun, crying, as they passed the spot where her father had been attacked.

Deok-gi paused before replying. Then, with regret in his voice, he said, "In a world like this, that was the only way for him to live with an uncorrupted spirit, with a clear conscience. Society is to blame for his grief, because it is without discipline or structure. It was an unfortunate, useless sacrifice that can't be undone."

When they arrived at the hospital, Deok-gi sensed that Pil-sun's father had only hours to live. Judging from his experience with his grandfather's death and by the way his eyes were glazed over, Deok-gi knew it wouldn't be long. Still, the father was conscious and glad to see his daughter. He recognized Deok-gi as well.

"I'm going with a glad heart, but how will you survive?" he stammered with difficulty to his family, tears streaming down his face. His wife and daughter wept, too. Deok-gi's heart ached to hear those words; this man has carried a heavy burden.

"Mr. Jo! I owe you so much. After I die, please be kind to them. I'm shameless to ask you this, but they have no one else to turn to."

"You're not dying, so please don't say that. Don't worry. Everything will be all right." Deok-gi comforted the old man, because he couldn't bring himself to say he'd take care of the man's family.

What should I do about his request? It could've been just a passing request. People have to worry about making a living all their lives, and as if that were not enough, they have to keep worrying until their dying moments. Deok-gi left the hospital with a heavy heart.

He thought of Gyeong-ae's father, though he had never met him. The old revolutionary must have asked the same favor of Deok-gi's father that Pil-sun's father had asked of him. Deok-gi remembered his mother's remark about following in his father's footsteps; her words haunted him.

After dinner, Won-sam trudged in while Deok-gi was reading the newspaper in the outer quarters. "I've come from the hospital."

"Has he passed away?"

"Yes. He died in the evening, so we closed the shop and went to the hospital."

"You could have phoned me. There was no need to come in person."

"They're having a funeral tomorrow, but they don't want to invite you—they don't want you to go out in the cold again. They said they'd be in touch after the funeral."

"They shouldn't do that. It would be different if I hadn't been involved from the beginning." Nevertheless, Deok-gi understood how they felt. He was grateful for their consideration, but he felt they were taking their solicitude too far by not notifying him right away.

"They seem to have few relatives, and it'll be difficult to cover the funeral expenses. They're going to use some money from the shop, but if you want to help, I thought I'd collect it for them. They don't know that I'm here—I've come on my own. I realize it's not my place to do this, but I had to do something." Won-sam was afraid that the young master might find fault with his impertinence, though Deok-gi didn't show any displeasure.

"You made the right decision. I'll have to pay my respects anyway, so let's go together."

"There's really no need for you to go. What if you get sick again, going out at night when you're already so exhausted?"

"What time will they leave for the grave?"

"A time hasn't been set yet, but it wouldn't make any difference if you paid your condolences later. It's as dark and chilly as a granary out there. Please just send them some money; that's what is most urgent."

Thinking he'd visit the next morning, Deok-gi wrapped up the money and took out some paper and candles left over from his grandfather's funeral. After sending Won-sam away with the parcel, he had second thoughts and decided he couldn't postpone his visit until the morning, especially when they'd grown so close. It was ridiculous to put off the visit because of the cold.

Because his mother believed that going out at night meant visiting women, Deok-gi always kept his coats in the outer quarters to avoid her nagging. Grabbing one as he left, he instinctively looked back.

A scolding seemed to be coming, not from his mother, but from the altar of his dead grandfather. *You're not studying. So what are you doing?* He realized that since his grandfather's funeral, he had become enmeshed in a three-ring circus. Even though he hadn't graduated from college, he had assumed the responsibilities of three households. Was it too much to take care of Pil-sun and her mother as well? But wasn't that what life was about?

It's all because of money. That's the only reason I'm harried, and the only reason people respect me. If I had nothing, who'd trust a schoolboy like me and ask me to take care of their family?

Won-sam was right. Paying condolences was not urgent. Money was. Pil-sun's father's request boiled down to money. He must have hoped that Deok-gi would help out with the funeral expenses. He wasn't asking Deok-gi to take care of his daughter because Deok-gi was a gentleman and would make a perfect son-in-law. Won-sam's plain words cut straight to the heart of the matter.

My father's involvement with Gyeong-ae may have started the same way. If my father hadn't been wealthy, her father would have asked other comrades for favors. My father and I find ourselves in similar situations because we both happen to come from a rich family, that's all. My father did things his own way, and I'll do things my way, according to my own character, ideology, and feelings.

With this revelation, Deok-gi repudiated his mother's comment that Pil-sun was "a second Gyeong-ae."

But what is money? Where does it come from? He asked these questions, yet he avoided answering them. He wanted to believe that he was now visiting Pil-sun and her mother to pay his condolences as Deok-gi, not as a benefactor.

He wanted to make sure that Pil-sun would not be spending the night in a chilly, dismal, wood-floored room. As he entered the hospital, it occurred to him that he hadn't sent enough money. He regretted not sending more, regardless of his feelings for Pil-sun.

Someone who was poor, whose lot in life was hard labor, shouldn't he at least receive an appropriate compensation for his pains? With this notion taking root in his head, it became clear to Deok-gi that looking after Pil-sun and her mother was his obligation, his duty.

Afterword

Korea had been in Japan's colonial clutches for twenty-one years when Yom Sang-seop's *Three Generations* appeared in 1931. This milestone in the history of Korean fiction was serialized in the Seoul daily *Chosun Ilbo* from January through September of that year. During the Japanese colonial rule (1910–1945), newspapers provided practically the only channel in publishing novels because the market was not mature enough to support long works of fiction except for a few eye-catching ones. A majority of writers, Yom included, started their careers as newspaper reporters, creating a climate in which journalists and literary figures commingled amicably. In turn, novels in newspapers tended to boost newspaper sales.

Dreaming of the Greater East Asia Co-Prosperity Sphere, Japan had begun to reinforce its colonial policy and flex its military muscle, with the northward advancement to Manchuria under way. Some Korean writers expressed their opposition to the colonial reality by joining the independence movement whenever opportunities arose or incorporating such material in their works. Others bowed to the Japanese imperialists' tactics of oppression and appeasement and participated in pro-Japanese activities.

Yom, born in Seoul in 1897, went to Japan to study in 1912. He finished high school there and entered Keio University. After finishing only a semester, however, he joined a regional newspaper as a journalist. He had been studying literature on his own and, in 1919, he joined forces with Hwang Seok-u to create a literary magazine. Soon after, he learned about the March 1 Independence Movement in Korea and became involved in planning a similar rally in Osaka, mobilizing Korean students and workers. He was arrested by the Japanese police and sentenced to ten months in prison at the first trial but was acquitted in the appeals court. He returned to Seoul in 1920 and joined the *Dong-A Ilbo* daily as a reporter. He participated in the founding of *The Ruins*, a literary magazine that would soon find a prominent place for itself in the Korean literary landscape. In 1921, his story "Frog in the Specimen Room" appeared in the literary journal *Dawn of History*, and, a year later, *On the Eve of the Uprising* (entitled *Cemetery* at its inception)—one of Yom's most defining works—came out.

He went to Japan in 1926 and devoted himself to writing fiction. He wrote two novels—*Love and Crime* and *Two Minds*—before he returned home in 1928, married Kim Yeong-ok, and joined the *Chosun Ilbo* daily as the head of its Arts and Science section. While at the paper, his third novel *Running Wild* appeared.

Three Generations invoked little interest while it came out in serial form, and no criticism on the work was published during the colonial period. It managed to evade the Japanese authorities' attention. Despite the novel's importance, it was published in book form only in November 1948, three years after Korea's liberation from Japan. At the time of publication, the author revised the second half of the book, making the ending more optimistic. Some critics believe that the revision reflects his changed outlook in the wake of the liberation. Compared with the serialized novel, this version focuses more on Deok-gi's family history than socialist activism.

The novel revolves around a passionate quest for new ideology and the negative climate that thwarts this quest; lurking behind the seemingly long-winded narrative is the author's critical eye. The characters in this work are not the figures involved in exciting adventures who take readers into the whirlwind of the times; rather, they are ordinary people carrying on their lives during the colonial period. Kim Dong-in, a well-known writer and Yom's contemporary, described Yom's works as putting readers under the weight of a "dull pain."

Three Generations depicts, in a prodding fashion, the mental landscape under the colonial rule from a pessimistic perspective. With the lively use of language of Jungin, or the traditional middle class, to which the author belonged, he manages to reveal the sensibility of this class, which played a pioneering role in the history of Korea's enlightenment (late 19th century). The story gives shape to the confrontation and conflict of three generations — the late Joseon Dynasty, the enlightenment period, and the colonial era.

The *Korean Literary History* (1997), penned by Kim Yun-sik and Kim Hyeon, assesses Yom as "revealing the limitations of the society at the time and simultaneously those of his own class." They go on to say, "Since the Korean society he criticizes is the one perceived by the Jungin class, he takes on the appearance of reactionism."

In 1924, with the formation of the Korean Artist Proletarian Federation (KAPF), proletarian literature became the mainstay of Korean literature. Yom challenged this faction. In a critical article entitled "Refuting Bak Yeong-hui's View in Discussing Newly Emerging Literature," he supported the national literature movement, with its basic thrust of "digging out what is Korean," which was in opposition to the proletarian literary movement, whose focus was the liberation of the oppressed. While his commitment to this liberation was unwavering, Yom insisted that the quest for Korean-ness should come first. He embraced tradition and the possibility of bringing new, unfettered life to traditional forms; he recognized the sustaining value of *sijo*, a traditional verse form (or folk song), with a conviction beyond nostalgia. He believed that a literary work was the reflection of the writer's character and moral influence and that traditional forms of literature could serve as vessels for the vision of the modern writer. In response, Kim Gi-jin, a core figure of the KAPF, disparaged Yom's argument as a "variation of ultra-nationalism, conservatism, and idealism."

While a disciple of traditional literary form in theory, in practice Yom used the novel to paint a broad picture of Korea's colonial era with a fresh perspective and a clear voice. He explores a handful of complex individuals forging their own lives within the context of a nation's history. The *Korean Literary History* purports: "*Three Generations* is not simply one of Yom's best works, but one of the outstanding literary achievements during Korea's colonial era. The work reveals his sense of reality in its full splendor and also vividly depicts multi-faceted interactions of different classes." It effectively reproduces a society in the throes of drastic change through the most concrete unit of society—a middle class family.

In *On the Eve of the Uprising*, Korean reality was perceived as a cemetery where the Japanese imperialists carried out their vicious exploitation. The authors of the *Korean Literary History* suggest that *Three Generations* is a more cool-headed rearrangement of society shaped by the remains of the pent-up anger that erupted in *On the Eve of the Uprising*.

Sim Hun, a novelist of the period, explains: "Sang-seop is known for his rich vocabulary. One of his special skills is his exquisite command of the expressions used in the homes of the former Jungin Class or merchant circles, in their full vulgarity. No one can compete with him in this respect."

It was only in the 1960s, however, that critics began to consider *Three Generations* a masterpiece of Korean fiction in the 20th century. Young critics, calling themselves the generation of the 1961 Student Uprising for democratization, published a stream of criticism on the work, contributing to raising the novel's status in the Korean literary canon. Their consensus is that through this work, Yom instills pride into the generation of citizens who did not receive a Japanese colonial education.

Yom was one of the few Korean writers who did not write in Japanese or publish pro-Japanese articles at a time when the Empire's suppression was at its worst. He lived in Manchuria from 1936 to 1945, at the height of Japanese hard-line policy—it is uncertain whether by choice or chance. What is clear is that Yom was at no point in his career under the thumb of the Japanese, and that he managed to remain true to his ideals.

Kim Chie-sou